THE GARMENT
&
SLINKY JANE

Catherine Cookson

CORGI BOOKS

THE GARMENT & SLINKY JANE
A CORGI BOOK : 0 552 14705 2

PRINTING HISTORY
This Corgi collection first published 1999
Copyright © Catherine Cookson 1999

including

THE GARMENT
Originally published in Great Britain by Macdonald & Co.
(Publishers) Ltd.
Copyright © Catherine Cookson 1967

SLINKY JANE
Originally published in Great Britain by Macdonald & Co.
(Publishers) Ltd.
Copyright © Catherine Cookson 1967

Set in 11/12pt Sabon by Kestrel Data, Exeter, Devon.

Corgi Books are published by Transworld Publishers Ltd,
61–63 Uxbridge Road, London W5 5SA,
in Australia by Transworld Publishers,
c/o Random House Australia Pty Ltd,
20 Alfred Street, Milsons Point, NSW 2061,
in New Zealand by Transworld Publishers,
c/o Random House New Zealand,
18 Poland Road, Glenfield, Auckland
and in South Africa by Transworld Publishers,
c/o Random House (Pty) Ltd,
Endulini, 5a Jubilee Road, Parktown 2193.

Reproduced, printed and bound in Great Britain by
Cox & Wyman Ltd, Reading, Berks.

THE GARMENT

Catherine Cookson

CORGI BOOKS

PART ONE

As she stared at the black, frost-patterned panes of glass the voice that had been whispering at her became loud in her head. 'Put it out,' it demanded. 'Go on, put it out.' And her eyes flashed to the light above the dressing-table to the left of her, then to the switch at the side of the window, and she imagined that her whole body, arms, legs, head, and even her bowels, rushed forward to the central point that was the little brass knob when all she did was lift her arm slowly and, after hesitating for a fraction of a second, switch out the light. As it snapped the clear outlines of the room from her gaze she closed her eyes, waiting for the panic to rise in her, but it only fluttered, a stationary flutter, for through her lids she could feel the soft-toned radiance of the four wall lights.

The fluttering took wings. 'Now these,' commanded the voice.

But that would mean walking the whole length of the room from the window to the door where the wall switches were. She couldn't do it . . . it would be all right going, but it would be the coming back . . . in the dark.

Before the thought had dissolved in her mind

she was walking towards the bedroom door, and as she put her finger on the first of the two switches she fixed her eyes on the floor. After the click her eyes did a swift hopping movement around the room, and then she felt slightly dizzy. All was merged now in a soft green glow. It was like looking through water. The white bedroom suite was no longer white but a delicate shade of blue; the bed, with its quilted coverlet, floated like a pale gold oblong box gently back and forth over a sea bottom, for the mustard carpet had taken on the appearance of moving sand; the rose curtains on the long window at the far side of the dressing-table looked almost blue, even black where they touched the carpet. But those on the french window facing her seemed to retain their own hue and were the only things in the room recognisable in this unfamiliar light. Her body began to play tricks with her again. It was dry now and hard, knobbly hard and aggressive. Each particle of her was thrusting out, pushing, grabbing at the air to pull her towards the window. With a slight movement of her finger the last two wall lights disappeared and for a brain-screeching moment she stood in total darkness.

Although every artery in her body was clawing its way to deliverance and the window, she herself moved slowly, and when she reached it she put her two hands flat against the shivering glass, then, with only a slight intake of breath, she opened the glass doors and moved one step out on to the balcony.

She was out in the night, standing without light in the night. How long was it since she had looked at the night like this? She couldn't remember, she didn't want to remember. Her breathing became deeper, slower, steadier, it was as if she was emerging into the world, coming out of the womb, being born again, and all that had gone before was the experience of a past existence. As the air went deeper into her lungs she wanted to shout with the joy of relief, but she stifled it by clamping her lips with her fist. No more shouting of any kind, no more yells corkscrewing through her head, it was all over and done with. She had been born again. The only difference was, she would not have to wait for years before becoming aware of her surroundings, she already knew where she was. Of course she had always known where she was. No matter how bad she had been, she had always known where she was. At least in the daylight. But this was night, blackness around her, below and above her, but strangely no longer in her. She was facing the night and defying it.

There were no stars. It was a black night, she could not have picked a blacker with which to test her quivering courage, and she was suspended high up in the night and was no longer afraid . . . well, only a little.

Sit down and look around, she said to herself, then answered, It's too cold. But again she was obeying her courage and her hand was already on the wrought-iron chair that took up a third of the balcony.

When she sat down she put her hands between her knees and pressed them close. It was a childish action and she couldn't remember having done it for years, not since she was a girl and had first come to this house, as a bride . . .

The darkness of the sky seemed to thin itself out as she sat, and she saw against it a deeper darkness made by the pattern of the trees, some of which bordered the drive to the main road. The drive was to the left of her. Slightly to the right of her there was a break in the pattern, which had been made only recently when she had had the old beech cut down. There had been trouble about that. They couldn't understand it. Nor could she have expected them to, only she knew why she had had the beech cut down. Yet she mustn't be too sure of that. This thought brought a tinge of fear again.

In the day-time she could see, through the gap made by the beech, the fells, each rise, mould, hill and crag all known to her so well that even now she could see their shapes through the darkness. Apart from the cottage that stood out there, in the far distance, to the right, there was nothing at all, nothing for miles but the fells.

But to the left of her, beyond the drive and down the hill, lay the village. Five minutes' walk from the gate lay the village . . . lay the world. All the physical substance of the world was in the village. All the types in the world were in the village. There was James Buckmaster, butcher and greengrocer, small and thin, very thin for a butcher, not hearty and brawny. But why should butchers be hearty and brawny? They, like everyone else, lived double lives. Perhaps he felt hearty and brawny inside. Then Mr Brooke, who dealt in groceries and drapery and had part of his shop for chemist accessories and photography. Mr Brooke had a head for business. He delivered his groceries as far as ten miles away, and he was a sidesman of the church, and his wife didn't speak to the women who went into the towns to supplement their larder, yet what was a wife for but to support her husband? Ironic laughter began to rise in her on this thought and she suppressed it hurriedly and turned her mind to the residents of the village again.

Although there were no street lamps in the village it would not be dark, for Mr Barker of the Stag always saw to it that there were two lights at least burning outside the bar. Mr Barker was a nice man, a kind man. They said he wouldn't last very long, for he was drowning himself in his own beer. He had a very large stomach, but also he had a very large smile, so perhaps the smile would keep him afloat even when the beer threatened to drown him . . . Again there was laughter rising in her, but it had a touch of merriness about it this time.

Then Miss Shawcross, Kate Shawcross as she was called, the postmistress. Why was it that there was always a postmistress in a village, seldom a postmaster. She hadn't thought of it before, but she didn't want to think of Kate Shawcross, and her thoughts swung away to Peggy Mather, which wasn't really very far, for Peggy lived with Miss Shawcross – she was her niece. She was also cook-general at Willow Lea, and at this moment was down below in the kitchen preparing dinner, a Christmas Eve dinner, a family dinner. She pushed her mind deliberately away from Peggy

Mather, for there had returned to her body a slight trembling. She began comforting herself. This time tomorrow she would be able to think of Peggy Mather and lots of things that she hadn't dared allow herself to dwell on, for this time tomorrow she would know whether she was to be free or not. Don't look at it in that way. She chided herself for her thinking. And, now in spite of her efforts, her mind wandered back to Kate Shawcross and the post office and the matter of lighting. Kate Shawcross had never kept a light outside her shop to help the travellers through the village. Even the light inside the shop was a dim one and she put that out at closing time. Yet she was supposed to be a good woman. Going on the interpretation that she taught Sunday school and dressed the altar and had for years subscribed handsomely to this and that church fund, she was a good woman all right. Yet some people were not fooled by the interpretation, they knew why Kate Shawcross had been so liberal. Mr Blenkinsop, the verger, had put it very neatly one day when he said that her goodness wasn't so much because she loved God as God made man. That had been very neatly put, very neat. After his wife died Mr Blenkinsop had wanted to marry Kate Shawcross; they said it was because she was a warm woman, having come into a considerable sum from an uncle in Canada, a man she had never clapped eyes on. They also said that Kate was indignant at the proposal. So Mr Blenkinsop had his reasons for being nasty and they were to do with . . . God made man.

Again there was a quirk of laughter in her, but

this time it was not relieving laughter, for it was weighted and held in place by bitterness. The laughter subsiding, the bitterness rose. It came up through her body like a square weight and when it had reached her throat and lodged there she admonished it harshly, saying, Enough, enough. No more of that, either.

She raised her head and looked towards the village again. In the far distance, right at yon side, there was a faint glow straining up into the darkness. That, she knew, would be the reflection of Dr Cooper's lights. He had a light hanging over his front gate and another always burning in the surgery, and the surgery curtains were never drawn. When all the other lights in the village were out, even those at the Stag, Dr Cooper's front light remained on. He was a light in a dark world, was David Cooper. Everybody didn't think so; his ways were too advanced for the diehards. But to her he was alike a mother and father confessor.

The word confessor caused her mind to shy again, and she lifted her gaze in the darkness over the village, and immediately her eye was caught by what looked like a falling star, so high was it in the blackness. But she knew it was no star, it was the headlights of a car and they had thrust themselves into the blackness through the gate of Toole's farm which clung to the side of Roeback Fell. James Toole would be coming down to the Stag. They said he came to the Stag every evening to get away from his wife, who was also his cousin, for Adelaide Toole was a bitter woman. Well, small wonder with what she had lost.

Now her head sank down on her chest, for her conscience always talked loudly to her when she thought of Adelaide Toole. For Adelaide Toole's bitterness lay at her door. She said as always, I couldn't help it, I didn't start it. And this time she added, Did I? Did I?

She was looking towards the gap where the beech had once stood and through it towards the fells, and it was as if she was speaking to someone out there, for she whispered aloud now beseechingly, 'It wasn't my fault, was it?' She lifted her hands from between her knees and, leaning forward, placed them on the rimed iron of the balcony. It was as she did this that she heard her family return and an unusual commotion below her on the drive. Immediately she straightened up and sat still. And she told herself not to move, let them find her here. It would not prove to them, how could it, that she was on the threshold of a new life, but it would show them that she had at last ousted fear, and therefore there was no longer any necessity for worrying, or whispered family councils concerning her . . .

In a few minutes the room was plunged into light, and she turned around to face them. After staring wide-eyed at her across the distance of the large bedroom, they rushed to her, they poured over her, exclaiming, touching, patting, dearing and darling-ing, oh-ing and ah-ing.

Beatrice, plump, solid, already maternal as if the mother of twelve instead of a scarcely two-year-old was crying 'Oh, what's happened? Come in out of the cold. Oh! You're frozen, just feel your hands.'

16

And Stephen, already the gangling, lanky parson in embryo, exclaimed, 'Are you all right? What possessed you?'

Then Jane, a week off seventeen and not yet old enough to be diplomatic, really spoke for them all when she said, 'Oh, Mummy, you did give us a scare. Why did you put the lights out?'

With a movement of her head Grace Rouse spread her smile across them and said gently, 'I wanted to.'

In their amazement they could not resist looking at each other, and she turned from them in time to stop herself saying, 'Don't worry, your Christmas is not going to be spoilt; there are not going to be any scenes. Don't worry, my dears.'

'I'll get you a hot drink and I'll also have a word with Peggy.' Beatrice's voice was very matronly now. 'The light wasn't on outside either. The whole front of the house in darkness. I can't remember ever seeing it like that before . . . well, not for years. As Jane said, it scared the wits out of us. Sit down there, dear.' She put her hands on her mother's shoulders to press her into a chair, and repeated, 'I'll bring you a hot drink.'

Grace smiled rather sorrowfully to herself. Beatrice was very solicitous; she had been solicitous since she arrived yesterday. She wanted something – not for herself, of course, but for Gerald. Gerald would be wanting a loan, another loan. She had felt it coming for some time. Well, she was sorry but he was going to be disappointed. She hoped he didn't ask tonight, for her refusal would blur the festive atmosphere, and she didn't want that. No, she hoped he would leave it until Boxing Day, just before they returned home. Gently she disengaged herself from her eldest daughter's hand, saying, 'Don't fuss me, Beatrice. I'm perfectly all right, dear, and I'm going downstairs.' She walked away from them towards the door, and there she turned and surveyed them, and as if they were children once again and she was explaining something to them that was a little out of their depth, she said, 'You can't stand still. Your grandfather used to say, "If you don't push on forward, you'll be kicked back." I think I'll push on.' Then she laughed, a reflection of the joy-tinted laughter that had at one time characterised her. And on this she opened the door quickly and went out on to the landing, for she knew she was embarrassing them.

She had taken three soundless steps when she stopped again, her narrowed eye drawn across the wide space that was furnished more like a room than a landing, to the head of the stairs where hung the picture of her late husband. The heavy, gold-enamelled openwork frame stood out from the white wall, with the painting of the man in his dark clerical attire appearing to be painted on the wall itself, the whole giving the impression of three dimensions. She was used to the picture, she passed it countless times each day, but she never looked at it, at least not with her eyes, yet her mind was nearly always on it. Even now she did not look at the figure but the frame. The top was entwined in flowers, live flowers that would surely die tomorrow, and at the bottom, clipped into the frame, were two vases, and these were filled with anemones.

Jane was at her side now, her voice soothingly soft, almost a whisper. 'I put them there, I've been thinking about him all day. It's over a year now . . . and . . . well . . .'

Grace moved forward away from her youngest daughter towards the head of the stairs and when there she did not stop, but as she passed the picture the eyes of her mind looked up at it and a voice from the dark depths of her which would not be repressed cried, 'Blast you!'

Before her feet touched the second step the fear was back and she was attacking yet beseeching it at the same time: 'No! No! Don't start again, don't think like that. That kind of talk must stop too. There must be no more vileness. Let it end. For God's sake, let it end. I'm afraid no more.' The voice in her head took this up and yelled with a semblance of the old panic. No more. Do you hear? I'm not afraid any more.

By the time she stepped into the hall there was only the echo of the voice with her, and she paused a moment and drew in a shuddering breath before looking round at her family walking in single file down the stairs, their expressions perturbed, each in its own way. Swiftly she put out her hand and caught that of Jane and drew her close. This action deepened their perplexity, but on Jane's face there was also a look of surprised pleasure as hand in hand they crossed the hall towards the drawing-room.

Beatrice and Stephen did not follow them. After an exchange of glances they moved down the stairs into the hall and turned towards a narrow passage and to a door at the far end, and just as

Beatrice was about to go into the room the sound of her husband's voice coming from the direction of the kitchen, where he was having a jocular exchange with Rosie Davidson, Peggy Mather's occasional help, made her pause and wait until he came into sight. Across the distance she beckoned to him, and when he joined them the grin slid from his face and he asked in an undertone, 'What's up?'

Beatrice made no reply but went into the study, the two men following her, and not until the door was closed and she had seated herself in a great leather chair by the side of the fire did she answer her husband. She said briefly, 'It's mother.'

'Oh!' It was expressive, and Gerald paused before he went on, 'What's wrong now?'

'Nothing's wrong; apparently everything seems to be all right. You'll never believe it but we found her in her room with all the lights out, standing on the balcony. Didn't we, Stephen?'

Stephen had taken up his position with his back to the fire. He liked standing this way . . . his father had always stood like it. Winter or summer, his father had taken up this position, with his back to the fireplace . . . he could always feel his father's presence strongly in this room.

He realised that the eyes of his sister and brother-in-law were hard on him and that he hadn't answered Beatrice's question. He stretched himself, neck upwards, again in the manner of his father, giving the impression that he had been debating his reply, then he said, 'She seems no longer afraid of the dark. In fact, I would say she's no longer afraid of anything.'

'Well, it's long overdue.' Gerald twitched his tweed trousers well up his legs before sitting down opposite his wife. 'It's a pity she couldn't have got over her nerves earlier, it would have saved us all a lot of worry.'

'And Daddy.' Beatrice looked towards the desk that stood between the two windows which were replicas of those in the room directly above. The desk was long and solid and took up quite a large space between the windows. The only articles on it now were an ink-stand, a tray, a blotting pad and a framed photograph. It was at the photograph that Beatrice was looking, and her eyes showed a film of moisture as she murmured, 'Poor Daddy.' The door of her conscience was tightly closed as she thought this.

Gerald uncrossed his legs, then, pulling a pipe from his pocket, he proceeded to fill it while he repeated to himself, 'Poor Daddy.' Well, there was no doubt he had had a time of it, but to be honest with himself, it was a phrase Gerald frequently used, to be honest with himself he had felt no real sadness at his father-in-law's departure, even though the old fellow had always, except on one notable occasion, been decent to him. To his mind he was a type you couldn't get to the bottom of. Hearty and all that, jocular, always ready to help you, with advice at any rate, but still there was a something . . . he had never felt easy in his presence. Yet of the two, give him the old man every time, for his mother-in-law, he had to admit, gave him the willies. If the old man had never made him feel entirely at ease, she always made him feel darned uncomfortable. She looked at you as if you were something the cat had brought in, with that air about her as if she were royalty. And after all, what was she? A coal merchant's daughter, that's all she was. Of course . . . he gave a little hicking laugh to himself . . . he wouldn't have minded being that particular coal merchant's son and having a share of the dibs he had left. She must be rotten with money. Yet with all of it she was as mean as muck. A clarty thousand to Beatty for a wedding present. He would like to bet she could have given her five and never missed it. True, she had settled another thousand on Yvonne when she was born, but she had tied that up so it couldn't be touched until the child was twenty-one. She might have been near barmy these past few years, but her business faculties hadn't been impaired, that was a certainty. Now there lay before him the job of tapping her.

His tongue came out and rubbed the fringe of his short, fair moustache. What if for some reason she didn't catch on to the idea and Livsey sold his share of the garage elsewhere . . . ? She couldn't do it. What was seven thousand to her, anyway? Pin money. Just look at this house, like a luxury hotel, with the stuff that was in it. But the snag was, she didn't like him. He knew she didn't like him, so what if she didn't rise to the offer? The thought was unbearable and brought him almost with a spring to his feet. This action had to be explained to the startled and enquiring glances of his wife and brother-in-law, and, never at a loss, he asked quickly, 'Where's Yvonne? I've just thought, I've never heard her. Is she asleep?'

'Asleep! No, don't be silly. She's at Miss Shawcross's. She begged me to let her stay for half an hour or so. Stephen and I had just slipped down to the church, and she was finishing the altar. She would have us go back with her to the house. She talked all the time about the new man. She can't stand him, she still considers it Daddy's church, she always will.'

Gerald made no comment on this, but he thought, Daft old bitch. Another one rotten with money. Why was it women who were always left money? Buttoning up his coat, he looked at Beatrice and said abruptly, 'We'd better go down and fetch her, she'll be sick with excitement and you know what that means. And then we've got the tree and the parcels to see to.'

At the reminder of the Christmas chores Beatrice sighed, letting out a hissing breath that spoke of boredom.

When she had left the room, followed by her husband, Stephen, his back still to the fire, started a swaying movement. From his toes to his heels, his eyes half closed, his hands, his back, his buttocks and calves soothingly warm, he rocked himself gently into a reverie . . . He liked this room, he loved it. He looked upon it as his; in fact the whole house was his. Well, as good as, he was the only son. Beatrice had a place of her own, and the way things were going Jane wouldn't be long before she left too. That would be determined tomorrow, he supposed, when the man turned up. He wondered for a moment what he might be like. That he was a lecturer at one of the colleges in Durham was something, anyway;

she wasn't letting herself down like Beatrice had done in marrying Gerald Spencer. Beatrice had hurt him over Spencer more than he would care to admit. Spencer was a type, and that had been proved conclusively when the marriage had to be rushed. Funny about that. The business had upset his father terribly yet he remembered his mother hadn't turned a hair. He knew exactly how his father had felt about it, for he had felt the same, nauseated, repulsed in some way – the whole thing was beastly.

The swaying which had lulled began again, and almost with a challenge his thinking made a statement. 'You'll never marry,' it said, and he took it up. No, he'd never marry because priests should never marry; you couldn't serve two masters, and as far as he could make out a wife was a master. And then there was the other side of it, the physical side. He actually shuddered on this thought. The Catholic Church had an advantage over the Church of England in the fact that they forbade their priests to marry. He sometimes wished, but just faintly, that he was in the Church of Rome. There the pattern was all cut out. There you were really a priest and your actions decided for you, but could you be a priest with a wife and children hanging around you? No, the title reverend or vicar was more suitable. He suddenly stopped his rocking and chided himself for his cynicism. But immediately he reverted to it. It was no good hoodwinking himself, he wanted to be known as a priest, not a vicar or a parson or a reverend. A thought coming directly on top of this minor explosion caused his lids to blink rapidly over his near-sighted hazel eyes: Would his mother marry again? The thought settled itself and continued. That's if she became really . . . quite all right. She had money and was still youngish and was what could be called good-looking. He had heard it said that she had been beautiful when she was young. He couldn't see it himself. Although she was his mother, her face didn't appeal to him. The eyes were too large for the face, and wide-eyed women, he understood, weren't supposed to be intelligent. He liked intelligent women, women who could talk of other things besides furniture and cooking. Of course there was her music, but on the whole she was just a domesticated woman . . . But what if she should marry again? It would mean another man in the place that was his father's . . . living or dead, would remain his father's. This house could never be another man's house, that was except his, and he would rent it but never sell it, and one day he would come back and live here, perhaps sooner than he expected. Having a bishop for a great-uncle, and having been called after him, might be of some use after all . . . Yet suppose his mother really did decide to marry again and go on living here?

As with Gerald, the thought was not to be borne, and he quickly went out into the hall and through a side door which led directly into the garage where the holly was stacked in a corner, and he began sorting with careful precision small pieces that would hang from the china bracket that surrounded the drawing-room. In his selection he was careful to pick nothing that would scratch the delicate grey walls . . .

Grace was now sitting on the drawing-room couch, relaxed as she had not been for months, even years. She was listening to Jane telling her, and in some detail, how she had met the most wonderful man in the world. Why was it, she thought, all girls of seventeen talked the same when this thing hit them? It was sad, even terrible, that the illusion should be an integral part of life; there was no way of jumping over it or side-stepping it, it had to be gone through. The only comfort was, that at that age you weren't aware of how naked you were to others, nor how tiring or boring or really painfully lovable. At that age you talked young, and why not? Why not indeed.

'Yes, darling, I'm listening.'

And she went on listening to how Jane had met the man of her dreams. His name was George Aster, and despite his being fifteen years her senior she knew it was the real thing. Grace hoped so, from the bottom of her heart she hoped so.

'I feel awful, Mammy, about having fibbed to him over my age, but, anyway, I look eighteen, I know I do; and I'm not telling him until after the holidays and things are settled in some way; and he means to have them settled, he's determined.' She gave a nervous giggle then added, 'You'll love him, Mammy.'

'Well' – Grace smiled dryly now – 'I may not do that exactly. Mothers-in-law are not supposed to, you know, but already I feel that I like him.' As she said this she edged herself out of the depths of the couch and to her feet and went towards the fireplace, thinking, Who wouldn't have affection for the man who is promising you freedom . . . It was dreadful to think like this, as if she wanted to be rid of Jane. But that wasn't true, oh no . . . no. She hadn't expected her to talk of marriage for a year or two yet, perhaps even longer, and she had faced up to the fact that not until the future of her younger daughter was secure in one way or another could she say to herself, 'Now . . . now I will live.'

But what if Jane should repeat the pattern that had been her own life? This George Aster was even older than Donald had been when they married. She mustn't let this happen, not even to save herself. She saw her reprieve sinking into the years ahead, and the panic began to rise in her again. But she quelled it. Age had not been the sword that hung between her and Donald. It would have made no difference if they had been exactly the same age, none whatever.

'Since I have felt like this I have understood about you and Daddy.' Jane looked towards her mother's back, slim as a girl's but stiffer. The shoulders had for the moment lost their droop and appeared unusually straight, and it seemed to be to them that Jane appealed, 'Mammy, I feel I must talk about Daddy. You mustn't mind any more. Not being able to mention him has shut him out somehow, and today, especially today, I have felt him near, as if he was sort of . . . well, I can't explain rightly, but sort of demanding to be let in. That's why I put the flowers on his picture . . .'

'Stop it, Jane!'

Grace's sharp cry seemed to slice off Jane's voice, and after staring at her mother's back for a moment she bowed her head and bit hard on her lip.

There followed a lull full of unease, then to break the tension came the sound of carols from the driveway and at the same time the drawing-room door opened and Stephen entered, his arms full of holly.

Grace turned to him, as if in relief, and asked, 'Are there just the children?' Her voice was quite calm now, and Stephen nodded to her, saying, 'Yes, about a dozen of them I would say.' His voice had a stiff, stilted sound.

'Will you see to them?'

He did not immediately reply, but laid the holly down by the fireplace and then said, 'Andrew's at the front door.'

'Andrew?' Grace repeated the name as if it was unknown to her. 'Oh, I thought he wasn't coming back until Boxing Day, or thereabouts.'

'Well, he's here at the door.' Stephen straightened up and his voice reached a high level as he asked, 'Why can't he use the back door?'

'Don't be silly.' It was Jane answering as she rose from the couch. 'You know Peggy would hit him on the head with the frying-pan if he dared put his nose in her kitchen . . . "Hell hath no fury . . ." But why should he, anyway?'

'Well, it isn't his place to come to the front door.'

'Stephen!' For the second time in minutes Grace's voice appeared to come out of the top of her head. The name was ejected so sharply that both Stephen and Jane held their positions as if competing in a game of statues. 'Don't speak like that, Andrew's not just a . . . a . . . he's a friend, who's always given us his spare time; he only took on the odd jobs and the garden to . . . to oblige your father. I've told you that before. Jane . . . Jane, go and let Andrew in.'

'Yes, yes, all right, Mammy.'

Stephen turned from his mother's stare and busied himself with the holly. He was consumed now by a disturbing anger. If he had his own way he knew what he'd say to Andrew MacIntyre, 'Go! And don't come back any more, inside or outside of this house!' He had never liked Andrew. And his father hadn't liked Andrew either, although he had never said anything against him; in fact he had never heard his father speak his name, but he still knew that he hadn't liked the man.

There were a number of things he himself held against Andrew MacIntyre. Not least of them that he had never addressed him as 'Mr Stephen' or 'Young Master Stephen' as the other villagers did. And then there was the fact that he did not call his mother by the title of 'Madam' or 'Ma'am'. It was odd when he came to think about it but he couldn't remember hearing him call her anything at all, no name whatever. It was as if he considered himself her equal, the equal of them all for that matter. That was why he kept himself apart from the villagers. He was too big for his boots, was Andrew MacIntyre, always had been. He did not chide himself that this was no Christian way to think. His feelings towards Andrew MacIntyre had long ago become a condition which had no claim to charitable thought.

The carol singers were now attempting 'Away in a Manger' in a variety of keys. The carolling became distinctly louder when the drawing-room door was opened, which was explained by Jane laughingly saying as she entered, 'Beatrice is back and Yvonne insists on joining in; half of them are in the hall . . . Here's Andrew, Mammy.'

The man who came forward into the room could have literally filled Stephen's description and not only with regard to his feet, for he stood six feet two inches tall, yet there didn't seem enough flesh on his body to do justice to his frame; it looked like the body of a young man that needed filling out. But the delusion was dispelled when you looked at the face, for there was hardly a trace of youth in it, not that it was lined or aged; the impression came rather from the eyes, deep-set brown eyes. And the impression was added to by the white tuft of hair that sprang away from the right temple. The rest of his hair was not black, merely dark, but it took on a hue of almost Spanish blackness in contrast to the white tuft.

'Hallo, there, Andrew; do come in.' Grace did not move from her place near the fire, but she lifted her hand and the gesture seemed to draw the man into the room. When he reached the head of the couch he stopped and she said, 'You're back sooner than you expected. We didn't think to see you until Boxing Day.'

'I left my aunt much better. She insisted that I come home for Christmas and I was nothing loath.' His voice was thick and deep and had not a Northumbrian but a Scottish burr. And his manner of speech was stilted and formal as if he had rehearsed what he had to say.

'Is she alone?'

'No, she's got a friend with her, so I felt justified in leaving.'

'Do sit down, Andrew.' She pointed to a chair and then went and sat on the couch, and as Jane sat down again beside her she did not look at her but groped out and clasped her hand.

'Why can't you get your aunt to come and live nearer, Andrew?' Jane was leaning forward asking the question. 'Living such a long way off.'

'She likes Devon.'

'You know what, Mammy?' Jane's legs were tucked under her on the couch now, and her face took on a mischievous twist as she said, 'I bet it isn't any aunt that Andrew goes to see. I'd like to bet it's a girl friend . . . what do you say?'

The sound of Stephen dropping the hammer on the floor, whether intentionally or unintentionally, brought all their eyes to him. He was looking at Jane, but Jane, having no fear of her brother, ignored his look and repeated, 'What do you say, Mammy?'

'I would say it is Andrew's own business.' Grace was looking at Andrew and he at her, then, moving his deep gaze on to Jane, he said softly, 'I came back because my girl lives here.'

Jane threw back her head and let out a gurgle of a laugh. Ever since she was eight and had proposed to him openly one day, saying, 'When I grow up will you marry me, Andrew?' and had realised that he was in some way shocked, she had taken a delight in calling him her lad.

'Jane has a friend coming tomorrow, Andrew,' Grace was smiling at her daughter.

'Yes?' Andrew's eyebrows moved up enquiringly.

'He's a special friend, Andrew.'

'Yes?' He looked at Jane and she exclaimed with a deep nod, 'Uh-huh.'

A piercing scream coming from the hall checked the monosyllabic exchange, and Grace screwed up her face against the sound as it was repeated again and again. There came now cries of 'Goodbye, goodbye. Thank you, goodbye. Merry Christmas . . . same to you. Goodbye,' followed by the front door banging, then into the drawing-room was borne Yvonne, kicking and struggling in her father's grasp, and yelling at the limit of her lungs, 'Want to. Want to. Down, Daddy. Want to.'

Gerald, stalking to the hearth, dropped the child none too gently onto the rug by the fire, and immediately his hands released her she stopped her screeching.

Yvonne looked round the company – there was hardly a tear stain on her face – then suddenly she laughed and, turning over on the rug lay on her stomach and kicked her toes into the soft pile.

'Something's got to be done in that quarter,' Beatrice nodded downwards. 'She's becoming a perfect little devil.'

'If you want to have harmony have a child in the house. What do you say?' Gerald addressed Andrew in a condescending, man-to-man style, and Andrew, getting to his feet, answered quietly,

'That's one thing I can't give my opinion on.'

'No, no, of course not. Well, you don't know what you've missed.'

Grace too rose to her feet and, looking at Andrew, she said quietly, 'You'll be on your own tomorrow, Andrew?' And without waiting for an answer she continued, 'Will you come and have dinner with us?'

Andrew was looking at the woman before him. Then his gaze moved from her to the members of her family, to Beatrice, the son-in-law, Jane and, lastly, Stephen. They were all staring at him, waiting he knew for his answer. He looked back at Grace again and it was a moment before he spoke. 'Thanks, I'd like that,' he said briefly. 'Good night now.' The good night was for her. Then, giving a nod that included the rest of them, he said again, 'Good night.' As he went towards the door he paused for a moment and, turning and looking back towards Grace, he said, 'A Happy Christmas to you.'

'And to you, Andrew.'

Their voices were low and level.

No-one saw him out, and when the door had closed on him the silence still held, giving him time to cross the hall.

Beatrice was the first to speak. 'But, Mammy,' she said, 'there'll be company, Jane's friend . . .' She paused to cast a glance towards Jane. 'George.'

'George will be all the better for meeting Andrew, Beatrice.'

'But Andrew will be awkward, Mammy; he'll be out of place, it's never happened before.'

'Andrew won't be out of place, Beatrice . . . I knew Andrew before I knew any of you.' Grace flicked her gaze quickly around them. 'I've never known him to be awkward in any company. Andrew is one of the family; I've always considered him so.'

And now she looked towards Stephen and she saw that his face was working. At this moment he was without his façade, and when she said, 'Well, Stephen, what have you to say about it?' she watched him wet his lips and wait a moment before speaking, and she knew he was going to great lengths to control his temper.

'Well, since you ask, and since you appear to be so much better, I feel that I should speak frankly.' He paused and she inclined her head towards him. 'It wouldn't have happened if Father had been alive, would it? And I can't see that the excuse is that he's alone tomorrow. He was alone on Christmas Day two years ago when Father was here and there was no talk then of inviting him to dinner, and I feel I know why.' Again he paused. 'Father didn't like the man, he never liked him. Why he kept him on I don't know, but there's one thing I know for a certainty: he would never have received an invitation to Christmas dinner from Father.'

Whatever effect Stephen's words had on his mother was not evident – except for a slight pressure on the lips her expression remained the same – but the effect certainly showed on the rest of them, for they all looked startled at his audacity. Then just as Grace was about to reply Jane broke in, her words tumbling over them-

34

selves, 'You . . . oh, Stephen, I don't know how you can say such things. Father did like Andrew, he did. As for George' – she glared at Beatrice now – 'if I wanted him to meet anyone it would be Andrew, and if he felt he was above meeting Andrew he wouldn't be the one for me . . . so there. You are nothing but a lot of silly . . . silly snobs. And snob isn't the right word either . . . Oh, I don't know . . . '

'Be quiet, Jane, it's all right.' Grace's hand was on her arm. Then she turned and looked at Stephen and her voice was very low, even gentle, as she said, 'What you seem to forget, what everybody seems to forget, is that I am still mistress of this house, and if I want Andrew to dinner I'll have him to dinner. Andrew is . . .' Her voice was trembling now. Her lids began to blink rapidly as she looked from one to the other, and when no-one spoke she turned away and made for the door. Having passed into the hall and closed the door behind her, she held on to the knob for some seconds, for her legs were shaking so that she felt she would drop, and to her dismay the sickly feeling of dread and anxiety was blocking her chest once more.

As she made her way to the foot of the staircase her walk became slightly erratic and she looked down at her legs. As she did so the expression on her face changed; the look of deep pain and anxiety seeping from her eyes was replaced by one of desperate urgency, and after supporting herself for a moment with a hand on the balustrade she did not mount the stairs to her room but crossed the hall towards the dining-room. It was imperative that she followed up the stand she had made in the drawing-room with a test. She would open the hatch to the kitchen and say to Peggy, 'Is everything going well, Peggy?' That alone would be a strengthener of courage.

When she opened the dining-room door Peggy Mather was bending over the table moving a cruet to a new position. Grace had spent most of the afternoon setting the table and now the voice of courage said, 'Tell her to put that back where it was,' but she wasn't brave enough to comply. And she walked into the room as if she hadn't noticed what Peggy was doing. Then she went and stood some way behind her, for it was easier to address her from behind.

The woman at the table was broad hipped, and as she bent forward her buttocks pressed themselves out of her print skirt bringing it up into a peak showing a pair of hard, fleshy calves. Even her bulk was intimidating. She had always stood a little in awe of this woman right from the very start, yet it was nothing compared with the feeling Peggy Mather had aroused in her these past few weeks.

She tried to speak now as mistress to maid, as if there was nothing more between them than that, but her voice failed her as she said, 'Is everything going all right, Peggy?'

'Why shouldn't it be? It isn't the first time we've had a dinner at seven instead of one . . . it's all the same thing.'

Grace watched the broad back straighten up. She watched her walk with her heavy step towards the service door, and when it had swung to behind her she sat down. Then, joining her hands together, she did a very unusual thing: she began to pray.

Less than half an hour later Stephen and Beatrice came to her room. Stephen came first. He looked slightly crestfallen and more youthful than she had seen him for some time, and when he apologised for his behaviour, saying, 'I'm sorry, nothing like that will ever happen again', she wanted not only to put out her hands to him but to take him in her arms. Yet all she did was to look at him kindly and say, 'It's all right, I understand,' and she did understand. She understood a little how he was feeling at this moment of contrition, for was he not her son.

When a few minutes later Beatrice came into the room and exclaimed, 'Oh, Mammy, I do like you in that grey, it looks super, I haven't seen you in it for ages,' she felt a little sick, a little sad, for she guessed that they had put their heads together, determined that the Christmas festivities should not be marred, at least through them. The incident that had happened downstairs was unfortunate, and the outcome of it they were waiving until tomorrow, she could almost hear her husband's voice endorsing their decision . . . 'sufficient unto the day is the evil thereof'.

For the first time in three years Grace went to sleep in the dark, and when she woke in the dark and found that she had been to sleep she was hardly afraid. There was a soft stillness about the room and the whole house, and she guessed that it was snowing. She told herself to get up and see, and then she remembered no more until it was morning, and she awoke again to a quiet stir about the house broken by excited cries from a room across the landing.

It was Christmas morning and Yvonne was opening her stocking. She had no desire to go and witness this event. When her own children had been small it had thrilled her to watch them unpacking their stockings, but Yvonne did not seem to belong to her, not even as a grandchild. She was a spoilt child.

As she lay she hoped that no-one would come and disturb her for a long while, for she wanted to savour this feeling that she had woken with, this feeling of newness, of courage, of having at least been able to conquer the dark. She stretched her long legs down the bed, then, twisting round, she lay on her stomach, her face buried in the pillow. She would make everybody happy today, everybody. And she would go to church . . . yes, she would go to church. That would please Stephen . . . Yes she would go to church. And this evening she would play to them . . .

It was ten o'clock before the breakfast things and all the debris from the presents were cleared away. She couldn't say that any of her Christmas presents had brought her delight. They were mostly things for use in the house; these no doubt they thought would please her, and she was sure she had conveyed that impression. Her gifts to them had been in the form of cheques, small ones, but they all, even Gerald, had received them with expressions of surprised delight.

She had a strong feeling that Gerald was trying to corner her. He had never left her for a moment last night. It had almost become embarrassing. He was too solicitous by far.

And now when she had come upstairs to get ready for church and he made the excuse to follow her by bringing some wood for her fire, she knew he had succeeded in his efforts and she must face up to it and get it over.

He stood outside her door calling, 'Fuel up, Mother', and when she said, 'Come in, Gerald', he entered, boisterous and gay, his arms laden with logs.

'That's kind of you, Gerald. I always feel guilty about my fire, but I can't stand electric fires and I have tried.'

'Why should you; you usually see to it yourself, anyway . . . If you can't have what you want in your own house it's come to something.' He pushed a log on the centre of the fire and pressing it home firmly with his boot added, 'And I don't see why you should have to mess about with fires either. Peggy's got nothing to do most of the time, only you to see to, and she's got help to do it at that.'

'Oh, she's kept pretty busy and there's nothing like fires for making work.'

Gerald straightened up and dusted his hands, then, turning and taking up a position not unlike that of Stephen he looked at her and said in a voice that could only be described as tender, 'You know, Mother, I haven't had the chance to speak to you alone, but I just want to say from the bottom of my heart that I'm glad to see you so much better.'

She turned from the dressing-table with a ring in her hand, and she looked at it as she slowly pushed it onto her finger. She even paused to admire its effect before saying, 'Thank you, Gerald; that's very kind of you.'

'Y'know, Mother' – Gerald let his head fall back onto his shoulders, then drop forward again before proceeding – 'if it wasn't that you are so much better' – he stressed the 'are' – 'I wouldn't, not for the world, say what I'm going to say now, and as time's short and they'll all be yelling for you in a minute, I'll come straight to the point . . . You know . . . or of course you don't know that Livsey is selling out, and he's willing to let his holding go as a sacrifice . . . Now' – he held his hand up as if he were directing traffic at the stop sign – 'I know that that word is suspect but nobody's going to put one over on me, not in my own line of business, so you can take my word for it that it just means what it says. Well, Mother, you know how I stand. I haven't got seven thousand pounds. I wish I had, and this is what I want to ask you . . . Mind, I'm not asking for a loan . . .' Again his hand was at the stop sign. 'I'm asking you to do a business deal. And this is it: will you buy Livsey out? You'll have profits, part control, the lot . . . Now it's like this . . .'

'Sit down, Gerald.' Grace's quiet tone checked him and she pointed to a chair. Then she drew the dressing-table stool near to her, and when she was sitting opposite him he put in hastily but in a less

40

strident tone, 'Well, just hear me out, Mother, before you say anything.'

'It's no use, Gerald.'

He made no reply to this but he smiled at her and nodded. He was used to this kind of beginning; he was also used to pressing home the point. One acquired the technique in the car business. 'All right, all right. Now just listen, just for a minute . . .'

Grace looked downwards to where her hands were joined tightly together and she bit on her lip before saying in a voice that was no longer quiet, 'It's no use, Gerald, you're only making it worse for yourself. I mean what I say, I can't help you' – she raised her eyes and looked straight into his round and to her unpleasant face as she ended – 'for the simple reason that I haven't any money.'

'What!'

His disbelief was scornful and it brought her head up and gave an edge to her voice. 'You can say "What!" in that manner, but I'm telling you the truth. I haven't any money, at least not your kind of money. It will come as news to you, I know, but I haven't had . . . what you call money for some time now.'

'What about the business?'

'It's mine in name only.'

'You were bought out?'

'No, I wasn't bought out in the way you mean. To put it briefly, Uncle Ralph speculated some years ago. As you know, he owned half of everything; something went wrong . . . many things went wrong and he was facing bankruptcy. The firm was taken over but still run under our name.

41

I was left with enough to put Stephen through college and see Jane settled.'

'But this place?' Gerald spread his arms wide, embracing the house. 'You can't run this on tuppence a week.' He refrained from adding, 'Cooks, gardeners, the lot.'

His tone jarred on her and she wanted to cry, 'What business is it of yours?' but she knew his hopes had been dealt a very hard blow, so she replied quietly, 'It doesn't cost so much to run as you might think, and in a very short time the house and everything in it will be sold.'

'Good God!' He was on his feet. 'And the others know nothing about it?'

'No, they know nothing about it. It won't concern them very much, anyhow. Stephen will have no use for a house like this, his home will be in a vicarage in some part of the country. And Beatrice is in your hands . . .' Grace paused here before adding, 'And Jane's future will be settled over the holidays – at least I hope so.'

'God Almighty!' Gerald was being entirely himself now. 'And you think they're not going to mind?'

'Oh yes, I know they'll mind and be disappointed.'

'Disappointed. Huh . . . ! Well . . .' He looked down at her. 'We . . . ll' – the word was drawn out this time – 'all I can say is that it's a damn fine kettle of fish.'

'I'm sorry you should feel so bitter about it, but after all, Gerald, it may surprise you to learn that I have dealt with you very generously. You've had two thousand pounds and more in the last three years. It was a very difficult thing to do to decide on giving Beatrice and the child that money when my affairs were in such a chaotic state, and no doubt in the future I may be glad of two thousand pounds. No, Gerald, under the circumstances your family has been treated very fairly.'

Gerald stared at her. There was a black rage welling up in him; her seeming indifference to his plight infuriated him. Not only had she killed his hopes of eventually owning his company but his future was dead also. He hadn't realised up till now just how much he had depended on her generosity to her grandchild and eventual legacy to her daughter. This woman had been a source of security for him, an insurance policy. If things didn't go right, well, there was always Beat's mother. Not a little of his present success was due, he knew, to his connection through marriage with Cartner and Cartner.

So bitter were his feelings that when Grace spoke again he did not hear her. But after a moment he turned on her and said, 'What did you say?'

'I was asking you, Gerald, not to tell Beatrice or the others about it just yet. Of course, they will have to know. You can tell Beatrice if you wish when you return home, but I'll explain to Jane and Stephen before the holidays are over.'

Gerald made no answer to this, but he thrust his lips out before bringing them in to form a tight line across his face. Then, turning abruptly on his heels, he left her.

It was some moments before Grace moved from the seat, and then she went slowly to the wardrobe and took out her mink coat, and when she had put it on she looked at herself in the mirror. She could up to a point understand Gerald's feelings. In a coat such as this, in a house such as this, it was hard to credit she was a woman without substantial means.

Apart from the child, Gerald had the house to himself; they had all gone to church, and even if Yvonne had not been sick he knew that he couldn't have sat through an hour of waffling feeling as he did. He was ready to explode. He looked to where his small daughter lay asleep now, curled up in the depths of the couch. She had a clarty thousand and no more to look forward to. That was eating him as much as the fact that unless he had a windfall of some kind or another he would remain a working partner in Livsey's for the rest of his days. And for that stuck-up cow to keep it to herself and she supposed to be ill, in the middle of a breakdown. She couldn't possibly have been as bad as she made out otherwise she would have blurted out the whole business among some of the other stuff she had spewed up. Enough to put you to shame, some of the things she had said, and it took something to make him blush, by God it did. She was a deep one, was his mother-in-law . . . But he just couldn't get over it . . . her broke. He swung round and looked at the room. Keeping up all this bloody pomp and her broke, it didn't make sense. And then the Christmas boxes. Twenty-five pound cheques to each of them, even the children. It didn't seem much when you reckoned it up, a hundred and twenty-five pounds, but a hundred and twenty-five pounds was a hundred and twenty-five pounds when you were broke . . . ! Broke, be damned . . . ! her broke likely meant she had a bare three thousand a year to survive on.

He must have a drink. Softly he walked past the couch and out of the room, and when he entered the dining-room he made straight for the cabinet standing in the corner. Opening its doors wide, he ran his finger along the line of bottles on the top shelf before selecting the brandy. And all this liquor. What did she keep this stuff for? Supposedly for her uncle and relations. That was my eye. She likely tippled on the quiet; there was no-one to check on her most of the time. Would you buy this amount of stuff if you were near penniless? He threw off a good measure of brandy, then as he stood savouring its warming effect he looked down at the empty glass and said aloud, 'She's lying.' His hand went out to the bottle again, and he was in the act of pouring himself out another brandy when the front-door bell rang.

Who the hell could this be? Not MacIntyre already? He hoped not. He didn't want to be stuck with him until the others came back.

When he opened the front door he saw standing there a man of medium height, dressed in a greatcoat and holding a hat in one hand and a small case in the other.

'Yes?' His enquiry was not convivial.

'I'm Aster.'

'Aster . . . Oh, good lord . . . come in, come in.' He closed the door behind the man. 'You weren't expected until one o'clock. Come by special train or something?'

The man was looking slowly around the hall, and he said with a laugh, 'No, hardly that, but a friend of mine was driving this way and offered me a lift . . . I took a taxi from yon side of the village.'

'A taxi? You were lucky. It's a wonder they came up this way with the snow lying . . . Here, let me have your things. I'm the only one in, everybody's at church. I'm Spencer, Beatrice's husband. You might have found an empty house, only my little girl was sick – excitement, you know. Up half the night waiting for her stocking . . . I bet you could do with a drink.'

For the moment Gerald had pushed aside his own concerns. He was playing the host in a way he would never have done had Grace been in the house.

He led the way across the hall. 'In here . . . now, what'll you have . . . ? Let's see.' He stood in front of the cabinet, again a door in each hand. 'We run to whisky, gin, rum, cherry brandy, brandy plain. Advocat . . . '

'Oh, a whisky please, neat.'

'A whisky neat. A whisky it'll be.'

'What a remarkable place.'

'Eh? Oh this . . . the house . . . yes. And you've seen nothing yet.'

'Jane didn't tell me. I expected a vicarage . . . you know, the usual kind.'

'Well, this is the vicarage, or was when the Reverend was alive. Anyway, it was used as such, but the real vicarage is at the other side of the village, near the garage . . . Oh, it's a long story. Jane will tell you some time, I suppose. Well, drink up . . . Cheers!'

'Cheers.'

'Sit yourself down.'

'Thanks.'

Gerald took up his stand on the hearthrug, and from his advantageous position he summed up the visitor. Well, all he could say was: he certainly wasn't much to look at. To hear Jane ramping on he had expected a six-footer at least and all that went with it. The fellow was no more than five foot five, tubby in fact, and looked his age. He might have the advantage on top . . . well, he needed it some place. But now it was up to him, he supposed, to keep the ball rolling until the others came in.

During this process and the next half-hour the man learned a great deal about Gerald, and, becoming a little tired of the theme, he skilfully turned the conversation to the house and garden again.

'You have some very fine trees here.' He stood up and went to the window. 'The willows are magnificent . . . Ah-h! That's a lovely sight, isn't it?' He pointed to where a large willow, its lower branches borne down with snow, stood in the middle of the wide stretch of white sun-gleaming lawn.

'Oh, that's nothing.' Gerald came to his side. 'Wait until you see those at the back.'

'It's a wonderful place . . . wonderful.'

Gerald made no answer to this, for the remark dragged his mind back to his own affairs. Aye, it was wonderful, he'd say it was wonderful, and according to her it was for the market. He wished they were back; he must tell Beatrice about the way things had gone and damn all promises to the contrary. This fellow, he was finding, was heavy going. Had nothing to say except enthuse about the place. He was turning from the window when his companion's exclamation of 'Good gracious!' brought him round again and he looked to where he was pointing to the path circling the lawn. 'That man . . . why, I know him . . . don't tell me he lives here.'

'MacIntyre . . . ? No . . . well, not in this house. He lives over on the fells. He does the odd jobs, part time, mostly at nights and week-ends. He's a farmworker really.'

'Really . . . ! Well, how strange.'

'Why, is he a friend of yours?' Gerald's eyes narrowed.

'No, no, I wouldn't say that. We've only met twice and then just for a few minutes each time. But he's the kind of man whom you couldn't forget in a hurry . . . he's got a white tuft of hair here, hasn't he?' He pointed high up on his temple.

'Yes . . . yes, he has.'

'That's him.'

They both watched Andrew follow the path that led towards the side of the house and the front door.

'Where'd you meet him . . . he hardly ever leaves these parts, except occasionally to visit an aunt in Devon.'

'It was there we met . . . Devon.'

'This last week?'

'No, some months ago – around Easter, to be correct. That was the second time. The first time was about two years ago. I lost my way when I was on a walking tour and came across him. I was making for Buckfast Abbey and got lost in a wood. You can, you know,' he smiled. 'I was thinking I was there for ever when I came on a clearing and a cottage. There was a field beyond. It was in the field I first saw him . . . It was most arresting, he was coming down the slope with his wife. It was rather a steep gradient and I think she must have slipped, for he pulled her up into his arms and swung round and ran with her down the remainder of the hill to the gate. I remember envying him his colossal strength . . . it was rather a beautiful sight, if you know what I mean, a man running down a hill with a woman in his arms. You don't often come across it in real life, you've got to go to the films to see anything like that these days, and then it's usually done by a stand-in Hercules.'

'He was with his wife?' Gerald's voice was low and his eyes were wide and he nodded his head slowly as he spoke.

'Yes. I didn't make my presence known for a moment or so, I didn't want to break in on the scene and . . . well . . . embarrass them, but even when I did show myself, and with quite a bit of preliminary noise, I remember I nearly scared the wits out of them, at least her, for she dashed into the house. It left me a bit mystified until he explained. She had seemingly been very ill and was still convalescent, and as they rarely saw

49

anyone in that isolated part my presence had evidently startled her.'

'Yes . . . yes, it would, I can see that.' Gerald was still nodding his head. Well, could you beat it? MacIntyre with a wife – a woman would be more correct, and tucked away in a nice secluded spot right in the heart of a wood. Well again, what d'you know? His mother-in-law's family retainer, who would be lonely on Christmas Day so must join the family circle, and while he was eating his Christmas pudding no doubt his mind would be in the woods . . . with the little woman. There was a loud snigger inside him. He couldn't wait to see Andrew's face when he was confronted with this fellow. It was a small world, wasn't it? Coincidences were funny things, upsetting things. He was going to enjoy himself today, mainly, he realised, not because Andrew's face was going to be red, but because of the disillusionment that was awaiting his mother-in-law when she learnt of the double life of her perfect odd-job man.

'I found him a most interesting man. He had a wide knowledge of trees. He walked with me and put me on the road to the Abbey. I remember wishing it had been longer. Then this Easter I went that way again and there they were as before. She's very shy, isn't she? Has she quite recovered?'

Gerald was saved from making a reply to this question by the sound of laughing voices entering the hall. The church-goers were back and Andrew would come in with them – oh he couldn't wait for this – so for answer he said, 'Here they come,

come on and show yourself.' He put his arm round the other man's shoulders and pressed him forward, and so it was almost side by side they entered the hall.

There before them was gathered the family. Beatrice was in the act of peeping into the drawing-room, Stephen was pulling off his muffler and coat, Jane had her back to them. She was in the fore-lobby gathering some late mail from the wire cage, but standing together like the central figures in a picture were Grace and Andrew. They had been joined in gentle laughter a moment before they looked towards Gerald and the man at his side. When the man came swiftly forward with outstretched hand Grace, with mouth agape as if she were being confronted by the Devil, shrank closer to Andrew. And then with a desperate movement she turned her face and body towards him as if seeking shelter from the advancing guest.

The man was shaking Andrew's stiff hand, and his now hesitant and perplexed tone pounded through Grace's head as he said, 'Well, isn't this the most unusual thing, I never thought we . . . we should meet again, not in this part of the country, anyway.'

There was a pause in the pounding, and when the voice came at her averted face saying quietly, 'I hope I find you better,' she knew with a great surge of relief that she was to be freed of this excruciating moment and that she was about to faint. As she clutched at Andrew and felt his arms supporting her, she heard Jane's voice crying, 'George! George! Oh, Mammy!'

PART TWO

1

Whenever Grace looked back to the incidents that occurred in the early years of her marriage her mind always picked on the first night Donald and she spent together. She could see herself sitting bolt upright in the bed waiting for him, her heart pounding so hard that she felt its jerking even behind her eyes. They were spending the night in an hotel in Dover before crossing by car ferry the following day to make their way through France to Rome, where they would stay for the next two weeks.

The bulbs in the bedroom were shaded to the extent of making the lighting appear dim, and she had sat peering through it towards the dressing-room door. The dressing-room had come as a pleasant surprise to her. When Donald had spoken of the booking he had referred to it as the room, not rooms, but it was so like him to be considerate of her feelings on this night.

When the intervening door opened and he entered the room in his dressing-gown, she was torn for the moment between two ways of greeting him, one with lowered head and the other with arms eagerly outstretched. She chose the latter, and when he was sitting on the bedside close beside her he took her face between his large hands, his fingers pressing her temples, and he stared into her misted eyes for some time before gently kissing her. And then he began to talk. With his voice soft and sometimes hesitant, he asked her: Did she know that love was God conceived . . . God distributed . . . given by Him to His creatures for the sole purpose of creating souls? Did she know that? Did she know that it was a most precious thing, a thing to be cherished, never to be squandered, as precious as the chalice holding the holy wine, to be sipped at, never to be gulped . . . did she know that? Consciously she knew none of these things, she was only aware of being lulled, almost hypnotised, by the magic of his voice. She only knew that he was wonderful, so kind, so understanding.

It was some months before she realised that the substance of his talk on their wedding night was the foundation on which their marriage was laid.

When finally he stretched his long length down beside her, there was a change in her feelings for which she could not account, for his tenderness proved to be enough for her. She did not miss the consummation of the marriage until, waking the next morning, she thought with a guilty start, Oh, I must have fallen asleep, and when she saw him lying looking at her, seeming even to be drinking her into himself, she wondered why she, of all people in the world, should have been selected for such happiness, and how could there be anyone so blind as not to see the wonder and goodness of her Donald. This thought took her mind to her Aunt Aggie. Aunt Aggie didn't like

Donald, never had from the day he came to commiserate with her on the tragic death of her parents in the car crash. He was too smooth, too good-looking, too much of a la-de-da, Aunt Aggie had stated openly. Her Aunt Susan and Uncle Ralph liked Donald, and both said that he was the kind of man her mother would have liked her to marry. For had not her parents moved into the best part of Newcastle so as to be able to give her a background that would in no way be incongruous to the boarding-school education they insisted on her having, and which was to prepare her to meet, and mate, with someone like Donald. Yes, they said, poor dear Linda would have been over the moon at her daughter's choice, for was not Donald Rouse, besides looking and talking like a gentleman, the nephew of a bishop.

Yet no approbation of her Aunt Susan and Uncle Ralph could make up for her Aunt Aggie's open hostility, for she liked her Aunt Aggie – loved her; she had always had a guilty feeling about her affection for her Aunt Aggie because she knew it was stronger than that which she had for her parents. But now she was finished with her Aunt Aggie; she couldn't be anything else after the things she had said about Donald, kept on saying about him even to the very night before the wedding.

'That fellow's after your money, that's all he wants,' that's what she had dared to say about Donald, who was a parson. On that last night Aggie had shouted so that she had rushed and closed the drawing-room door and begged, 'Oh, be quiet, Aunt Aggie. Donald will be calling any minute. Oh, how can you say such things?'

'I can and will. Somebody's got to say them; the others can't 'cos they're mesmerised – like you. Look, Grace.' Aggie's voice had dropped and there came a note of urgent pleading into it. 'Listen to me. He's a good-looking fellow granted, although he's old enough to be your father, but from my experience that kind of man doesn't look for a good-looking wife – not your type, anyway.' Her voice sank even lower now as she went on, 'Don't you realise it, Grace, you're not only good-looking, you're a beautiful girl. You could have anybody you had a mind to point at. I could name half a dozen men in this town who would jump if you raised your finger. The only reason they are keeping their distance at present is because you are so young and your folks haven't been dead six months yet. But that doesn't seem to trouble your parson friend. And another thing, if that fellow had wanted anything but money he'd have been married afore the day at his age, going on thirty-eight.'

Grace was crying now and had protested, 'Oh, Aunt Aggie, how can you?'

'I can and I will,' she had repeated over again, 'and I'm going to tell you this, Grace. It will be the sorriest day's work you'll do in your life if you marry that man the morrow. I tell you I know the type. They're like some of the great big whopping turnips you see, fine on the outside but boast inside. It's all the same with these big beauties, and you'll find you'll want more than a good-looking face on the pillow to get you happily through marriage. Aye, you will. And what about your music, eh? What about that? D'you think he'll let you go on with that . . . ? You wait and see.'

And now as Grace lay looking into the beautiful face she knew Aunt Aggie was wrong, so terribly wrong, and she felt sorry for Aunt Aggie, because for years she had been looked upon as the oracle of the family. Her father used to say nobody could hoodwink Aggie. She had a head on her, had Aggie. How many women after losing their husbands would, or could, carry on his job, and the tricky one at that, of buying and selling property? But Aggie had done it. Yes, Aggie was astute, and cute.

As Donald rose from the bed, his hand trailing slowly from hers, she forgot her Aunt Aggie, for who could think of a domineering, middle-aged, fat little woman when they were murmuring, 'Oh, darling, darling, I do love you.' Yet somewhere in her mind, she was vowing, I'll make Aunt Aggie eat her words. I will, I will. No-one, no-one in the world must dislike Donald . . . anyway, how could they?

By the end of the honeymoon she was a little tired of looking at architecture, Byzantine, Gothic, and the rest, and she was secretly looking forward to taking up her life at the vicarage, and, as she said to herself – doing things with it. She knew exactly what alterations she was going to make to that big, draughty house, but she knew that she would have to move cautiously, for Donald had emphasised, and strongly, that she must be prepared to live within his means. And to think that Aunt Aggie . . .

Donald had himself been only three months in the village of Deckford, and, as he said, was still feeling his feet. He was also, she knew, still smarting under the reason for his banishment from St Bernard's. He had made light of it when it happened, saying to her, 'You want to know the reason why I've got to go. Well, can you give me your undivided attention for the next few days to listen to the history of the Church – I'll have to start with the Reformation.' His voice had become sad as he ended. 'I am, as you know, innately what you might call High Church, and St Bernard's is innately what you might term Low Church. My job, when I was sent there, was to bring the two to a moderate meeting point, but I'm afraid my zeal has carried me over that point and annoyed a number of people, so I am being banished to a little village, but where, oddly enough' – he laughed here – 'they are rather partial to trappings.' It was on the day he told her this that she knew she loved him and couldn't live without him, and on the day he actually moved to Deckford he asked her to marry him and she fell into his arms . . .

But it was decreed that Grace was not to live in the vicarage at Deckford. The weather took a hand in her destiny, for during a gale, and only three days before they returned from Italy, one of the two large chimneys crashed through the roof and caused a great amount of damage. Uncle Ralph, taking things in hand, made it his business to find them temporary accommodation against their return. This accommodation was the home of the late Miss Tupping and called Willow Lea. The house and its contents were up for sale, and the business was in the hands of Bertrand Farley, Junior, who had been Miss Tupping's solicitor. Bertrand Farley saw no reason why the house should not be rented for a few weeks, for privately he could not see it being sold at any price. There was a slump hitting the country, and it was improbable he would get an early sale for a place such as Willow Lea . . .

So it was that Grace returned to a home which delighted her heart with its air of graciousness, and she determined right away that she was going to do all in her power to remain there, for her Donald, she saw at once, loved the house. Although he said not a word in its favour until a month later when they were about to leave it. It was this moment that Grace had been waiting for and she put into words what had been in her mind since she had first entered the door. Why shouldn't they live here permanently? Why couldn't they buy it?

What? Donald was up in arms. The suggestion met with a complete refusal. No, she knew the arrangement they had agreed on, they must live within his means. Of course he liked the house, but that did not mean, etc., etc. Grace was not deterred: she sent for her Uncle Ralph and Aunt Susie, and there was a meeting in the drawing-room during which Donald gradually, but only gradually, became amenable. Once his consent was gained, the rest was a mere formality.

Willow Lea was bought as it stood, furniture

included, at the bargain price of £4,000. There was only one snag that promised to be an irritant, a codicil concerning Benjamin Fairfoot, the gardener.

Benjamin had started with Miss Tupping's family when he was a boy, and when Miss Tupping had had a new house built for herself she and Benjamin Fairfoot between them had designed and created the gardens, and the codicil provided against Benjamin's dismissal. Whoever purchased the house must sign to the effect that he would be kept on as gardener, as long as he so desired.

Grace saw nothing in this to worry about, it did not even call for consideration . . . of course Benjamin would be kept on, he was part of the garden. She liked Ben, he talked Geordie and reminded her of old Jack Cummings, except that up to date she hadn't heard him swear. Jack Cummings had been one of her father's men when they lived next to the coal depot. She knew that it was because she liked to play around Jack and had acquired a little of his vocabulary that her mother had insisted on her being sent away to school in the first place.

Uncle Ralph's opinion of the codicil was much the same as Grace's own. 'Oh, that's nowt,' he said, 'I'd say you're lucky to have such a fellow as that thrown in. You're lucky altogether, me lass.'

Donald alone questioned the matter of Ben's compulsory employment, the reason he voiced being that they couldn't afford a gardener. Grace had laughed over this. 'We can afford three gardeners,' she had said, 'and a full staff inside

too. And, what's more, we're going to have them.'
It was a silly thing to say, taking things far too
quickly, and it brought upon her head a lecture.

'No, Grace, that'll never do. The gardener . . .
all right, because our hand is forced . . . and a
little help in the house, that'll be all right too. But
you must remember, Grace, that I'm just an
ordinary parson, and only by continuing as such
can I hope to hold my parish together. Any show
of undue affluence would be bound to estrange at
least one part of the community.'

She knew that he was referring to the folk
versus the others, and she sighed. She knew he
was right. Her Donald was always right, he was
so wise. He had explained all this to her before,
the difference between the folk, as he called the
villagers, and the others. Among which were
the Farleys, the hunting Tooles, the doctor,
and the schoolmaster in that order. Oh yes,
Donald was right.

From when did she first start telling herself
several times a day that she was happy? Before
she had been married three months? Yes, a while
before that. Her days at the beginning left her
very little time for private thoughts. Running an
eight-roomed house with the part-time help of
Mrs Blenkinsop, and getting initiated into the
duties of a parson's wife, which, besides visiting,
included taking an active part in the Women's
Guild, the Sewing Meeting and the Literary
Evening, the latter a new innovation instigated by
the vicar, left her a little tired by nightfall. Sometimes she would sit on the rug before the fire, her

head resting against Donald's knees, her hand on top of his hand where it covered her hair, and she would almost fall asleep listening to his endearments.

'My energetic little girl is overdoing it.'

'No . . . no, I'm not.' Her voice would often sound as if it was coming through sleep.

'I'm going to take you to bed and tuck you up.'

Whenever he spoke in this way she would be roused and say, with a sort of childish petulance which in no way suited her, 'Oh, aren't you coming, Donnie?'

'No, I'm not coming. Come along, up you get.'

She would be in his arms now and he would be putting on an act of mock sternness. 'How am I going to get any work out of you tomorrow if you don't get your sleep?'

'But, Donald . . . '

'No but Donald, it's bed for you.'

'Yes, and for you.' Her finger would be tracing the outline of his mouth.

'After I get my sermon finished.'

'But you did that last night.'

'No, I didn't get at it. I had to do the address I am giving on Saturday in Newcastle.'

'Oh, Donald.' Her head would fall wearily against him and he would carry her upstairs and into their room and drop her with a playful plonk on the bed. He never stayed while she undressed. When some time later she would be in bed he would come in again and stroke her hair and kiss her lips, and lastly her eyes, and tuck her up before putting out the light. Sometimes she would sigh happily, then drop off to sleep, but at other times, and more frequently as time went on, when this little scene was enacted, she would kick her legs down the bed or turn on her stomach and push her face into the pillow . . . She had not cried yet . . .

About this time her mind was lifted from herself by the fact, the stupendous fact, that Aunt Aggie was coming to visit them. It was Donald who had really brought about this minor miracle, for, from shortly after their return, he had voiced his opinion that it was a great pity her Aunt Aggie was estranged from them, and Grace must try to bring about a reconciliation. She had, on this occasion, received a little private sermon on the poison of malice and the health-giving properties of forgiveness, and as she listened she thought, Oh, if only Aunt Aggie could see him as he really is.

If at that moment Grace herself could have seen him as he really was she still would not have believed that her wonderful Donald could not suffer the thought that anyone could know him and find him not to their liking.

So Grace went to see Aggie, and again she went, and yet again, and at last Aggie said yes. Yes, she would come to see the grand new house . . . but just because she was interested in property, mind – that was the only reason.

The morning Aggie was due to arrive Grace sidled out of bed around six o'clock, very careful not to wake Donald, and began an onslaught of rearranging and preparation for the visitor. Mrs Blenkinsop, when she arrived at eight o'clock, did not take kindly to the bustle that was already in progress, and Donald, when he came down to breakfast, exclaimed, 'My! My! All this for the dragon. You never make so much fuss about me.'

'Oh, Donald, I do. You know I do. And besides, Aunt Aggie isn't a dragon. She's a darling really, once you get to know her.'

'She scares me stiff.' Donald was in a playful mood.

'Oh, that's funny.' She was laughing at him. 'I can't imagine anyone scaring you stiff.' She dashed at him now and, flinging her arms around his neck, kissed him.

'You're the one that scares people. D'you know what you do? You scare the pants off them.' She accompanied this latter with small jerks of her head, then giggled as she watched Donald's eyebrows move up.

'And where, may I ask, did you hear that edifying piece of news?'

'Ben.'

'Ben . . . Oh . . . when?'

'Yesterday, after you had failed to persuade him to move those hydrangeas.'

'Well?'

'I was coming up the drive, walking on the verge. I heard part of the persuasion, and then I heard him leading off to himself.' She fell into an imitation of Ben's voice. ' "Scare the pants off 'em down there" – he was meaning the village – "but he's not going to scare 'em off me. No, by damn!" '

'Tut! tut! You mustn't repeat words like that . . . But he said that, did he?' Donald disengaged

66

himself, and she looked at him in some surprise as he added, 'Well, we'll see.'

If he hadn't made the last statement she would have imagined that he was only amused, but now she could see that he was slightly annoyed. But as for him scaring any of his parishioners, it was, when she came to think of it, ridiculous, for his attitude towards them, she considered, was over-conciliatory, except when he was in the pulpit. When there, there was nothing conciliatory about him. At times, if she had dared criticise his sermons, she would have said in the idiom of her father, 'That was hot and heavy this morning.' But not for the world would she dream of criticising anything he might do with regards to his work. His business was putting over God, and all his energies were spent in that direction. Unbidden there came to her mind the picture of herself kicking her legs down the bed before turning on to her stomach.

The picture was not new, and because in some way it was a reflection on Donald she chided herself vigorously once again on its appearance. She was the wife of a vicar, she mustn't forget, and parsons were different, there were many things as the wife of a vicar she would have to make herself not only get used to but like. The latest was praying together, privately at night at the bedside.

It was around about the time of Aggie's visit that she began to look towards the nights with a slight dread, to see them as a time of conflict, and there was no-one she told herself to blame for this but herself. Certainly not Donald, Donald was wonderful. It was she who was at fault. The truth of the matter was that at rock bottom she wasn't good, there was a baseness in her. A burning, craving, unsatisfied, restless baseness. Oh, she knew herself and she must try, try hard to conquer this unworthy feeling.

There were times also when she wished she had someone to talk to . . . her mother or someone. She did not bring Aunt Aggie into the category of someone, she could never now talk to Aunt Aggie about herself – at least not when it related to her marriage. Aunt Aggie must be made to realise how happy she was with Donald and come to like him . . . Yet she wished there was someone . . . But had there been, could she ever have put into words what was troubling her? No. No. Never . . .

Everything was ready except flowers for the table, and she knew that these would have to be coaxed out of Ben. But that wouldn't be difficult, she had a way with Ben. She liked him and, strangely, she felt more at home with him than with anyone else in the village, but she was wise enough to keep this fact to herself. She ran now through the hall, out into the garden, and round the side of the house and just remembered to pull herself to a walk before she reached the greenhouse. This running everywhere was something that Donald had checked her for. But she never seemed to be able to get to places quickly enough, she had to run.

'Hello, Ben.'

'Mornin', ma'am.'

'I'm on the scrounge, Ben, for something for the table.'

And her vocabulary would, definitely, she knew, have brought a protest from Donald had he heard her. One was careful how one spoke both to the folks . . . and the others. Jokes were for the privacy of one's family, as also was slang . . . if it must be used. But this manner of speaking was an attitude that Ben knew and understood. She had learned from the little he had said about his previous mistress, and the great deal Mrs Blenkinsop had told her, that there had been no starchiness of man and employer between them. Looking at this wonderful garden she could understand that it could never have come into creation without sympathetic co-operation. Her attitude might not be similar to that used by Miss Tupping, but it was one that Ben in his surly way appreciated, and she was aware of this.

'Well now, what have we got?' He considered a moment. 'A couple of roses suit you?'

'Roses? Oh, Ben, marvellous.'

There was not more than half a dozen late roses left, and when lovingly he cut four of them, trimmed the stalks, and handed them to her she said with genuine feeling, 'Oh, that's kind of you, Ben.' It was as if the garden was his and he was bestowing a gift upon her.

'That's all right, ma'am.'

'Thanks, Ben.' She turned from him, forgetting not to run, and she took the path round the vegetable garden towards the back door. She was still running when she burst into the kitchen crying, 'Look, Mrs B, what I've scrounged . . .' Her voice trailed away and the hand holding out the roses moved slowly downwards as she looked at the young man standing near the dresser. He was in rough working clothes and had his cap in his hand, and after looking at her for a moment he said, 'Good morning.'

'This is Andrew MacIntyre, ma'am; he's come with a message for the vicar. I've just told him he's out.'

She laid the roses on the table, then asked, 'Is there anything I can do?'

'It's from Mr Toole. He says to tell the vicar that there's a mount for him for Thursday's meet if he cares for it.'

'Oh.' She sounded a little surprised. 'He usually phones.'

'He tried twice this morning but the line was engaged, and as I was passing this way . . .'

She was looking at him, waiting for him to finish, and when he didn't go on she said, 'Thanks.' Then again, 'Thanks, I'll tell him.'

He nodded his head once towards her, then, turning and looking at Mrs Blenkinsop, he said briefly, 'Good morning.'

From the kitchen window Grace watched the tall, rather gangling figure cross the courtyard before she asked, 'Is he in our parish, Mrs B?'

'Lord alive, I should say so. But I saw by your face, ma'am, that you hadn't come across him afore. And that's nothing unusual, he scarcely comes down to the street unless he has to. He's from Peak Fell, in the cottage up there.'

'As far away as that. That's likely why I've never seen him in church.'

'Huh! You're not likely to see any of the MacIntyres in church, ma'am. If they're anything they're at the opposite pole from the Church of England. They're Scots and a close family . . . All Scots are dour, don't you think, ma'am?'

'I haven't met many, Mrs B.'

'Well, from my experience I'd say they are. The MacIntyres have been in the village around fifteen years – quite a while it is, fifteen years – but nobody knows much more about them than on the day they came except that she was a teacher of sorts and he was crippled with arthritis . . . laziness I would say, for he can get around on his sticks when he likes. He hasn't done a bat to my knowledge in all the years he's been here except carve little animals and such which he sells now and then. It's yon Andrew they live by, and if you ask me—' Mrs Blenkinsop's voice stopped abruptly, then she added, 'The vicar, ma'am, I've just caught sight of his tails flying.'

'Oh, is it?' Grace stopped herself from bounding towards the door, and, picking up the roses from the table, she said, 'I'll do these in the cloakroom, they'll be out of your way there.'

But the green baize door of the kitchen had hardly swung to behind her when she ran across the hall and into the study.

'Hello, darling.' She flung her arms around his neck, the roses still in her hand, and as they waved about the crown of his head she cried excitedly, 'See what I got out of Ben, four of his best; I've got him eating out of my hand.'

He closed his eyes and refused to look at her as he said with mock severity, 'Conceit and pride ill becomes a vicar's wife.'

'Oh, Donald.' She dropped her head onto his

71

shoulder and began to giggle, then after a moment she raised it quickly, when, with more than a touch of censure, he commented, 'It's a pity they've been cut. I think they would have looked better and remained alive longer if they had been left in their natural setting. There are so few now and it was so nice to see them in the garden at this time of the year.'

She loosened her hands from behind his head, then, after looking at him for a moment, her gaze dropped and she said softly, 'Yes, yes, I suppose you're right, Donald, it was very silly of me to ask him for them. I rather pestered him. I'm sorry.'

That the roses had been cut had vexed Donald, but his vexation would only be aggravated if he knew that Ben had done the cutting without any pressure. She had been stupid to brag about him eating out of her hand. So again she repeated, 'I'm sorry.'

'Well, they're cut now.'

'Don't be vexed.'

'I'm not.'

'Kiss me.'

He kissed her and then turned away, and she exclaimed with nervous, false jocularity, 'I've got a present for a good boy.' She paused before delivering it. 'There's an invitation from Mr Toole; he says there's a mount for you at the meet on Thursday.'

His head came round and his eyes brightened with pleasure. 'He called?'

'No, he had phoned twice this morning and couldn't get through so he sent one of his men with the message, an Andrew MacIntyre. Have you met any of the MacIntyres? I never knew they existed, and I thought I had met everybody from miles around.'

'Oh, the MacIntyres.' Donald's neck stretched out of his collar and the smile left his eyes. 'Yes, I've met the MacIntyres. Dyed in the wool bigots.'

'You've visited them then?'

'Yes, shortly after I came here.' He paused, and when he continued his voice had a rasping sound. 'When you get an ignorant bigoted Scot there's nothing much more can be added to the description.'

'But the young man seemed quite nice.' Her comment sounded tentative.

'Oh yes, I should say he's all right, at least on the surface, for he's bound to have his father in him somewhere. But I suppose there must be a deal of good in him, for I understand that Toole has taken a great interest in him since he was a boy, and he's no fool where men are concerned. At one time he wanted to send him to an agricultural college, but the father would have none of it. Of course his point of view is understandable: the boy is their only means of support.'

'Is the father really ill?'

'Not so ill that he couldn't be better if he tried, and that's Doctor Cooper's version too.'

'What a pity – I mean that the boy couldn't have gone to college.'

'Yes, it was. But then if Mr Toole hasn't been allowed to help him, the daughter is going to do her best.' This last was accompanied by a pursing of the lips and Grace cried delightedly, 'You mean Adelaide . . . she's . . .'

'Yes, head over heels I should say, and if her father allows it, and it's probable, for he likes the young fellow, yon Andrew MacIntyre will fall very firmly on his two big feet.'

'Oh, I hope it comes off. I like Adelaide . . . she seems full of life.'

'It is whispered that she has a temper.'

'And what is wrong with that, Mr Donald Rouse?' Donald had recovered from his slight irritation over Ben and she could tease him.

'Everything.'

'Are you serious?' Grace dropped her head to one side.

'Yes, I am serious, Mrs Rouse. I think a woman with a temper is something to be abhorred. Just think what it leads to, temper of any kind, but in a woman . . . a bad-tempered woman . . .'

'Oh, Donald,' she broke in on him, 'I must see to the table, and these flowers, but do come along, darling, and tell me all you know about bad-tempered women.' She made a grab at his hand and turned to pull him after her, but found herself jerked back to him.

'You're not taking me seriously.'

'No, Donald dear, I am not.'

'Do I suspect you're laughing at me?'

'I wouldn't dare laugh at you, sir.' Her face was straight but her eyes were shining, and she was striving not to giggle. She was happy inside, she loved Donald in these playful exchanges. The nights were forgotten. She could tell herself she adored him.

'You must not laugh at me, I am a very nervous

man at the moment. In a short time I am to eat before your aunt.'

Her head went back and her laugh rang out, 'Eat before your aunt. Oh, that does sound funny, Donald . . . This is the house of my aunt . . . *ce ci est la maison de ma tante.*'

As her laugh soared again his hand went up quickly to silence her on the sound of the front-door bell ringing, then he punched the air and hissed, 'Miss Shawcross. You see what you've done, almost made me forget. Look, come this way.' He drew her quickly across the room and through the french windows, along the terrace and through a similar window into the drawing-room, and there hastily closing the window behind him, he chided her with raised finger. 'I meant to get this explained before she came. It's about the play.'

'The play?'

'Yes; you see, what I hadn't fully understood before was that she had always played the piano for the children, not just last Christmas, and when . . .'

'But it was all arranged that I should play, I chose the music and—'

'Yes, yes, I know, my dear, and her playing is atrocious, we all know that, but it would hurt her so much if this little duty were to be taken away from her. I've felt for days that there was something wrong, and when she approached me this morning I discovered . . . well, that was it . . . the play. I told her that of course you hadn't understood, and if she would call up during her dinner hour you would let her have the music, she's quite willing to work to your choice . . . Oh, my dear, don't look so disappointed.'

'But I wanted to play for the children, Donald, I've been looking forward to it.'

A flatness had come upon her day. Playing for the children at the Christmas concert and Nativity play was to constitute her first real social engagement as the vicar's wife and she had given to it quite a lot of thought. It was actually Donald himself who had suggested she should do this. There were not more than fifteen children from the scattered community who attended Sunday school and they offered material that had no artistic claim, but this had in no way deterred her – in fact it had set her a challenge. The Christmas concert and Nativity play was going to be the best ever heard or seen in the village. She would show them that although she was very young to be the parson's wife she was capable, very capable.

Donald was patting her cheek and saying quietly, 'I've got an idea to show off your talents on a much larger scale . . . an evening concert, you could let yourself rip at that. What do you say?'

At this moment she was too disappointed to be other than herself, so the only reply she made to this solace was with her eyebrows. She gave them an upward lift.

'Oh, my dear, come along.' There was the slightest edge to his voice now. 'What is there in playing for children; much better to make your début at a proper concert. One of the Miss Farleys plays the 'cello, and Blenkinsop, although you mightn't credit it, is no mean hand with the violin.'

'All right.'

'Come on then, smile. If your Aunt Aggie sees you like this she'll swear I'm starting to beat you and she'll say, "I knew it. I was right." '

She gave him a playful push and he squeezed her hand before going out on to the terrace towards his study and Miss Shawcross.

Blast Miss Shawcross. Grace gave no girlish sign of guilt on this thought. She was getting a little fed up with Miss Shawcross. This wasn't the first time during her short sojourn in the village that her opinion had had to be waived in favour of that of Miss Shawcross. There had been the business of the new literary group and its procedure. Miss Shawcross's suggestions had been followed because Miss Shawcross did such an amount of work for the church and it was only fair to give her a little say in this new venture. There had also been the dressing of the altar. The brass vases Grace considered looked too heavy when filled with flowers and she had substituted two silver ones, but the week after their arrival they had been relegated to the dim corners of the altar, and the brass ones were back dominating the scene.

'Let the matter be,' Donald had said, 'it's not worth a fracas. She has done the altar for years, in fact since she was a young girl; until now she has almost come to think that it belongs to her.' And then he had added, 'The church means so much to her, you'll have to remember that, my dear.'

And now the play – Miss Shawcross had won again.

This latter thought came to Grace in the form of a shock. She was made aware that she was in the midst of a contest, a contest which required the use of guile, and she could see quite plainly that if she was even to hold her own she would have to avail herself of this guile. The picture presented looked rather nasty, and she turned from the window and shook her head as if trying to throw the whole business off. Miss Shawcross was an old maid, a stuffy, prim old maid. She would tell Aunt Aggie on the quiet about Miss Shawcross and they would have a laugh. Yes, that was the best way to deal with Miss Shawcross, laugh at her.

Grace was bursting with pride and happiness. Aunt Aggie liked the house, she had thoroughly enjoyed her lunch, and, what was more – oh more important than anything else – she seemed to be getting to like Donald. Donald had gone out of his way to be charming to her and in Grace's opinion he was irresistible. Aunt Aggie would have had to be made of stone if she hadn't melted under this treatment.

There was one incident that Grace feared might throw a spanner into Aunt Aggie's capitulation. This was when Donald, taking the key from his waistcoat pocket, went to the sideboard and, unlocking the cupboard door, drew out the lead-lined wine box. In the box were four bottles and a number of glasses and then he turned and looked at Aggie, saying, 'What will you have? Sherry sweet, sherry dry?' He pointed to the bottles in turn, 'Sauternes . . . ? Or whiskey . . . Irish?' He laughed, and Aggie replied, 'I think I'll have the Sauternes, thank you.'

Grace could see that Aunt Aggie was slightly puzzled. The only glasses on the table were those for water, and when Donald placed the glass of wine before Aggie and another by the side of her plate, she felt that some explanation was due, and just as she was about to give it Donald raised his hand in his customary fashion and said brightly, 'Leave the explanation to me, my dear. 1 am the culprit and I must answer for my sins.' Before continuing he went and pushed the wine tray back into the cupboard, locked the door, then took his seat again, and, leaning across the table towards his guest, he said, 'The truth is, I'm a secret tippler, Aunt Aggie.'

There was a peculiar gleam in Aggie's small bright eyes as she said flatly, 'Well, that wouldn't surprise me in the least.'

'Oh, Aunt Aggie . . . ! and you, Donald.' Grace turned on him. 'You'll have her believing that . . . It's because of Mrs Blenkinsop, Aunt Aggie.' Grace's voice was a whisper now as she leaned towards her aunt. 'Parsons and their wives are not supposed to have wine with their meals, it would be all over the village . . .'

'Let us stick to the truth, Grace,' Donald put in quietly. 'It is not that parsons are not supposed to have wine with their meals, parsons are not supposed to be able to afford wine with their meals. There's a fine point there. But I'm a crafty man, Aunt Aggie. I married a woman with money who could afford to pander to my secret craving.' Donald did not look at Aggie as he said this but lifted the glass to eye level and twiddled the stem between his fingers. And he kept his eyes on the glass as he ended, 'But there is nothing I enjoy more than a glass of wine.'

From across the table Aggie nodded slowly at him, before saying, 'Well, at least I'm with you there, for if there's anything I like better than a glass of wine meself, it's two glasses of wine.'

The vicar let himself laugh at this triteness, and Grace thought how odd it was that these two should agree on the one point which she had dreaded might be the means of widening the gulf between them. Donald's system concerning the wine came under the heading of duplicity, and she hadn't expected her aunt to condone it. No, she had expected her to attack it, with a 'well, what did I tell you?' She was very relieved.

Lunch over, the atmosphere all she could desire, she lost no time when she was alone with Aggie in bringing before her notice the virtues of her husband. That which she felt would impress her aunt most was the fact that he would not allow her to use the car for visiting, nor would he use it himself for such a purpose. Moreover, there was the fact that he insisted they could only afford Mrs Blenkinsop for half days. And finally, he only had three pairs of shoes and he wouldn't buy any more until at least one pair was worn out.

'Well, he can't manage to wear more than one pair at a time, can he?' Aggie's dry remark was delivered without a smile and brought Grace to fluster. 'Yes, Aunt Aggie, but you understand what I—'

'Yes, yes, I understand all right.' Aggie patted Grace on the knee. 'Don't frash yourself, child. We'll get along all right, I suppose, when we get to know each other a bit better, but don't you work too hard at it or you'll wear yourself down to your hunkers . . . I'll accept the fact that you've married a saint.'

'Oh, Aunt Aggie.' Grace had her head half lowered as if she had been caught at some misdemeanour, but when Aggie burst out laughing she joined in and threw her arms about her aunt and hugged her, crying, 'Oh, now I want nothing more.'

'Sit down and don't rumple me.' Aggie pushed her into a chair, then asked, 'What are the folks like around here, nice?'

'Yes. I'll take you through the village in a little while and you'll see some of them for yourself. I said they were nice and they are, all except one, a Miss Shawcross.'

'Miss Shawcross? Who is she?'

'The postmistress.'

'Ah, the postmistress, middle-aged, a church worker and . . . after the parson.'

Grace's eyes were wide as she exclaimed, 'You're a witch, Aunt Aggie – that's Miss Shawcross.'

'Is it, by gum?' Aunt Aggie bristled in mock anger. 'Come on then, let's have a dekko at her.'

Grace's laugh was high and free. Oh, it was good to be with Aunt Aggie again. She wanted nothing more now – nothing . . . ?

Some time later in the afternoon, after Aggie had visited the church and met Mr Blenkinsop, had been introduced to Dr Cooper as he came out of Brooke's the grocer's, had met Sep Stanley the baker and, like Grace on her first visit, had been given a hot buttered roll, they made their way to the post office and Miss Shawcross, and they were careful not to exchange glances as they entered.

Aggie Turner's shrewd eyes immediately saw that Miss Shawcross was quite different from her own jocular description; she was younger than she had expected, she was bigger than she had expected, and immediately she found that the woman claimed her sympathy, and this she hadn't expected either. As she looked into the large, plain face, she thought, 'It's a pity. By, it is that, for if he had come here before he had seen Grace that time of the accident, here's the one who would have been Mrs Rouse. At least she would have had a damn good try, and I would have said good luck to her.' This woman, she thought, would have made a far better parson's wife than her niece ever would, no matter how hard she kept on trying, and she was trying so hard at present that it was painful to watch her, and all because she was clean barmy about the man. Yet it looked as if she herself had misjudged the fellow, for, going by his present behaviour, he wasn't squandering Grace's money. But, of course, Aggie's business acumen prompted the thought, he had got quite a bit out of it already and in a way that brought no pointing finger at him. He had a fine house and furniture, and he was living much more comfortably than he could ever have hoped to do on his own income. Still, she must be fair. Apparently he had his principles and was living up to them. Moreover, she was glad to know he had his own frailties. She had liked the touch of the wine business at lunch.

'What do you think?' asked Grace, when they had left the shop and were walking circumspectly through the village.

'I'm a bit sorry for her. Now! Now! Wait till I finish.' Aggie discreetly raised a finger. 'I also think I'd go very carefully. Don't pull her to shreds in front of him, of – of Donald. Your best plan, you know, would be to try to get to like her.'

'Oh, Aunt Aggie.'

'All right. It's only a suggestion, but remember you'll have to live with her for a long time.'

On this Grace let the matter drop – she was very puzzled at her aunt's reactions to Miss Shawcross, and not at all pleased.

The afternoon was sunny and even warm, and so they made their way on to the fells, Grace's primary idea being to show Aunt Aggie the village from the top of Roebeck Fell. An hour later, after much talking and laughing, they found themselves on top of Peak Fell from where you could see nothing for miles but the rolling hills, and Grace said, 'What does it matter, we'll go halfway down the valley and take a cut up to Roebeck Fell.'

'That you won't, not today,' said Aggie. 'I've got the feeling my feet are worn down to my knees already. We'll take the shortest cut for home and soon.'

'Oh, sit here for a while longer, Aunt Aggie. Isn't it beautiful!' She stretched out her arms to embrace the scene. 'You know something: this is the first time I've been on this fell. It's more beautiful than any of the others.'

'Yes, it's very beautiful.' Aggie nodded as she looked round. 'That's if you like it wild. There's not a habitation to be seen. I can't say my fancy bends this way. I'm more comfortable in Northumberland Street in Newcastle.'

'You've got no poetry in you. This does something to you.'

'Aye it might' – Aggie's voice had dropped, as it did when she was aiming to be funny, into the north country idiom – 'but aal Aa knaa at the minute is that A'm froze . . . Look' – she sought for a handkerchief – 'me nose is runnin'.'

'Oh, Aunt Aggie!' Grace's laugh rang out over the hills as she pulled Aggie up towards her, saying, 'Come on, then, let's be moving. There must be a shorter cut down than the one we came up by.'

Aggie's statement that there were no habitations on the fells was proved wrong when after walking not more than ten minutes they came upon a cottage. It was two-storied and made of rough quarry stone. It looked stark and ugly and had none of the warm mellowness attached to the houses in and around the village, many of which were built of the same material. The front door of the house led straight on to the steep road which had levelled itself out for a short distance at this point.

They were some yards from the house when they heard the shouting. The raised voices spoke quite plainly of a row in progress. Grace looked at Aggie and Aggie pursed her lips and nodded as she commented under her breath, 'Skull and hair flying.' The voices ceased before they reached the house, but just as they passed the door it opened and a woman and a young man stepped into the road, then came to an abrupt halt as they stared at the two women opposite them.

The young man Grace recognised as Andrew MacIntyre and the woman she took to be his mother. It was odd, she thought, that during all the months she had been in the village she hadn't seen him, yet here she was meeting him twice in the same day. 'Good afternoon,' she said.

The woman moved her head just the slightest as she murmured, 'Good afternoon.'

'This is my mother. This is the vicar's wife, Mother.' The young man was looking at Grace as he spoke.

The woman inclined her head slowly and Grace said, 'How do you do, Mrs MacIntyre?'

'Very well . . . ma'am.' She seemed to have some difficulty in adding the ma'am.

'You have a beautiful view.' Grace half turned from them.

'Yes, it's a grand view,' said the woman.

'And a grand walk up to it,' came wearily from Aggie. 'I'll be glad when I get off my feet.'

Whether or not this was a hint to be asked in to take a seat for a time the woman did not rise to it, instead she suggested a short cut for their return journey. 'You can halve the distance,' she said, 'and come out behind Miss Tupping's . . . I mean your house, ma'am,' she added apologetically. Then, turning to her son, she said, 'You'r going down. Will you show the ladies the way, Andrew?'

The expression on the young man's face did not alter, so there was no means of knowing whether he was vexed or pleased, and when he spoke he looked neither at Aggie nor at Grace.

'If you'll come round this way,' he said.

After saying goodbye to Mrs MacIntyre they both followed him round the side of the house. Grace, going first, looked at his back. It was very slim, especially around the hips, and his walk was slow as if he had all the time in the world at his disposal . . . yet he had come through the door of the house quickly enough. He must have been rowing with his father; it couldn't possibly have been his mother, her glance was too soft on him. He was very like his mother; he had the same eyes, round and brown, almost black, but his hair wasn't as dark as hers.

'Are you all right, Aunt Aggie?' She turned now to where Aggie was picking her way carefully down the steep, rock-strewn path, and Aggie replied, 'Yes, I'm all right, as long as it doesn't get any worse.'

'Your mother said this path leads to the back of our house. Does it go down through the wood?' She was speaking to his back.

'Aye . . . yes.'

As she slithered over the rough ground she remarked, 'I wouldn't want to take this short cut often,' and she laughed to soften any suggestion of criticism.

'It isn't usually as bad as this. The rain's loosened the rocks. My mother didn't think when

86

she suggested it. I'm sorry.' He had stopped and was now looking beyond her towards Aggie.

'Oh, I don't mind.' Aggie's voice was re-assuring. 'As long as it shortens the journey I'll put up with it.'

'Well, it does that.'

As they went on again Grace thought, He's got a nice voice. Unlike his face and disposition there was nothing surly about it. It was a warm sort of voice, with the Scottish 'burr' thick on it. He might have lived in Northumberland for years but he hadn't lost the Scottish twang. She felt she wanted to listen to it, but his economical use of words offered little opportunity.

At one part the path crossed directly over a stretch of stone road, and she remarked, 'This looks a good road, where does it lead to?'

'The quarry.'

'Oh, I didn't know there was a quarry about here.' She looked at his averted face.

'It's not worked now.' His tone did not seem to invite further enquiry and she did not press the matter further.

A few minutes later they entered the wood and when they came to where three paths met in a small clearing he spoke without turning, saying, 'We fork left.'

Ten minutes later they emerged quite abruptly from a narrow path between the brambles into a field not more than twenty feet wide, and there, bordering its other side, was the hedge of Willow Lea.

'Well I never!' With this mundane exclamation Grace looked around her.

'So we've arrived,' commented Aggie dryly a moment later. 'And thank you very much.' She nodded at their escort. But after gazing towards the high hedge she looked up at him again and demanded, 'But can you tell us how we're going to get over that?' She pointed across the field.

'Oh, there's a gate farther up, at the far end, Aunt Aggie,' Grace put in. 'It's locked, but if I shout I'll make Ben hear – the greenhouses are just to the right of it.' She turned now and looked at the straight countenance of the young farm-worker, and, smiling, she said, 'Thank you very much for bringing us and for showing me the path. I often go into the wood, but I've always had to get in by the main road.'

He nodded as he looked at her but made no comment. Then, touching his cap, he said briefly, 'Good-day.'

It was meant for both of them, and Aggie said, 'Goodbye and thanks,' but Grace found herself answering him with his own words. 'Good-day,' she said.

As they moved along the field towards the gate, arm in arm, Aggie commented with a chuckle, 'By, he was pleasant, wasn't he? I've laughed me head off.' And Grace, quoting Mrs Blenkinsop, stated authoritatively, 'Oh, it's likely just his way, all Scots are dour.'

That Aunt Aggie's visit had been a great success was borne out as she stood in the bedroom adjusting her smart toque hat in the mirror. As she did this she looked to where Grace was standing behind her, then with lowered eyes she said, 'I'm glad to see you happy, child . . . and I suppose this is the time I should admit to being wrong, eh?'

'Oh, Aunt Aggie!' Grace pulled her round from the mirror and Aggie protested, 'Now look what you're doing, mind my hat . . . this bit of nonsense cost me a pretty penny, let me tell you.'

'Oh, Aunt Aggie!'

'Don't keep saying "Oh, Aunt Aggie!" and don't think that I'm going to join Susie and Ralph and start dribbling over him, that I'll never do.'

'That'll come, there's plenty of time yet.'

Aggie gave her a sharp push and sent her laughing on to the landing, crying, 'Donald! Donald! She's braying me!' and Donald, from where he was waiting in the hall, shouted back, 'Well, it's about time somebody did, for I've got to confess I'm not up to it.'

The atmosphere was homely and happy, and surrounded by it they waved Aggie and her car off down the drive, then turned and went into the house arm-in-arm.

This, Grace felt, had been the happiest day of her life, even happier than her wedding day. If she remembered the incident concerning Miss Shaw-cross she looked upon it now as one of the pin-pricks that parsons' wives are called upon to endure. There was always at least one Miss Shawcross in every parish.

Even when at ten o'clock Donald said he couldn't come upstairs just yet as he had some writing to do, which would take about an hour, her happiness still remained at an even keel. She spent rather longer than usual getting prepared for bed, then sat propped up reading.

She stopped reading before eleven, and when at half-past there was still no sound of movement from the room below, her legs jerked themselves down the bed and she turned onto her stomach.

At twelve o'clock she was tossing and turning from side to side in an effort to stop herself from going down to the study. He did not like that, she knew he did not like that.

When later, after what seemed like an eternity but was not more than twenty minutes, she heard him coming up the stairs and creeping quietly into the room, she was lying on her side, her face buried half in the pillow and half under the bedclothes. And when she felt him standing at the bedside looking down at her she made no movement. He had hoped to find her asleep; he was finding her asleep.

She pulled in the muscles of her stomach, screwed her eyes tight and bit her tongue . . . she still hadn't cried.

2

The musical evening took place at the end of January. Miss Shawcross started it off with a song. It was as well, Grace thought, that she was accompanying herself, for certainly nobody else could have followed her rendering of 'The Barcarolle'. Yet she was clapped roundly when she finished. She was followed by Miss Farley playing the 'cello. Miss Farley looked bored. Next Mr Blenkinsop was widely acclaimed with his violin solo; the comic sketches of Mr Thompson, the schoolmaster, brought forth laughter and a great deal of guffawing, but Grace did not consider he was funny at all, for he exaggerated the Geordie dialect beyond all recognition. Her own proposal to do a Tyneside sketch had been quickly squashed by Donald, and she had been given to understand once again that one did that kind of thing in private, not in public, and especially did this apply if you were the vicar's wife. He had chosen the pieces that she should play, they were 'Mazurka in A Minor' by Chopin and 'Serenade' by Schubert.

Her playing was received well but not enthusiastically. But later, when the concert was over, being brought to an end by yet another song from Miss Shawcross, she was congratulated by young

Dr Cooper and his wife. 'Look in some night,' he said, 'and give us a treat.' And his wife had added, 'Yes, do come. I've been wanting to ask you for ages, but you're so busy I didn't like to bother you.'

Grace knew that this was a gentle dig at their, or at least Donald's, connection with the Farleys and the hunting Tooles, but she liked the doctor, and his wife too, and she promised to make a date on which to visit them.

Of the others only Bertrand Farley told her that he had enjoyed her playing, and as he stood at the school-room door he held her hand just a fraction too long and his eyes seemed to boggle more than usual as he looked at her. 'You know, I think you should have made the piano your profession . . . but you got married instead, eh?'

There was a look in his eyes that caused her to turn away with a mumbled 'Excuse me' under the pretence that someone was claiming her attention. She didn't like Bertrand Farley. She didn't like any of the Farleys, for that matter. She had the idea, and correctly, that they imagined they were the lords of creation, at least in this part of the world, and acted accordingly. Being solicitors who repre-sented most of the inhabitants of the village and surrounding country helped the illusion.

She found Donald in the vestry with Miss Shawcross. Donald had his back to her and Kate was standing in front of him. It was impossible not to notice the expression on her face – the only description Grace could give to herself was that it looked alight – her lips were parted, her eyes were shining, and in this moment she did not appear as

Grace usually saw her, a plain, heavy-faced woman. She looked even beautiful.

At her entry Donald stopped talking and turned towards her, saying, 'Well, that's over. And what a success. I was just congratulating Miss Shawcross on her wonderful performance.'

Kate Shawcross had neither moved nor taken her eyes from the vicar, but now her head drooped in a girlish fashion that brought her, at least in Grace's eyes, back into focus, for the coy action made her look silly. She still did not look at Grace as she flustered, saying, 'Now I must see to the clearing of the room.' It could have been that Grace had never entered the vestry, at least for her.

It was on the point of Grace's tongue to make some cutting remark, some slighting, scathing remark on the foolishness of the woman, but, remembering Aggie's warning, she forced herself to remain silent.

Donald seemed in high good humour, and as they were walking up the hill towards home, her arm tucked into his, he suddenly remarked, 'And it was a success without the aid of the bagpipes.'

She turned and looked at him in the dark. Andrew MacIntyre had refused his invitation to play the bagpipes at the concert. She did not know what had transpired between them, but she knew that the refusal had annoyed Donald. Yet this had happened weeks ago, and now Donald was speaking of it as if it had occurred only today. She knew that his mind at this moment was filled, to the exclusion of everything else, with the fact that someone had refused an appeal of his. The tone of his voice when he spoke of Andrew MacIntyre was the same as he used when speaking of Ben.

She was silent for the rest of the way home because she was sad. She had been sad since the concert ended, for not once had he mentioned her playing. And now the sadness was intensified because it was being fed by a disturbing thought: Donald was being vindictive. Lesser men could be vindictive, but he wasn't in the category of lesser men; and, moreover, he was a vicar, and even ordinary men of the Church should be above vindictiveness.

Strangely, it was on this night that she first cried, not because Donald had once again evaded loving her and was now gently snoring, but because she had a feeling that she couldn't sort out. It was as if she had lost something.

It was in the spring of 1937, when Grace had been married ten months, that Uncle Ralph spoke to Aunt Susie, and Aunt Susie thought they had better consult Aunt Aggie and see what she had to say about the matter. So they got together and talked about the subject nearest to their hearts. The matter was so serious that they did not start on their high tea before they took it up. Uncle Ralph came straight to the point as he stuck his thumb down into the broad bowl of his pipe, saying, 'Well, Aggie, let's have your opinion of her.'

'What do you want me to say?'

Both Ralph and Susie looked at her and Ralph

said, 'We want to know what you think'; and Susie put in, 'Is she pregnant, Aggie?'

'Not that I know of.' Aggie turned her gaze on them both.

'She talks to you, Aggie,' said Susie, her lips a little prim now. 'She's always talked to you more than to me, or even to her own mother. Linda used to say that.'

'She may talk to me,' said Aggie, 'but she tells me nothing that she doesn't tell everybody she meets, and that is that she has the most wonderful husband in the world.'

'Well, I just don't know what to make of her.' Ralph lit his pipe for the third time. 'She's jittery, Aggie; she's not the girl she was last this time, and she's as thin as a rake.'

'Have you thought of speaking to him?' asked Susie.

'What!' Aggie rounded on her sister-in-law. 'You mean me to talk to him and ask him what's wrong with his wife?'

Susie had risen to her feet, and her head was up and her chest was up and her chin out as she said in a tone that could only be termed huffy, 'Well, you needn't bawl at me, Aggie; it was only a suggestion. Why' – she looked at her husband – 'you would think I had asked her to commit a crime.'

She turned her back on Aggie, and Aggie said, 'Oh, don't take it like that, Susie; it was never meant like that. But it was the suggestion that I should talk to him. Why, I could no more do that than I could fly across the Tyne. You might as well know that I don't like him any more than I did afore she married him. I thought I might, but no. I put on a front for her now, and on the surface everything looks all right, but I've never liked the fellow, and I never will and that's the truth of it. But I don't want to be prejudiced. He seems to think the world of her and she of him. Nevertheless, now that we are on the subject, I can tell you that I feel, and I've felt it for months . . . there's something wrong somewhere.'

Both Susie and Ralph stared at Aggie. That she had admitted to feeling there was something wrong was to them paramount to stating the actual cause, which from their expression could have been some dread disease.

The outcome of the meeting was that Ralph must speak to Donald. But Ralph did not like this idea at all. Donald was a nice chap, none better. He paid little heed to Aggie's opinion of him; women had prejudices against men, it meant nothing. Vaguely he thought Aggie's opinion of Donald was mixed up in some way with him being a strapping handsome fellow while her own man had been a little titch of a bloke. A live wire doubtless, but he hadn't been a figure of a man that would attract a woman. Yet he had attracted Aggie, or had she just taken him because she was getting on and chances were few and far between for her at the time? It was a deep question this; the further you got into it the more muddled you became. He was back to where he started: Aggie was prejudiced.

During the following week Ralph dropped in to Willow Lea and he had a chat with Donald on the quiet, the result of which left him with the impression that Donald, too, was worried about his wife. His manner at first had been stiff and evasive and suggested to Ralph that this was his house and what happened in it was his concern alone. Yet before very long he was admitting that yes, he had been a trifle worried over Grace losing weight and energy during the last few months. But no, he could not give any reason for it. He had added that her happiness was his one concern and he spent his private life solely with that concern.

Ralph's report took the line that Donald was a grand chap, and if there was anything wrong it didn't stem from him. Donald, he said, had suggested a number of times that she see the doctor, but Grace had pooh-poohed the idea. However, now he meant to insist.

Later, when Susie and Aggie were alone together, Susie commented knowledgeably, 'It's the first year. Things are often difficult, you know, in the first year.' She made this remark as though Aggie had never been married, but Aggie let it pass . . .

Donald, true to his word, arranged that Grace saw the doctor; in fact he forestalled any opposition on her part by telling her that Dr Cooper was coming that very afternoon to look her over. He made this statement with studied casualness across the dinner table and showed no reaction to Grace's defiant rejoinder, 'Well, he can go away again; I won't see him.'

'Don't be childish, Grace . . . please don't be so childish.'

Grace lowered her eyes towards her plate. She had an almost uncontrollable desire to jump up and beat her fist on the table and yell at him, 'I don't want a doctor, you know I don't need a doctor, you know what's wrong with me.' The thought when it reached this point acted as a shock and steadied her, and her mind gabbled hastily, 'Oh dear, dear God, don't let me think such things.' She raised her eyes and looked at the crown of his bent head, the hair falling away in shining waves, without a streak of grey anywhere. It looked strong and virile, he looked all strength and virility, and yet . . . The heat enveloped her neck, it spread upwards to her face and downwards to her waist and again it brought a feeling of shame to her. In contrition she wanted to spring up and fling herself on him and say, 'Kiss me. Oh kiss me, darling.' She knew that he would kiss her, he never kept her short of kisses, but they were kisses without fire, bloodless kisses, passionless kisses . . . Yes, that was the word: passionless kisses.

For over three hundred nights she had slept with Donald and his kisses were withering something in her, that something that had been wonderful, beautiful. Its going was stripping the flesh from her bones; she had lost eighteen pounds in weight in the last few months. This thing that was dying in her had the symptoms of a disease, and she felt, and not hysterically or morbidly but knowledgeably, that she could die of it; if she didn't do something soon she could die of it. Yet the cure did not lie in her hands, it lay in his.

She watched him now as he excused himself and rose from the table, and he turned his back to her as he said, 'You'll remember that I go into Durham this afternoon for the meeting. I don't know what time I'll be back, maybe about seven. It's a glorious day, perhaps you'll feel like a walk after seeing the doctor.'

She heard her own voice saying quite calmly, 'Yes, I think I'll take a walk over the fells.'

He was winding his wrist-watch as he said, 'But you'll wait until he comes, won't you, Grace?' It was an order put over in the form of a request, and she answered flatly, 'Yes, I'll wait until he comes.'

It didn't matter whether she saw Dr Cooper or not, he couldn't do anything for her . . .

David Cooper walked into the house un-announced about three o'clock. He had, over the past few months, been a number of times to Willow Lea to play bridge, and the vicar and Grace had visited his home a few times. These were social visits, return courtesy visits, when everyone was on his best behaviour, when it would have been practically impossible for a doctor or even a psychiatrist to get underneath the façade, yet he knew things weren't right with the vicar's wife. To him she was a high-spirited girl who was being clamped down. She wanted an outlet; a family would be the solution. That was likely the whole root of her present trouble. He had wanted to ask the vicar about this when he had suggested looking her over, but he found it difficult to talk to him. There was a reserve that emanated from him, together with his manner of always taking charge of a situation that was very . . . off-putting. The vicar, the doctor thought wryly to himself, was the man who was always the interviewer and never the interviewed.

'Hello there!' He stood in the centre of the hall calling, his eyes moving between the elegant drawing-room and the stairs, and when Grace appeared at the stair head he said again, 'Hello there!'

'Hello,' she said, and as she came down the stairs she wagged her finger playfully at him, 'Renee is always telling me how busy you are, and this is a sheer waste of time.'

'Yes, I think it is myself.'

'There you are then, so why bother?'

'Simply because I'm being paid for it. I've got to eat, and a wife to support, and with quads due in two months' time I just can't afford to turn down offers like this, easy money . . . Where are you going, upstairs or downstairs?'

'Quads.' She had to laugh. Then she turned from him, adding, 'Upstairs, in my lady's chamber I suppose.'

Not more than ten minutes later he was putting his stethoscope back into his case and Grace was asking from the dressing-room, 'Well, am I going to die and you're afraid to tell me?'

Some seconds passed before he answered and then he said, 'There's nothing wrong with your body that I can see . . . what's on your mind?'

There was no answer to this, and a few more minutes elapsed before Grace came into the bedroom. She was fastening the belt of her dress and she asked, 'What do you mean?'

David Cooper puckered his face up, and, giving an impatient shake of his head, said, 'Don't let us stall, Grace. You're worrying about something. Come on, let's have it.'

'Worrying?' Her eyebrows moved up in surprise as she stared him full in the face. 'What would I have to worry about?'

'You tell me.' He was returning her stare. 'Do you want a family?' He watched her blink, then lower her gaze from him as she said, 'Of course I want a family; every woman does – at least most do. Is there anything wrong in that?'

'No, that's definitely the right outlook . . . Does Donald want a family?'

'Well . . .' She turned away. 'Yes . . . yes, I suppose so.'

He looked at her as she walked towards the window, and said quietly, 'Do you mean to say you've never discussed this?'

'There's been no need, it's understood.' In the silence that followed her remark she thought, Of course it's understood. Love and marriage were for the sole purpose of creating souls, hadn't Donald said that? . . . Oh – she closed her eyes and chided herself – she must stop this way of thinking about Donald.

Dr Cooper left the matter where it was and came to her side as she stood looking down into the garden, and after a moment he remarked, 'There's old Ben still at it. He's aged since he lost Miss Tupping.'

'Has he?' Grace turned to him. 'Of course, I wouldn't know; he looks the same to me as when I first saw him. I like Ben.'

'I'm glad you do. He's a funny old fellow but as straight as a die. He had one interest in life and that was his mistress. They were more like father and daughter.'

'Father and daughter? I've always been under the impression that Miss Tupping was old.'

'Not old as people go, she was only about forty-five.'

'Really?'

'Yes. She was under sentence of death when she had this house built, you know, and she started on the garden expecting to give it the last year of her life. The earth repaid her and gave her nine more years. She was my first patient, and I had to pass sentence on her . . . And the day she died I found Ben lying on the ground behind the greenhouse crying into the earth.'

Grace made no comment. The picture the doctor conjured up before her was too deep and sad for comment. She looked down on the stooped back of the old man and asked what seemed an irrelevant question. 'Why have you stayed here all these years?'

'Because it's a healthy place.'

'Healthy?' She turned her head towards him again, her eyes narrowed. The way she had repeated the word healthy conveyed a question which might have been interpreted as having said, 'What have doctors to do with healthy places? It was in the unhealthy places, surely, that they were needed.'

He lifted his gaze to the beech that bordered the lawn and replied, 'Renee's had TB. She went down with it the first year we were married.'

Again she could find no comment. She had never guessed that Renee had been ill, she looked strong and robust and so boisterously happy now that she was having her first child after ten years of marriage.

Renee had infected her with all the excitement about the coming baby. That was until the last few weeks, when she had come to think of her new friend with something that could only be called envy. But now she was filled with contrition and not a little shame. Renee with TB and Ben lying on the ground crying. Why had David told her these things – to take her mind off herself? Well, whatever his reason it had certainly achieved something, for she felt better, not so deflated. She had a sudden longing to be alone, to make new resolutions to herself, resolutions concerning patience and understanding, resolutions to think less about herself and her own feelings and more about . . . Donald and his needs . . . But what were his needs? This last was flung at her from a section of her mind that had become surprisingly analytical in the last month. This section would tear things apart and present them to her and say, 'Stop hoodwinking yourself.' Once it had said, 'Tell Aunt Aggie,' and she cried at it, 'What! Do you think I'm mad?' This section was becoming rather frightening, for it was taking on a permanency and almost creating another personality, so much so that she referred to it as a separate person, at times saying to herself, 'Take no notice.' Once it had frightened her by saying, 'Aunt Aggie was right, you know. He didn't want the actual money, just the things the money could buy. Look at what he's had lately, that rigging out of the choir boys, the new hassocks, chairs for the church hall, and now he's touting for the five hundred to close the subscriptions for the screen. Well, I'll see him in—' 'Shss! Shss!' she admonished the voice that was an echo of her father's.

'What are you going to do with yourself this afternoon?' said the doctor.

'I thought of having a walk on the fells.'

'Good idea. The higher you get, the better the air. Walk until you're tired. How are you sleeping?'

'Not too well.'

'I'll send up some tablets for you, just enough for two or three nights. It's a habit you know, this sleeping business.'

'Everything's a habit.'

He was at the door now and he turned and looked at her for a moment, then nodded and said with a smile, 'Yes, you're right there; even living is just a series of habits.'

The doctor gone, Grace went upstairs again and changed her shoes and picked up a coat. Then she crossed the landing to the storeroom. A door from this room led to an outside staircase which had two purposes: that of a fire escape and an easy means of carrying the fruit into the house. This side of the house, which was the back, was accessible to the orchard. Last year, under Ben's direction, she had packed the fruits away.

As she passed the greenhouses she hailed Ben, and he came to the door and, looking from her light coat to the sky, he said, 'You makin' for the fells, ma'am?'

'Yes, Ben.'

'Ah well then, I wouldn't go far.'

'No?' She looked at him in surprise. 'And it such a beautiful day?'

'Aye, yes now. Be different in an hour or so's time. Look over there.' He pointed over the top of the trees to a small group of harmless-looking clouds, and he added, 'That's a sure sign. Bet you what you like we have rain afore we have tea.'

'Oh, don't say that, Ben.'

'I do, ma'am, so be careful.'

'I will, Ben, but I'll be back before tea.'

'Do that, ma'am, do that.' He nodded and gave her what was to him a smile.

She let herself out through the gate, and within a few minutes was in the wood taking the path that she had first come to know when she had walked behind Andrew MacIntyre.

It was strange, she sometimes thought, that she had seen Andrew MacIntyre twice on that one day and only twice since. The first time was on the road above the village. He was in a field which was somewhat higher than the road and his head was on the level with Adelaide Toole's as she sat on her horse. They were both laughing and she remembered that they looked young and happy. She remembered also that after seeing them she was left with a feeling of loneliness, not because they looked and sounded happy but, strangely, because they were young. Adelaide was her own age, yet she had felt old enough on that day to be her mother, for it was a day following a night when she had cried herself to sleep. Adelaide had greeted her cheerily on that occasion, but Andrew MacIntyre had not spoken, he had merely inclined his head towards her and his face had taken on a sober look, but only until she had passed on. She knew this because she had not gone far along the road before their joined laughter came to her again.

The next time she had seen him was one day not more than a fortnight ago. She had passed the cottage on the fells at least a dozen times since the autumn and had seen no-one at all, but this day they were all outside looking at something on the road, Mr and Mrs MacIntyre and Andrew MacIntyre, and when she came up to them she saw that it was a small terrier bitch with puppies. A different scene from that which she had come upon the first day she had passed the house, for now the mother and son were laughing at the antics of the pups and the father was looking on. Mr MacIntyre she saw should have been a tall man, but he was very bent and stood with the aid of a stick. His body looked like that of an old man but his face was that of a man in his fifties. Neither Mrs MacIntyre nor Andrew had introduced him to her, and after passing the time of day with them, and remarking on the sweetness of the puppies, she had continued on her way feeling as if she had trespassed on their property. They were using the road as if it was their garden, and she was left with the impression that she had walked through it without asking permission.

She now climbed up through the wood until she reached the flint road, and here she hesitated as she had done once or twice before when she had the desire to explore the quarry, really explore it. She had been as far as the end of the road and looked over the barbed wire into the vast crater that the workings had left. The water in it, the accumulation of the rainfall of years, was blackish and forbidding, and it had always checked her adventurous desire to walk round the perimeter of the quarry or to find out if there was even a way around it, for from the end of the road there was no sign of a path. Yet from her first visit she knew that someone went into the quarry, for in one place the barbed wire had been pressed down to make easier access.

So today when she looked at the wire she thought, 'Where one can go another can' and she was under the wire and in the enclosure of the quarry before the thought had finished in her mind.

Once over the wire fence she stopped. It was strange, but she had the feeling that everything was different on this side of the wire; it was as if the quarry had no connection with the wood. The atmosphere in the wood was soothing; here only a few steps within the wire, she felt a surge of unrest, even fear. When she found herself half turning towards the wire again, she murmured aloud, saying, 'Don't be silly' and then, surprised at the sound of her own voice, she closed her eyes and smiled.

There was no possible way of her getting to the edge of the crater from where she stood, for bracken, bush and bramble had entwined to make an impregnable barrier at least thirty feet wide, and only because this sloped downwards could she see the water. And from this distance she guessed she must be looking almost into the middle of the quarry.

The only way clear enough for walking was by the wire fencing, and this did not lead to the quarry but away from it. Yet she had only followed it for some yards when she saw to the left of her the narrow cutting in the wall of bracken. It was just wide enough for one person to walk through, and as she stood looking at it there came to her again the feeling of fear, but this time it was intensified and she had the urge to turn like a frightened child and dash out of the enclosure.

Was the land boggy and this feeling a warning? Tentatively she put her foot among the grasses, but the ground felt rock-like. Hesitating no more, she entered the path. Although it was open to the sky, it seemed dark inside. She walked quietly and slowly, wondering with a quickening of her heart beats what she would find round the next corner, for the path twisted and turned continuously until it came abruptly to an end.

She was now looking on to what appeared to be a small lake. The water was still. There was no life to be seen on its surface and no indication of any underneath. Between her and the water's edge lay about ten feet of baked mud and this stretched away for some distance, looking for all the world like a deserted beach. At the far end there rose, almost vertical, a wall of rock jutting out towards the water. It was as clean and bare as if it had just recently been sliced. There were boulders of rock mounting one on top of the other to the right of her, and her only path now seemed to be the mud beach. Fascinated, she walked along it towards where it skirted the wall of rock.

There was not more than two feet between the water and the point of the rock and she had her eyes cast down on the water as she rounded the point. And then her hand came up across her mouth to stifle her exclamation of surprise. There, not a couple of yards from her, lay Andrew MacIntyre. His hands behind his head, his eyes were closed as if he was asleep. But she hadn't time to wonder or make her retreat, for the next instant he was on his feet and staring at her . . . They remained gaping at each other until she gabbled, 'I . . . I'm sorry. I . . . I didn't know . . .' As she had felt she was trespassing through his garden when she had walked down the road past his house, now she had almost the feeling that she had barged into his bedroom. He and his family seemed to create a privacy about them that was most disconcerting.

'I was out for a walk.' She was still trying to explain.

His blank silence was unnerving, and she was on the point of turning with what dignity she could muster and making her escape when he spoke, and the tone of his voice brought an immediate show of relief to her face, for he said, 'Don't go, please don't go. You see, I thought you were a sort of . . . of apparition.' His voice was so quiet, his expression so gentle, his manner so easy, that for a moment she didn't think she was looking at the dour Andrew MacIntyre.

'You see, very few people find their way around here.'

'Yes, yes' – her laugh was nervous and high – 'I can understand that . . . it's a weird kind of place.'

She looked up to the wall of rock that towered above them. Then, turning her gaze to the water, she said, 'It's a wonder people don't come here to swim.'

'It smells too much when it's stirred up.'

'Really?' She was looking at him again. 'It's a pity. Well' – she smiled up at him – 'I must go and leave you to your reading.' She glanced at the book lying on the ground. 'I'm sorry I disturbed you.'

'You didn't disturb me.' His voice had changed, it was as if he was contradicting her now. And then he added, 'I was just about to make my way homewards, anyway.'

She watched him bend over and pick up the book, and as he straightened up she turned away and went round the point of the rock again.

They walked along the mud beach, and when they came to the narrow, bramble-walled passage, he led the way, and it was very like the day he had shown her and Aunt Aggie the short cut down to the back gate, for she was looking at his back and he was silent now as he had been then. It wasn't until he lifted the wire up to allow her easier passage through into the wood that she made herself speak, and then she asked, 'Are you going to the farm now?'

He shook his head. 'No; this is my day off, I wouldn't be here else. The quarry is only for high days and holidays . . . or when you want to escape and be by yourself.'

'Oh, I'm sorry.'

'I didn't mean that.' His face was dead straight.

'It's all right. I understand.'

'Look. Look here.' He was bending slightly towards her. 'You don't understand.'

'Yes. Yes, I do.'

'No you don't.' His brows were drawn together, his voice was harsh, and now his face looked not only dour but grim. 'There are times when you want to get away from people – not all people – just . . . just some people . . . and I wouldn't have said that if . . .'

As he hesitated she put in quickly, 'Well, that's what I mean, that's what I understand, the desire to get away from some particular . . . people.' She had nearly said particular person. She understood how he felt all right . . . oh, she understood perfectly, and her knowledge made her fearful.

She was looking intently at him, and becoming aware of a number of things at once: that his expression had changed yet again and his whole face now looked gentle; that he had a nice mouth; that he never addressed her as Mrs Rouse or ma'am; that he was young, and strangely was making her feel young, even younger than him; and, lastly, that here was someone who would kow-tow, or bow, to no-one, and that was why Donald didn't like him. It was this last thought that dragged her wandering mind and feelings abruptly into line again.

She had a strong desire now to get away from him, even to run. She conquered this by assuming an air of sedateness, and as she pulled her eyes from his face and moved away she said, 'Ben says it will rain before tea.'

He was behind her now, but keeping at a

distance, as his voice told her when he answered after a pause, 'He's right.'

When they came to where the stone road ended she turned to him and said with stiff politeness, 'Well, goodbye.'

He was standing some yards from her, his deep brown eyes looking almost black. 'Goodbye,' he said.

They both seemed to turn away simultaneously, he going up the steep incline that led towards his home, and she cutting across the hillside towards the main road.

When she reached the road she did not go down to the village but skirted it and came out near the little cemetery that backed the church.

There was no-one in the cemetery and the vestry door was closed, but the main door was open and she went in and walked between the six stone pillars of the chancel, then turned towards the alcove where the little side altar was, the children's altar. And here, on the single wooden kneeler, she knelt and with her hands tightly clasped and her head down she prayed, prayed earnestly. And as she prayed, Ben's promised rain began to beat on the roof.

Andrew MacIntyre had not taken more than a dozen long strides when he stopped and, turning abruptly, watched, from his vantage point, the vicar's wife scurrying along the path between the trees towards the main road.

He'd never had such a surprise in his life . . . never. To be thinking of her, then to open his eyes and see her standing dead in front of him. It had shaken him. Why had she come into the quarry? It must have been her first visit, and he could take it for an omen. He had gone in there to decide for good and all what he must do. He had come to the point where he had made up his mind that the madness that was growing in him must be cut out; for it could lead nowhere. There was a 'gift horse' waiting for him to saddle. He had known for two years now what was in Adelaide's mind, but had made no move in that direction, not only because of her father, and the hell he might kick up, but because Adelaide herself aroused nothing more in him than sincere liking. Even now, when he sensed that old Toole had had it out with Adelaide and she had brought him round to her way of thinking and he might even welcome him in the uplifting capacity of son-in-law, even this could not make him see Adelaide in the light of a wife.

Although he had worked for Toole for years he had never felt inferior to him – and that was another thing that made life and the future difficult, for he considered his own mother a better woman in all ways than his master's wife. His mother had been educated, whereas Mrs Toole had at one time gone to the village school. Of course everybody tried to forget this, but would they forget he was a farm labourer if he aspired to Adelaide Toole. As for his father – on this thought Andrew's lip curled back from his teeth – if it wasn't for him they wouldn't be in the position they were today. For himself it didn't much matter . . . he could fend . . . but his mother, tied up there for life. Why did women do it?

Why? Was some part of them mentally blind? Her, too. He could now only pick out the colour of Grace's dress as she jumped the ditch to the main road, but her face was vividly before him. She was different from anyone he had ever come across, sweet and kind, and intelligent. You only had to listen to her to know that. Yet she had picked a fellow like Rouse . . . Parson! Psss! Big-headed nowt! With that air of authority as from God himself. His stomach had turned the first time they had met. He had wanted to start an argument with him, to tie him up with the flaws in his own doctrine . . . and he could have done just that. Hadn't he been brought up on the Bible? So much so that he had, as a child, thought that his father had written the book. But this was getting him nowhere. Recriminations were useless, he had learnt that too. The main thing was that she was unhappy . . . he knew she was unhappy. What was he to do? What could he do? Would she be like his mother and go on all her life suffering because it was her duty . . . ? God, no!

3

Miss Shawcross had come to tea. She was sitting in the drawing-room to the side of Grace and opposite Donald, and Donald was playfully chaffing her. Donald was always playful with Miss Shawcross; it could be said he treated her like a beloved sister. It certainly couldn't be anything else. This thought brought Grace's cup to shake gently in its saucer, but not with laughter.

'Can you see us all running over the fells taking pot-shots at the German parachutists?'

Miss Shawcross made a sound that was a cross between a laugh and a giggle; it was a sound that irritated Grace.

'But there' – Donald's voice was serious now – 'I mustn't joke about this matter, war's no joking matter at all, and if the worst comes to the worst we will undoubtedly all do our bit . . . Now about the rota, Kate.' He leant forward. Then his jocularity returning, he said, 'But have a piece of this sandwich cake, it will give you strength for the battle.'

Kate Shawcross's laugh filled the room. She laughed, with her eyes closed and her head down. She stopped laughing as abruptly as she had started, then, taking from her bag a sheet of foolscap paper, she began to explain the rota.

Grace sat looking at them as they earnestly made their arrangements for their part in the coming war. It was early in September, 1938. War was in the air. Any minute now it seemed that England would be at war: they had already been issued with gas-masks, and there was talk of digging holes in the ground and sleeping in them. The thought of war did not frighten her except when her mind settled on children. Grown-ups could fend for themselves, but children, especially the little children, like those in the Infants in the village school . . . She did not question that her concern for the children was because her mind was thinking of nothing else these days. Children, children . . . a child. What if she had a child and it was killed by a bomb. She shuddered from head to foot, then became strangely still as a voice said from within her, 'I'd chance it.'

She looked at Donald again. His face was serious now, beautiful and serious. No wonder Kate Shawcross could not take her eyes from him. She was being talked about in the village for running after the vicar, but that did not seem to trouble her, she seemed oblivious of everything in life but this man.

The feeling of annoyance, scorn, and even jealousy that Grace had felt at different times over the past two years towards this woman had vanished as if they had never been. Now she had for her another feeling. It was pity. For Miss Shawcross was in love with a shell . . . a shell filled with God. There was no room for a woman inside that shell, except as a mother or a doll . . . Donald was a man with a doll. She herself was the doll, sometimes to be kissed, fondled . . . and forever frustrated.

This time last year she had come to look upon God as her rival for Donald. This feeling had gone on for some months and had been a terrifying experience. One could not pit oneself against God and yet she had attempted to do just that. Thankfully it was brought to a sudden end one day when Donald took her on a visit to a friend of his in Harrogate. This man was also a parson. He was a good man, it showed in his face, and he had seven children . . . men could be men of God and still men.

She had been married to Donald seven hundred and eighty-four nights. This way of thinking worried her. She didn't think she had been married just over two years, she counted the time in nights. And each night now seemed to bring fresh terror to her, for she would lie awake seeing one more new aspect of the man by her side. She had faced the fact many months ago that Donald was a man who should never have married. One fear-filled night she had almost turned on him and shaken him out of his sleep to cry at him, 'You have committed a sin, you who are always preaching against sin; you have committed the worst sin against human nature. Do you hear me?' She had got up that night and crept from the room and went, of all places, into the storeroom because there she could open the door and look out into the night without fear of anyone seeing her. Although each night she dissected him and looked at his lack and weaknesses, she was still in love with him. She knew that he had a vindictiv streak in him, submerged but nevertheless there. She knew that he had a cunning knack of getting his own way. She knew also that he used the pulpit to strike, and not only in the defence of God. No-one could answer you back when you were in the pulpit. Yet she felt that in part he was a good man, never ceasing to go out of his way to help someone. Perhaps it was more correct to say, he got others to do that. Anyway, she supposed organisation was part of his job.

'And where are you going to put this big brawny piece?' Donald put out his large white hand and touched Grace's face.

Miss Shawcross turned her eyes from the vicar and, looking at Grace, said, 'Oh, I haven't put you down anywhere because of you not feeling too well.'

'But we can't have this, she's got to do her bit.' Donald was looking tenderly towards Grace, patting her hand the while. 'We'll have to put her on the diplomatic staff, eh?'

Miss Shawcross laughed at this and Grace said, 'Can I fill your cups?'

Fifteen minutes later Donald left the house with Miss Shawcross. He was going to visit the Tooles, as Mrs Toole was in bed with phlebitis.

Long after they had gone Grace sat in the drawing-room, staring out through the french windows into the garden. She knew she had reached a point where something must be done. She could not go on like this any longer, she must speak to Donald, come out into the open. Aunt Aggie had said to her only last week, 'Isn't it time you started a family?' And she had made no answer to this. A few months previously she would have come up with some excuse such as, 'Oh, there's plenty of time for that.' And then there was Dr Cooper saying, 'You know you can't live on tonics. Nature is a tonic and you've got to use her.' He had paused before he added, 'You understand what I'm saying?' She had nodded. Yes, she had understood perfectly what he was saying and tonight she was not going to be baulked. It wasn't that she hadn't tried to bring the matter into the open a number of times, but whenever Donald felt that the subject was broaching he kissed, patted and teased and put the situation on ground from which it was impossible to say, 'I want a baby'. But tonight she would close her ears to his prattle. She turned her head slightly to the side on this thought. It made her sad to realise that she could think along these lines, terming Donald's beautifully modulated words as prattle.

At seven o'clock Donald had not returned and she went out into the garden in search of Ben. Ben had no set hours, and Grace found that when in the old man's company she forgot herself and her worries. Perhaps it was because that in character he was closest to the men amongst whom she had been brought up, those on the Tyne. From Ben she saw reflected traces of her father and Uncle Ralph, and old Jack Cummings.

She found Ben clipping the top of a lonicera hedge. Without any formal greeting he addressed her immediately, saying, 'He said take two feet off this.' He never gave Donald any other title but 'he'. 'If I was to take two feet off un you would see the top of the tool-shed from the front drive. 'Twouldn't do, an' I told him.' He turned his small bright eyes on her. 'See what I mean, ma'am?'

'Yes, Ben. Yes, I do.' Then she asked enquiringly, 'The vicar said he wanted two feet off?'

'Aye, this afternoon just gone, he came out here and said it should be taken down altogether. Too dark green he said it was . . . did you ever hear the like, too dark green? Why, I never did. And I pointed out to him that it's the darkness of this here hedge that acts as a background for the lavender and such.' He pointed to the side, and Grace, looking towards the bushes, said, 'Yes, yes, I see.'

'Miss Tuppin' planted this hedge, ma'am, because it was quick growin'. "We don't want to see the roof of that black shed from the drive, do we, Ben?" she said. And I said, "No, ma'am, we don't want that." "Lonicera is the thing," she said, "it's quick," and there she put it.'

Ben was talking easily about his late mistress these days and Grace knew it brought some solace to him to be able to do so. She also felt that she was the only one to whom he talked in this way and she gave him the opportunity whenever she could.

'Ma'am.'

'Yes, Ben?'

'Only yesterday I came across a recipe of me mother's, it was for reviving an appetite. It's a mixture of herbs and I brought it along for you.' Ben did not look at Grace as he spoke but went on cutting slowly and expertly at the hedge. 'I remember me mother sayin' it would make a man eat like a horse.'

He stopped now and, laying down the shears, drew from his pocket a square of yellowed paper. Opening it slowly, he handed it to Grace.

In the swift glance she gave the paper she made out the words dandelion and rosemary. Then she looked at him and said softly, 'Thank you, Ben, it's very kind of you.'

'Well, what I say is' – Ben was at the hedge again – 'these new-fangled medicines . . . well, you might as well drink dish-wattar. The old recipes are lost or forgotten an' so people die.' His voice sank on the last words and Grace knew he was thinking of his beloved mistress, and she wanted to say, 'But you kept her alive for nine years, Ben . . . you and the garden,' but all she said was, 'Thank you, Ben'; then added, 'I'll have it made up, I promise you.'

He did not turn towards her, not even to nod, and she walked slowly away reading the prescription that was to make her eat like a horse. Oh, Ben, dear Ben, it wasn't herbs that she needed to put on flesh.

She stopped and looked around the garden, then looked towards the back of the house. She should be as happy as a princess in a fairy tale; in this atmosphere she should be relaxed and at ease, her body should be afloat, and in harmony, whereas it was a mass of jangling nerves, and only needed a sharp word to set the tear ducts quivering. With a sudden spurt she ran towards the house, through the hall, and up the stairs into her room, and, throwing herself face down on the bed, she cried into her hands. Why had this to happen to her? She wasn't bad, she wasn't wicked, she only wanted . . . she only wanted . . . wanted . . . wanted. Her brain was yelling the word, 'wanted . . . wanted . . . wanted.' Then as her fists clutched up handfuls of the eiderdown, it added on a voiceless scream, 'To be loved . . . to be loved . . .'

Donald did not get back until just on dusk. From her bedroom window she watched him coming up the drive. When he did not come in the front door but skirted the house, she knew without bothering to ascertain that he had gone to look at the hedge to see if Ben had carried out his orders. Tomorrow there would be words and a battle of wills between them. There had been words before when Ben had usually emerged the victor, and doubtless he would do so again, and in her heart she was with him. Not because he was right in this case as he had been in most of the others, but because it hurt her somehow to see him ordered about in what was, spiritually at least, his garden, and, moreover, he was an old man. It was odd, she thought, at this moment, that Donald never brought his Christian attitude to bear with Ben, and he should have done so, if only to try to get him to attend the services.

She reached the hall just as Donald entered it. She did not fly to him now as she had once done and fling her arms about his neck. She saw immediately that he was annoyed, very likely with Ben, but when they got into the drawing-room it was not of Ben he spoke but of the Tooles. Mrs

Toole wasn't well at all and she was worried about Adelaide. Apparently things weren't going as they should with Adelaide. It was all to do with that MacIntyre fellow. They had been like second parents to that boy. Mr Toole had gone so far as to indicate to him that he would be welcome as a son-in-law, but the fool had done nothing about it. It was hurting both Mr and Mrs Toole, not to say anything about Adelaide.

She went and stood in front of him, and, catching hold of his hands, brought his attention to her. 'Donald . . . Donald, I . . .' Here she stopped and her heart gave a number of thumping beats before she finished, 'I would like to talk to you.'

Did she see a shadow come over his eyes, or was it that he was still feeling annoyed with Ben? It was his way when annoyed about one thing to talk about something entirely different . . . this was another trait that she had reluctantly been forced to recognise.

He released one of his hands from hers and, putting it to his brow, said, 'Yes, yes, of course,' then added, 'you don't have to ask like that . . . like . . . like a parishioner. If you can't talk to me, who can you talk to?' He followed this in the very next breath by saying, 'Is there any coffee on hand? My head is thumping – it's the heat, I think.'

Slowly she released his hand and without a word turned from him and went into the kitchen. Taking the percolator from the stove she placed it on the tray that was standing ready and carried it back into the drawing-room, and there she poured him out a cup of coffee before sitting down.

The coffee finished, he lay back in the chair, stretched out his legs, and sighed. Then with eyes closed he said, 'Now, my dear, what is it you want to say?'

Her body felt cold and rigid. Could one look at a man sitting in a chair with his eyes closed and his legs stretched out and say, 'I want a baby . . . come up to bed and love me, I want a baby,' or words to that effect?

Her silence brought his eyes open but he did not move. 'Is it important?'

'Yes.'

He closed his eyes again and remained motionless, and she continued to look at him. His body seemed to have spread over the chair; she did not see it as a beautiful body any more. It was soft and flabby, even fat in parts. It was only when he was standing stiffly upright or striding along, his tails flying, that he gave the impression of an athlete. But she knew his body was no athlete's. She looked at his black-clothed legs and the thought came to her that she had never seen them without a covering of some sort, and only twice had her hands felt their bare flesh . . . Were all marriages like this? No, no – she gave this answer emphatically to herself – all marriages could not be like this, or else the madhouses would be more full than they were now. This thought lifted her swiftly to her feet, and the movement brought his eyes open again and he stretched himself and said, 'Oh, I wish I hadn't anything more to do tonight. Well, my dear, come along, what is this important business you want to discuss?'

'I'll talk about it upstairs. Will you be long?'

'Only about half an hour.' He rose and came towards her. And now he put his arm about her shoulder and said, 'You go on up, I won't be long.'

Did the look on his face say he understood? Did it promise something? She stared intently at him for a moment before lowering her eyes. Then slowly disengaging herself from him, she picked up the tray and went out of the room . . .

In spite of the balcony window being wide open the bedroom was hot and the air heavy. Her undressing was slow, for her mind was not on it. That is, not until she was on the point of picking up her nightdress from the bed, when her hand became still and she looked at the bundle of drooping voile. She looked at it for quite a long while before releasing it from her hand and turning round. And now she began to walk about the room as she had never done before. It was a strange feeling to walk about like this, unclothed. Back and forward, up and down she walked. And as she walked she listened, and just after the half hour was up she heard movements in the room below, followed by the sound of the front door being locked.

As she heard his steps mounting the stairs a tremor passed over her and she became still. She would time his steps across the landing, and when he opened the bedroom door she would be in the act of walking across the room. But when he opened the door she was sitting at the dressing-table, her naked back to him, and the entire front of her body gleaming at him through the mirror.

There are moments in a lifetime when all the five senses of the body are in agony at once. It is torture that dare not be repeated often. It is a torture that breaks the mind before the body. At such times you can smell your own humiliation, you can taste your own despair. You can feel the actual recoil of the other's revulsion. You can see the disgust squaring a mouth to leave the teeth bare. You can hear the hateful crying of self-denouncement.

Grace experienced this agony when through the mirror she met his look, for not only his expression but his whole body showed his reactions to her nakedness. It shrivelled her up. She couldn't endure it. It was as if he was being forced to look at some debauched creature. He looked like a trapped priest. As she clapped her hand over her mouth she cried through her fingers, 'Don't look at me like that!'

'I'd put your nightdress on; it ill becomes you to act in this way, Grace.'

Even before the deadly cold words were finished he had turned and closed the door, not quietly as was his wont but with a bang. With her hand still tightly pressed across her mouth she stared wildly into the mirror and she saw there, not her own flesh but a verse of Genesis:

'AND SHE CAUGHT HIM BY HIS GARMENT, SAYING, LIE WITH ME: AND HE LEFT HIS GARMENT IN HER HAND, AND FLED, AND GOT HIM OUT.'

He had looked at her as Joseph must have done on the wife of his Egyptian master . . . but she was no-one else's wife, she was his wife . . . but he didn't want a wife, not to lie with. She had clutched at his garment with her naked body and what had happened? He had got him out.

Oh God! Oh God! Her body dragged itself round away from the mirror, but although she stared about the room she could see nothing, for her vision was blurred. Yet she was not crying. She bent over and covered her face with her hands, 'Oh God! Oh God!'

She was still muttering 'Oh God! Oh God!' when she made a sudden rush towards her clothes and, tearing at them, began frantically to dress herself again.

When she had zipped the side of her dress up her movements stopped. Her two hands underneath her armpits, she looked down at the carpet and asked, 'Where will I go? Aunt Aggie's . . . No, no.' But her Aunt Aggie would understand, she knew she would understand. Yet how could she put into words what she had done to bring about this situation? And would anyone understand this unbearable feeling of rejection . . . ? She couldn't go on, she couldn't. She was unclean. He had stamped her forever as something unclean.

She went through the storeroom without switching the light on, and when she ran down the iron steps to the garden the night appeared light in comparison. Hardly pausing in her running, she snatched the key to the garden gate from the nail just within the door of the greenhouse, and when she had unlocked the gate she did not stop to close it, or to remove the key, but ran across the narrow belt of grass and into the wood.

She had never been in the wood at night before, not even in the twilight, and if she had been in her right mind the darkness would have terrified her. But there was no room for terror in her at this moment, there was no room for anything but shame and a desire to be rid of it as soon as possible. She ran with her arms outstretched, warding off obstacles, and when she stumbled for the third time she went flat on the ground. As she lay breathless and dazed she imagined in the stillness all round her that she could hear the sound of footsteps. Still she was not frightened, only determined that the footsteps should never catch up with her.

She was running again and her feet told her when she had reached the stone road. She flew along it with a surety, as if she could see her way ahead, and she was at the wire fencing before she realised it, for its impact nearly knocked her on to her back. It was as she bent under the wire that she saw the light of a torch spreading into the trees, but she was in the enclosure and she knew that he would never find her here, not until she had done what she had come to do.

She had never told him about her visits to the quarry, she did not think he even knew of its existence. Once through the narrow lane of brambles she did not make for the mud beach but began to scramble over the shoulders up towards the top of the shelf of rock. At the far end there was a sixty-foot drop, and at the foot of the cliff there was no mud, just huge lumps of quarrying stone overgrown with bracken.

When the sharp stinging drops of rain hit her face, they pierced through the unbalanced state of her mind and brought her climbing to a gasping halt, and she thought for a moment with normal surprise, 'It's raining.' Then once again she was scrambling frantically upwards. She could hear quite clearly now the sound of Donald running, and she knew that her own footsteps were leading him to her, and she cried to herself, 'If he touches me I'll kill him, I'll kill him – kill him.'

When her feet reached the comparatively level ground on the top of the quarry the blackness, intensified by the rain, took all sense of her bearings from her and she ran this way and that not knowing in what direction the edge lay. When the torch flashed over her, she blinked into it before turning and rushing blindly away. A second later she was struggling like a wildcat. It was only when she realised that the arms that were holding her were hard, not soft and flabby, that she became still.

'There, there, you're all right. Go easy, don't be frightened.' The voice enfolded her, soothing her. She remained still against the man, her head resting on his shoulder until she began to shake as if with ague. A torrent of tears seemed to have solidified and blocked her throat, stopping her breath and causing her to heave as if she was being suffocated. When his voice came again, saying with deep gentleness, 'Don't be frightened, nothing can harm you', it was too much. She made a sound that could have come from an agonised animal before the tears spurted from her eyes, nose and mouth at the same time.

'There now, there now, don't, don't cry so. Look you're getting wet. Put this round you.' She felt him putting his coat over her shoulders, she felt herself being led back down over the boulders, and she was only vaguely aware that they had passed the rock point and the place where she had first seen him lying.

'Sit down here a minute, it's dry and out of the rain.' He lowered her to the ground, and when his hands left her she turned and lay on the earth and buried her face in her arms.

After some long time his voice forced its way to her, saying, 'No more now, no more. You'll make yourself ill. Come on, sit up.'

But she could not sit up. Her body was being rent apart with her weeping, and he said no more, only patted her gently until slowly, gradually, the turmoil subsided and she lay quiet and exhausted.

As she stared into the black inkiness of the earth, her mind began to settle and find its balance once more, and it came to her that she was lying up here in the quarry beside Andrew MacIntyre and that he must think her insane. Slowly she eased herself up into a sitting position and, her words checked by her jerking breath, she said softly, 'I . . . I don't know what . . . what to say. I don't know what you must think of me.'

'I think you're very unhappy.'

She felt herself jerk as if she had been prodded. She could not see him but she knew that his eyes were on her.

'You've been unhappy for a long time, haven't you?'

She felt her face stretching with amazement. Nobody had known how she felt, nobody had known that she was unhappy. She had seen to it that she had talked and laughed as usual, and Donald had seen to it that he was very sweet to her, even lovable, in public.

She heard her voice, hardly audible and still uneven with her sobbing breath, asking, 'How – how did you know that?'

'I've watched you.'

'Watched me?' She turned her face full in his direction, and now she could just make out the dark outline of him. She had not met him more than a dozen times since she had seen him lying on the beach here. That encounter would always remain in her memory, for it had driven her to church. She remembered praying that day that Donald would love her and that she would never stop loving him. She had never come across Andrew MacIntyre in the quarry since that day. She had only come here when, like him, she felt she would be alone. Her encounters with him had been on the road or at the Tooles' when she had seen him working on the farm.

'You're not happy with him, are you?'

As she had flown only a few minutes ago from the house she now wanted to fly away from this man.

'Why did you marry him?'

She heard herself saying softly, 'I loved him.'

'You thought you did.'

'You mustn't say such things.'

'Why? Because you're the parson's wife or because you won't face up to the truth?'

She felt his hand groping towards her, and when it covered hers she made no resistance.

'I don't know your name, your Christian name, they always call you Mrs Rouse up there. I've given you all kinds of names . . . what is it?'

Her mind was starting to whirl again but in a different atmosphere, and her voice was just a whisper as she said, 'Grace.'

'Grace.'

She shuddered and blinked in the dark, terrified now of something she couldn't name. She made an effort to get away from it by saying, 'I . . . I must get back,' but she made no move to rise. And then she asked, 'Why were you in the wood?'

'I was coming from work.' He paused, then said hastily and below his breath, 'No, that isn't true. I was standing on the edge of the wood – I often go down there – and I heard you running through the garden. I thought you were having a game with someone. You passed me not more than an arm's length away, and I waited to see who was after you, and when nobody came I knew you were in trouble. I think I knew it from the minute I heard you running.'

Her head was bowed low now as she asked, 'Why were you down there?'

There was another considerable pause before he gave her an answer, and then it was not to her question. 'That day you appeared round the bend there, I'd been thinking of you; I was thinking of you that very minute and I opened my eyes and there you stood. I'll never be able to explain what

I felt then, but I can tell you now. I knew then what I had guessed from the first time I saw you: I knew you were for me, the only one for me, parson's wife or no.'

She knew a moment's horror and made to scramble to her feet, but his hand, without moving, held her to the ground. 'Don't be frightened – you have nothing to fear from me. Sooner or later you'd have to know. Things happen like this, no matter what people say, and it happened to me that day in your kitchen when I first set eyes on you.'

She turned her face towards him again and her expression was full of wonder now. This was Andrew MacIntyre, the dour Scot. He was talking with the ease which she attributed only to men like Donald, and he was telling her . . . What was he telling her? That he was in love with her? Again she recalled the day she had run from the quarry through the woods to the church, and there came to her now the real reason for her praying. She, too, had known it then, but would not face it; she was the parson's wife and she loved her husband. But she was confronted with it now and some part of her still protested loudly: 'This mustn't happen. It is wrong, this mustn't go on. There must be nothing between me and Andrew MacIntyre. It would be a situation that would be unbearable. Andrew MacIntyre, Mr Toole's man . . . Andrew MacIntyre, a farm-worker . . . Andrew MacIntyre who lives in the little stone cottage on the fells . . . Andrew MacIntyre, who was dour, unsociable, taciturn and who wouldn't play the bagpipes at the musical evening.' On this last thought something faintly resembling a laugh passed through her, and she found herself turning her body towards him and allowing a breath of a whisper to say his name, 'Oh, Andrew.' The next minute she was enveloped in a storm of weeping again. When his arms went about her and she felt herself pressed close against him she did not protest in any way, and when a short while later she felt his mouth moving against her temple she said again, 'Oh, Andrew.' Of her own will she moved her mouth up to meet his. And when with a sudden jerk his body pressed hard against her and bore her sideways to the earth she did not shrink away.

The passionate abandon with which she gave herself to him both startled and elated her, and the knowledge that she was being loved brought compensation for her husband's rejection and gave her a shield to hold up against the look that the sight of her nakedness had brought to his face. She had, as it were, had a painful abscess lanced, and the relief was indescribable. Somewhere at the height of the ecstatic, swirling pinnacle of released joy she thought that those lines in Genesis were being justifiably reversed. It was the Egyptian who would not lie with her, but Joseph had, and his cloak was over her and she knew he would never lift it from her.

4

'Oh, girl, what have you done? And I'm not referring to that MacIntyre fellow either, although I think he's a swine of the first water.'

'He's not, Aunt Aggie.' Grace brought her head up from its dropped position, 'He's not.'

'Well, I have me own opinion and I'm going to stick to it. But it's your life I'm referring to; you've made a mess of it, and I'm going to say right now I told you so. But there, it's done, and now there's no way out for you that I can see, for if I know Mr Donald there'll be no mention of divorce. He should never have married in the first place. I knew it, I had a feeling about it, but now that it's done he'll bring God on to his side and fasten you to him for life.'

'I don't care. I've made up my mind, I'm going to leave him.'

'And take up with this MacIntyre fellow?'

'Yes.' She was looking straight ahead.

'Is it all cut and dried?'

'No.' She turned and looked full at Aggie and her voice shook as she pleaded, 'Don't condemn me, Aunt Aggie; you don't know what it's been like.'

'Condemn you?' Aggie came swiftly forward and put her arms about her. 'Oh, lass, I'm not condemning you, I'm only sorry from the bottom of me heart that it needed to happen. The only criticism I've got to make is that I could wish you had gone off the rails with somebody nearer your own class. To take up with . . . with that kind of fellow, and after the education you've had.'

Grace sighed. 'Don't forget, Aunt Aggie, after all Dad was a coalman.'

'He was nothing of the sort,' put in Aggie indignantly, 'not in that way. He managed his own business and was on a footing with men like old Arthur Wentworth, councillors and such. And there's Charlie Wentworth. There's not a time that I meet him but he asks after you.'

'You don't know Andrew MacIntyre, Aunt Aggie. He's . . . he's . . .' she could not find the words with which to describe Andrew and his effect on her. She only knew now that the feeling she had for him had been breeding in her for some time and that it was different from anything she had felt for Donald. She could now look on the love she had borne Donald as a girlish infatuation; she could even term it a 'pash' on a parson. She leant against Aggie's high breast and released the breath from her lungs as she said, 'You've got no idea of the relief, Aunt Aggie, now that I've talked to you.'

'You should have done it earlier – I knew there was something wrong. There should be some way of stopping men like him marrying at all.'

Grace moved her head against Aggie, shutting out the light as she said, 'It was the look on his face; I don't think I'll ever forget it to my dying day.'

'Nonsense.' Aggie's body gave a quick wiggle of impatience. 'You can get that out of your head as soon as you like. He's no man, never was. I knew that from the minute I clapped eyes on him. Why, my Arthur never wore a thread of anything from the day we married, and I might as well tell you now I didn't either.'

Grace's eyes were closed but she could not conjure up a picture of her Aunt Aggie running around naked before her husband, but she could still see the look on Donald's face.

'That man's as full of pride and conceit as an egg's full of meat, and that's all he's full of, for the rest he's boast. I told you that right at the beginning: he's as empty as a watery turnip . . . What did you tell him afore you left?'

'I just said I was coming to you. But I'm not going back, Aunt Aggie, I'm not. I can't, I just can't.'

'All right, all right, there's nobody forcing you. I'll phone and tell him that you're not feeling too good and you're staying the night, that'll give you a breathing space.' She stroked Grace's hair back from her temples and then added softly, 'Don't worry, child, things will straighten out. Rest yourself there till I put the car away.' She patted Grace's head, then added, 'There's one thing I'm thankful for and that is, Susie and Ralph are away. You won't be having any committee meeting on the matter and that's something.'

She smiled, but Grace could not return it. The committee meetings would eventually take place, they were merely being postponed. She sank deeper into the chair. Strangely now she found she was relaxed as she had not been since the day she became Grace Rouse. She no longer felt herself to be Grace Rouse, a parson's wife, and she could never again be Grace Cartner, the gullible, romantic-minded girl. Was she already Grace MacIntyre? Perhaps. Andrew had said last night that this kind of thing happened. Most people, nice people, would say that it didn't, not in a snap of the fingers like that. Yet it hadn't been a snap of the fingers, it had been maturing quietly for two years, justifying itself by some inward call that each had heard. Her call to him must have been loud and clear, for he recognised it and accepted it at once. He was much wiser than she. His wisdom was a natural part of himself and had nothing to do with learning. Last night, just before he had let her go, he had said, 'Tomorrow morning you will loathe yourself, but when you do, remember this: I love you, and no matter what happens I'll go on doing just that.' He had added with just a trace of humour, 'I'm not dour for nowt.'

How right he had been. She had loathed herself, but thankfully this feeling had not lasted.

When she had returned through the garden last night she had been surprised to hear the church clock striking twelve. In just two hours her world had completed a somersault. The light was still on in the bedroom, there were also lights on in both the drawing-room and the hall, and she saw from the head of the stairs that the front door was wide open. Had he gone to the village to raise the alarm? She doubted it. To admit that his wife had run away would cause a loss of face. She couldn't see him risking that until he was absolutely sure that she wouldn't come back when her tantrum was over. That was the name he would give to the episode.

She was crossing the landing going towards the spare room with some of her clothes when he came up the stairs, and just for a moment she felt sorry for him, for he had a frightened look about him. But her sorrow was short-lived, for immediately on sight of her his whole countenance darkened and subdued anger bubbled from his lips as he demanded, 'Where have you been?'

When she turned from him without answering and pushed open the door of the spare room he strode quickly after her, and from the doorway he reprimanded her, saying in the same tense, subdued tone, 'It's about time you grew up, Grace; this is no way for a woman to act. Don't you realise you are no longer a girl being petted and cajoled by your . . . family?' The stress he put on the word family brought her eyes flashing round on him. His private opinion of her family had come over in the intonation he had given the word.

As she looked at him standing there filling the doorway with his bulk, she realised with surprise that she no longer stood in awe of him. An hour ago she had given herself to another man; she had sinned, a grievous sin, and yet because she had sinned she had the courage to look fearlessly at this man who had been to her as a god. If her journey into the darkness had resulted in nothing more than running wild through the woods and the quarry until she had come to her senses and returned penitent to this house, she knew that her abasement would have been complete, but on her wings of flight she had stopped to sin and in doing so had gathered courage into her body, together with a new and extraordinary feeling of easement. She had been unfaithful and in this moment she was exulting in it.

'Don't you realise that you've had me worried sick?'

It was on the point of her tongue to say, 'Yes, so much so that you got a search party out to look for me,' but instead she said flatly, 'I'm very tired, I want to go to bed.'

She watched him draw himself up even straighter. 'You're not sleeping in this room.'

'Well, if I don't I won't sleep anywhere else.' As she said this she made the movement of turning round a casual act. Then going towards the chest-of-drawers she added, 'I'd like to be left alone.'

'Grace . . . Grace, do you know what you're saying?'

'Yes, I said I'd like to be left alone, to sleep alone.' She looked at him over her shoulder. 'You shouldn't find that wish difficult to grant.'

She saw the blood slowly leave his face until it looked a pasty smudge of flesh and became one with the colour of his eyes. Even his lips looked grey.

'We'll have this out in the morning.' His voice, his whole body, emanated bluster.

When the door closed on him she felt a momentary feeling of triumph that settled into scorn.

Her remark at least had struck home. His façade of working late, sermons to write, talks to rehearse, of being very, very tired, had at last been penetrated. No more would he be able to hide behind such lies. But Donald never lied, he simply evaded . . . skilfully evaded.

She did not go to bed but sat by the window looking out on to the back garden and she wondered just why she had put up with the situation all this time. There were two answers. Ignorance of the sexual side of marriage, and a natural diffidence to speak of this side to anyone. When she had entered into her marriage she felt she was equipped with all the necessary knowledge. You loved a man, you slept with him, the outcome was a baby. You became aware of this when your periods stopped and you felt sick. It took nine months to have a baby and during this time your husband worshipped you. And had not millions of women got by on no more knowledge than that? But how had the others made out? The ones that had been led up the garden path and then had the door quietly shut in their faces – had they gone to their mothers, or their doctors, or their priests and poured out their pain? Perhaps. But there would be others like her who had been able to do none of these things. Then had they gone mad, had a nervous breakdown, or been gladly seduced?

She, she knew, had been on the verge of a nervous breakdown, but now she was saved. She had been gladly seduced.

She sat on until the night began to lift and the dawn appeared. She had been sitting with the eiderdown hugged around her and now she pushed it off and made her way quietly out of the room and downstairs to the kitchen. There she made herself a cup of strong tea. She had no fear of being joined by Donald. The sound of his snoring as she crossed the landing had told her that, however much his mind was troubled, it was not preventing him from having his sleep out.

Back in her room she once more pulled the eiderdown about her, and as she gazed out into the swift rising light she tried to see into the day ahead and to what action she should take.

At what point in her thinking she fell asleep she did not know, but she was woken with startling suddenness by the sound of Ben's voice yelling from the garden. She sat up, blinking her eyes rapidly, not sure for a moment where she was, and then as she rose painfully from the cramped position in which she had been sleeping Ben's voice came to her again. When she put her face close to the window-pane she could see him near the greenhouse. He was standing waving his arms about and still yelling. What was happening? What was the matter? She could see no-one else in the garden. Then, as she watched and saw him coming towards her window, she knew he was making for the side of the house and the kitchen door. Hurriedly she smoothed down her hair and her dress. She still felt dazed with sleep, and her eyes seemed full of sand. On crossing the landing she saw that Donald was already about, for the bedroom door was wide open and there was no sign of him.

As she entered the kitchen she saw Ben through

the far open door; his fist was clenched and shaking in front of Donald's face, and he was crying at the top of his voice, 'Sawed down her hedge, did you? Sawed it down, you cruel bugger! That's what you are, you're no man. Well, this is the finish for me. I'll not work for you another minute, no, not if I was starvin'. Do you hear?'

'I told you I wanted that hedge cutting well down; I told you quite plainly yesterday and all you did was to take an inch or so off the top.'

'You go to hell's flames. I know why that hedge was put there in the first place an' I told you.' He thrust his hand outwards in the direction of the drive. 'There's no green hedge there now, is there? No, all you can see is a tarred roof. Nice, isn't it? But if it hadn't been that it would've been somethin' else. You were just waitin', weren't you? Giving your orders right, left and centre about things you know nowt about. Playing God Almighty inside and outside the church. Well, let me tell you, mister, you're not comin' God Almighty on me. I'm on to you and your ways. I saw through you from the start. It's folk like you that cause murder, aye it is that. Well, now I'm finished. You get me cards and me pay ready and I'm downin' me tools. And I'll say to you me last word . . .' Ben's old face quivered upwards. 'You're a two-faced, mealy-mouthed nowt, and a cruel bugger into the bargain, and there you have it.'

The old man turned away, and after a moment Grace stepped slowly out of the kitchen and into the yard and looked at Donald. She saw that he was going to great lengths to control himself. And when she spoke to him it was not so much a question as a statement. Coldly she said, 'You cut down that hedge? You must have got up early this morning and purposely gone out to cut down that hedge, Ben's hedge.'

'It is not Ben's hedge.'

'Then it is my hedge.'

His face became scarlet and his jaw-bones seemed to lift from their sockets before he said, 'Very well, Grace, since you emphasise your ownership, I shall make arrangements for us to return to the vicarage – it is still available.'

As she turned from him, his voice rapped at her, 'Where are you going? I forbid you to go near that man.'

She stopped and, turning round, looked at him. And there rose to her tongue Ben's words, 'You cruel bugger', and it was as much as she could do not to repeat them. But had she said them they would not have surprised him any more than when she said, 'You can forbid me to do nothing that I want to do.'

She left him with his eyes wide open and his lips apart, and as she hurried round the house towards Ben she kept saying to herself, 'It's impossible, it's impossible', for she knew in this moment that she had not only ceased to love him but that she almost hated him. He must have risen early this morning, not to come to her and try to sort out the events of last night, but deliberately to cut down a hedge that he must have known would be a wanton thing to do. Ben had disobeyed his orders, so Ben must suffer. Ben, although he did not know it, was also suffering because she had disobeyed her master's orders.

When she came upon Ben he was standing at what last night had been a thick trim hedge. The main stems of the lonicera had been sawn through and pulled away. They lay in a heap at the side of the path; all that remained of the hedge now was a straggly torn mat of bush about two feet high.

'I'm sorry, Ben, oh I am.' She stood by his side, but he did not reply; only his head drooped lower and he shook it slowly from side to side before turning away towards the greenhouse. When she followed him and he still wouldn't say anything to her she realised that the old man was crying. It was as she watched the tears sliding from one wrinkle to another that she knew she must go away, she must leave this house. She said to Ben's stooped shoulders, 'I'll come and see you, Ben, I'll get you a garden of your own, I will, I promise you.'

Ben's cottage on the other side of the village had nothing more than a pocket handkerchief of a garden, and she knew how the old man would miss his work, so she was not just using soothing words but meant what she said when she made him the promise. He still gave her no answer and she turned about and went quickly towards the house . . .

When half an hour later she came down the stairs wearing a light costume and hat and carrying a case she was confronted not only by Donald but by Mrs Blenkinsop, and this situation could not have made things easier for her, for, ignoring Donald and looking straight towards the older woman, she said, 'I'm going to my aunt's, Mrs Blenkinsop, she isn't very well.'

'Oh, I'm sorry to hear that, ma'am.'

Grace knew that at the moment Mrs Blenkinsop believed her, and Donald did nothing that would tend to make the situation other than a natural one, for he followed his wife out and along the side of the house to the garage. But once in its shelter his wrath burst over her, but in a controlled quiet way that would not carry beyond her ears.

'What are you playing at, Grace? Don't be silly. You can't go running off to your aunt's because we have a little misunderstanding. Go for a drive and then come back, but don't go near your Aunt Aggie's. I . . .'

'You forbid me?'

'I'm asking you not to.'

'I'm going to Aunt Aggie's and I'm going to talk to her. I should have done this a long time ago. If I had I wouldn't have served my time to become a nervous wreck.' She opened the door and got into the car, and from there she looked up at him. 'In a very short time I would have had a breakdown and everybody would have been sorry . . . not for me, oh no, but for you. That the poor vicar should have a wife with nerves.'

They were staring at each other, and she saw his eyes change colour. She had noticed this before. It was as if he drew over them a thick veil of protection. She watched him gulp before speaking.

'Of course you're suffering from nerves, and it's because you've been acting like an hysterical girl for months.' His voice became lower still. 'There are more things in marriage than silly romance, and one of them is duty. You seem to forget that you have a duty to me.'

'Ask Miss Shawcross to take it over.'

'Grace, how dare you! You are both uncouth and coarse.'

'Yes, yes, I suppose I am. I come from that kind of stock. You have never thought much of them, I know. You don't really think much of anyone below the standard of the Tooles and Farleys, do you? The folks and the others – remember? The cheque-book buyers versus those with cash.'

She pressed the self-starter, and when her foot came off the accelerator and the noise in the garage subsided she heard him say, 'It's unbelievable, I can't believe it. What's changed you like this?'

'Oh, Donald!' She was talking through her teeth now. 'For God's sake don't be such a hypocrite.' She leant towards him until her face was not more than a few inches from his, and actually hissed at him, 'You're trying your damnedest to get confession going in the church, aren't you? Then I'd advise you to set an example and go and be your own first penitent. That should give you the answer . . . What's changed me . . . Huh!'

'Grace, wait; I beseech you, wait.'

The car moved out of the garage; they were in the open now and there was Mrs Blenkinsop at the kitchen door. She smiled a farewell and Grace returned the smile, even lifted her hand in a wave, and then she was off along the drive, out of the gate and on the main road. Away, away, and she was never going to come back.

Aggie did not go out immediately to park the car but went into her office and hastily wrote a letter. Then, after she had installed the car beside her own in the converted stables at the end of the cul-de-sac, she hurried down the main road and to the pillar-box and there posted the letter. As she returned to the house she thought, 'He should get that first post in the morning. Today's Wednesday; I should have word back by Friday and something should be settled at the week-end. That's if the light of day hasn't brought him cold feet . . . the young swine . . .'

The following morning at half past eleven no-one could have been more surprised than Aggie when, answering a ring at the front door, she was confronted by . . . the young swine himself.

Andrew MacIntyre had his hat in his hand, he was wearing a brown suit and thick-soled, highly polished boots. 'I got your letter.' His attitude was characteristic and to the point, as was Aggie's reply, 'Have you flown?'

'No I came on me bike, it's me day off.'

Aggie glanced behind her. There was no sign of Grace, and she said quickly, 'Come in. Go into that room.' She pointed to the left. Then, closing the front door, she glanced towards the stairs before following him.

As Aggie took her seat at her desk she said curtly, 'Sit down.' And when he was seated she looked at him squarely and said, 'Well!' then added, 'This is a nice kettle of fish. You know what you are, don't you?' She jerked her head towards him, and when he made no reply she added, 'Well, what have you got to say? Nothing, I suppose.'

'I've got plenty to say but I'll wait until you're finished.'

Well! She said the word this time to herself as she sat up straight and scrutinised him. He certainly was no weak-kneed youth, but still he wasn't going to get it all his own way, she was going to give it to him hot and heavy, by gad she was. 'All right then. I'll have my say. What do you mean by . . . by . . . ?' Now she was stuck for the right words. She could hardly say 'raping my niece?' nor could she say 'taking down a married woman?' Grace, by her own account, had been more than willing. But she had to say something, so she finished, 'by ruining my niece's life?'

'I haven't ruined her life; that was done the day you let her marry him.'

She didn't say, 'I didn't want her to marry him, I would have stopped it if I could,' but snapped back at him. 'Nobody could have stopped her, she was in love with him. She was potty about him.'

'What did she know about it? She had been tucked away in school.'

'How old are you?'

'I'm twenty-four.'

She was surprised, he didn't look that old. 'Oh, and I suppose you know all about it, and would have done better than him?'

'Aye, I would that. And I would now, but it isn't always possible to do what you want.' For the first time Andrew looked away from Aggie and his voice took on a softer note as he ended, 'I'm sorry about what happened.'

'Oh?' Aggie raised her brows. 'Are you telling me that you want to back out?'

His eyes came up swiftly to her again. 'No, I don't want to back out as you call it, but there are circumstances . . .' He wetted his lips. 'I've no money; at the end of the week I won't have a job – I've given me notice in – and I have to support my parents.'

Aggie nodded her small head. 'Oh. Your prospects are very bright, aren't they? And what do you expect us to do about it . . . ?' Her words were cut off by Andrew getting swiftly to his feet.

'I don't want . . . us . . . to do anything about it. The matter lies between her and me.'

'Well, there's one thing: she's got enough money to keep you both.' Her eyes, narrowed now, were tight on him.

'Well, she won't be called upon to use it, not on me.' His words and tone now caused Aggie's head to droop slightly. Then it came up with startling suddenness as she said, 'You're not going to take her away then?'

'I'm not going to take her away.'

Aggie was now on her feet, her head tilted to look up into his face. 'Then may I ask what you are going to do?' she demanded angrily.

'I'm going to stay where I am.'

'You mean to stand there and tell me that you're going to stay . . . ?' Aggie stopped. 'Well, she won't go back. What do you say to that?'

Aggie watched the skin around his mouth pale

before he said, 'That will be up to her.' Then, drawing in a sharp breath, he added, 'Now can I see her?'

Aggie continued to look at him for a moment longer. She couldn't make him out. Things had not gone according to her plans. After the pre-liminaries were over and the shouting had died down she had seen him installed on a farm, a farm of his own – Grace's money could run to it easily. But here he was telling her he wasn't going to leave Deckford. She did not say another word as she left him, but when she got upstairs into Grace's room the words tumbled out of her.

'He's downstairs – no, not Donald, Andrew MacIntyre.' She took Grace by the arm and shook her none too gently. 'I know what you've got in your mind, but let me prepare you for a disap-pointment: he won't leave Deckford. He's left his job, by the way – why, I don't know – but he won't leave the place. Again why, I don't know, but that's for you to find out.'

'How did he know I was here?' Grace's voice was scarcely audible.

'I wrote last night and told him. I expected a reply some time tomorrow, but there he is, as large as life, downstairs in the office. Go on now. But mind, things are not going to go your way, I'm warning you.'

Slowly Grace descended the stairs. She was nervous, a little afraid, a little bashful, more than a little ashamed to face this man. Andrew in the dark had been a boy matching his youth with hers, but in the daylight she knew he would be Andrew MacIntyre and another being. But all these feelings disappeared when she entered the room and, after closing the door, stood with her back to it looking across the small space towards him.

He made no move towards her but just stood, his eyes bright and dark, returning her deeply troubled stare. It was the hunger in them that reached out once more to the loneliness in herself and within a second she was in his arms, her head on his shoulder, her mouth pressed into his coat, muttering over and over again as she had done the night before last, 'Oh, Andrew; oh, Andrew.'

He did not attempt to kiss her, but after a moment he pressed her from him and put her into a chair beside the desk, and, drawing another one up close, he asked, 'Has your aunt told you anything I've said?'

'She said you were leaving the Tooles.' She did not now ask why – she knew. And then she ended, with her face screwing up in some complexity, 'But she said you won't leave the village. Is this true, Andrew?'

'Yes, I can't leave there.'

'But why?'

'My people.'

'But, Andrew, listen to me.' She leant forward and gripped his hands. 'I'm not going back there. I never want to see it again, or anyone in it. You told me the other night that these things can happen. Well, I believe you, for now I know it. I want to go away with you, Andrew, and I have enough money to set us up in any kind of business, farming or anything. And if Donald won't divorce me it won't matter. If it came to the point . . .' Now she stopped and looked away from him towards the face-curtained windows and she repeated, 'If it came to the point I could have it annulled.'

'Oh, Grace, what have I done?' He was looking at her hands. 'I should never have let that happen the other night. I know now I shouldn't. I knew it at the time, yet I've been livin' these past months just to hold you.'

'You're sorry?'

'No, no, I'm not. No, be damned, no never that. You know I'm not sorry – not for myself, that is. But for you. You would, I suppose, have gone on; like my mother you would have gone on.'

'I wouldn't, Andrew. I couldn't have gone on, I was heading for a breakdown. I never slept properly for months. I was ill. I know I was ill, and no matter what happens I'll never regret the other night, Andrew . . .' She looked up into his face. 'You mightn't know it, but you not only saved my life, you saved my sanity. If I had gone down through the wood the way I came up something would have snapped in me.'

'Oh, Grace.' He gently touched her face. Then his eyes dropped from hers and he shook his head slowly from one side to the other. 'What I want to do now is take you up and run with you to where nobody will ever find us. But I can't; I can't, Grace. I can't leave her.'

'Her?'

'My mother.'

'Your mother?' The surprise and disappointment in her voice brought him to his feet and he turned his back on her as he said, 'For twenty years she has worked and slaved after my father. Her life has been sheer hell. He is crippled with arthritis, as you know. Besides that, his mind is crippled an' all. He hates people, everybody, even me. Most of all me, I think. She won't leave him and I can't leave her. If she knew of this she would tell me to go. It is because I feel for her as I do that I am capable of loving you as I do. I can love you and let you go. I can love you without even touching your hand again. I have done, and would have gone on doing it.' He swung round to her now. 'That might be hard to believe but it's true.'

'But . . . but, Andrew, what's to be done? I can't go back there. At least' – she lowered her head as she murmured – 'I hadn't thought I'd be called upon to.'

'Don't come back because of me. Whatever you do, don't do that. I can see you at times . . . if you still want me to. I'll have to find fresh work, anyway, but that won't be difficult now – they are crying out for farm-workers.'

'Andrew.' She reached up her arms to his shoulders and said, 'Let me give you a farm.'

With one step he had moved from her reach and the small space between them seemed to widen. Then with a motion of his hand as if he was flinging something away, he said, 'No, not that. Never that. Don't you offer me that. I am one who must make his own way, and as far as I can see that'll never be very high, but nevertheless I must make and pay me own way. Don't ask me to be another soft-seated parson.'

'Oh, Andrew!' The hurt in her voice brought him to her and he pulled her up into his arms and held her close as he said, 'I didn't mean it like that. I just wanted you to know I want nothing from you but – but yourself.'

He was silent now, holding her hard against him, and as she felt the trembling of his body it came to her quite quietly, and therefore clearly, that whatever Andrew MacIntyre said his word would be her law. Mentally they might be poles apart, for she did not know the trend of his mind as yet, but physically they were as one, and because of this, if nothing else, she would be capable of enduring anything to remain near him.

And so it was.

'Do you mean to say you are going back to that house to live with him all because that pigheaded Scot won't move from the village?'

'I've told you, Aunt Aggie, why he can't.'

'Nonsense! His people could come and live near you, for that matter . . . something could be arranged.'

'His father is a bitter man, he won't leave the cottage. He hates the sight of people and he rarely sees anyone up there.'

Aggie made a complete circle of her drawing-room before she spoke again. 'Well, it beats me. What if Donald starts changing his tactics and making demands on you, futile or otherwise?'

'Don't worry, he won't do that – that's one thing I'm sure of. If I wasn't I don't think I could go back.'

'And how long do you expect to live under that strain? You'll only be able to see Andrew MacIntyre when you sneak into that quarry. Don't be silly, girl, it would break you.'

'Yes, yes, I agree with you it might, but nevertheless I must give it a try. Even if I don't speak to him, I know he'll be near and at hand if I want him. And it'll be a different kind of strain. I'll not break under this strain.' She shook her head slowly from side to side.

'Oh, to think your life has come to this. And they made game of Charlie Wentworth and thought he wasn't good enough for you because he was only second clerk in Raynors' office.' Aggie looked at her in dismay . . . 'Well, when do you propose to go?'

'I'll go back this afternoon.'

'My God!'

There was no-one in the house when Grace arrived. Mrs Blenkinsop had gone home. The trolley was set for tea as was usual. The house was the same as when she had left it yesterday morning, yet not the same, and she knew it would never be the same again.

She was standing by the window of the drawing-room when Donald came up the drive. He stopped in his tracks when he caught sight of her, yet he did not enter the house through the french windows but went in through the front door and came into the drawing-room from the hall.

When she felt him standing behind her she gave a slight shudder, and when his hands came on her shoulders and turned her towards him she did not resist.

'Grace.' His voice was low, soft and full of forgiveness. 'Are you feeling better?'

'I'm feeling all right.'

'I'm glad to see you again. I've missed you; the house has been so empty.'

She looked up into his face. His expression was gentle and beguiling, but no longer did she see any beauty in it. Had she ever loved this man? Had she ever been mad about him? Yes, yes. There was no use in denying that. And he could have turned the girlish love into a passion that would have burned fiercely down through the years. The thought, down through the years, brought another shudder to her body. Would she have to live in the same house with him until they were old, or one or other died? No, no, she couldn't. Something would have to be done, something would have to happen. But in the meantime she would stay. She felt no sense of guilt at the thought of deceiving him. He had deceived her as no man should deceive a woman. His deception had amounted to torture, and he was all the more guilty because he set himself up as an example to other men. He who wasn't and could never be a man.

'Come and have some tea.' He went to put his arm through hers, but she forestalled this by walking ahead of him towards the trolley. As she busied herself pouring out the tea, he went and stood with his back towards the empty grate, his hands linked behind him, and he talked, talked as if nothing had happened between them to shatter the harmony of his days. He talked about the shadow of war that hung over the country and the preparations the village was making to meet it, and as she listened she knew that the incident of yesterday morning and Ben would not be referred to again. As for what happened in their bedroom the other night, that was already something he had buried so deep that it could never be uncovered.

'Mr Baker from the Stag has been very good. He has a small cellar attached to the main one. He's offered it for a shelter until we get things under way, that's if it becomes necessary, and we'll soon know that. Brookes says that food will be very scarce. He suggests we stock up; or, to be more correct' – he gave a little laugh at this point – 'it was Mrs Brookes who suggested this. I was talking to the doctor. He seemed to think he might be called up and seems worried over it, because of Renee, I suppose. Yet I should have thought at his age he would have been eager to go. He's just turned thirty.'

She would have liked to have asked point blank, 'Will you go?' He was thirty-nine. Men of that age could go. Oh, she wished . . . She turned her head sideways away from the thought that sprang into her mind. She mustn't desire that – that was bad, vile, much more so than betraying him with another man.

When he came and sat beside her on the couch and took hold of her hand she drew it quietly away from him and, joining her fingers together, she pressed them for a moment between her knees before saying, 'If I am to stay here, Donald, I want a room to myself.'

She was staring ahead and did not see the reactions of her words on him, and it was some little time before he answered her, and then neither the tone of his voice nor his words surprised her, for he said evenly, 'Very well, it will be as you wish.'

He was relieved. She knew he was relieved, and for a moment she felt a fierce anger rise against him. He was a cheat, a hypocrite, he was also a coward. It might seem incongruous knowing her feelings towards him at the moment, but she would have felt less bitter against him had he made some protest against her request. And then he did, but in a way that deepened her scorn.

'There is only one favour I would ask of you, it will only be for a couple of days.' He refrained, she noticed, from saying nights. 'I heard from my uncle – you know, Uncle Stephen; he would like to see me and proposes staying over the week-end. He is due in Edinburgh on Monday next and proposes coming here on the Saturday.' He rose now and went to the fireplace and took up his old position but with his back towards her, and from there he said, 'He would think it unusual . . . you understand?'

Her anger almost burst from her now. It bubbled inside of her, and it was as much as she could do to remain still. Face must not be lost, his face; the proprieties must be kept up for the bishop. She wanted to turn on him and yell 'You hypocrite!' and not only 'You hypocrite!'

but to give it an adjective, an adjective brought from the memory of the years in the little house at the head of the coalyard, and in spite of her anger its appearance in her mind shocked her slightly.

5

It was now the middle of October and Grace knew for a certainty that she was pregnant and she was both elated and slightly distraught. She knew that the child was Andrew's, and yet . . . The yet would loom quite large at times, for there would come back to her again and again the incident that occurred during the bishop's stay. She thought of it as an incident, an isolated, repulsive, even dirty incident. She also thought: Aunt Aggie was right again. Donald had made love to her. Whether his intention had been to convince himself of his potency or to appease her she did not know; she only knew that she had been sickened and repulsed and she had been left wondering why she had longed with a burning longing for almost two years for this to happen. Added to this was the frightening knowledge of the complete change in her feelings towards him. She would not have thought it possible for any human being to change so completely. If, two years ago, someone had confided in her, saying, 'My husband is not capable of loving me', she knew she would have said, 'Poor soul', and she would have been thinking, not of the woman, but of the man. She would have been sorry to the heart for the man, for, after all, she would have reasoned that sex was only part of marriage. You read that that was so . . . Moreover, hadn't Donald said so. But now she could curl her lip at that statement. Sex was marriage – at the beginning, anyway. For the marriage to go right, that one thing had to be right. All things stemmed from it – harmony, peace, peace of mind and body, and, the most important thing of all, learning to like your man. And there was small chance of liking in the daylight a man whom you didn't like in the dark. There were extenuating circumstances, she knew, such as when a man was crippled, and a woman sublimated herself in a selfless love for him. But Donald wasn't crippled . . . and yet, in a way, he was – he had been born crippled. Realising this, she asked herself why she wasn't sorry for him, why she wasn't kind to him in her heart, and the answer came to her that it was because she knew him to be a cheat. He must have known his own make-up before he married her. He had felt the need of a mother to pet him, a doll to play with, and a woman to run his house and assist in his church, preferably one with a nice bit of money, but he had never wanted a wife.

There was one thing at least that the incident had achieved: it had given her an alibi. But at the present moment she didn't care if she had one or not, things were bound to come out.

She went into the kitchen now to see about dinner, and Mrs Blenkinsop looked at her closely and exclaimed, 'By, ma'am, you look peeky.' And then she added with motherly concern, 'You're not yourself these days at all, ma'am. Why don't you lie up for a while and have a good rest? It's the aftermath, all that excitement about the war that never was. Everybody's feeling it one way or another, the village is as flat as a pancake. It's funny, ma'am, but I could bet me bottom dollar that half of them's disappointed.'

'Oh, I wouldn't say that, Mrs B.'

'They are, ma'am. It would have given them the opportunity to carry on dizzy-lizzying all over the place, throwing their weight about.'

Mrs Blenkinsop mentioned no names but Grace knew she was referring to Kate Shawcross. Mrs B didn't like Kate Shawcross.

'About lunch, Mrs B.'

'Well, ma'am . . . yes now, there's the rabbit Mr Toole dropped in, or I can mince that chicken, whatever you like.'

'I think we'll have the chicken.'

'Just as you say, ma'am. Speaking of the Tooles' – Mrs Blenkinsop moved towards the sink, lifting in a stack of dishes as she spoke – 'that Adelaide is getting her name up, I'm afraid.'

'Yes?' Grace did not turn away from the prattle of her cook, it was only through Mrs Blenkinsop that she knew of the real happenings in the village. People did not speak their minds to the parson's wife, and her nothing but a young girl after all.

'Well, since Andrew MacIntyre started at Tarrant's farm she's gone out of her way to be on the road nights when he's coming back. You would think she would take a hint, wouldn't you? Mr Blenkinsop said it made his ears red when he heard her.'

'Mr Blenkinsop heard her?' Grace was looking

at Mrs Blenkinsop's profile, and the older woman went on washing the dishes, nodding down to the water as she said, 'Yes. He was in the field just above the road, beyond the cemetery you know, ma'am, at the back there. He was going to drop down to the road when he heard them. She was accusing him of egging her on and he was denying it. And then you know what he said, ma'am?' She turned her eyes towards Grace. 'He said, "Have I ever as much as kissed you?" That's what Mr Blenkinsop said he said . . . I ask you. Then she snapped back at him, "No, but you've wanted to." Can you imagine it, ma'am? Her saying a thing like that to Andrew MacIntyre. Lowering, isn't it, for, after all, although they treated him a cut above the rest, he was only a farm-worker. Then he said, "It's all your imagination," and stamped off. But mind, as I said to Mr Blenkinsop, he's a fool. She's the only child and it's a fine farm, one of the best around here, and it could be his just for the lift of his finger. "Yes," I said to Mr Blenkinsop, "that lad must be daft." '

'Perhaps he doesn't love her, Mrs B.'

Grace was turning away when Mrs Blenkinsop laughed aloud. 'Oh, what's love to do with it? If he doesn't love her afore he'll love her after, and a good farm and plenty of dibs would help things along. Aye, it would that . . . Love? Huh! And the chance to get into the county fringe. Not that the Farleys would take kindly to him, and some of the others likely wouldn't recognise him at first, but things are changing fast and time wears people down, and if there should come a war – well, you know what changes wars make, ma'am.'

Grace left the kitchen. Had she stopped Andrew from having a good farm and plenty of dibs and getting into the county set? No, she wouldn't hold herself responsible for that. He could have plenty of dibs now, her dibs, if it was dibs he wanted, and as for the county fringe! She couldn't see Andrew in that set. Unlike Mrs Blenkinsop, she didn't look upon the Tooles as being of the county fringe. But nevertheless she felt sorry for Adelaide Toole. She liked Adelaide, the little she had seen of her.

What would Andrew say when she told him about the baby? It was a week since she had seen him, a week since she had been held in his arms. Why hadn't she told him then? What would Donald say when she told him about the baby? She felt sick on this thought, and her mind felt dizzy and muddled, yet even so one thought remained clear. They would both have to be told.

As she crosssed the hall there came a ring at the door bell, and when she opened it there stood Dr Cooper, and on the first sight of him she knew a sense of relief. Here was someone she could tell.

'Well, how are you this morning?'

She smiled at him, and as she closed the door she said enigmatically, 'Different.'

'Different?' His thick eyebrows moved upwards. 'Now what do you mean by that?'

'Come in here, into the morning-room – I've lit a fire. It's a bit chilly this morning, isn't it?'

'Yes, there's a nip coming. But never mind

about fires or nips, tell me what is this mysterious difference?'

She turned and faced him, her face looked sad, 'I'm going to have a baby.'

'You are?' His voice was level. 'That's good news, very good news. Are you sure?'

'Positive.'

'Oh well, that's done me out of a job. What does Donald say to this stupendous news? Is he overwhelmed?'

'I haven't told him . . . not yet.'

His eyebrows moved upwards again and he nodded his head. 'And when may we expect the arrival?'

'I'm about five weeks.' She did not say six. What was a week, anyway? But she asked herself: was she already using the alibi?

David Cooper looked at her. Here was a young girl going to have her first baby and talking flatly and unemotionally about it, as if it was her fifth or even her seventh. The doctor went back on his thoughts as he said to himself: young girl? She was no longer a girl, and whatever had happened to her – and he didn't lay the change down to her pregnancy – it had changed her into a woman, and not a very happy one either. Something was wrong here and he couldn't get to the bottom of it. It had been all over the village a few weeks ago that she had dashed off in a car early one morning and left the vicar. It was over the busines of Ben and the garden. If it hadn't been that the whole place was agog waiting for a war to start that incident would have raised much more gossip than it did. And so she was going to have a baby?

If this had happened in the first year it would doubtless have smoothed things over, but now he wasn't sure. He wished she would talk.

'Can I tell Renee?'

'I'd rather you didn't, not yet.'

'Just as you say . . . I suppose I'll have to look you over. What about tomorrow afternoon? And stay and have a cup of tea, Renee's always delighted to see you . . . I won't tell her, she'll think it's just a check up.'

'Thanks, I'll come down.'

'Well, I must be off.'

'Won't you stay and have a coffee?'

'No, no thanks, I'm off to the Farleys. Papa Farley's got rheumatism – we used to call it gout. Do you know that Bertrand Farley has joined up . . . the army? I saw him in his uniform yesterday; it does something for him. I won't say he doesn't need it.' He gave Grace a dig with his thumb, and she laughed. They laughed together, and as they crossed the hall her laughter rose much louder than the joke had warranted.

She was still laughing when she returned to the breakfast-room, but when she stood before the fire with her foot on the fender and her hand on the mantelpiece her laughter stopped abruptly and with her teeth clamping down on her lip she began to cry – painfully slow tears.

It was Andrew, after all, whom she told first. Not from within the security of his arms under the shelter of the rock wall in the quarry, but on the open road outside an empty cottage at Culbert's Cut. She had come once again to look at this place, wondering whether she would buy it, and having done so would it then be easier to persuade Ben to accept it? It was going for three hundred pounds. That was quite a bit for this type of property, but what was three hundred pounds compared with Ben's idle hands? The cottage stood alone, about a quarter of a mile from the village, and the land around it was flat and open.

When she stepped from the garden gate onto the road and saw the lorry coming towards her she did not look at it twice, until its stopping drew her attention. And then she saw Andrew. He got out of the cab and stood beside the door, and she stood by the bonnet of the lorry. There was four or more feet between them, and this space held the village and any covert stroller like Mr Blenkinsop.

'Hello, darlin'.' The soft low burr of his voice gave the words a deepened caress, and her heart was warmed and eased by the endearment.

'You look whitish; are you all right?'

She did not answer for a long moment as she hesitated in her mind whether to tell him or not. She had imagined giving him her news with her face resting against his, but it might be a week, even two, before they would get the chance to meet again, and so she said, 'I'm going to have a baby, Andrew.'

No muscle of his face moved, but his eyes darkened. And then he asked softly, 'Are you glad?'

'Yes, yes, Andrew, I'm glad . . . are you?'

'Yes, yes. But it's you, if you're happy about it, that's all that matters.'

'Oh, Andrew.'

Their bodies were taut and still and their glances were held fast links of a chain.

'The only thing I'm worried about is later on.' Her voice was trembling. 'I won't be able to go up to . . . to the quarry.'

'Don't worry about that, we'll work something out . . .'

They were still staring at each other. The danger was imminent; she knew that in a moment she would fall against him. She said quickly, 'I must go.'

'Yes . . . Grace.' His hand was lifting towards her when swiftly he changed its direction and swung himself up into the cab. As the door banged she stepped away from the bonnet and now she was below him. He had his hand on the wheel but did not start the engine; he looked down into her eyes and said, 'I love you, lass. You're . . . you're the most beautiful thing on earth . . . An' . . . an' I worship you.'

The gears were rammed in and he left his deep glance on her as the lorry moved away.

He said things at odd times like that, things that brought fire to her heart. His verbal love-making was jerky yet in a way profound and beautifying . . . If only . . . if only . . . She turned round and walked down the road towards the village and Ben's cottage. If only they could be together, live together, mellow together. It was strange but in this moment she did not think of him as he was now, but her mind was filled with the desire that they should be old together.

*　　*　　*

Andrew had his eyes on the road as he drove the lorry but he was not seeing it. He avoided the potholes by instinct, for between him and the road were his thoughts which seemed to be written large on the windscreen, and nowhere among them was one of elation at the news Grace had given him. One thought stood out from the rest: it said, 'Leave the damn place. Take her far away. You can't expect her to put up with it.' There was no answer to this on the windscreen, for deep within his bones was the pull of the woman in the windswept stone house on the fell. He had felt this pull and her need of him even from the age of three. They were so close that it seemed at times as if the cord had never been cut between them. She had said to him the other day, 'I'm not asking why you left Toole, you'll tell me in your own time, but I had to tell your father something so I said you had a row about your wage – he would understand that.' He had looked at her drawn face and said, 'Stop worrying, I'll tell you some time.' But as close as they were, could he tell her, tell her he was fathering a child to the parson's wife? If he did he knew it would bring his release – but he couldn't do it – not even for Grace . . .

Not even for Grace.

Almost two more weeks elapsed before Grace could bring herself to tell Donald. She had done a great deal of thinking during this particular time, and it revolved mainly around whether she should go away or stay here. There were two things against her going away. First, she would see less of Andrew than she did now; second, and this was the point that was having more bearing with her as each day of her pregnancy advanced, if she went away the child would be born illegitimate, whereas if she stayed it would be sheltered by Donald's name, for she knew him well enough to be sure that he would do anything rather than suffer the public indignity of her lapse. These two things became bands as strong as steel, hawsers holding her in place. Yet the more she now saw of Donald, the stronger became the desire to get away from him.

During the past few weeks Donald had developed a sullenness. He might be relieved that he was sleeping alone, but the fact that he was not the instigator of this arrangement was apparently having a delayed action. He no longer made any pretence of playing the lover; there was no kissing and petting and dear-little-girling now. Often there was not even a good night between them. He also had an added irritation to bear . . . the garden. It was the time of year for cutting, and clearing, and there were great patches of browning Michaelmas daisies, phlox and other perennials giving striking evidence of neglect. Peter Golding, the man who had followed Ben, had left over a week ago, the job, as he said, being too much for any one man. And he had added, he wasn't serving his time to be a Ben Fairfoot.

Grace knew that Donald had been furious over this, and she had heard him say to Mrs Blenkinsop, 'Lazy blighter. I'll do it myself in my spare time. A couple of hours a day will keep it well under.' But apparently he hadn't had any spare time, for the garden had not been touched. As Ben had said, Donald knew nowt about gardening. Moreover, she knew that he didn't like work – not that kind of work, anyway.

And now came the day when they got the spare time gardener, the day when a new era of her life began. It happened that she had been sick. She was slightly sick in the mornings, but on this day there had been fish for lunch, cod, and the oil must have upset her stomach, for in the middle of the afternoon she felt ill, and she had no ease until she vomited. She lay down for a while until the desire for a cup of tea took her downstairs. It was as she stepped into the hall that Donald let himself in through the front door, and on the sight of her he came towards her, asking quietly, 'What is the matter? Are you ill?'

She shook her head and turned in the direction of the kitchen, and when he followed her and repeated his question she placed her hands flat on the kitchen table, her weight on them, and, looking downwards, she said quietly, 'I'm pregnant.'

He was silent so long that she was forced to turn and look at him, and when she saw his face some understanding of his inner plight came to her and pity welled in her for him. His expression was a mixture of disbelief and blank amazement, but over all there was a look of wonder.

'You mean . . . ?' He wet one lip against the other, then, moving his head slowly from side to side, he brought out, 'Oh, Grace!' Then on a higher note, 'Oh, Grace!' She could imagine him going up the scale chanting her name until he burst into song. It was pitiable. Then like a great benevolent figure he flung his arms out wide. He was forgiving her for being a silly hysterical girl. He was forgiving her for being a demanding wife. He was forgiving her for her unpredictable conduct on the particular night some weeks ago when she had struggled like a wildcat, and necessity demanded he put his hand over her mouth in case his uncle should hear her protests. Definitely he was forgiving her this last, for look what he imagined it had achieved.

'No, no, don't touch me, leave me alone.' She sprang back from the enfolding arms and he stopped nonplussed for a moment. Then, smiling gently, he said, 'All right, all right.' And after a great intake of breath he asked, 'But tell me, are you happy about this?'

She could look at him and say quite truthfully, 'Yes, yes, I am very happy.'

'You'll feel differently now, Grace. Things will be different.' He was standing close to her, looking down on her bent head. 'I told you, didn't I, that things shouldn't be rushed. There comes a time—'

'Stop it! Stop that talk.' She moved away but turned her eyes full on him. 'I've listened to too much of that kind of talk. I want to hear no more of it.'

His face had taken on a pinkish tinge, and he remained quiet for a moment but still looking at her. Then he said, 'Very well. All right, don't let us argue.' His manner was placating and his voice was like warm oil; he was soothing the mother-to-be. 'Go and sit down and I'll bring you a cup of tea.'

Slowly, almost mechanically, she walked into the drawing-room, saying to herself over and over again, 'I can't bear it, I can't. I won't be able to stand it, I won't. I must tell him, and now, today, this minute, now.'

When he brought in the tray of tea his step was almost tripping, and if there had been a laugh anywhere in her she would have laughed, he looked so comic. She was momentarily relieved when he did not sit on the couch beside her but walked with his cup slowly to the window and stood there looking out into the garden. It would be easier to tell him over the distance. On this thought there returned to her the spasm of pity, for she could almost see him thinking. She could almost feel his pride, his sense of achievement. He imagined he had accomplished what he never expected to accomplish: he had proved himself to be a man. His back was straight and his shoulders spread wide with the glory of it. And then he turned to her and, as was his wont when deeply concerned with one thing, he talked about another, and so she did not tell him that he was suffering from self-delusion, for his words set the pattern of her future.

'I've engaged someone for part-time in the garden. It's that Andrew MacIntyre. He's only on four days over at Tarrant's so he'll do at least two days for me, and likely get through as much in that time as the others did in a week. I won't say I would have taken him if there had been choice of . . . Why, Grace . . . !'

As the cup fell out of her hand to the floor with a clatter and she fell over sideways she heard his voice echoing as if through a gigantic empty hall, 'Why Grace! Why Grace! WHY GRACE!'

6

In June 1939 Grace gave birth to a son; he had blue eyes and features that could be traced to neither Andrew nor Donald nor herself. If at this early stage there was a resemblance to anyone it was to her own father. The birth left Grace quieter inside and changed her still more. It intensified her feelings for Andrew, it created a passionate love for the child, and strangely enough created in her a tolerance towards Donald. She called him Stephen.

She had the baby at home for reasons best known to herself, and she did not stay long in bed after the birth but was up and actually had taken a walk in the garden by the ninth day. It was a Thursday and the nurse had put the baby in the pram under the porch, and Andrew MacIntyre, who was mowing the front lawn, came and looked at the child. He looked at it for a long time, and then he smiled at its mother . . .

On 3 September war was declared, and Grace hardly noticed it except that it brought to her a fear for the safety of her child. But for that and the fact that Andrew had now to take a full-time job at Tarrant's which after all was a blessing in disguise for it deferred his call-up she might have ignored it altogether. Her life was wrapped around the child to the exclusion of apparently everything else. That the vicar's wife took no active part in the village's stand against this war passed unnoticed. The vicar's wife wasn't strong and having a baby had taken it out of her more than somewhat.

As far as the duties of a parson's wife pertaining to the parish were concerned Kate Shawcross filled that bill. And this, too, passed without comment. Kate Shawcross was a wonderful organiser. Everybody knew that and in this time of crisis was glad of it. Kate went to the extent of seeing to the arrangements in the cellar below Willow Lea. Andrew MacIntyre had constructed some wooden bunks in the cellar, also a cupboard for holding stores. Miss Shawcross saw to a carpet being laid, bedding being brought down, first-aid equipment put ready to hand, candles and matches in case of emergency . . . two boxes of matches, for the vicar was naughty, he was always walking off with matches . . . she even soaked dozens and dozens of newspapers into a horrible pulp with which to seal the cracks in the boards that had been nailed over the ground level window of the cellar . . . 'In case of gas, you know.'

When the first air-raid warning sounded over the village Grace did not have to be told to remember her drill. She did not know whether it was a practice or a real warning, but she grabbed up the child and flew with him down into the cellar. She did this almost nightly for the first fortnight of the war and nothing happened. From this time onwards she had ceased to fly, but on the sound of the air-raid warning she would gather up her belongings and the child in an unhurried fashion and make her way downstairs.

Donald was the centre hub of the village administration, and during these first few days of fevered tension he acted more like a general than a parson. Each evening found him at the ARP post in the school-room, where he was second in command to Colonel Farley. If the colonel was on duty from six to ten, Donald took over from ten to four. From time to time the air-raid warnings sounded and excitement ran high.

But in the weeks that followed, things, not only in the village but apparently in the whole country, settled down like a monotonous routine, and for everyone, with the exception of Kate Shawcross, life in the school-room became sightly boring.

It was the first Christmas of the war and Aunt Aggie was coming to stay. Aggie rarely came to the house, and Grace was more than a little surprised that she had accepted the invitation to stay over Christmas. Besides the reason that she wanted to see Aggie and talk to her there was another reason that made her visit doubly welcome. She knew her Aunt Aggie would look after the child and enable her to see Andrew for a while. There was no-one in the village she could call upon to stay in the house while she went out – where could she say she was going in a blacked-out village? It was weeks now – no, months – since she and Andrew had even touched hands. They had glimpses of each other, they spoke at times, but the world of the village was looking on.

If it hadn't been for the child, life would have been unbearable.

That night when she had first heard that Andrew was coming as part-time gardener and had fainted, Dr Cooper had kept her in bed for two days, and during that time she had been tormented by a number of different feelings, not least among them that the situation would take on something of indecency if Andrew came here to work. And the question kept coming to her: why had he done it? Why had he placed them both in such a position? She didn't get the answer to this until she had stood in the greenhouse looking at him. It was quite in order for the vicar's wife to go down and speak to the gardener, quite in order, and no-one could hear what she said to him in the greenhouse. Besides which, the all-round view would have shown anyone's approach. The only thing she had to be careful of was her expression, she had to veil her desire. She had learned to do this when speaking to Andrew, but on that day she had looked at him with her heart in her eyes as she asked, 'Why have you done this, Andrew – it will be unbearable?'

'Not more than not being able to see you for days on end . . . perhaps weeks on end later on.'

'But, Andrew, we'll give ourselves away.'

'I won't.' He kept looking down on the box of soil, his hands moving slowly over it. 'I told you that I could love you without seeing you or touching you, and that's true, but when he asked me to take this on it seemed like a gift. It was too good to pass over.'

'But I'm afraid . . .'

'Don't be afraid.' He lifted the box up and as he placed it on top of a number of similar ones he said, 'I'll stay on as long as you do. When you're ready to leave just tell me.'

Andrew knew her feelings with regard to the child bearing a name. He, like her, knew that Donald would never divorce her. He would have given a great deal to see her away from this house; not that he was jealous of Donald, there was nothing to be jealous of – to him Donald was like a huge drum with a pea rattling inside, he despised him. It was Grace herself he was thinking of, and in this particular his conscience would trouble him, for was he not the real reason why she stayed put.

They worked out a simple means of signalling when they were to meet in the quarry. If the loop wire was removed from the staves that leant against the oak near the gate, then he would be waiting for her. Very often in the early days of her prgenancy the loop would be off but she couldn't get away. Donald would be in or someone would have called, so therefore the vicar's wife would not take her stroll out through the bottom gate and quietly along the field and up through the wood. One moonlight night as she entered the wood on her way to the quarry she bumped into someone in the shadow of a tree, and she only stopped herself from collapsing in fright on the sound of the well-known voice. It was Ben Fairfoot; he had held her arm as he repeated, 'Why, ma'am, I'm sorry, I'm sorry. I wouldn't have scared you for the world. I'm sorry, ma'am, I'm sorry.'

She was so shaken by the encounter that she could not go on. 'I was just taking a stroll, Ben.'

Poor Ben. On no account had she been able to persuade him to take the cottage at Culbert's Cut. There could only ever be one garden for him, and he had been walking round it . . . on the outside. He had not asked her where she was going, anyone else might have done so.

Then there was the night that she had slipped out feeling safe because Donald was taking a meeting in the village hall, only on her return to find David Cooper in the house.

'You've given me a scare,' he said. 'Where have you been, out in the dark?' And then he had looked at her shoes, at the mud around the rims. He had been puzzled, for it hadn't rained for days.

When you played a game like this you had to be careful; there were so many things you had to be careful about. Parson's wife or no parson's wife, people had the way of putting two and two together. Yet there still remained the fact that the name 'parson's wife' was like a banner held up to advertise morality. She wouldn't have believed it had she not experienced it. She could stop and talk to different men in the village and no wrong thought of it, but had any other woman been seen indulging in this way, then the heads would have got together and the tongues would have wagged. But as the parson's wife she was merely helping her husband to bring men to God. It was laughable really, but she never allowed herself to laugh over it.

Now that Andrew, with every minute of his

time taken up at Tarrant's, no longer came to do the garden and odd jobs, the quarry was their only means of contact, and their meetings were arranged by a few casual and enigmatic words while running into each other in the village or thereabouts. One such meeting had been arranged for the night after Boxing Night and Grace prayed it wouldn't snow, for apart from it being almost impossible to do that climb in the snow there would be the matter of footprints.

But on the night after Boxing Night Donald unexpectedly stayed at home. He had a slight cold and he made this the excuse for evading the duty attending the men's meeting in the schoolhouse, and as it wasn't his night to be on duty in the ARP section his conscience apparently wasn't troubled. Grace, in a turmoil of disappointment and agitation, knew that the cold was but an excuse to remain in the house and give him further opportunity of showing off his parenthood to Aunt Aggie.

All through Aggie's visit he had carried, played with, and talked incessantly to the child. He had even insisted on bathing him, which ceremony Aggie did not give herself the pleasure of watching. It was as if he was yelling at her, 'Well, isn't this proof? No matter what she told you, you can't get over this.' He played the father in such an outsize way that Aggie's teeth became continually on edge. His voice at this moment was floating down the staircase, and when Grace, on her way to the kitchen to get the baby's bottle, passed her in the hall, Aggie's eyes turned upwards in their sockets as she exclaimed, 'I don't know how you stand it. Does this go on all the time?'

Grace smiled. 'Not so much, not at such a high pitch. It's for your benefit.'

'Yes, I thought so.'

There came a ring at the kitchen-door bell and Grace turned from the stove, the child's bottle in her hand, to answer it, and when she saw Andrew's tall figure framed in the dark, her hand with the bottle went involuntarily to her mouth. She glanced quickly round before saying, 'Come in.'

'I have a message for . . . for him.'

She closed her eyes for a moment, then said, 'Oh. Oh, I see.' She walked to the other side of the table, it was safer at this distance. He was still looking at her as he said, 'Mrs Rolland, the shepherd's wife, she's dying. I was passing along the road and he was waiting for me. He asked me if I would take a message to the parson and the doctor. His wife had taken a turn for the worse.'

'Poor thing. She's been ill for some time, hasn't she? And away up there all alone. Yes, yes, I'll tell him.' She talked of the sick woman but she wasn't thinking of her, and as she was going from the table she looked round at him and murmured under her breath, 'Wait.'

Andrew waited. He stood stiff and straight with his cap in his hands, and when in a few minutes Donald swung into the kitchen he answered the vicar's, 'Oh hello, Andrew' with a plain 'Good evening'. He never addressed him as 'sir'.

'You have brought a mesage from Mr Rolland. Do you think she is dying?'

'He seems to think so.'

'Dear, dear. Well, I must go . . . yes, I must go right away.' He turned round as if looking for his things, and as Grace entered the kitchen Andrew said, 'I took the same message to Dr Cooper. I told him I was coming on here. He said he would wait for you.'

'Good. Good. I don't fancy a bicycle ride over the fells tonight. Good . . . good. Get on the phone, Grace, and tell him I'll be there in a few minutes. And by the way' – he turned to Andrew – 'you can't have had any tea.'

'No, but that's all right.'

'Oh, you must have a cup of tea or something after coming all this distance out of your way. Now it's no problem, just wait a minute.'

On this Donald disappeared beyond the green baize door, and Andrew did as he had been bidden for the second time – he waited.

In a few minutes Donald reappeared, he was tucking a scarf into his overcoat. 'She won't be a minute, just giving the nipper his bottle . . . or handing the job over to her aunt.' He jerked his head and laughed. He was treating the gardener to his line of jocular equality which he found had a two-fold use: it put ordinary folk at their ease, but at the same time kept the picture of the upper stratum from which he addressed them in the forefront of their minds. This he accomplished with his voice: his words were ordinary, yet the tone in which he delivered them was anything but.

Andrew said nothing, not even when Donald gave him a hearty 'Goodbye, then' before going into the hall again. He merely inclined his head. But when he heard Donald's voice calling upstairs from the hall he shut his eyes for a moment and repeated to himself, 'Goodbye, my dear.'

There came the sound of the front door banging, and a few minutes later the kitchen door opened. But it was Aggie who entered.

'Well. Hello there,' she said.

'Hello.'

Oddly enough Aggie had not seen Andrew since the morning in her office fifteen months ago, and she was surprised at the difference in him. Although he seemed as thin as ever he looked bigger, taller and definitely much older. From the change in him it could have been five or six years since that morning.

'Go on up and see the child.'

'But . . .' he hesitated, his eyes widening.

'She wants you to . . . she's waiting. Do you know your way?'

'No.'

'Up the stairs, second door on the right.'

As he went to pass her he stopped and smiled at her, and as she saw what the smile did in almost transfiguring his face she could understand in some part how this dour Scot had come to captivate her niece.

Grace had told her only this morning that he had never yet held the baby in his arms, and Aggie had already made up her mind to rectify this unnatural position by arranging for him to come to her house when Grace and the child would be there. But now there would be no need for her to be a partner in this form of deception. Yet for all that she said, 'If you should be in Newcastle any time you can look me up if you like, I'm in most nights after five. The phone number is Temple 3567 . . . it's easy to remember, 3567.'

He looked at her, his face grave now as he savoured all that her brusque, off-hand invitation implied.

'Thank you.'

He did not move away and she pushed him now with her voice, saying, 'Go on then, get yourself up, and make it snappy.'

Andrew had never been beyond the kitchen nor yet had he seen much of the interior of the house from the outside . . . he had always kept his eyes trained away from the windows when working in the garden . . . and so now the luxurious comfort of the hall, and drawing-room glimpsed through the open door, attacked his natural pride and temporarily brought his native arrogance low. She was used to all this yet she had picked him, and she had loved him . . . did love him. After a moment's pausing, he bounded up the stairs. What were chairs and carpets, anyway? They hadn't brought her happiness, only he had been able to do that. Only he could go on doing that.

The second door on the right was open and Grace was standing in the middle of the room with the child in her arms. Slowly he walked forward, and when he stood in front of her she held out the baby to him. He looked down on it lying in its snowy-white drapery and hesitating, he motioned to his working overcoat.

'Take him.'

He took him . . . This was his son . . . his son.

As he held him and looked for some sign of himself in the laughing eyes and the gurgling, dribbling mouth, his thighs began to tremble, then his knees and finally his arms, and Grace, watching him, laughed gently before saying softly, 'He's beautiful, isn't he?'

'He's like his mother . . . Take him . . . I – I'm—'

Grace laughed again, and, taking the child from his arms, placed him in his cot.

They stood side by side now looking down on the baby, until Grace, placing a woolly duck in his hands and touching his cheek, gently whispered, 'Good night, darling, good night.'

Andrew said nothing, the sight of the child in the cot dragged at his eyes, and when Grace, having lowered the light, said, 'Andrew,' he seemed to have difficulty in turning round to her.

They were facing each other in the dim light of the room. The door was closed. It was an opportunity to fall into each other's arms, but neither of them made a move in this direction. Although the desire to throw herself on him was almost overpowering, Grace could not bring herself to love Andrew within the walls of this house, and strangely she sensed the same reluctance in him. She smiled tenderly at him, her heart in her eyes, and as she had touched the child's cheek so now her hand went out and touched his. In a moment it was caught and pressed across his mouth. She gave a sharp gasp of breath as if the kiss had been on her lips and had checked her breathing. Unable to rely on the strength of her good intentions for a moment longer, she turned about, pulling her hand from him, and made for the door. Slowly he followed her.

Aunt Aggie was not to be seen when they got downstairs and, in the kitchen once more, Grace said, 'I'll make you some tea.'

'No, no, don't bother; my mother will be waiting with it ready.'

'How is she?'

'Oh, she's all right – she's altering my kilt.' He gave a wry smile now and drew his hand down the side of his face. 'Did you know I'm playing the pipes on New Year's Eve?'

'No. Oh, Andrew, where?'

'Here, at the do in the school.'

'No . . . ! When was all this arranged?'

'Oh, the do's been talked about for weeks, but I only said I'd play the other day. I . . . I thought perhaps it being for the Civil Defence and New Year's Eve . . . you . . . you might be there.'

'I would love to go; oh, Andrew, I would . . . and see you in your kilt.' She laughed. 'Will you play-in the New Year?'

'That seems to be the idea.'

'I must come. Aunt Aggie will stay a little longer if I ask her. And, Andrew—' She paused and her voice sank to the merest whisper. 'I'll do my best to get up tomorrow night, I can't tonight.'

His hand came out and gripped hers. 'I'll be there.' His eyes dropped from her gaze for a moment and he turned her hand over in his and looked at it, and then, pressing it close between his two palms, he said, 'Just in case you don't manage it and I don't get a chance to speak to you on New Year's Eve I'd better tell you . . . I've got to register.'

'Andrew!' She sounded aghast. 'But I thought, being a full-time farm-worker, you were deferred.'

'Yes, so did I. But there it is. They're putting women on so I suppose that's the answer.'

'Oh, Andrew . . . Andrew.' She could think of nothing else to say, for she was enveloped in anxiety. Anxiety for his safety, anxiety at the prospect of her loneliness when he would no longer be up on the fells, a mile away, but nevertheless near.

'Does your mother know?'

'No, I haven't told her yet.'

'Do you want to go?'

'Want to go . . . to the war?' He screwed up his face. 'No, I certainly don't. Want to stick bayonets into fellas and blow their brains out? Want to go to the war?' His voice was vehement now and he shook his head. 'The pipes rouse no clan spirit in me. I'm no fighting Scot, although I'm proud of coming from across the border. But war . . .' Again he shook his head.

'Oh, Andrew.'

She realised from his outburst that he had strong opinions about this war. So far they had never been able to discuss anything other than themselves because their moments together were short and precious but she could see now that he must have done some thinking about the war because he, like all the other young men, would be called upon to fight it, not like Donald and Colonel Farley playing at soldiers in the village. Oh – she shook her head at herself – she supposed she wasn't fair to them, because if there was such a thing as an invasion they would certainly fight. But invasion was a long, long-off chance, and in the meantime she knew that they and most of the older men enjoyed this game of war. It was like an outsize toy with which they could safely play without being held up to ridicule.

'I must talk to you somehow.' His voice was earnest.

'When will it be? I mean when do you register?'

'The third of January, but I may not be called up for weeks.'

Again she said, 'Oh, Andrew,' and the next moment she was in his arms and they were kissing – a short, hard, intense, hungry kiss. It seemed to be over before it had actually begun and he had gone through the door pulling it after him quickly in case the light should show, and she leant against the back of it, her arm crooked and her face hidden in it. What if he were killed and she were left alone? Without Andrew she would be alone. Even the child, somehow, wouldn't count without Andrew.

Aggie stayed and Grace went to the New Year's Eve party. The partitions between the three school-rooms had been pushed back and every seat that lined the walls was occupied, even while the centre of the floor was taken up by those indulging in the Lancers, the barn dance or north-country reels. At one point in the evening when the laughter and dancing were at their height, Grace's conscience pricked her with the thought that Aggie would have enjoyed all this and it had really been a bit thick asking her to stay and look after the child, especially on New Year's Eve, but Aggie had assured her that all she wanted this particular night was bed and a book and perhaps a glass of hot whisky and sugar.

Although Grace could see Donald laughing and chaffing with one and another she had the feeling that he wasn't enjoying himself; the affair was a little too rowdy for him. What was more, no church function, dance or social, had gathered anything like this number into the school-rooms. It was the excitement of war, uniforms, and the uncertainty of seeing another Christmas perhaps that had brought the village out. She had not yet seen Andrew.

At five minute to twelve the whole company joined hands and the building swelled to the thunder of 'Auld Lang Syne'. Then on the stroke of twelve Mr Blenkinsop raised his fiddle high in one hand and his bow in the other and cried 'Quiet! Quiet, I say . . . ! Listen! Here he comes!' And there, as if from far away across the fells, came the sound of the pipes. Andrew was coming down the main street. Grace's heart began to leap with a strange excitement. Nearer and nearer came the drone. The faces about her were gleaming expectantly, waiting for the moment to burst into cheering when the piper came round the black-out curtain. They were all looking towards the doorway at the end of the hall. Her heart was pounding. It was a moment filled with sentimentalism, patriotism, custom and tradition, even if of another country; but for her was added the knowledge that the piper was hers, and that he was playing for her alone, bringing in the New Year for her alone. There came a great burst of cheering as a hand jerked the curtain aside and Andrew MacIntyre, his kilt swaying, the pipes held high, marched into the room.

Her heart swelled with possessive pride; he looked so gallant, taller than ever in the kilt, handsome, fierce, even war-like. But he wasn't war-like, he didn't want to go to the war, he hated war.

The piper did a round of the room, then came to a stop in the centre of the floor and dead opposite to her. But this was not noticeable, for she was one of dozens standing in front of him.

As he finished on a long wail he was blotted from her sight. Everybody was milling together, 'Happy New Year! Happy New Year! Many of them, damnation to Hitler! Oh, we'll Hang out the Washing on the Siegfried Line.'

It was some ten minutes before she saw Andrew again. He had made his way casually towards her. She saw that he was laughing and his eyes were bright, and she wondered if he had had a drink or two. Funny, but she didn't know whether he took anything.

'Have you really got a clan, Andrew?' This was from young Barker, the publican's son.

'A clan! I should say so.' Andrew threw out his chest. 'The Clan MacIntyre.'

Those around laughed. Andrew MacIntyre was a fine player and he was in fine form tonight. Nobody could remember seeing him like this before.

'Have you a war-cry?' the boy now asked.

'We have that . . . Cruachan! Cruachan!'

'What does it mean?'

'Aw, it's taken from the name of a mountain.'

'An' do you ever shout it?'

'Oh, aye, whenever I see a Campbell.'

'A Campbell. Why for?'

'Och! Because they pinched our land from us, the thieving rogues.' Andrew was now talking the thick Scots accent and everyone about was laughing. 'We made the mistake of giving them money instead of a snowball and a white calf.'

'Away! He's pulling your leg, boy.' They pushed at young Barker.

'I'm not, I'm not. It's the truth I'm telling you. Once a year the MacIntyres paid for their land with a white calf and a snowball and it's not so very long ago either. But once they started paying in money the rent went up.'

'Oh, he can tell a tale. By, he can! And what a player, eh? Never would have believed it.'

Pride rose in Grace. He was not just a farm-worker, he was Andrew MacIntyre with a clan. He had behind him something that the ordinary man didn't have – tradition, clannish tradition. But what was a clan? All Scots had clans, in fact they were one big clan. She laughed at herself now. With or without the prestige of a clan she loved Andrew MacIntyre . . .

At half past twelve, as the vicar's wife was handing out refreshments, Andrew MacIntyre approached her and asked her for the pleasure of the Lancers. There was nothing wrong in this – parson or peasant, publican and lawyer were equal on this New Year's morning. So Grace danced with Andrew for the first time. They were both light on their feet, their steps fitted, and as they got into the dance they became dangerously near forgetting where they were, for after changing partners and coming together again their glances would become entwined. Their faces full of youth and love, they could see no-one else. Yet no-one seemed to notice them – this was New Year's Day – perhaps with one exception, Dr Cooper. He had slipped in for a few minutes to see the fun and his attention had been caught by Grace Rouse and young Andrew MacIntyre, arrayed in his kilt, dancing together. They were both young and somehow they matched.

The danger must have made itself apparent to Andrew, for, the dance ended, he left the hall, after saying to a number of people including Grace, 'I'll have to be making my way over the fells; my mother'll be waiting up for her first foot.'

Almost at the same time as Andrew went out Bertrand Farley came in. He was accompanied by two other officers, and if there had been a doubt in Grace's mind as to whether Andrew had had a drink, there was no such doubt on looking at Bertrand Farley, for he was very merry.

That the entry of the three officers put a slight dampener on the company and took away some of the spontaneous informality, bringing in its place a stiffnes to the men and a false decorum to the women, was not all Grace's imagination. But this could not last, this was New Year's Day, and soon two of the three officers were dancing.

When Bertrand Farley asked Grace to dance she wanted very much to refuse. Andrew had gone, the night was over for her, she wanted to get back home, but Donald wasn't in sight and she could hardly make a move without him. Several pairs of eyes were on them wondering how the vicar's wife would deal with young Farley and him bottled, and she saw that the least embarrassing thing would be to accept his invitation. Should she refuse, he would likely start on a bout of maudlin persuasion.

The dance was a waltz and they had been circling erratically for only a short time before he gave an exaggerated sigh, and, bringing his face down to hers, he whispered, 'Know somethin'? I promised myself this the first time I saw you. "She'll be a spiffin' dancer," I said. "I'll dance with her one day," that's what I said. Know somethin'? . . . I think you're the best looker in Northumberland . . . honest.'

He stopped in his dancing, pulling Grace to a halt. She had made no comment, and so he said, 'You don't believe me?' His bulbous eyes looked as if they were going to drop out of their sockets.

'Do you want to go on with the dance?'

The floor was so packed that the incident passed unnoticed.

'Look . . .' His arm drew her more tightly to him. 'I know girls . . . I know women . . . all types, all classes. Oh yes, little Bertrand's been around.'

He was coming to a stop when she said, 'We'd better sit down.'

'No, no.' He waltzed her more swiftly now. 'I'm not drunk, don't think I'm drunk. I've had a few. It's New Year's Eve . . . no . . . New Year's Day. We're at war, d'you know that? And little Bertrand here might go and be killed. Any moment little Bertrand might go and be killed and then you'll be sorry you weren't nice to him.'

'Will you stop being silly, or do I have to sit down?'

For answer he waltzed her even more quickly. But when he stumbled and nearly brought them both to the floor she forced him to stop and said coldly, 'I think we'd better sit down.'

'All right, all right, anything you say. You order, I obey. And how! Let's sit on the balcony, eh? In the moonlight on the balcony. That's what the villain does. When the villain's going after the parson's wife he takes her on the moonlight in the balcony.'

At this verbal mix-up Grace laughed. She had to be annoyed or she had to laugh . . . she decided to laugh.

'What you want is a pot of strong coffee.'

'Anything you say. Lead on. Coffee it is. Coffee it must be. There's nothing stronger in this joint, I suppose. Old Barker's sold out. We called in there; he was as dry as a haddock. Not even any droppings. That's what war does. Expects you to be a brave little boy and no fire water . . . Daft.' He talked as he rocked gently behind Grace along the passage towards the school kitchen.

There was only Mrs Twait and Kate Shawcross in the kitchen, and Grace, looking at Mrs Twait, asked, 'Is there any coffee left, Mrs Twait?'

'Yes, plenty.' Mrs Twait lifted up the jug from the stove.

'Happy New Year, Miss Shawcross,' Bertrand Farley was bowing low to the postmistress; and with a look that held no touch of Christian spirit or yet the spirit of a new-born year, Kate passed him without a word and left the kitchen.

'There, she thinks I'm drunk. I'm – I'm not drunk, am I?' He now appealed to Mrs Twait. And Mrs Twait's small compact body began to wobble with her laughter and she said, 'Well, I wouldn't say you were drunk, Mr Farley, but at the same time I wouldn't say you were a kick in the backside off it.' On this and a high laugh she also left the kitchen.

'Here, drink this.' Grace handed him a cup of black coffee. She had never liked Bertrand Farley, but at this moment, strangely, she saw nothing to dislike in him. He was silly, empty-headed, he was drunk and, who knew, as he said, he might be dead this time next year.

'Thanks. Thank you, my fair lady, my fair goddess of the pukka parsonage.' He took a drink of the coffee and then made a horrible grimace. 'Ooh . . . ! Oooh, my God! What stuff! Nevertheless thanks . . . Grace . . . Nice name, Grace. I made up a poem about you once. Ah . . . that surprises you, doesn't it, that I can write poetry? Oh, I'm a deep one. You must get to know me. What about it, Grace – what about getting to know me?'

'Don't be silly.'

'I'm not being silly, honest to God. Serious, thought about it a lot. What you say, eh? What about it? I'll write another poem about you . . .

about Grace . . . Darling. Ha ha! That's funny, Grace Darling!'

She had turned from him to put the jug on the stove when his arm came round her shoulders. 'Grace Darling.'

Now she ceased to be amused and was on the point of shrugging herself away when a voice spoke from the doorway. It said 'Grace,' and they both turned to see Donald standing there.

'Are you ready for home?'

'Yes. Oh yes.' She moved hastily forward.

'I . . . I was just telling your . . . your wife . . .' Bertrand Farley walked unsteadily towards Donald. Then, shaking his head, he said, 'What was I telling her? Oh yes.' He now thrust his finger towards Donald's chest saying, 'You've got a very beautiful woman, Mr Vicar, do you know that? You're a lucky bloke, do you know that, eh? And there's something else I'd like to tell you. You know I've always wanted to tell you this. That girl, that beau . . . beautiful girl should have stuck to the pian . . . piano; an' another thing . . .'

'I'm afraid I haven't got time to listen.' Donald's voice was deadly cold. He stared with almost open hatred at the blinking eyelids and blurred pupils of young Farley before turning from him and walking hastily down the passage after Grace . . .

Ten minutes later they were going up the hill towards home and for the third time since leaving the hall Donald said, 'You must really think me a fool, I heard what he said. He called you Grace, darling, and a man doesn't do that on the spur of the moment, drunk or not. You can't tell me that.'

Grace had already given him the true version of this episode . . . she had stated her defence . . . and now she remained quiet until they reached the drive to the house when Donald, still talking, said, 'You forget your position. You're the vicar's wife; you frequently forget that, and . . .'

'And Grace Darling was the lighthouse-keeper's daughter,' Grace cried flippantly. 'I tell you, Donald, he was quoting Grace Darling, he wasn't calling me Grace . . . darling.'

They were in the drawing-room now. The fire was blazing merrily, Stephen's first Christmas tree was sparkling in the far corner of the room, the holly was lying in strips at the foot of the coloured plates that lined the rack high up round the walls. The setting looked like a picture you would see on a Christmas card, charming, warm and inviting, yet at this moment she hated it and the whole house . . . and its master. Its master most of all, for there he stood, determined to go on with his cross-examination until she admitted the truth. What truth? She had told him the truth. She turned her back on him and closed her eyes as he said, 'Well, supposing I wasn't hearing aright, were my eyes deceiving me when I saw him with his arm about you?'

She had had enough; she couldn't stand the sound of his voice a moment longer, she would have to combat it with something. Swinging round, she said, 'No, they didn't deceive you, no more than my eyes did when I saw you holding hands with Kate Shawcross in the vestry.' If she had levelled a tommy-gun at his chest he couldn't have shown more surprise, and she cried at him,

'Yes, yes, now I'm the accuser and you are on the defensive. Dear, dear Kate,' – she mimicked his attitude and his voice – 'what would I have done without you? Dear . . . dear Kate.'

'Be quiet! Be quiet!' His face was as red as a turkey cock's. 'It wasn't like that at all, you misunderstood.'

'Oh yes, I – I misunderstood.' Her head went back on a harsh laugh. 'All right then, I misunderstood, but nevertheless you were standing in the vestry, her hands tightly locked in yours, and she was gazing up at you in adoration.'

'Be quiet, will you! I know the time you are referring to. It was nothing like that at all. I was merely thanking her for all the work she had done.'

'Yes, yes, I understand, and consoling her because she was disappointed there wasn't going to be a war and she wouldn't be called upon to run the village besides running the church.'

'Grace, if you dare say another word!' He was standing near her, towering over her.

'Yes, what will you do?' She waited while they glared at each other. And then she added, 'Because a drunken man talks a lot of damn nonsense you accuse me of encouraging him. You say I did it in front of over a hundred people because I danced with him. Yet I see you with my own eyes making love to Kate Shawcross—'

'Don't say that! Don't say that!' His voice thundered at her in denial. 'I wasn't making love to Miss Shawcross.'

'No, you weren't Donald, and I believe you, for you're not capable of making love to anyone.' She

200

thought for a moment he was going to strike her. There was a terrible look on his face. But this could not daunt her and she gabbled on now, 'But Kate Shawcross doesn't know that; she thinks you're in love with her, and if it wasn't for me she would be mistress here, and of the church . . . Oh, don't let us forget, of the church.'

'You're out of your mind, woman; you're out of your mind altogether.'

'I'm not out of my mind and you know it, and I don't care about Kate Shawcross being in love with you. I'm sorry for her, for she's being deceived.' Her tongue was running away with her. She was on the point of adding, 'as you are being deceived', and the next moment she would have flung at him the name of Andrew MacIntyre. But the drawing-room door swung open and Aggie stood there in her dressing-gown. She stood looking from one to the other in silence, then she said, 'I'd be a little quieter if I were you. Besides waking the child, people away on the road will hear you, and there'll be plenty going up and down on this morning, at any rate.'

'This happens to be—' Donald had reached his full stature and his face had taken on a purple tinge on sight of Aggie.

Aggie raised her hand. 'All right, all right, don't tell me. This is your house and you are the master in it and you can shout as much as you like. But it doesn't appear to me to be very seemly for the vicar and his wife to be going on like this on New Year's morning. Unless of course there's an excuse because you are drunk . . . And of course that's not something that can be ruled out altogether, is it?' Aggie's tongue too had run away with her, and with that last crack she knew she had closed the door on future visits to the vicarage . . . Well, that wouldn't worry her, she'd had more than a bellyful of the big sanctimonious 'I am' during these holidays. How that girl put up with it she didn't know. She returned Donald's furious glare with a disdainful glance, then went out. And Grace, after one last look at her husband, followed her.

Not until they were in Aggie's room and Grace had sunk onto the edge of the bed did they speak.

'He's found out?'

'No, no.' Grace moved her head from side to side. 'You'll never believe it but he thinks I'm having an affair with Bertrand Farley.'

'Bertrand Farley? That goggle-eyed fathead?'

'That goggle-eyed fathead.'

'In the name of God!'

'Yes, Aunt Aggie, in the name of God,' and then she added, 'That's the second time I've been on the point of telling him the truth and something's happened.'

'Are you sorry?'

'I don't know. I really don't know, Aunt Aggie.'

7

It was in October 1940 that Deckford had its first
raid. It was on a Tuesday night and it started at
half past seven.

The inhabitants complained that the war had
changed the village out of all recognition. What
they really referred to was the RAF camp that had
risen in the valley only a mile to the west of the
village. It was a fighter base and both night and
day planes flew backwards and forwards over the
fells until, as some hardy souls said, they couldn't
get to sleep if they didn't hear them. And then
there were the RAF men themselves. Every day
the village street was like market day in Morpeth,
and on Saturday afternoon there was as much
chance of getting a bus into town as of chartering
a private plane.

And the evacuees. There were not so many as
yet, but enough to make competition rather keen
to billet airmen who were living out with their
wives, for such couples meant more money and
less trouble than looking after somebody else's
bairns.

But there was no doubt that the countryside
around the village had changed completely. The
moorlands were studded with pyramidal shapes
of concrete, rolls of barbed wire met you at every

turn, and men had started to work on the far side of the quarry again, cutting out great slabs of rock where the workmen had left off years previously.

This last had come as a great blow to Grace, for Andrew, now in the Highland Fusiliers, was stationed in Scotland, which was, after all, not very far away, and after the first two months of square-bashing he had managed to slip home every other week. Following one period, when they hadn't been able to meet for nearly six weeks, Grace began to visit her Aunt Aggie every Saturday. Most times she took the child with her, but when she didn't Mrs Blenkinsop stayed on until her return. If on her visit she did not see Andrew there would be letters awaiting her from him, and in Aggie's comfortable little secluded house she would sit in peace and peruse them, then write at length about what was in her heart. Such was the pattern of Grace's life during the first months of 1940.

Saturday, 1 June, 1940, was a fateful day – it saw the end of Dunkirk. Three men from the village and Bertrand Farley, all in the same regiment, were known to be in the retreat, and nothing had been heard of them until three o'clock in the afternoon when Colonel Farley came rushing down to the ARP centre, his bloated, lined face aglow. He had just had a call from Dover: Bertrand was all right, as also were Ted Bamford and Steve Brignall. The colonel was on his way now to the blacksmith's house to tell Mrs Bamford the good news concerning her son.

The following week Bertrand Farley came home and Grace ran into him in the village street. He had an aura about him – he had been in Dunkirk. But to Grace there seemed to be only one apparent change in him: he had lost some flesh. His manner was still perky, even more so than usual. In spite of the trouble he had caused her at Christmas she could not help laughing at him. It was odd but she found that she even liked him a little now. He was silly, he was harmless, he was what her Aunt Aggie had called him . . . a fathead.

Miss Shawcross, looking into the street through the side of the black-out blind which she kept permanently drawn, saw at that moment the vicar's wife laughing with Captain Farley. The vicar's wife laughed too loud, she thought; she did not seem to realise that she had a position to uphold. Miss Shawcross shook her head. Poor, poor vicar. Even in her most revealing moments Miss Shawcross never allowed herself to allude to the vicar as Donald.

It was that same afternoon that Miss Shawcross asked the vicar if he knew that Captain Farley was home. She had seen the Captain talking to Mrs Rouse in the High Street.

A few days later Colonel Farley gave a small party, a sort of thanksgiving for the safe return of his son, and to it were invited the vicar and his wife. Grace knew that Donald would have liked to refuse the invitation but had been unable to see his way clear to do so, and she was well aware that his weather eye was on her from the moment they entered the Farleys' house. She smiled wryly to herself when, after a game of bridge had been proposed and two tables had been made up, she and Bertrand Farley were left adrift. She had refused Bertrand's invitation to play the piano, saying she had not kept up her practice and would rather not. But when he suggested they should look round the garden she accepted. He was not drunk tonight, he would not be silly.

She felt no compunction that Donald's bridge would be affected, and although she did not think the scene of New Year's morning would be enacted again she was quite prepared to undergo the same silent and censorious displeasure as that to which he had treated her for the most of January, for she preferred this to his jocular, bouncing, daddy-boy act.

Yet, being fair, she knew that the daddy act was not all pretence, far from it. He had a deep affection for the child; in fact she could give it another name – a possessive love. On one occasion she had come across him holding the boy tightly to him with the child's head pressed closely into his shoulder. His own eyes were closed and on his face had been a look that had touched her and drew from her a surge of conscience, and for a moment she had wished that the child could have been his.

There were two results of her walk in the garden that night. The first: the disquieting knowledge that Bertrand Farley was really in love with her, yet he had not made love to her in any way. The odd thing was he hardly spoke to her once they had left the house, but while they sat on the garden seat he had looked at her in telling silence, then had abruptly got up and walked away.

The second: when Donald and she returned

home, after a journey during which no word was exchanged, Donald went straight to his study and there must have exceeded his daily drop . . . for the following day she found that quite some inroad had been made into a fresh bottle of whisky.

Sometimes on a Sunday when she would listen to him expounding from the pulpit she would wonder how, in his own mind, he reconciled the fact that their well-stocked wine-cabinet was supplied by the black market. Not through Mr Barker at the Stag – oh, no, that would never have done – but through Uncle Ralph. Uncle Ralph had friends and could get most commodities that money could buy. Nor did Donald question that he always had butter on his bread and bacon every morning. No. No. Men weren't supposed to notice trifles like that, their minds were taken up with higher things, they just ate what was put in front of them. She often smiled sadly to herself.

The months of summer wore away and so October came. The Battle of Britain had been won, but night bombing was on in earnest. On the Monday night before the attempted raid on the aerodrome, Colonel Farley, Farmer Toole, Dr Cooper, Mr Thompson and . . . Miss Shawcross came to the vicarage to hold a meeting regarding the coming influx of evacuees. They were to be mostly children from the shipping districts of the Tyne. Before the meeting was over Bertrand Farley called. He was in possession of a service car and had come to pick up his father.

The meeting in the study over, Donald, ahead of the others, opened the drawing-room door to see Bertrand Farley standing in front of Grace and to hear the tail-end of his words.

After an exchange of greetings, the committee broke up, and when they had all gone, Donald, without speaking or even looking at Grace, once again went to his study.

The next night the air-raid siren went at seven o'clock. They were sitting in the drawing-room at the time and the sound apparently startled Donald. From the look on his face he might never have heard an air-raid siren before. He had not left her for a moment since teatime and Grace had begun to puzzle over this. Usually, following tea, he went either down to the village or into his study. But this night he had sat with her, even followed her into the kitchen. And now when the sirens went he exclaimed aloud, 'No! Oh no.'

Before the wail had died away Grace had rushed upstairs and collected Stephen, and when she reached the kitchen Donald was waiting for her. He had already donned his top coat and gas-mask. After switching off the lights he opened the door and guided her out and around the side of the house.

The night was black, but he did not switch on the torch until they reached the shelter, then he shone it on the steps for her to enter. Once inside and the door closed, he switched on the light. Then, looking round, he said, 'You have everything. I'll have to go, you'll be all right?'

'Yes, yes, I'll be all right.'

He seemed to be on the point of speaking again; instead he jerked his head with a half-angry helpless gesture and, turning from her, went up the steps.

She had reached out her hand to pick up a book from the top of the cupboard to take to the bunk with her when she heard the click, and her glance darted towards the steps and the cellar door. The sound was like the key being turned. She must have imagined it. Her hand had descended on the book when she swung round and went swiftly up the steps to the door and turned the knob. She knew that her face was registering blank amazement. Why had he locked the door? He had locked her in. She felt a slight tremor of panic rising in her. What had he locked the door for! What if a bomb dropped and she couldn't get out? 'Donald . . . Donald!' She looked upwards, yelling at the ceiling which was the floor of the hall. 'Donald . . . ! Donald . . . !' He couldn't have gone away, he couldn't. 'Donald . . . ! Donald!' After a moment she tried the door again, shaking it viciously. Then slowly she walked down the steps.

'Mm . . . mm . . . Mumma.' The child began to winge.

'Go to sleep, darling; it's all right, it was only Mummy calling.'

'Mumma.'

'There, there, don't cry. It's all right, it was only Mammy. Go to sleep. Ssh!' She sat patting Stephen, her eyes looking upwards. What had made him lock the door? He had been acting funny all evening, at least he hadn't acted to his usual pattern. Why had he sat with her? He had never sat with her after tea, not even when they were first married. There had always been something he wanted to do about that time . . . Then the answer came to her. It came in the picture of his face as she had seen it in the drawing-room doorway last night when he stood looking at Bertrand Farley. Bertrand Farley's leave was up. More for something to say than anything else she had asked him, 'When do you go back?' and he had replied, 'Tomorrow. Report Wednesday o-seven hundred.' His jocular front was well in play again. 'But they don't get anything out of me, I travel in the small hours, so I needn't make a move until eight tomorrow night.' . . . Eight tomorrow night. No. No. It was too funny. But she remembered Donald had gone straight into his study without a glance at her . . . He thought she had intended seeing Bertrand Farley off, so he had locked the door, locked her in here, and anything could happen. Didn't he realise that she couldn't possibly leave the child even if she wanted to? She sat down in the basket chair near the little table and, putting her elbow on it, rested her head on her hand.

The more she thought about the situation the more she was filled with anger . . . and then fear. She hated being locked in. As a child if she went home and found her mother out she would not lock herself in for safety but would open both the back and front doors, so leaving herself a way of escape. She had never been able to sleep in a room when the door was locked. She had never even locked her door against Donald, not that she had any need to.

It was about ten seconds to half past seven

when she heard the sound of the planes and instinctively she knew they weren't ours. Their drone was heavy and different somehow. And then the first bomb dropped. The sound of it crashing into the earth was like great teeth grinding down into cinder toffee, and as she flung herself from the chair onto the bunk over the child the light in the low ceiling flickered twice, then went out.

'Mumma . . . Mumma . . . Mumma.'

'It's . . . it's all right, darling. It's all right, Mammy's here.' Her voice was trembling, her whole body was trembling. Oh God! Oh God! What if one fell on the house and she couldn't get out of the cellar? There came now the distant sound of the pop-pop of anti-aircraft guns, followed by the low, thick murmur of a plane seemingly crossing straight over the house. In the inky darkness she looked upwards, too petrified for a moment to move. Then the earth shuddered again.

'Mumma . . . Mumma. Dadda . . . Dadda. Stevie . . .'

'It's . . . all right . . . darling. Mam . . . Mammy's here.' She could hardly get the words through her chattering teeth.

There came more thick, dull droning, then the great tremor that ran through the earth seemed to run straight through her, and it was followed by another and another . . . They were bombing the village, the little village. Why the village? There was nothing in the village . . . The aerodrome. They thought they were bombing the aerodrome. Jesus . . . Jesus . . . she should pray, but she couldn't pray. She couldn't pray. If only there was somebody with her, somebody to speak to. Oh, Andrew! She didn't want to die without seeing Andrew . . . And the child. Oh, God! Don't let anything happen to my child. If only she had a light . . . The candles – of course, the candles. 'There, darling, lie still, lie still. Mammy's going to light the candles, Mammy's going to make a light. There now.'

She moved backwards off the bunk and groped towards the top of the chest where the books were. There was a candle already in its holder next to the bookrack. With trembling fingers she lifted it up and groped round the broad saucer rim for matches. There were no matches on it. Her fingers, like a blind man's, spread over the books and over the top of the chest. When she had covered its entire surface the panic whirled through her body and corkscrewed through her head, and she only stopped herself from screaming aloud. He couldn't have taken the matches, he couldn't have taken the matches. She was on her hands and knees feeling around the legs of the chest, around the floor. He couldn't have taken the matches. He was always picking up boxes of matches, but he couldn't have taken these matches, he couldn't . . . And he had gone off with the torch. She remembered seeing that in his hand as he went up the steps.

He had locked her in, he had deliberately locked her and the child in, and they were bombing the village. But he couldn't have taken the matches. 'Andrew . . . Andrew, he has taken the matches, I haven't got a light, I can't light the candle . . .' She was scrambling about on her hands and knees near the table now and she gripped at its thin leg with both hands and whimpered. Steady, steady. Don't scream. Go and lie down, put your face into the pillow, it will be like night. Go to sleep. In this instant there came another thud, and as the foundations of the house trembled she flung herself forward in the direction of the bunk, dashing her forehead into the woodwork.

'Mumma!'

As she smothered the child to her there came a different sound still – it was that of a falling plane. As it screeched on its downward plunge it seemed so near that she drew her head right down between her shoulders as if avoiding contact with it. It was only a matter of seconds before she heard the crash but they appeared like long, long minutes to her. Had it fallen in the wood? It had fallen somewhere near. People would soon be milling about and then she would shout and they would break the door open.

There was no sound of any kind now, not the sound of bombs or planes, or human footsteps. Nothing. She turned her eyes from the pillow and looked upwards. The blackness was thick. She had heard of pit blackness which was darker than pitch blackness. This was the pit blackness that the miners had to endure when they were in a fall and the lights went out. Oh God! If only some-body would come. They would all be in the village. Had anyone been killed? Had Donald been killed? She hoped he had. Yes, she did, she did. He had locked her in and taken the matches.

Be quiet, don't say things like that, they're wicked. Well, wasn't he wicked? He was a walking hypocrite. She hoped . . . Be quiet! be quiet!

'Mumma! Mumma!'

'Don't cry, my love.'

The child began to cry loudly now, and above his wailing she imagined she heard the sound of a car. She rose from the bunk and groped her way up the steps to the door. After a moment of waiting and no further sound coming to her, she called, 'Hello! Hello! Is there anyone there?' Only silence answered her, as deep and thick as the blackness about her. Suddenly she was thumping on the door with her fists, yelling, 'Open the door! Open the door! Help! Help!' She thumped until her arms ached and she dropped onto her knees exhausted.

The child was quiet now as if he, too, was listening. But her fear must have threaded its way to him, for as she stumbled down the steps, panic swamping her, he let out an ear-splitting scream.

Feverishly she gathered him up in her arms. Somebody must come soon. Donald would realise how frightened she must be locked in here and come hurrying back. Any minute now he would come hurrying back. He must come soon, he must. This unnatural quietness, this darkness would drive her . . . She did not finish but hugged the child closer to her and began to rock him.

A short while later, when he had dropped off to sleep again and still there was no sound, she stood up peering into the blackness. Then groping towards the chair she carried it carefully to the side of the steps where the window was, and, standing on it, she began to pick and claw at the packing between the boards. But Miss Shawcross had done her work well. She might have mixed the paper with cement for all the impression Grace could make on it. She knew there was no possibility of getting out this way. All she was aiming at now was a little slit of lighter night to penetrate this inferno of blackness.

When she found that her efforts were fruitless she got slowly down from the chair and carried it back in the direction of the table. And the quietness that was about her settled in her. It was an awe-filled quietness in which she watched her mind throw off restraint and drag up from its deep chambers repressed recriminations of the last three and a half years. When it began, as it were, handing them to her, she took them and delivered them in low, staccato sentences. 'I hate him! I loathe him! He's cruel. Ben said he was a cruel bugger, and he is. A Christian, a man of God. Huh! A man of God. Bloody hypocrite! Bloody . . . bloody . . . bloody.' Her swearing was brought to a sharp stop by the familiar, but now muffled boom of the clock in the hall above striking eight. She looked up – only eight o'clock. She felt she had been in this darkness for hours. But why wasn't there any sound? What had happened in the village? Had any of the houses been hit? Oh, if only someone would come soon. She hoped it wasn't him. She prayed it wouldn't be him. For she might do something. She might even kill him. 'Young wife stabs minister. Mind turned through darkness . . . no matches . . . no matches.'

She was still sitting at the table when the clock chimed the half-hour and at the same time the all-clear went. The next sound that came to her was the strokes of nine o'clock. She still hadn't moved.

The swearing was now confined to her mind, like the sound of a gramophone being played in a distant room, unintelligible but still there. She had been in this thick blackness for one hour and a half. Everybody in the village must be dead. Donald must be dead. Some time, perhaps tomorrow morning, somebody would come. She turned her head away on the thought of not being found until tomorrow morning. She knew that after tonight she would never be the same again, never feel nice inside again for in spite of her double life she felt herself to be . . . a nice person still. But when you swore in your mind, you couldn't be nice, and if she was left all night and the swearing got worse, if she was left here until tomorrow morning until the Air Force got round . . . she shuddered from head to foot . . .

When she heard the sound of footsteps to the left of her she turned her eyes slowly upwards towards the door, and when the key turned in the lock she did not rise and rush towards the steps but closed her eyes against the painful brightness of the torch.

She could say nothing, not even when she heard his voice, slower than usual, different somehow, asking, 'Why are you in the dark?'

The torch was lying on the table now, between them, and she was on her feet, her hands gripping the edge of the table, and she leaned forward, crouched over it like some wild animal ready to spring. And the words that came from her lips were thick and guttural.

'You . . . you cruel b . . . beast . . . swine. You . . . you locked me in . . . you locked me in!'

'Grace!' His voice was low yet commanding. 'Grace, be quiet. Don't talk to me like that. Why didn't you light the candles?'

'You . . . you took the matches.'

'Oh my God!' She saw him put his hand to his head.

'You bloody—!'

'Grace! Listen to me, Grace!' He had her by the shoulders. 'Be quiet! Don't dare say such words, do you hear, don't dare! Listen to me. Something dreadful has happened this night.'

'Yes . . . yes . . . ' she flung his hands off her and stumbled backwards. 'I know that. You tried to send me mad, didn't you?'

'Is she all right?' The voice came from the top of the steps and Grace looked up to see the dim outline of Kate Shawcross. There seemed something different about her voice too, there was something different about all their voices.

Kate Shawcross . . . Kate Shawcross. He wouldn't lock her in, oh no. 'I was locked in,' she cried.

'Grace!'

With a wild movement she bent down and gathered the child to her, and like someone drunk she went up the steps and into the glorious star-filled night that in comparison with the blackness she had lived in for several eternities was like the brightness of the sun.

As she passed her, Kate Shawcross asked in that different voice, 'But why are you in the dark?' and Donald, his voice laden with contrition, answered, 'It's me, I must have picked up the matches.'

'Oh no, vicar, no!'

Kate Shawcross now ran on ahead into the kitchen, and within a few seconds three candles were glowing. In their light Grace turned her furious wild gaze on them both, her mouth open to speak, and then her lips closed. They were both filthy, their clothes were torn, and underneath the dirt that hid their faces they had the same kind of pallor. As she looked at Miss Shawcross the postmistress suddenly put her hand out to a chair and, turning it round, sat down, and Donald, going swiftly to her side, said, 'I'll get you something.'

'No, no, it's all right.' Miss Shawcross looked up at Grace. 'It was dreadful! I'll never be able to forget.'

Grace turned her eyes slowly towards Donald and he said quietly, 'They bombed the village. They were trying for the airfield . . . Mrs Blenkinsop . . .'

'Mrs B . . . ?' Grace's lips just formed the word. 'Dead?'

Donald nodded.

Grace hitched the child further to her and sat down.

'And Mrs Cooper. Poor Mrs Cooper.'

Grace turned her wide staring eyes on Miss

Shawcross now. The postmistress's head was bent and moving from side to side and the tears were raining down her face.

Stupidly Grace said, 'Renee dead?' Then she looked up at Donald again. 'The child?'

'She's all right.'

'David?'

'His leg is hurt, they've taken him to hospital. Renee must have just left the child in the shelter and gone indoors for a moment.'

'And old Ben Fairfoot.' Miss Shawcross was crying unrestrainedly by now.

'Ben? Ben? Dead?'

Miss Shawcross nodded her head deeply. 'And the three Cummings children . . . my Sunday-school children, and Mrs Watson . . .'

Grace watched her head sinking lower now, the tears dropping onto the table from her chin, and all she could say to herself was, 'Ben? Oh! Ben.' It was odd but it was Ben she was most sorry for. Yet he was old and would have died soon, and Renee was young. Renee had fought TB and conquered it, now she was dead. And Mrs Blenkinsop, she would never come into this kitchen again. Never again would she say, 'Mornin', ma'am,' never again would she give her the gen on the village, the undercover news. Poor Mrs B . . . But Ben . . . Ben. Before these dreadful happenings her own ordeal sank away into a pocket and rested temporarily.

'Don't cry, please don't cry.' Donald was standing at the side of Miss Shawcross. He did not touch her, not even to put his hand on her shoulder. Grace would not have minded if before her eyes he had taken her in his arms and comforted her, kissed her.

'You must have something to steady you, we must all have something.' He turned round and left the room, his step heavy and slow, and when he returned he brought three glasses and a bottle half full of whisky.

'Drink this.' He handed Miss Shawcross a glass three parts full, and when without glancing at it she shook her head, he said, 'Drink up.'

'I . . . I don't usually, Vic . . . ar.'

'There has been nothing usual about tonight; you must drink it.'

Grace watched Miss Shawcross coughing and spluttering as the whisky hit her throat. She watched Donald finish his full glass of raw spirit at one gulp and when almost immediately he replenished it she made no comment to herself, for, as he had said, this was an unusual night . . . Picking up her glass and easing the child on to one arm, she rose from the table, and she said no word to either of them as she left the kitchen.

Fifteen minutes later she was sitting in bed, a candle burning to the side of her. She was sitting propped up, staring ahead. Renee Cooper, Mrs Blenkinsop and Ben. There were others, but these were the three she herself had known, and now they were no more. Had Ben met up with Miss Tupping? She hoped so – oh, she hoped so. Perhaps Miss Tupping had already started a garden . . . Stupid thought, all stupid thoughts, meeting and coming together. All balderdash. When you were dead, you were dead, blown into a thousand pieces . . . No, no, she mustn't think like that. It was better, more comforting, to think that at this moment Miss Tupping was leading Ben along the grassy path of a beautiful garden, a pattern of the garden that she had left behind. And there would be a lonicera hedge, a high lonicera hedge. She could see Ben and Miss Tupping standing before it and Ben would say, 'Well, here's one he won't cut down.' She was thinking stupidly, spitefully. She mustn't think like that; it had been a dreadful night for him, for all of them.

She heard Donald returning from taking Miss Shawcross down to the village. She waited to hear him come upstairs and go into his room, but some little time elapsed before the sound of his footsteps came on the stairs. A few minutes after his door had closed on him it opened again, and then hers opened. He opened it as he knocked.

Slowly he crossed to the side of the bed, and when he was standing above her he muttered thickly, 'I'm sorry, Grace, very, very sorry. I did wrong. For – for – forgive me.'

She looked up at him. Like Miss Shawcross he was crying. Whether he would have cried without the aid of the whisky she did not know but she realised with a start that he was tipsy, quite tipsy, and he looked both pathetic and ludicrous. She said flatly, 'It's all right, it doesn't matter.'

'But – b-b-but Grace, I'm sorry.'

She moved restlessly against the pillow. 'It's all right, I've told you. Anyway, in comparison with what happened tonight, it's nothing.' Yet even as she spoke she knew that the terror she had experienced in the blackness would remain with her for a long time. She did not think it would take twenty years to conquer it.

'Grace. Grace.' He was bending over her now, his hands on the bed.

'It's all right, I've told you, Donald. Go to bed; you'll feel better in the morning.'

'I – I can't go to bed, not by myself. I keep seeing them. I want comfort, Grace. Let me lie . . . lie in your arms.'

'No, Donald, no. You won't get to sleep.' She moved away in the bed and put her hand out in a protesting movement as he bent further over her. 'Go to bed. Please . . . Please, Donald.'

'Oh, Grace, Grace. I'm unhappy, Grace.'

She closed her eyes against the wave of revulsion that swept over her when she saw him slide to his knees, but when from that position his arms groped for her, her eyes stretched and she said firmly, 'No! Donald, no!'

'Grace . . . oh, Grace.' He had hold of her.

'No, Donald, no! I tell you no!' She was shouting now.

'Ssh! Ssh! You'll . . . you'll waken the nipper. Just let me . . . me lie . . . lie here with my head on your breast like this.'

'No. No, I've told you. Donald . . . Donald, do you hear me? Get away!' Oh God! God in heaven! An unusual night he had said. What an ending to an unusual night!

She closed her eyes tight and the clock in the hall struck ten.

8

Grace had a new cook. She was not only a cook but a general help too, and full time. Her name was Peggy Mather. She was twenty-eight, big and of a surly disposition, and she was Miss Shawcross's niece. Why she had chosen to evacuate herself to this out-of-the-way village Grace did not know. The reason she gave was that she was fed up with the raids on the Tyne. Yet she showed no fear when the air-raid warnings went, and no matter what anybody else did she went stolidly about her work. What had really brought her from Newcastle to live with her aunt whom up to date she had rarely visited, Grace did not know and did not care, she was only too relieved to have her in the house, for now added to the household were David Cooper and three-year-old Veronica.

Young Dr Cooper was no longer young Dr Cooper. His small, slim stature had always made him appear years younger than he was, but the night of the raid had banked the years on him with one blow, and now he looked a man of fifty, not thirty-eight. After only three weeks' stay in hospital he had returned to the village, and in spite of protests plunged straight away into his practice; and as there was only a heap of rubble where his house had stood he had accepted without protest the invitation from the vicar to make his home with them.

It was in the morning-room at Willow Lea that he held his surgery. The expensive Persian carpet that had covered the hall had been taken up, chairs lined the walls between the doors, and the table was laden with old magazines.

Grace cast her eyes on the untidy jumble on the table as she crossed the hall towards the morning-room with a small tray in her hand. It always irritated her to see books and magazines thrown down open, but when a patient's turn came he or she just threw the reading material onto the table, never thinking.

She knocked at what was now the surgery door and David Cooper's voice called, 'Come in.'

'Oh, it's you, Grace. No more out there?'

'No.'

'This snow doesn't seem to have frozen the 'flu. If you ask me it's snowing germs. The whole Barker family are down now, mother and five kids.'

Grace put the tray down on the end of his desk. David talked a lot of shop these days, in fact he talked nothing else. It was over five months since the raid, but he was still fighting off the memory with work and talk of work.

'Drink that up while it's hot, David.'

'Thanks, Grace . . . Grace . . .' He was writing something rapidly on a prescription block and did not look up at her as he went on, his voice a low mumble now, 'Don't you think we'd better have a talk?'

She had been on the point of turning away but she stopped and looked down on his bent head. His hair was thin on the top, the rest was pepper-and-salt and had a grizzled look. She sat slowly down in the patients' chair to the right of him.

'You're pregnant, aren't you?' He still continued writing.

'Yes.'

'I remember asking you this question once before . . . does Donald know?'

'No.'

'Why haven't you told him?'

There was a long pause, and then she said, 'Because it isn't his.'

His eyes darted to her. Her words were like a jab in the arm penetrating his inner apathy.

'What are you saying?'

Her eyes dropped from his and she joined her hands together and pressed them tightly in her lap.

'Just that. Donald isn't capable of giving any woman a child.'

David bent forward; his hands went out and took hers from her lap, and as he gripped them he asked, 'Stephen?'

'No . . . and yet.' She shook her head violently. 'Oh, I don't know.' Then again she said, 'No. No, he couldn't be.'

He stared at her blankly. So this was it. He had always known it really . . . nerves didn't go to pieces like hers had done for nothing. Yet when Stephen had come he had thought he must have been wrong. Poor girl. Poor Grace. 'Can you tell me who it is . . . ? Farley?'

Her head swung up. 'Bertrand Farley?' She smiled sadly. 'Oh, David, not you too.'

The doctor moved his head ruefully. 'Well, I can't think of anyone else and I knew he was gone on you. You only had to look at him when you were about.'

'It should be funny, but it isn't . . . Bertrand Farley.' She closed her eyes for a moment, then, looking at him again, she said rapidly, 'Donald thought there was something between us and on the night of the raid he locked me in the cellar. He thought I'd made arrangements to meet Bertrand. When the lights went out I was in the dark, the black dark.' She said slowly now, 'He had gone off with the matches . . . You know his habit. Oh, David, it was terrible . . . Oh, I know, David, it was nothing to what happened in the village. I know what I experienced was nothing compared with that, I know, I know' – she kept moving her head – 'but it had a funny effect on me, David . . . David, I'm no longer nice inside. I no longer like myself, if you know what I mean.' She moved her hands within his. 'I find I'm swearing all the time inside, inside my head. I started to swear at Donald down there in the dark that night, and now sometimes for hours on end I'm swearing, and it frightens me, David.'

'Now, now.' He patted her hand. 'Don't worry. It's nothing to worry about, not really, especially now that you've talked of it. That's the main thing to do, talk about it, don't bury it. Look, I'll give you a tip. When the opportunity arises swear out loud – that's the best way to stop the underground stuff.' He squeezed her hand and smiled faintly as he said, 'I do quite a bit of swearing inside too. We must get together one night and have a swearing match, eh?'

He was comforting, so comforting. He was looking at her now quietly, waiting for her to go on, tell him who the child's father was. She started by saying, 'I suppose you think I'm dreadful . . .'

'Now, my dear Grace, don't be silly. I'm only sorry, sorry to the heart for you. And, strangely enough, sorry for him, too . . . Donald, I mean . . . Yes. Yes, I am.' He nodded his head. 'You know, I can confess to you now, I've never cared much for him, there's always been a something. I suppose my subconscious knew all the time about his trouble, and it is trouble, you know? It's an illness. He's not the only one, there are thousands like him, you'd be surprised. He should have gone and got advice.'

She actually laughed at this. 'Advice . . . ! You don't know Donald. He's so eaten up with pride he'd rather die than admit he's in the wrong about anything. So he tries never to do anything wrong.' She made a harsh sound in her throat. 'He's a vicar and he lives by the book . . . and . . . oh God . . .' She shook her head, then ended abruptly, 'Andrew MacIntyre is the father of my children.'

His gaze was holding hers and she couldn't help but feel a little hurt when she saw the look of blank amazement take up his whole expression.

'Andrew MacIntyre? Grace!'

'Oh, David, don't be shocked. Andrew is a fine man.'

227

'Yes, yes, I have a high opinion of Andrew, but . . .'

'Yes, I know what you are thinking: he's a farm-worker. But he's not just a farm-worker, he's a very intelligent man, a good man.'

David blinked. He was bewildered. 'Does Donald know?'

'No, but he soon will. I managed to get over Stephen but not this one.'

'How far are you gone?'

'Four months.'

'Have you any idea how he'll take it?'

'Yes, he'll forgive me and make me promise to give up . . . sinning. He'll also suspect about Stephen.'

'It's cruel, you know, Grace.'

'Yes, I suppose it is.' She paused a moment and then continued, 'Yes, I suppose it is. Stephen's become his private world.'

'When are you going to tell him?'

'Not until I must.' Quickly now she covered her eyes with her hand and murmured, 'I want to go away. Oh David, I want to go away. I want to take Stephen and go right away.'

'You can't do that. You mustn't do that.'

'You're just thinking of him now, aren't you?'

'Yes, and no. I'm sorry for him, Grace. A big, bouncing individual, so maimed . . . don't ever think of taking the child from him, don't. Leave him his illusions.'

She got slowly and steadily to her feet. 'Your coffee's got cold, David.'

His hand went out towards the cup, and she said, 'Leave it, I'll get you some fresh.'

There were no more words between them and she went out of the surgery . . .

It was that same night when the children had been put to bed and David had gone out to answer a call that Donald stood with his back to the blazing fire, and, after rocking backwards and forwards on his toes for a moment, looked down at his shoes and said quietly, 'Haven't you got something to tell me, Grace?'

Her body actually jerked upwards in the chair, and when she turned her face sidewards and looked at him she realised with a shock that he was smiling and her thoughts began to spiral in her mind, the words knocking against each other, pushing for place. No! No! God! It's impossible. He's not such a fool. A bloody fool! Don't swear. Only a stupid fool would . . . A stupid . . . Don't swear, I tell you . . . Be quiet and think . . . He thinks . . . he thinks that night . . . the night of the raid.

For more reasons than one she hated to look back to the night of the raid. It was over five months since that night and she was only four months pregnant. Had it been the other way about there would have been no risk, but could she get away with being four, five, or more weeks overdue? She must talk to David.

In the meantime she bowed her head under Donald's fatuous glance and tried to stop the spate of swear words that were now skating about in her brain.

9

It was a bright day in April, 1943, when Aggie let herself in the front door of her house. She was cold and tired, and all she wanted was to get a hot drink and her feet up for a while, but she had hardly closed the door behind her when the telephone bell rang in the office.

That would be Susie to see if she was still alive. If a bomb dropped in Wallsend Susie expected a splinter to hover over Newcastle to pick her out. Susie never gave her number or said the usual 'Hello', she always started with, 'You all right, Aggie?' and seemed very surprised when she learned that Aggie was all right.

Aggie lifted the phone. 'Yes . . . yes, this is Temple 3567.'

'Hold the line.'

She waited, and then at the sound of a voice coming over the wire her eyes widened and she said, 'Oh, hello, Andrew.'

'Listen, Aunt Aggie, I haven't got a minute.' He called her Aunt Aggie now and she liked it. 'Tell Grace I'll be passing through any minute, perhaps tonight or tomorrow at the latest, and if luck holds we'll make a stop. Tell her that, will you?'

'Yes, Andrew . . . Hello . . . ! Are you there? Andrew . . . Andrew!'

He had rung off. Well, that was short and sweet, anyway. Perhaps that meant that he shouldn't have been on the phone at all. They were coming down from Scotland and going some place, the south likely; there was something in the air, in the air of the whole country, a sort of waiting. Churchill had something up his sleeve. Well, she'd better get on to Grace. She didn't fancy having to be the bearer of this message – it was weeks now since Grace and Andrew had seen each other, he hadn't even been able to get a forty-eight-hour pass. She picked up the receiver and gave Grace's number, and when the thick voice of Peggy Mather came on the phone asking, 'Who is it?' she said brusquely, 'Tell Mrs Rouse it's her aunt.'

'She's bathing the baby, she's busy.'

'Well, be kind enough to tell her that I want to speak to her.'

That fat, sullen piece. Aggie didn't like Peggy Mather, and she knew that Peggy Mather returned these sentiments. She stood waiting, moving from one cold foot to the other. Poor Grace, having to put up with that surly creature all day! Her on the one hand and the Laughing Cavalier on the other . . . Oh, that man got her goat completely. What with his smarmy ways and that smile of his, and always playing the big daddy-boy . . . Eeh! It was fantastic when she thought of it. Those two children that he held up as his own private achievement . . . He almost put placards on them . . . and neither of the bairns his. It was – it was fantastic . . . She didn't know how Grace stuck him, stuck the whole set-up.

Something would have to be done. When Andrew came out of the army there would have to be a showdown. She picked up a pencil and started doodling on a pad. Would he come in with her? Would he make an estate agent? Well, he would have to have a job of some sort, something different from farmwork too, something with money in it . . . and prospects, because he wouldn't live on Grace, that was a sure thing, and very much to his credit that was. She liked Andrew, she did. She wished things had been different. There was a strength about him that was older than his years. He was like a . . . 'Oh, hello there, Grace.'

'Hello, Aunt Aggie. Are you all right?'

'Yes, I'm all right. You sound just like your Aunt Susie, that's how she starts.' She heard Grace laughing, and then she asked quietly, 'You alone?'

'Yes.'

'I had a phone message, somebody will be passing through at any time. With luck they'll stop in the village. Could be tonight or tomorrow, he doesn't know.'

There was silence, and Aggie said, 'Hello, are you there?'

'Yes, yes, I'm here, Aunt Aggie. When did you get to know?'

'A few minutes ago.'

'Thanks, Aunt Aggie, thanks.'

'Well, I'll be off now. I've just got in and I'm perished both inside and out; the wind's enough to cut you in two. How is it there?'

'Oh, it's a lovely day, sunny, even warm.'

'You're lucky. Goodbye, my dear.'

'Goodbye, Aunt Aggie, and thanks . . . thanks . . .'

Grace put the receiver down and, going slowly into the drawing-room, stared out into the garden to where Donald was hoeing between slightly erratic rows of vegetables. There was no semblance of Willow Lea's beautiful garden left. All the beds now had been utilised for food, and Donald had learned with back-breaking patience the art of growing it. Even so, his labours would have shown very little result if it had not been for his power of organisation which roped in the help of all ages at the week-ends.

She walked nearer to the window, everything suddenly racing inside of her. She must get the children in and bathed. He might be here tonight, Andrew might be through tonight. But how would she know? Would he come here openly? Why not, why not? If he didn't find her at their new rendezvous he would come here. He would see her. Whatever happened he would see her. Oh, Andrew . . . Andrew. Her eyes were tired straining at the mental image of him. She often thought that if anything happened to him she would have no picture of him, only that which was in her mind. And yet that wasn't so. She just had to look at Beatrice to see him. Beatrice had his eyes and his straight, strong nose. The nose mightn't make for beauty in her later on but it would give her character. Beatrice would grow up like Andrew, but Stephen wouldn't. She looked to where Stephen was now working side by side with Donald and Veronica Cooper. He had something of Andrew's extreme thinness and sometimes she imagined she saw Andrew's profile when the child looked upwards, but there the resemblance ceased.

It was always painful for her to witness the child's adoration of Donald. Whatever Donald did was the pattern which the boy set himself out to copy. He had even managed to imitate the inflection of Donald's voice.

Over the last four years Grace had watched, often with boiling anger, Donald manoeuvring for first place in the child's affection. And the same process was being enacted with Beatrice. She should be glad about this, she sometimes thought, but she wasn't. Beatrice had been born about ten days before time, which made her over three weeks late in Donald's reckoning. At one period she could almost see him checking up in his mind, going back to a particular Saturday when he had seen her and Bertrand Farley getting off the Newcastle bus. They had been laughing, and when Bertrand went to help her off the step she had slipped and nearly fell. Donald had been coming out of the church gate at that moment.

But he must have reassured himself, for from the moment the child was born he claimed her as his own.

She called now from the window, 'Stephen! Veronica! Come along, time to have your bath. Come along now.'

'Oh, Mummy!' Stephen turned his eyes towards her. 'Just five minutes.' Not waiting for her answer he looked up at Donald and asked, 'Just five minutes, can't I, Daddy?'

Donald straightened his back and, placing a

hand on his hip, he turned round and called, 'Just five minutes.'

'Goody. Goody, goody, goody.' The two children began digging furiously with their small spades, and Grace grated her teeth against each other for a second. This was the pattern. Wonderful Daddy, wonderful Uncle Donald, able to get them five minutes by just saying the word. And he could get them chocolates when nobody else could get them chocolates. He would read them stories when nobody else had time to read them stories. He could take all fear of the nasty aeroplanes away from them by simply saying, 'Kneel now and say "I am in God's hands. No nasty bombs will fall near me. The Good Shepherd is protecting me and no harm can come to me".' Wonderful psychology that turned a man into a god, a god that granted your every wish and had the power to make others do the same . . . But Andrew was coming tonight or tomorrow. She would see Andrew. If it was only for five minutes she would see Andrew, and things would balance themselves for a time. It was only when she saw him that she seemed to be able to see straight; when she needed comfort she could not even go upstairs and read his letters, for they were all at Aggie's. His last letter had said, 'On my next leave I'm going to tell my mother, although I've an idea she knows something already. Before the war I thought that nothing could make me leave her to the mercy of my father, but you see I've just had to, and she will be the first to see that my duty lies elsewhere now. The war can't go on for ever, so we must face up to things together. The sacrifice will be on your part as always. I love you, you are never out of my mind, I worship you, and as long as I live that's how it will be, Grace.'

She asked herself for the countless time since receiving that letter what he actually meant by sacrifice. Did he mean leaving the children with Donald? No, he couldn't mean that, he wouldn't want her to do that. No, he meant the sacrifice of her good name, for there would be no such thing as divorce. Or would there? Views were changing even in the Church. High Church people were getting divorces. But if she was divorced Donald might lay claim to the children . . . he would be the offended party. Yet if she went into court and told the truth . . . Court. Go into court and say that Donald . . . No! No! She could not expose him like that. Her head began to whirl as it often did these days, the words racing round one after the other. She must keep calm . . . keep all her wits about her, that could wait, Andrew could be here at any minute.

The convoy stopped in the village at twelve o'clock the following day. It comprised twenty-five lorries laden high with irregular shapes over which tarpaulins were tightly drawn. Besides the twenty-five drivers there were nineteen other men, two corporals and two sergeants, of whom Andrew MacIntyre was one, a first lieutenant and a captain. The convoy had been on the move since six that morning. They were to have an hour's halt.

Andrew had taken the hill towards the vicarage

at a gallop and only pulled himself to a stop when he entered the drive. When he knocked on the kitchen door and it was opened by Peggy Mather he gave a start of surprise and then stared at her for a moment. He had seen that face before, and he suddenly remembered where. But that was of no importance at the moment. He asked quickly, 'Is the vicar in?'

Peggy Mather looked at him, not only at his face but taking him all in, and it was evident that she liked what she saw, for she smiled and said, 'No. Can I do anything for you?'

'Is Mrs Rouse in?'

'Yes, she's somewhere about; she was in the garden a minute ago.' As she stepped out from the kitchen to look along the path, Grace came round the corner, and after only a slight hesitation in her step she came forward and held out her hand, and Andrew took it.

'How are you, Andrew?'

'Very well.' He turned round and nodded towards the maid before moving off on to the drive with the vicar's wife, and slowly they walked towards the main gate again.

They did not walk close and they talked generally, Andrew telling her where they were parked in the village and the length of time they were allowed to stay. And then at the gate, turning and facing her squarely, he murmured low and thickly, 'Oh, I want you in me arms. Oh, Grace.'

She was staring up at him, no veil on her feelings now. 'You really must be gone in an hour?'

'Yes, I'm going to dash up home. I won't be more than fifteen minutes. Can you be there?'

'Yes, I'll be there.'

'Oh, God! Grace!' He still stood. 'It seems years since I saw you . . . touched you.'

'Go now. Quick. Fifteen minutes, I'll be there.'

Before turning into the drive again, she watched him sprint up the road. Her head was quite clear, and she made it her business to go through the kitchen before crossing the hall and out into the garden by the drawing-room window. She also looked in at the sand-pit where the three children were busily constructing a castle. She did not speak to them or disturb them, but went hurriedly down the garden, past the greenhouses and out through the bottom door. She kept her pace steady until she entered the wood, and then she began to run. She crossed over the stone road and went on upwards in the direction of the cottage. Their new rendezvous was a clump of shrubbery some way from the path. It was a place that any couple might have used, but never before had they been there except in the dark, but this was no time for discretion. In little over half an hour he would be gone.

It was doubtful whether the presence of Donald himself could have kept them apart at this time. For it came to her as she stood waiting in the shelter of the thicket that there was an urgency about this convoy that portended long separation, not just weeks, but months, even years. Perhaps for ever. What if Andrew went away this time and never came back . . . She heard his feet racing down the path. The next minute he was before her and they were holding each other as if attempting to exchange their bodies.

'Oh, my darlin'! Oh, Grace, Grace! Let me look at you.' He held her face between his hands. His eyes seemed to lift each feature separately into the storehouse of his mind. Then he shook his head slowly. 'They talk about their women. Oh my God, but it sickens you. They've got women, but I've got . . . you.'

'Oh, Andrew. Oh, Andrew.'

'Don't cry, darling. Don't cry. It won't be for long. It can't be, and then we'll be together, you understand – together.'

Before her lips could part to speak, his mouth was on hers again and they swayed drunkenly for a moment until, without breaking their hold, they lowered themselves to the ground . . .

The bliss was still on them as they stood folded quietly together, and it was in their last kiss, soft and tender, that they were wrenched apart by a harsh, grating voice exclaiming with awful condemnation, 'God Almighty!'

Grace stared open-mouthed with shock and fear at Mr MacIntyre where he stood supporting himself by two sticks not more than three yards' distance from them.

'Why you dirty sod! To think that a son of mine . . . And the parson's wife. God Almighty!' He raised his stick. 'Get out! Get to hell away . . . out of it!'

Andrew had pushed Grace behind him and his voice was ominously low as he growled, 'Be careful what you're saying or else I'm liable to forget who you are.'

'Dashed in just to see your mother, did you?' The old man's eyes seemed to gleam red. 'Does she know about your fancy wife?'

'I've warned you, mind.'

'Warned me?' The old man was shouting now at the top of his voice. 'Well, let me warn you, you bloody upstart . . . Show your face in my door again and I'll brain you. So help me God! As for her, the dirty faggot, and a parson's wife . . . Huh!'

Grace flung her arms upwards, straining at Andrew's uplifted hand. 'No! No! Andrew! No . . . ! Oh no!'

'Get out of me sight.'

'Out of your sight? Aye, I will that, I'll get out of your sight, me cock-o'-the-midden.' The old man was thrusting forward with one of his sticks now, emphasising his words. 'I'll get out of your sight and into that English ranter's afore I'm five minutes older. And it isn't the day or yesterday I'll tell him that this started; I've had me suspicions. Her slinking about the road. Aye, I'll away.'

Still clinging to Andrew's arm, Grace watched the old man turn and hobble drunkenly through the trees with an erratic agility that belied the fact that he was utterly crippled with arthritis.

'Oh, Andrew, Andrew, he'll tell him.'

'Yes, he'll tell him.' Andrew's voice was flat. 'He's been wanting something on me for years, to hit at my mother with, and now he's got it, God blast him! But it's no use trying to stop him short of shooting him. He'll tell him.'

He turned his face slowly from his father's

disappearing figure and looked at Grace, and after a moment he said, 'Perhaps it's for the best, for neither of us would have had the heart to bring it into the open. I've always known it, even when I wrote that letter. First it would have been the children, and then not wanting to hurt him. Perhaps, after all, this is the best way, a clean cut. One way or another you will be free now. But, oh God!' He bared his teeth and jerked his head, 'If only I had a day or two and hadn't got to leave you to face this alone.' He rubbed his hand swiftly around his face, and then asked, 'What will you do? Go to Aunt Aggie?'

Grace shook her head dazedly. 'Yes, yes. I suppose so . . . Oh, Andrew, I don't know where I am. It's all happened so suddenly. Somehow I can't believe it . . . and at the last moment like this.'

'Look, Grace . . . Oh, dearest, don't look like that . . . Oh God, if only I had another hour or so. As it is, I'll have to dash back and tell my mother.' He caught her to him and kissed her hard and quickly once more, then, taking her by the hand he ran with her through the wood upwards towards the cottage.

Mrs MacIntyre was standing on the road, it was as if she had been looking over the fells in the direction her son would shortly be moving along the main road. Her face was tear-stained, and it was evident that she had been crying bitterly, for her voice broke as she exclaimed, 'Oh, boy, what is it?'

'Dad . . . he found us together. He's gone down to the vicar.'

'In the name of God, no . . . ! Oh, why didn't you stop him?'

'Stop him? How could I? If he hadn't told him today he would have told him the morrow. You know yourself he's been waiting for something like this for years.'

Mrs MacIntyre was not looking at her son now, but at Grace, and now she exclaimed in a gabble, 'He mustn't, he mustn't tell him . . . The children. Have you thought of the children, and Andrew not here to take your part? You cannot stand alone.'

Grace could find no words to answer this and Andrew cried, 'But how can you stop him, Mother? Anyway . . . look at the time, I've got to go. It's no use.'

'I'll stop him, I can stop him.'

'You? Don't be silly, Mother.'

'I can.' She was standing straight and tall facing him, yet already poised for flight. 'I have one hold over him. He's terrified at me leaving him.' Before she had finished speaking she was off round the corner of the house, flying down the path to the wood . . .

All at once Grace became quite still inside. During the past shock-filled moments she had been strangely afraid of Donald knowing. Now she thought: it's as Andrew says, it'll be a clean cut. They never would have been able to do it. If Mr MacIntyre reached Donald before Mrs MacIntyre caught him, well, that would be that, she would face up to it and get it over and thank God. Yes, thank God.

It was as she thought thus the air-raid siren

sounded and she gave a startled gasp and exclaimed, 'The children!'

They were running down through the wood again. When they reached the quarry road they branched off, and in a few minutes he had lifted her over the ditch and they were out of the wood and tearing down the main road towards the curve that would bring them in view of the vicarage gates. But before they reached it the plane soared over them and they actually saw it drop its bomb.

Within a split second Grace found herself picked up bodily and thrown in the ditch, and when Andrew dropped on top of her, the earth heaved and trembled as it had not done in the village since the night of the big raid.

'Oh, Andrew! Andrew! The children! The house!' Her mouth was full of dirt.

'Wait . . . wait, he's coming back.' The plane soared over them again and then was gone. There was no more sound; it was as if it had been sent to deliver a message and had done so. Andrew rose and pulled her to her feet and they were running again, flying towards the curve in the road. When they rounded it they both stopped dead; side by side and close together they stood leaning forwards as if frozen in flight. There was a haze of dust pouring upwards from a big hole in the road opposite to where the vicarage gate had been and on the verge of the road some way on this side of the hole lay a huddled form which Grace knew to be Mrs MacIntyre.

Andrew had reached his mother before Grace had covered half the distance, and when she came up to them he had turned her over and was shouting, 'Mother! Mother! Mother! Mother?' There was a deep cut across her brow and blood was pouring over her face.

Grace, with her hand across her mouth, murmured, 'Is she . . . ?'

'No. She's alive.' He wiped the blood swiftly and tenderly from her face, then cast his agitated gaze up at Grace as she gasped, 'The children, Andrew, the children.'

As she dragged herself away from his side she was aware of men in uniform racing up the hill towards them and then, like someone in a daze, she was stumbling round the crater. There at the other side and what had been the beginning of the drive were two men bending over the torn, twisted body of Mr MacIntyre, and about a dozen yards farther up the drive, lying on his back, his head near the root of a tree, was Donald. She made to run towards him, then stopped, her hand over her mouth again, this time because she knew she was going to vomit. The guilt that was filling her was turning her stomach – not the guilt of loving Andrew but the guilt bred of thoughts that had escaped in less time than it had taken for the bomb to explode . . . She hoped he was dead . . . Oh, no! No, no, no.

She must have paused for only a second, for she was bending above the white, blood-drained face as a voice to her side said, 'He's breathing. It doesn't look as if anything's hit him. The blast likely knocked him against the tree.' She watched the khaki-clad figure lifting Donald's head, and then the man said, 'Yes, it's as I thought. He's bleeding a bit there, but it doesn't look much.'

'Oh, ma'am, you all right?'

Grace straightened her back and turned dazed eyes on the wiry figure of Mr Blenkinsop, and as she did so she took in that the place was now swarming with people and two men were running towards them with a stretcher. As they came up one of them said, 'Coo! It's the vicar, poor—' He did not add the epithet.

She watched them lift Donald onto the stretcher. She did not speak or make any move towards them; and then Mr Blenkinsop, taking her arm, said, 'Come on away out of it, ma'am, up to the house.'

The house? No, she must go to Andrew and his mother. Poor Mrs MacIntyre! Her poor face . . . But there were the children. She startled Mr Blenkinsop by tearing away from him up the drive. But she had not gone far before she pulled herself to a stop. What was she thinking about? The bomb had dropped at the gate, and if the children had been with Donald there would be evidence of them.

As Mr Blenkinsop came panting up to her side, Peggy Mather appeared at the head of the drive and she called coolly, 'Who's got it this time? That was near enough. The house almost bounced.'

Peggy Mather had never used the prefix 'ma'am'; and although its lack was on occasion decidedly noticeable, Grace had never had the nerve to enforce it. When Donald had pointed out it was her place to do just that, she had said it wasn't worth the bother. Peggy Mather was only temporary . . . the war over, she would go. In this moment of shock, fear, and revulsion, she was further startled to hear herself exclaiming in a high voice, 'When you speak to me in the future, Peggy, will you kindly address me as ma'am or Mrs Rouse. Now, where are the children?'

Peggy Mather's features had contracted until they looked like a piece of dried leather. The fact that she was taken aback was evident, and after a moment, during which she glowered at her mistress, she said with telling flatness, 'Round the back where you left them . . . ma'am.'

The verger, taking hold of Grace's arm once more, said soothingly, 'We'll go and have a look ma'am,' and he led her away towards the back of the house, and as they went he told himself that the poor thing was suffering from shock or she would never have stood up to that one like that. A good job, too, and not afore time. His Mary, God rest her, would never have talked to the young mistress without a ma'am, but that Peggy Mather! He didn't know why Miss Shawcross kept her in her house; if she knew half of her carry-on she wouldn't.

It was with something of wonder that Grace looked down on the three children. They had apparently not moved out of the sand-pit. Stephen looked up at her now and explained, 'There was a big bang, Mammy, and Veronica said it was a bomb and wanted to go into the shelter, but I told her it wasn't 'cause Daddy said God wouldn't let any bombs drop today because it was so nice and sunny. And, anyway, I told her if it was a bomb you would have been here, wouldn't you, Mammy?'

She did not answer, only stared down on them, thinking God would not let any bombs drop today.

'What are you making?' Mr Blenkinsop was now bending his creaking joints over the sand-pit and looking down on Beatrice, but it was Stephen who as usual answered for them all. 'Oh, she's just muddling, she's still trying to build a castle. But I'm building a dugout, and Veronica's building a God-house.'

'Huh! Huh!' It was in the nature of a deep chuckle from Mr Blenkinsop. 'A God-house, eh?'

'Yes, that's what she calls them. But Daddy says God hasn't got a house, just churches. Veronica's silly . . . You are! You are!' He pushed her, but she showed no resentment, only laughed, and went on industriously poking holes in a square of sand. And as Grace now looked down on her the words began to revolve in her mind, A God-house . . . A God-house . . . a God-house, until they turned themselves into a mad-house . . . a mad-house . . . a mad-house.

'Oh, there you are.'

Miss Shawcross came hurrying towards them, and as Grace turned from the sand-pit there penetrated the whirling maze of her mind the thought that Kate Shawcross looked distraught. And it also came to her with a strong feeling of impatience that this woman had the power to imbibe the essence of any event, for she looked at this moment as if she had partaken of the actual experience of the bombing.

'They're taking him to hospital . . . the vicar?'

'Yes.' Grace nodded.

'He . . . he was wounded? And . . . and you let him go alone?'

Something slipped in Grace's mind, lifting the haze from it, and her voice was cuttingly cool as she said, 'He wasn't wounded, he had merely struck his head on a tree-trunk.'

'But . . . but you . . . ?' Miss Shawcross's voice was breaking, 'you let him go alone?' Her words faded on a note of recriminating judgement.

Grace found herself rearing upwards, her head going back and her small breasts thrusting out. This woman . . . this woman to criticise her, and in front of Mr Blenkinsop. She had stood enough . . . she had put up with enough all these years one way and another. Kate Shawcross had usurped her position right from the start – yes, right from the start. How dare she! She would show her that she had reached her limit. 'When you speak to me, Miss Shawcross, will you kindly remember that I'm the vicar's wife.'

Twice in less than five minutes she had done what she had never dreamed of doing during the seven years of her marriage . . . pointed out her position as the vicar's wife. She saw how ludicrous the situation was. Now, when she had ceased to be the vicar's wife, when Mr MacIntyre had made it unnecessary for any more posing or lying, she was laying claim to the supposed privilege.

As she walked past Kate Shawcross, whose whole face was twitching, Mr Blenkinsop said in a small placating voice, 'There, there, we're all upset, very upset. There, don't take on, Kate . . . there now, there now.'

His voice was soothing, and Grace had the impression that he was patting Miss Shawcross's arm. Patting her arm . . . she would like to slap her face. Yes, she would . . . Why hadn't she gone to the hospital with Donald? She was not only repeating Kate Shawcross's question but asking the question of herself now. Why hadn't she gone? They would have let her. But she'd had to see to the children, hadn't she? Had it been Andrew lying there what would she have done? There was no need to answer that question.

She did not make her way into the house through the kitchen because Peggy Mather was there, but went towards the front door, telling herself that she must sit down, if only for a minute, before going back to the gate. She felt sick and faint . . . oh, she did feel faint. As the earth came up suddenly to meet her she heard Mr Blenkinsop's voice crying, 'Steady . . . ! steady . . . !'

When she came round she was in the drawing-room and a voice was still saying, 'Steady . . . ! steady!' but this time it was David's voice. 'Now drink this up.'

She drank some bitter stuff from a glass, then he gently lowered her head on to the couch again.

After a moment of blinking she looked wearily up at him. 'David.'

'Don't talk.'

'I must. Mr MacIntyre . . . is he . . . is he dead?'

'Yes.'

Dazedly she watched him look away, rubbing

at his chin, and when his eyes came back to her he said, 'He's never been down as far as this for years; in fact I've never known him come to the village. He must have come down to the road with his wife to see Andrew off.' He paused. 'You know, of course, that Andrew was passing through with a convoy?'

She stared at him, not saying a word. He knew all about her – that is, up to now. But she couldn't tell him the dreadful truth that she was responsible for Mr MacIntyre's death. It was she who had killed him, not the bomb. He never came down to the road, no, and he wouldn't have come today but for her. She saw him lying in a twisted heap. She saw Donald lying against the tree. Had he managed to tell Donald everything before the blast blew them apart? Mr MacIntyre would have wasted no time, he would have out with it. Yet if they had been standing together wouldn't Donald have received the full force of the blast too? Perhaps they hadn't met . . . perhaps Donald was just coming towards him down the drive . . . perhaps, perhaps. The thoughts were trailing around in her mind. She felt sleepy. That stuff in the glass . . . she made an effort to rise, saying, 'I must see . . . see.'

'Go to sleep.'

'No, David, I must see . . .'

'There now, go to sleep. That's it.'

As David Cooper stood looking down on her he thought with analytical coolness that it was a pity the position of old MacIntyre and the vicar hadn't been reversed. Then Donald would have been saved a great deal of mental agony, which, when this was over and Andrew MacIntyre was home again, he would certainly be called upon to face. He could not see any evasive action, no matter how skilfully used – and he had come to recognise this vicar as an expert in this field – being proof against these two young people and their needs. As for Grace, the vicar's death would have given her a reprieve, a mental reprieve. When Andrew MacIntyre had given her the child it had saved her from a breakdown, yet now she was heading fast that way again. The cure was in a way turning out to be worse than the disease. He wondered why old MacIntyre had been down on the road with his wife; he hadn't for a moment believed the reason was the one he had suggested to Grace. If he had gathered anything from his visits to the cottage over the years it was that Douglas MacIntyre hated his son while the mother loved him too much. This latter, no doubt, could in the first place have accounted for the old man's spleen, added to which he was full of the pride and bigotry which self-education engenders in some Scots. No, Mr and Mrs MacIntyre had not come down to the road to see their son off. Of this he was certain.

He did not know what the outcome of all this would be, but he hoped he wouldn't be living in the house when the balloon went up. It was very awkward. Although all his sympathy lay with Grace, there were definitely two sides to be taken into account.

10

'The man's not all there, he can't be. Do you mean to say he hasn't mentioned it in any way?'

Grace shook her head slowly. 'Not a word.'

'Not a word?'

'No, Aunt Aggie, not a word.'

Grace looked beyond Aggie's broad figure towards the window and the garden, a gaily flowered window-box, and she remarked to herself that there hadn't been a thing out in the box the last time she had sat here. She was finding like Donald, she could be talking of one thing while thinking of another. She should be keeping her mind on what she was telling Aunt Aggie; instead she was thinking of the window-box.

She had not seen Aggie since three days before the bomb dropped, and that was well over a month now. On that fateful day Aggie had taken herself off to Devon to have a week with her late husband's sister, but the week had spread into four, for Aggie had got her nose into some property – not selling it this time, but buying it. She had, during her stay there, purchased three houses. One of her purchases she was very enthusiastic about, a dilapidated cottage in a wood near Buckfastleigh. She had apparently picked it up for a song, and not with the idea of letting when the war was over, as she intended doing with the other two, but of making it a place where Grace and the children could go in the summer for the holidays. Grace's thoughts now hovered about this cottage; it seemed to be the very answer to her present need. If it could be made habitable she would take the children there and be away from everybody – Kate Shawcross and Peggy Mather, all the faces in the village – away from Aunt Susie and Uncle Ralph and their 'committee meetings'. Her thoughts touched on everyone but Donald.

But what about Mrs MacIntyre? The last words Andrew had said to her over the phone were, 'Will you see to my mother, Grace?' and she had promised with loving emphasis, 'Yes, oh yes, I'll see to her, darling. Don't worry, I'll see to her.' Perhaps Mrs MacIntyre would come with her when she came out of hospital . . . perhaps. But what if she were really blind? No, no, she mustn't be blind, she couldn't be blind. They could do such wonderful things now, she couldn't be blind. Oh no! The protest against Mrs MacIntyre's blindness became loud in her head. She couldn't be made to carry that weight on her conscience too, Mrs MacIntyre's blindness.

'But one way or another he could have mentioned it.'

'Yes, Aunt Aggie, one way or another he could.' She found she was repeating everything Aggie said.

'Is he aiming to push you round the bend?'

'Whether he's aiming or not, he's succeeding.'

'Well, be damned, it's up to you, girl, not to let

him. If old MacIntyre did tell him, why doesn't he come out into the open with it like a man, and if he doesn't know everything why doesn't he speak of the bombing? He came off pretty lightly, anyway.'

'He's supposed to be suffering from shock.'

'Shock be damned!'

'Yes, that's what I've been saying to myself. About this cottage, Aunt Aggie, how many rooms did you say it has?'

'Six – but mind, they're just boxes.'

'And it is furnished?'

'Yes, if you can call it that. It was left as it stood at the beginning of the war and the stuff wasn't very great then.'

'Could it be made habitable?'

'Oh yes. My, yes, of course it could. I'm only saying it isn't another Willow Lea, but it will be a grand little place when it has a good clean-up and some attention. All it wants is a handyman on it for a few weeks. I'm going down there in the summer and I'll rake out somebody and get the place ship-shape.'

'It will be ship-shape before that, Aunt Aggie.'

'What do you mean, girl?'

'I've got to find some place, some place for the children, some place where he won't think of looking for us. I'm just going to pick them up and go. It wouldn't be any use asking him if I could, even for a few months, he wouldn't hear of it. He'd just shut me up. In one way or another he'd shut me up . . . and effectively. No, the only thing is to pick them up and go.'

Aggie was staring down at her niece. 'So you've

made up your mind at last?' she said quietly. 'Well, I'm glad to hear that. Sometimes I've thought you must be barmy, for anyone else in your place would have made the break after Stephen – if not before; and you know, sometimes I've thought he's got some weird power over you, keeping you there. It's as if he's got you inside an elastic band, and he's just got to twang it and back you spring.'

'Well, Aunt Aggie, I won't spring back this time. My mind's been made up for me . . . I . . . I'm pregnant again.'

Aggie's eyes and mouth, even her whole face, seemed to spread outwards before she exclaimed, 'God Almighty! Are you out of your mind altogether to go and do a thing like that? Oh! God above!' She waved her two hands as if in supplication and then said angrily, 'But why weren't you careful? I warned you, girl.'

'How could I be careful, Aunt Aggie, when I wasn't expecting to have to be. He only had an hour remember, and half of that was taken up with seeing his mother. I didn't think there would be any need for care. These things just happen and you can't say at such a time as that, "No . . . no, I'm not prepared for it" . . . It's no use, Aunt Aggie, it's done. And don't look so upset. I'm not. It had to be this, it had to be something like this to bring things into the open. Andrew said that day, "Let my father tell him, it needs something like this to bring matters to a head", but that didn't work out. Or if it did, Donald's holding on to it like a secret weapon. But he can't hold on to this one. He won't be able to turn his back on this rising fact, or make any claim to it.' With a crudeness foreign to her she patted her stomach, then rose to her feet. And as she got up Aunt Aggie sat down. Of the two, she was the more agitated.

Grace looked down at Aggie now and asked, 'Have you told Aunt Susie and Uncle Ralph about this cottage?'

'No, I only got in last night and I haven't been round there yet, although she was on the phone this morning to see if I was all right, all in one piece. I'm to go round there for tea.'

'Then don't tell them about the place, Aunt Aggie, because if Donald started working on Uncle Ralph he would soon give himself away. Uncle Ralph is a strong believer in the rights of husbands.'

'But you'll have to let me get something done to the place before going in, the roof's leaking at one side.'

'Could we go down and see it?'

'Yes, we could make the trip, say, next week-end – I couldn't do it this.'

'That'll do. I'll ask Aunt Susie to have Beatrice. Stephen will be all right at home. I'd like to be settled in it within three months.' She did not say, 'Before I start to show.'

Grace now went and stood near the window and looked down on the window-box. 'You know, Aunt Aggie,' she said, 'I've got a feeling I'm going to enjoy carrying this one. Donald would have to stretch his imagination some to lay claim to it. There will be nothing he can do about it, and you've no idea what a feeling of relief that is.

Knowing that I won't have to witness any more daddy-boy acting. That in itself was a form of torture. Oh, Aunt Aggie, what an odd life I've had.' She turned round now and smiled at Aggie, but Aggie could not return the smile – she was crying quietly.

Four months later Grace was still at Willow Lea but poised, as it were, for take-off. One incident after another had managed to delay her flight, two of the most important of them being that handymen and materials with which to repair the cottage were difficult to come by, and not until just over three weeks ago had it become ready. Then Stephen went down with measles, followed in turn by Beatrice and Veronica. But now there were no more obstacles. She did not think of Donald as an obstacle, for he would know nothing until they were gone. She hadn't been idle during the past weeks. Everything was packed, and, to make things easier for her, she was no longer under the keen eye of David. Three days ago he had taken up his new home in rooms over Stanley's shop. He had taken on a housekeeper, a Mrs Maitland, a war widow with a child of three, and Grace felt, and hoped sincerely, she would soon change her name to Cooper.

She was already penning in her mind the letter which she would write to Donald later tonight telling him she was leaving him because she was going to have a baby, whose father was also the father of Beatrice and Stephen. She would tell him not to try to find her, for if he should and made to claim the custody of the children she would have to speak, and in court, about things which would be embarrassing and painful to both of them. So it was better, etc., etc.

Over the past few weeks she had been taking certain of their clothing and belongings to Aggie's, and she was going now to get a box from the top of the nursery cupboard in which to pack some toys. In her own room she had just taken off the loose three-quarter length overall she usually wore, presumably to keep her dress clean when dealing with the children. The ritual of the four-o'clock drawing-room tea had ended, partly from choice and partly because meals since the advent of David's coming into the house had been some-what erratic, so her wearing an overall, it being an attractive one, had brought no comment from Donald.

She was reaching to the top of the cupboard and had the box actually in her hand when her attention was drawn towards the door . . . and Donald. He was staring at her. Her vocabulary had no words with which to describe his look. His eyes were not on her face but on the globe of her stomach, which was accentuated by her skirt and her extreme thinness.

He stepped slowly into the room, closing the door behind him. They had the nursery to them-selves, for the children were at this minute racing across the drive, their yells rising up to the open window.

She did not try to cover herself up; there was nothing to do it with anyway, except her hands, and these she kept hanging idly at her sides as she looked at him, thinking that she would have given anything to avoid this. She had tried, she had done her best, he had treated her for months now with coldness, almost ignoring her for days on end, except when in the company of David or visitors, when his manner was so skilfully general that no-one could have picked out of it any particular attitude towards herself.

'You . . . you're . . .'

'. . . Yes, I am.' Her voice was quiet and held no tremor. She did not feel any fear of him at this moment, nor any shame at the admission. At last, at last, the air was going to be cleared. The dreadful years of lying were finished, her life would be open and aired, and from this day forward she would keep it aired. If she was forced to live in sin, well and good, it would be all right with her.

That's how she was feeling one moment, the next she had her hands in front of her face shielding herself as she cried, 'Don't! Don't!' In a split second Donald had whipped up from the nursery table a large, heavy, cutglass water jug. It seemed impossible that it wouldn't crash down on her head. She cowered almost double, when from the crook of her arm she saw it fall against the nursery cupboard, still held in his grip. Not until it had slid some way down the door did he release it, to fall to the ground with a crash but not to break.

She staggered back now away from him towards the wall. His face looked blue as if he was going to have a heart attack. He looked enormous standing there, his eyes pouring out their hate of her. Then much like those of an old senile man, the muscles of his body began to twitch. His legs, his arms, his face, he looked all atwitch. With a swaying movement he turned and faced the cupboard door and, putting his arm on it, he leant his head against it.

Still against the wall Grace stood and watched him. She was trembling all over. She had always guessed that something like this would happen, that's why she had wanted to get away without having to bring the matter into the open. He had nearly hit her with the jug: the suave, polished, controlled minister had nearly hit her. The blow might have killed her, and the child. She had dealt a blow to his pride that all his veneer was no proof against.

He turned now but did not move away from the door, seeming afraid to leave its support, but he looked across the room to where she stood and after gulping twice in his throat he muttered, 'You – you've brought me to this, you've made me . . .' He looked at the jug, then his head drooped suddenly forward and he swung it from side to side. 'You've done this to me, shamed, humiliated . . .'

At this moment Beatrice's voice bordering on tears, came from directly below the open window, screaming, 'No! Stevie. No, don't, Stevie.' Stephen answered but his words were not distinct and there followed another high scream from Beatrice.

Grace, knowing that Stephen must be up to something, wanted to go to the window, but she couldn't take her eyes from Donald. At this moment her whole being was filled with pity for him. She watched him stagger like a drunken man towards the low nursery table and stand with his knees against it for support. His body was still twitching and it twitched forward across the table as he groaned out under his breath, 'You're debased . . . no better than a street woman . . . a whore.'

Her pity vanished. 'Who's to blame for that?' She did not allow him to get anything in but went on quickly, bitterly, 'Well, tomorrow I'm relieving you of my debased self, I'm going . . . and for good.'

He pulled himself upwards, and as Beatrice's screeching reached an ear-splitting crescendo he thrust out a shaking hand towards the window and demanded in awesome tones, 'The children, you'd leave the children?'

'No.' She shook her head. 'No, I'm not going to . . .'

As if he were jumping bodily into a breech to prevent some fatal catastrophe he now flung his arms wide and began to move in the narrow space between the table and the wall with the gestures of a rapidly animated clockwork being, and as he moved he shouted, 'You can't leave my children . . . my children. You would leave them motherless and with disgrace on them. Do you hear? Disgrace!' The jerking movements, stopped for a second before he went on, again gabbling, now almost incoherently, about his children, his children. Grace looked at him. He was like a child putting up a defence mechanism. He would not listen to the words that he knew she was about to say, 'I'm taking the children with me.' He would not admit such a possibility. If he talked fast enough about his children, then she couldn't possibly say she was taking them. His attitude now was like that of some backward individual who had only the sound of its voice to prove its power.

Suddenly she shouted as she sometimes did at the children, 'Stop it! This minute! Stop it, I say!' And when he stopped and stood staring at her, the sweat running down his face, she said in slow definite tones, 'I'm leaving tomorrow and I'm taking the children with me. Do you hear? And . . . and I'll tell you now . . . they're not your children.' There, it was out.

He bent low and placed his hands on the table looking like some great orang-outang in this attitude. His voice even held some animal's guttural quality when he said, 'They are my children; you'll never get them from me . . . never. Do you understand that? Never will those children leave my side, I swear on it.'

'Stevie! Stevie!' Beatrice's voice was still screaming from the drive, and Grace shivered now as her calmness seeped from her and fear took its place.

In his bent position, with his head up, they were on eye level and they stared at each other while Beatrice screamed. They stared at each other until slowly Donald straightened himself up and, groping for his handkerchief, wiped the sweat from his face. He stood looking downwards for a few minutes taking in great breaths of air, and then, in a voice more like his own now, he said without looking at her, 'I want to hear no more, and I will forgive you if you will promise before God that this will never happen again.'

'I don't want your so-called forgiveness, and I give no such promise.'

His head came up slowly and he stared at her again. 'Grace . . . I said I would forgive you. Don't you realise just what it has taken for me to say those words? I'm a priest of God, but I am a man and you have done me a most grievous wrong, the most grievous wrong—'

'Grievous wrong? Huh!' It was a laughing sound but the muscles of her face did not stretch. In her head was a rising spate of swear words, which some part of her was trying, unsuccessfully, to press down. She nodded quickly at him now as she said, 'Once again I'll say to you: don't be such a bloody hypocrite . . . Grievous wrong . . . Oh, my God!'

'Stop that swearing. I won't have it, do you hear? Call me hypocrite or whatever your trivial mind suggests, but I won't have you swearing in my presence . . .'

'Mammy! Mammy! Mammy!' The words rose up in a paroxysm of screaming, and such was their intensity they forced Grace to the window, and as she went there threw bitterly over her shoulder, 'Grievous wrong.'

Even as she glanced out of the window she was only giving a fragment of her attention to the child who was kneeling on the gravel below beating her little fists as she screamed, for her mind was still full of words, dreadful words, wanting to hurl them at Donald. Then in another second Beatrice had her whole attention, for, following the child's petrified gaze, she saw to her horror what had all this time been eliciting her screams. Stephen was climbing the trellis work that led up to the nursery window. It was used as a support for the delicate tendrils of the clematis, and he was now more than halfway up it. Instinctively Grace's hand went to her throat. She knew she must not shout at him, but the fears and tensions of the last few minutes came over in her voice as she exclaimed, 'Stephen!' The boy looked up, startled. Then, pleased to see that she was witnessing his daring feat, he called, 'Look, Mammy, I can climb . . .' Looking up at her in his moment of triumph his head had gone too far back. As he released his hand for the next pull, he overbalanced, and to a scream that out-did Beatrice's he fell onto the drive.

Grace was out of the room, down the stairs and onto the drive in a matter of seconds. Beatrice's screams had reached the point of hysteria now, but there was no sound at all from Stephen. As her arms went round him to gather him up she was thrust roughly aside. 'Don't touch him!' Donald spoke as if her touch would defile the boy and brought up in her an emotion that bordered on rage. But she had to stand aside to see him lift the child and carry him indoors. As she watched him disappear into the drawing-room with the limp figure in his arms she forced herself towards the telephone, and there rang up David, and as she gave the number she was surprised to hear herself still muttering, 'Grievous wrong. Grievous wrong.'

* * *

At nine o'clock that night Grace phoned Aggie, and when she heard the brisk tones saying 'Hello' she said without any preamble, 'Stephen's had a fall, Aunt Aggie. They think he might have fractured his hip-bone. He's in the Cottage Hospital.'

'No!'

'Yes, Aunt Aggie.'

'And you were to come tomorrow.'

'Yes, Aunt Aggie.'

'It's fantastic.'

'That isn't all. He's found out about the other . . . and you'll be pleased to know I'm to be forgiven.'

'Aw! Girl.'

'He won't let me have the children . . . The elastic band has pulled tight again, Aunt Aggie.'

'My God!'

11

Grace's third child was born on 1 January 1944, and she called it Jane. Donald was confined to bed with 'flu at the time, and so any lack of interest he might have shown was not observed.

Stephen did not like the advent of another sister, for it took some of the limelight away from his iron-bound leg. Beatrice did not care one way or the other; so Grace seemed to have her daughter to herself. And this state of affairs went on until the child was six months old. Donald, to Grace's knowledge, had never looked at the baby, and she was glad of that. At least this child would be hers, for Beatrice had long ago followed in Stephen's footsteps and was Daddy's little girl. But Jane was hers and would remain hers.

With the birth of the child Grace developed a philosophy, perhaps a negative one, but nevertheless it had the becalming effect of acceptance. It was no use, she told herself, she would struggle no more. She would take things as they came – what had to be would be. She had her child – it was as if she had only one – and Mrs MacIntyre.

It was strange the comfort that Andrew's mother had brought to her in the past months. It should have been the other way round – but no, it was Mrs MacIntyre, now almost blind but for a faint light in the left eye, who gave her comfort while at the same time killing any hope for future reprieve from the life she was at present leading, for, as Mrs MacIntyre said, her sight was now in the ends of her fingers and these had become familiar over the years with every article of furniture in her home. Moreover, when she stood outside her front door she did not need anyone to point out what lay in front of her. The air on her face, mist-laden, wet, warm or stinging with snow particles, told her how the fells would be looking at that moment . . . Was there any hope, then, that Andrew would leave his mother alone in the cottage, 'and go and live his own life a little way off', as she would say to Grace? 'But not too far, so that he could look her up betimes?' No, the pattern was already set.

But her new philosophy said: 'Don't worry. Wait and see, take it in your stride.' That was until the morning of her twenty-sixth birthday, which Donald had not acknowledged. From that day she no longer told herself to take it in her stride: she told herself to fight.

The telephone had rung as Donald was crossing the hall and he picked it up, and as she went into the drawing-room she heard him say, 'Oh, hello, David', and then a long pause and, 'I'm very sorry'. A few seconds later he was standing in the drawing-room. She was gathering some papers up from the table, her back to him, when she realised he was looking at her. This hadn't happened for a long time, not since the night in the nursery. She turned and faced him.

'David has just phoned. He tells me—' He

paused, 'They have heard that' – his voice sank – 'that Bertrand Farley's been killed in action.'

She allowed him to hold her gaze as she thought: Oh, poor Bertrand . . . poor fellow. But as she looked at him her mind told her why he was giving her the news of Bertrand Farley's death in this way. He thought, he actually thought, that Bertrand was the father of the children. No bubble of laughter rose in her at this revelation – only a faint sense of wonder at the knowledge that this could prove that he knew nothing about Andrew. And yet against this supposition was the fact that he had never once mentioned anything concerning the bomb being dropped. Nor had he ever spoken of its effect on Mrs MacIntyre.

She turned from him and sat down on the couch, and it took all her control, when he stood in front of her, his gaze directed down on her as he said, 'I'm sorry. You know that, don't you?' not to cry out, 'Don't be such a bloody fool!' This was the first time she had sworn inside her head for a number of weeks, and it brought the usual feeling of sick revulsion against herself and she cried out at it, 'No not again, don't start that again.' After a long, silent moment Donald left her and the spate of words died away.

But that very afternoon they returned in force. It was when Donald looked at the child for the first time. Not only looked at her but took her up in his arms.

She was standing at her bedroom window looking towards the sand-pit. The pram was near the edge of the pit and she saw Donald coming towards it to tell the children as always that he was at hand again, for never did he return to the house, even after an absence of only an hour, but he made his presence known to them. Stephen was not in the pit but sailing a boat on the small fish pond some distance away, and on the sight of Donald he sprang up with the hampered agility of the iron supporting his leg and made a dash towards him, and once again, perhaps for the fourth or fifth time that day, he was lifted up high. Then it was Beatrice's turn, for whatever Stephen had she must have too. Even if she hadn't demanded it Donald would have seen that she got it. It was with one on each side of him that he walked towards the pram and, standing in front of it, looked down on the gurgling, fat and anything but pretty face of Jane. He stood for a long time like this while the children jabbered and talked and prodded their sister in various ways. Then through the open window Grace heard his voice remonstrating with them gently, 'Now, now, Stephen, you mustn't be rough. No, Beatrice, no, not like that.' When she saw him bend slowly forward and pick the child up into his arms her stomach seemed to turn over. The sensation was similar to that created by an enema – sickly sweat-making. And what followed next did nothing to lessen this sensation. She saw her husband carry the child to the garden seat, where, placing her on his right knee and putting his arm about her, he took hold of her right hand, then with his left hand he drew towards him Stephen's right hand and placed Jane's podgy fist in it. Then, taking hold of Stephen's left hand, he joined it to Beatrice's left with his own. There was now formed a circle and the circle was almost encompassed by his two arms. The ritual had been accomplished without a word. Daddy was showing them a new game and the children's faces were alight. Words were not necessary.

The feeling in Grace's stomach had brought a weakness to her legs, and she leant against the stanchion of the deep window-sill and in the silence of the room she talked to him, spitting out the words, 'You won't do it! No, by God, not with her you won't! You shan't take her from me. No, Donald, I'll play you at your own game . . . You . . . ! You . . . ! You . . . ! You're inhuman, you must be. Oh the cruelty . . . You . . . ! You . . . ! You . . . ! . . .'

The new phase was given its seal on the Sunday following this ritual of possession, for Donald preached a sermon on 'Forgive us our trespasses'. She was sitting in their pew, Stephen on one side and Beatrice on the other, and Donald, standing above her in the pulpit, asked the congregation how could they expect to be forgiven for their shortcomings if they did not forgive others, and not just for small sins, but for grievous sins. The sin of unfaithfulness had been bred like a germ through this war, but sins, like germs, must be attacked and exterminated. Yet who would think of exterminating the man because he carried in his body the germs of, say, influenza. No, you could kill the germs and save the man. So it was with sin. And he told them they were incapable of forgiveness unless they became humble . . .

Grace was rearing inside. Unless you were humble. My God! Humble! Donald humble! And these poor Air Force fellows in the congregation and those girls. They would all be thinking he was at them. She wanted to turn to them and say, 'Don't worry, it's not you he's getting at.' Forgiveness . . . unless ye become as little children . . . humility . . .

She looked straight at him, but he did not once let his gaze rest on her. Humility. What about stealing? Practised, calculated stealing. Not the stealing in a passion-inflamed moment of another man's wife. That was a clean thing, almost a virtue, compared with the daily, hourly, sucking in to himself the lives . . . the whole lives and emotions, the loyalty and love of two children whom he was determined now made into three . . . Humility!

She just had to see Aunt Aggie.

When later that same day she made a flying visit to Newcastle she flung her arms wide as she asked Aggie, 'What can I do? I feel helpless against such . . . such wiliness. Oh, I could go, but . . . but it's Stephen.'

In reply Aggie made a statement which was not an answer. 'The unnatural swine,' she said, 'blast him to hell's flames.'

12

As one nerve-strained day melted into another Grace fought Donald in every way she could to resist his usurping of Jane. The conflict was all the more intense because no mention of it was made by either of them.

The ill-effect of the situation on Grace was added to when she had to face the fact that never would she be able to take Stephen away from Donald. She might as well drain off the boy's blood and expect him to live as separate him from the man he called Daddy.

The whole pattern of her life was becoming unbearable; only the sight and touch of Andrew could have brought her easement. But Andrew was in Italy. From North Africa and Sicily he had gone to Italy. His letters from there awaited her at Aggie's every Saturday morning, but they nearly always ended with, 'It won't be long now, it's nearly over, it's near the end.'

When the end finally came, hope for a time brought colour back into her face if not flesh on to her bones and she thought continually, 'Maybe tomorrow. Maybe tomorrow. Maybe tomorrow.' But it was many months later, and peace an accepted thing, before she saw Andrew.

One Friday night, at six o'clock, Peggy Mather,

in the act of putting on her coat and wrapping a scarf around her head against the snow blizzard that was raging, heard the telephone ring, and she was about to pull the back door open to leave when she heard it ring for the second time. She stopped. The vicar was making so much bloomin' noise in the nursery with those bairns that he couldn't hear the bell. And where was she? she wondered. She stamped across the kitchen and through the baize door into the hall, and when the phone rang again she picked it up and said, 'Hello?' After a moment she put it down and went to the bottom of the stairs and yelled in her loudest voice, 'It's for you – ma'am!' Never once did she use the word ma'am without giving it a telling quality.

Grace was in the bathroom tidying up after having bathed the children, and she only just heard the call. When she got to the top of the stairs Peggy Mather, from the folds of her scarf which she was now pulling over her mouth, muttered, 'Phone.'

'Thank you, Peggy.' Grace screwed up her face and cast her eyes in the direction of the nursery, from which were issuing high-pitched, gleeful yells.

When she took up the phone Aggie's voice came immediately to her saying, 'Hello there, you been asleep?'

'No, Aunt Aggie, but there was so much noise going on upstairs I couldn't hear the bell.'

'How are you?'

'Oh . . . you know . . . as usual.'

'How are you off for beef for the week-end?'

'Beef, Aunt Aggie? Well . . .' Grace shook her head as she repeated, 'Beef? Not at all, we've had mutton for the last four weeks. I'm sick of the sight of it. Can you get me a piece of beef?'

'Yes, a prime bit, real Scotch.' Aggie laughed at this point and added, 'And not from under the counter either.'

Grace was smiling into the phone. Aggie sounded happy, even excited; she was always digging up something on her rounds. She knew so many people. But a piece of beef!

'Grace.'

'Yes, Aunt Aggie?'

'Hold on to something, I've got a surprise for you. In fact it's the Scotch beef in person.'

Grace moved the phone from her ear and looked at it, and then it was tightly pressed against her flesh as a voice, a low, deep voice, came over the wire saying, 'Grace . . . Grace.'

She closed her eyes and gripped at the edge of the telephone table, for not for the life of her could she utter a sound.

'Grace . . .' The voice was lower, deeper. 'Grace . . . darling, are you there . . . ? Grace.'

Her mouth was open, the words were swelling up in her ready to pour out, when she heard Aggie's astringent tone calling sharply, 'Grace . . . ! Grace, do you hear me? Are you there?'

'Yes. Oh, Aunt Aggie!'

'Is anybody about?'

Grace shook her head again and was on the point of saying 'No' when she heard the door of the nursery close overhead and Donald's footsteps coming towards the stairs, and she said hastily:

'Yes, Aunt Aggie, yes.'

'You'll be in tomorrow morning, then?'

'Yes, Aunt Aggie.' Donald was in the hall now and she forced herself to talk. 'I've got enough coupons to get Beatrice the outfit that we saw. Yes, I'll be over in the morning . . . and . . . and meet you. Good night, Aunt Aggie. Good night.'

She put the phone down as Donald went into the study and, running upstairs towards her own room, she paused on the landing for a moment and looked towards the nursery. She should dash in there now and gather them to her and cry, 'Children! Children! Your daddy's come home. Three years and you haven't seen your daddy. But he's home now, home for good, for ever and ever and ever. Just like the fairy tales. Yes, just like the fairy tales, for ever and ever.'

13

Grace paused for a second before inserting the key into the lock of Aggie's front door. In spite of the snow on the ground and the knife-edged air she was sweating and trembling with it. She had not slept all night waiting for this moment, and now that it had come she was filled with a mixture of shyness, elation, and dread – the dread centred round Andrew's reactions to her changed appearance, for she felt that she was no longer beautiful. It was impossible to feel as she did inside and still remain beautiful, and there was the evidence of her mirror to prove it. She was thin to the point of drabness, the bones of her face pressed forward through her skin, her eyes no longer sparkled, her blond hair now appeared tow-coloured to her and hung limply, without life. Would Andrew see her as she saw herself? The key seemed to turn of its own accord and the door swung open to reveal Andrew, an outsize, bronzed Andrew, standing rigidly posed halfway up the stairs.

'Grace.'

He did not leap towards her but advanced slowly, taking one step at a time, his eyes riveted on her.

When he reached the foot of the stairs she

hadn't moved from the open door. Not until his arms came out towards her and he spoke her name again in a tone so deep it was akin to a groan did she fling herself forward into his arms.

'Darling, darling! Oh, Andrew!'

His mouth was moving in her hair, over her brow, around her face, and all the while she kept repeating his name, 'Andrew, Andrew.' When her mouth was covered with his the tenseness seeped from her body, and she seemed to fall into him, right through his hard bony frame into the centre of his being.

Clinging together, they went into the sitting-room, and, still together, they sat on the couch; and together they lay back, not speaking now, and kissed their fill.

It was some time later when Grace whispered, 'Aunt Aggie . . . where is she?'

'She had important shopping.' Andrew smiled whimsically. 'She's very tactful, is Aunt Aggie.'

They both laughed softly . . .

Half an hour later Grace lay gazing into Andrew's face. It looked healthy and attractive, made more so by the unusual white tuft of hair to the side of his brow. Her fingers moving over it lovingly, she said, 'It might have killed you.'

'It might, but it didn't . . . it didn't even give me a week in hospital . . . I was never lucky.'

'Oh, Andrew!'

'Only in finding you . . . there's no-one in the wide world like you.' He had her face cupped in his two brown hands.

'You still think that?' Her question had a plea in it, and he pulled her towards him and held her tightly as he said, 'I'll go on thinking it until the day I die.'

There was a silence between them now until he asked softly, 'Tell me, how are the children?'

There followed another silence before she answered him, and then her voice cracked as she said, 'Fine, they're fine.' In the silence she had pictured herself on the landing last night after she had received the news of his coming, when she had wanted to run into the nursery and say to them, 'Children, your daddy's home.'

A strange sadness was now enveloping her; it was seeping into the joy of the moment, depriving it of harmony, of its high pinnacle of easement, and all because it had been impossible to say to her children, 'Here is your daddy,' and also impossible to watch the light of ownership, the pride of the creator, as Andrew looked on his children after a long separation.

She had longed, ached, lived for this moment, and she told herself that this was heaven and she desired nothing more. She thrust at the sadness, pushing it away, denying herself incompleteness, denying that a vital section of herself was even now in the nursery at Willow Lea.

When Andrew, with a soft yearning in his voice, said, 'What does Stephen look like?' she refrained from saying, 'Like you,' as he had refrained from asking, 'Does he look like me?' but she compromised by saying, 'Tall, thin,' and then added, 'He could be dour at times.'

They laughed together at this, and he playfully punched her cheek before he asked, 'And Beatrice?'

She ran her finger down the bridge of his nose, saying, 'This is in evidence and I don't think it's going to add to her beauty.'

He touched his nose and the twinkle deepened in his eyes as he remarked, 'It's a decent enough neb . . . at least my mother always said so.'

'Mothers are prejudiced.'

'Are you prejudiced?' He was pressing her head into his neck now and she nodded it against him as she murmured, 'Yes, very much so.' Then she added softly, 'Wait until you see Jane. She's like her name, plain and podgy, but she's a darling.'

'Yes?' He went on stroking her hair, pressing her face into his neck, keeping it hidden so that she would not see his expression and she knew this. In yet another silence that followed she knew that they were both stalling, warding off the time when Donald's name must be mentioned.

The sound of a key turning in the lock relieved them for a moment, and when the drawing-room door opened they were leaning against the back of the couch, their faces wreathed in smiles, each with a hand outstretched towards Aggie.

'Will you have a drop of soda with it?'

'No, I'll take it neat, thanks, Aunt Aggie.'

Aggie handed the glass to Andrew where he sat at the side of the fireplace, then, sitting opposite to him and bending forward, she asked quietly, 'What is it, Andrew?'

Andrew swirled the drink around in the glass, looking at it the while, and then, leaning his head against the back of the chair, he cast his eyes ceilingwards before saying, 'The war was easier than this – at least I could handle my part of it.'

'Something gone wrong between you and Grace?' There was an anxious note in Aggie's voice, and Andrew brought his head quickly from the back of the chair as emphatically he said, 'No, no, not between her and me.'

'What is it then?'

'It's the children.'

'Oh.' Aggie nodded her head slowly.

He finished the whisky, and after putting the glass on the table at his hand he bent forward, and, placing his forearms on his knees, he looked at Aggie and said, 'You know I had visions of picking her up the minute I got home, her and the children, and my mother as well, and going off somewhere. I was even prepared to live on her money until I got a job . . . I knew it wouldn't take me long to find work. I even played with the idea of accepting your offer' – he smiled a little here before adding – 'even when I knew it was the worst service I could do you. I'm not made for selling things. Anyway, I knew I wouldn't be out of work. Wherever there was soil and cattle I would find a job. It seemed easy, simple, when I was all those miles away. It even seemed simple a week ago today when Grace and I met in this room, but it's simple no longer.'

'Did you go to the house?'

'Yes, I went to the house.' Andrew now turned his eyes towards the fire. 'I wasn't looking forward to meeting him. I felt . . . well, a bit scurvy somehow. That was before I saw him and then all that feeling went. I can't explain it, but when I

280

looked at him any remorse at my underhand dealings vanished. He didn't appear to me like a man at all. I hadn't the feeling I had betrayed a man. When he stood there with Jane in his arms and said to me, 'You haven't seen Jane, have you?' I could have taken it in different ways – that he was taunting me, for instance, telling me he knew all about everything, and yet I reasoned that if that was the case, then it would be impossible for him to act as he was doing at that moment, for he was jolly and laughing and his face looked open. I couldn't credit any man with the power of being so subtle, of being able to act such a part.'

'Where was Grace in all this?' Aggie put in.

'She went into the house. I don't think she could stand it.'

'I don't think so either.'

'You know, Aunt Aggie, I'd been a bit perplexed the first few days because Grace didn't talk about the children, but when I stood on that drive and saw him with the three of them I understood, for if ever I saw three bairns adoring a man it was those three . . . my three.'

His face was turned completely away from Aggie now, and she could only see his profile, with the ear and jaw-bone twitching. After watching him for a moment she said, 'I've been afraid of this, but it's something you've got to face up to. I, meself, have had to face it, Andrew . . . Grace can't take those children away from that man. Jane perhaps yes, but not the other two, and never Stephen, and she won't leave them and come to you without them.'

'I wouldn't want her to.' His voice was brisk and the words clipped.

'Well then, you've got to look at this thing squarely. You give her up and go away, or you carry on as you are.'

He had turned on her first words and now he answered them by saying, 'Oh, Aunt Aggie, don't be silly,' and then, moving his head from side to side, he added hastily, 'I'm sorry, but you know what I mean. There's no separating Grace and me whatever happens – it's one of these things that's there for life.'

'Well then, you've got to face the consequences, and don't forget, there's your mother – she won't leave the house. You're as tied as Grace is.'

'I know that only too well, but the awful thing is, Aunt Aggie, that I want the children more than ever now because of yesterday.'

'Yesterday? What d'you mean?'

Aggie watched Andrew pull himself to his feet and walk to the window and back before saying, 'Stephen said he didn't like me.'

'What? Stephen said that?'

'Yes.'

'How did that come about?'

'It was when I was on the point of leaving. Grace came out again; she was standing by the boy, purposely I think, and she said to him, "Say goodbye, shake hands with Andrew" . . . I went down on my hunkers and held out my hand, and . . . and he backed away from me and put his hands behind his back and said, "I don't want to, I'm not going to." Grace spoke to him sharply. I could see that she was vexed, so I made my goodbyes, and had just turned away when the boy said clearly, "I don't like him, I don't like that man" . . . It brought me round in my tracks like a bullet.'

Andrew's eyes were looking into Aggie's, and the pain in them struck at her so sharply that she put out her hand and gripped his, saying, 'Don't take any notice of that. Why you know what, I remember telling my own dad that I wished he was dead and I would like to bury him, and I was only eight.' She laughed at this point.

Andrew, ignoring the joke, said, 'Yes, yes. I've thought of all that about kids being funny and saying unpredictable things, but the unusual thing about it was that he . . . the vicar . . . never checked the boy. Grace was all het up, but not him; he didn't even react like a normal man in such a situation and threaten the lad with a skelped backside or something like that. He just stood there with a smile on his face. I felt dreadful, Aunt Aggie, I don't think anything will ever hurt me as much as hearing that child say "I don't like him". I felt in that minute that I couldn't risk going through anything like that again and I'd have to get away. I felt like that until I reached home and saw my mother sitting before the fire. She hadn't said much since I returned, but she must have sensed that there was something wrong and she started to talk. She told me she was all right and that she would manage, she had managed all the time I'd been away, and I was to make my own life . . . make my own life. And there she sat staring into nothing and all through me, and she was telling me to make my own life, and as I looked at her sitting there it came to me that I had no say in the matter, either about Grace, or the children, or her. If I left the fells that minute it would be alone, for neither Grace nor the children nor she would be with me. Nothing had seemingly altered; it was as if I had never been away . . . well, there it is, Aunt Aggie.'

Aggie said nothing; she was searching for words that would be of comfort to him. He had, she realised, already faced up to the situation before he came to her and he wasn't finding it pleasant. She rose and picked up his glass from the table and, going to the cabinet, she poured him out another whisky, and then she said an odd thing, 'Do you think Stephen's yours, Andrew?'

He did not take the glass from her but stared with narrowed eyes into her face before saying, 'What makes you say a thing like that, Aunt Aggie?'

'Here, take it.' She thrust the glass at him, then, sitting down again, she went on slowly, 'Well, a number of things. The lad's disposition, for one, for he's like neither you nor her in ways. Then his looks. There's not a feature of yours in him that I can see, Andrew. But the main thing that's set me thinking this is a bit of reading I did recently, it was by a doctor and he was on about . . . you know . . . well, about impotency. He said – the writer – he was a doctor – well . . . ' She hesitated, embarrassed in her attempt at this delicate explanation. 'Well, he said a man could be nearly impotent and yet be able enough to give a woman a child. Impotency didn't mean he . . . well, he wasn't fertile . . . These things have been in me mind a lot lately and I couldn't say anything to Grace. And if it was his you wouldn't feel so badly about the lad's rudeness, now would you?'

The whisky still remained untouched in Andrew's hand. He seemed to have forgotten it; he even seemed to have forgotten Aggie for the moment; and then, with a sudden lift of his arm, he threw off the drink in one go and put the glass down. 'I'd rather go on thinking he was mine even if he hated me guts, Aunt Aggie.'

'Aye, I suppose you would . . . it's only natural. There . . . I was just trying to ease you.'

He touched her hand. 'I know, I know.'

14

So the pattern of life was resumed, dominated by the circumstances that their love had created. Andrew went to work once again on Tarrant's farm with the promise of promotion . . . 'Perhaps to manager, who knew?' Mr Tarrant's own words.

Grace, once the jigsaw had fallen back into place again, tried to accept the situation. She had Andrew and that was all that mattered, she told herself. For days her mind would stay at a level of acceptance, until some subtlety of Donald's would send it spiralling upwards into a spasm of aggressiveness and hatred. One such occasion was when she came across him holding Jane high above his head; he was wriggling her fat body between his big white hands as he chanted over and over again, 'Daddy's girl, Daddy's girl,' only to break off and ask the question of the laughing face, 'Whose girl are you?' and then to give the answer, 'You're Daddy's girl.' It was a form of indoctrination.

She found the scene sickening, even sinister. There was something almost unclean in his insistence to lay claim to the children, especially this last one. She asked herself time and again how, knowing that the child wasn't his, he could try to project himself into her mind as her father. The words hypocrite and mealy-mouthed had ceased to have any meaning with reference to him. His attitude, his entire approach to life, needed words and exclamations that she herself was not capable of giving. She only knew that more and more proximity with him repulsed her. She shrank inwardly from him as if from something unclean. His sexlessness was more repulsive in its way than the extremes of a lecherous old man, and the miming of a father-figure more frightening than mad fantasy, and she was experiencing mad fantasy at nights now. In spite of Andrew's return – or perhaps because of it, because he was so near and yet so far – her nights were filled with dreams, mad fantastic dreams, dreams that she was wallowing among reptiles, flying, armless, legless, slithering white bodies, eyeless, mouthless, that turned themselves into hands, great soft white hands belonging to neither man, woman, nor child.

Then there was added to the complexity of her life something that was both irritating, and in a way humiliating, for Peggy Mather started to set her cap at Andrew. Openly, blatantly, she waylaid him, and openly she was rebuffed. As Adelaide Toole – now married to her cousin – had waited for him on the road as he returned from Tarrant's, so now, on certain evenings, did Peggy Mather. And as time went on and she made no headway the atmosphere in the kitchen suffered.

When they were together at Aggie's, Andrew would laugh about the situation with regards to Peggy Mather, as also did Aggie in an endeavour to make Grace see the funny side of it. But this Grace could not do; although Andrew was still only a farm-worker and she felt no shame in loving him, the fact that she was in a way contesting with a woman like Peggy Mather hurt her pride.

And then there was the cottage. She had never hoodwinked herself as to the reason why she had bought the cottage from Aggie. When it had failed to serve the purpose of a refuge for her and the children, she could have forgotten about it, but no, she determined to buy it, to make it her own, and not with the intention of it being a holiday home for the children. It was to be a place where she could be with Andrew alone for days, but strangely, except on two occasions, it never worked out like that. Andrew first saw the cottage during the second week after he was demobilised, when, accompanied by Aggie, he took his mother there for a short holiday. From that time on it became known in the village that Mrs MacIntyre liked, every now and again, to visit her sister in Devon. If during this time the vicar's wife went away for a week-end or a day or so to Harrogate or Whitley Bay with her aunt, who in their wildest dreams would connect the two incidents? Donald? Only once did he phone the hotel in Harrogate, and then Aggie answered him. Grace had gone on a day's coach tour, she herself was a little off colour. Late that night Grace phoned the house . . . and from the hotel in Harrogate.

The strains that this particular way of life imposed on her began to show as the months mounted and fell into years, and the stolen hours with Andrew seemed to have less power as a soothing salve as time went on. As the children grew, the silent battle for their love between her and Donald grew more intense. There were days when they did not exchange a word, not even at mealtimes, but communicated with each other through the children. 'Go and tell Mammy so and so. Go and tell Daddy this or that.' This form of strategy hoodwinked practically everybody except David Cooper.

In the village the parson's wife was known as 'a nervy piece', which was odd, they said, when the vicar himself was such a jolly chap, and so fond of the bairns . . . by, he was fond of them bairns.

At one period David Cooper felt bound to warn her of where she was heading. 'The brain is like a boil, Grace,' he said. 'Give it enough anxiety poultices, and it will come to a head and burst.'

The boil in Grace's brain took ten years to reach this point, and when finally it did burst it was not through the application of a heavy poultice but through what could be termed a light dressing in the form of Donald repeating a statement he had made many years previously . . . he was going to engage a part-time gardener . . .

It was on an August afternoon in 1957 that Donald made this statement, but it was preceded earlier in the day by an incident with Stephen.

The boy had locked his door, and when Grace went to go into his room and found the door shut against her she asked for an explanation. Stephen, a slim, tall youth, still looking like neither his father, nor his supposed father, nor yet herself, told her that Donald had suggested him locking his door because he was being pestered by his sisters and it prevented him from getting down to study.

'Very well,' she said, 'then leave the key where I can get it. Peggy must clean the room and I want to see to your school things.'

When with a coolness that could have been termed insolence he answered her with, 'I'm not leaving it about, Peggy can come and ask for it,' she suddenly screamed at him, 'Stephen!'

Stephen, his face paler even than usual, was standing looking at her with a frightened look in his eyes when Donald bounced up the stairs.

'What's the matter?' He glanced quickly from one to the other. Then, his gaze coming to rest on Grace and his voice dropping into a tone of reprimand, he said, 'Screaming like that! What is the matter?'

'It is about the key, Father. I locked the door.'

'Oh! Really!'

The vicar closed his eyes for a moment. Then, looking at Stephen, he said quietly, 'Leave it to me,' and indicated that the boy should go down-stairs. And he waited a moment before looking at Grace again. Then, still in a subdued tone, he said, 'Have you no control, yelling like that? Aren't you aware that Beatrice has two friends in the garden? What will they think?'

Her tone was as low as his but of a different quality as she hissed back at him, 'I don't care what they think. Do you hear? I just don't care what they think.'

'Well, you've got to care, especially what . . .

what ours think. They are young people growing up, full of impressions, they are—'

'Oh, my God! Be quiet before I . . . I . . .' She choked, then gasped, 'Full of impressions! Yes, they are full of impressions. And what have you done with their impressions over the years?' She was thrusting her face up to him now. 'I've just seen the result of your impressions. My son dislikes me . . . Impressions . . . impressions . . . my son dislikes me. Do you hear? He was coolly insolent to me. He was showing me one impression you have given him of me.'

Donald, his face stiff and white, looked back at her, and his words were still quiet as he went on, 'I am not going to argue with you, now or at any other time. That's what you want, isn't it, to brawl and argue. Splash your emotions all round the house for everybody to hear. I never have argued and I'm not going to start. The only thing I'm going to say is that, whatever your son thinks of you, I'm sure you deserve it.'

As she watched him walk away there came a strong animal desire in her to leap on his back and bear him to the ground. She rushed into her room and, gripping the bed-rail, stood looking down on to the bed. He had achieved what he had set out to do: made her son dislike her, and without saying a word against her, for he was too clever to malign her. He had done that: turned her son against her. She wanted to run to Andrew, just run to him and look at him and become calm. Andrew could make her feel calm. But Andrew was in Morpeth, at the market with the cattle.

It was nearly two hours later when she went downstairs and into the dining-room, and saw through the open french window that Peggy had set the tea near the willow tree. In the far distance behind the line of firs she could hear voices coming from the tennis court, a recent addition to the garden. She was about to step on to the paved terrace when she saw Donald coming across from the court accompanied by a young man. She recognised him as Gerald Spencer, the brother of Beatrice's school friend who lived in Morpeth. He was in some car business. She didn't like him, he was too brash, but his sister seemed a nice girl. The tennis players now came round the trees, Beatrice and her friend, Stephen and Jane, and Jane as usual was not walking but hopping and dancing from one foot to the other, waving her racket over her head. And now she threw it up in the air yelling, 'Mammy! Mammy! We beat them, Joyce and I beat them.' She raced across the lawn and did a war dance in front of Grace, and Grace, putting her hand out, said, 'Jane, stop a minute.' She was listening to what Donald was saying to the young man.

Donald's arms were stretched wide and he was saying, 'Not for love or money, they can make so much more in factories, you know. I've been without help now for nearly three weeks and it's beginning to look like it.' He gave his ha-ha of a laugh. 'I'm not much of a gardener. I did try my best during the war, but, truthfully speaking, I'm not a man of the soil.' Again there was the ha-ha. At this point he turned a chair round for the guest and looked towards Grace, yet as she stepped across the terrace he continued as if unaware of her presence, 'I'll get a part-time man as I did before the war, just a few hours a week, and things went very smoothly then.'

'If you are anything like we are, you'll find the part-time ones as difficult to come by as the full-time ones.' The young man buttoned up his coat, then unbuttoned it. It added an air of authority to his words.

Donald was handing the guest a sandwich as he replied, 'Oh, well, you know, you're in the town and we're in the country. People are different in the country. Oh' – he turned his head between Grace and the young man – 'I forgot. You have met my wife, haven't you? Yes, of course you have. What I mean is, you've seen each other today?'

The young man shook his head in denial and smiled, but Grace remained still. Somehow she was waiting for Donald to go on and he did. As she poured the tea out he sat down on the left of her and, stretching out his legs, carried on the conversation, addressing her through the guest this time. 'I thought of asking Andrew MacIntyre again,' he said.

That was all.

The cup Grace had in her hand clattered to the tray, bringing all eyes to her, and as Donald's hand came out to rectify the damage she smacked it aside and, getting up from the chair, rushed into the dining-room. But she hadn't reached the hall before he was behind her.

'Grace!' It was an order and not a quiet one now. She took no notice but sprang up the stairs, and when from the foot his voice cried again, 'Wait! Do you hear me? Come here this minute!' she turned. She was at the head of the stairs now, and looking down on his upturned, outraged countenance, she cried, 'You . . . ! You . . . !' The saliva was spluttering from her lips. 'You'll bring Andrew MacIntyre back as your gardener. With just a lift of your little finger you'll bring Andrew MacIntyre . . .'

'Grace!'

'To hell with you! You try to stop me talking, go on!' Her voice was rising. 'You swine! You swine of a parson! You cruel, sadistic, unnatural swine.'

She saw him bounding toward her, taking two stairs at a time, and when he gripped her by the shoulders she struggled to free herself, yelling now, screaming now, mouthfuls of abuse. The boil had burst . . .

She was on the bed and he had one hand over her mouth while with the other he pinned her shoulder to the mattress. Her straining, staring eyes saw the amazed faces of the children in the doorway, and when Donald cried, 'Get away and close that door!' she saw Beatrice and Jane disappear, but not Stephen. Staring-eyed she watched him moving timorously towards the bed and heard Donald cry angrily, 'Get out of here at once.'

Donald did not look at the boy, and when he realised that Stephen was not obeying him he yelled, 'Get out! Do you hear? Go on, get out . . . Ring Uncle David . . . now, at once.'

As she struggled to draw breath into her

panting lungs through her nostrils she was aware that something had burst in her head. It was in a way a relief. Words were still pouring into her mouth but she couldn't get them out. Cunningly now she became calm, and when she stopped struggling Donald slowly relieved the pressure on her mouth and shoulder. She waited, watching the seconds as it were, waiting to pick the right one. When it arrived she gave a leap and was free from his hands and in a second was on the other side of the bed and the poison from the boil was once again flowing. But now it was more terrifying, for she was laughing at it, and him . . .

'The gentle parson. Dear, dear Vicar. Dus yer mother want any coke? dus Kate want any coke? I mustn't talk Geordie. Oh no, it isn't refined. You've shut my mouth for years, haven't you? But no longer, no longer. The children mustn't hear me. The children . . . our children . . . Oh, that's funny. Our . . . our . . . OUR children! Stay where you are! If you come near me I'll tear you to bits, I will! I will . . . !' She was screaming now, her arms hooked, her fingers clawed . . .

When she felt her nails tear at his flesh the laughter stopped in her and she was enveloped by fury alone.

Once again she was on the bed, glaring up now into his blood-spattered face. He was holding her from all angles. One of his knees was pinning down her legs, with one hand he was gripping her two wrists, while with the other he kept her mouth shut. He was visibly worn out and was showing it when the door burst open and David came into the room. But he did not release his hold on her, he merely turned his face silently towards the doctor.

Grace became still as, over the rim of Donald's hand, her eyes beseeched David, calling loudly to him.

'Let her go.'

'You must give her something first.' Donald's voice was thick.

'I will in a minute. Let her alone.'

'But . . .'

'Leave her alone.' The words were more like a bark, and Donald, after a moment's pause, lifted his limbs one after the other cautiously away. And when he stood at the foot of the bed wiping his face with his handkerchief, Grace hitched herself up into a sitting position and, grabbing at David's hand, started again, 'He's . . . he's a devil, David . . . a swine . . . a bloody swine. You said I should . . .'

'Now, now, Grace.' David's voice was quiet.

'But, David, David, I can't stand any more . . . I'm going away . . . I'm going away now, to-night. I must get away. I'll take Jane. He's got Stephen . . . I'll never have Stephen . . . David, Stephen doesn't like me, he doesn't. My son doesn't like me. Oh, I must get away. I'm going . . . You . . . you bloody . . . !'

'Now, now, stay where you are.' David took one hand swiftly out of his case on the side of the bed and stopped her from rising, at the same time speaking to Donald over his shoulder, saying, 'It would be better if you went.'

When Donald did not move, Grace with another spurt of energy made to rise from the bed, and David, holding her hard now, said soothingly, 'Now, Grace, be still. Lie quiet and let's talk this over . . . eh? Look, stay still just a minute. Do that for me, will you?'

After a moment he took his hands away but kept his eyes on hers as he went to his bag again, but Grace was staring past him now at Donald, and although she didn't move she began to talk once more. First in a low mixture of abusive swearing, then suddenly her voice rose almost to a scream, and David, the syringe in his hand, said, 'Quiet, quiet; they'll hear you in the village, Grace.' He smiled tenderly down on her.

'Let them, let them, David . . . They laugh about the vicar's wife in the village, do you know that? I'm one of the war-time jokes . . . the vicar's wife locked herself in the cellar the night of the raid. Everyone else turned out to help but not her, oh no. She dropped the key and couldn't find it. That's rich, isn't it? She dropped the key and couldn't find it. And when the lights went out, there were no bloody matches either . . . for why? 'Cause the vicar had swiped them, that's how it goes, the vicar had swiped them. Serve her right. Oh!' She put her hand quickly towards David's. 'That hurt, David. What is it? What are you doing? I'm going away . . . Kate Shawcross set that yarn around, but he told her. You told her, didn't you?' She leaned forward, glaring at Donald. 'Dear Kate. Dear, dear Kate. When I'm gone you'll have her here, won't you? She liked this house, I can't leave it a minute but she's up here . . . Oh, I know, I know. I've got a spy, too. You'd like to know who it is, wouldn't you?' Her voice was becoming quieter. 'Oh yes, you would, so you could take it out on him an' all.' She did not mention Mr Blenkinsop, and she addressed herself now to David, but with her glassy stare still on Donald. 'D'you know what his latest is, David? You'll never guess, not in a month of Sundays, you'll never guess. The sadistic swine. He's going to ask Andrew to come and do the garden . . . just like that.' She snapped her fingers. 'As if he was a serf, so he can torment me and make me pay for my—'

Her voice was cut off on a gulp as her mouth was once again compressed but this time vertically as David gently pressed her cheeks together and said, 'There now, no more of it . . . And why shouldn't Andrew MacIntyre do the garden, eh? Although I don't see where he'd get the time.' He shook her face gently as he stared down into her eyes, compelling her to silence. 'Andrew's a good gardener, none better, which I've often thought is an odd thing in a farmer. Now, now,' he pressed his hand tightly across her chest, 'lie still, you'll feel better in a minute. You're going to sleep now. There now, there now. Lie still, that's a good girl, that's it.'

It was some minutes later when he released his hold on her and she lay limp looking at him. Her lips moved slowly as she said, 'David . . . Jane . . . I want Jane.'

'Jane will be all right. There now, close your eyes. Jane will be all right. I'll see to Jane.'

When her eyes were closed David stood watching her, and when her hand slid off her chest he raised her eyelid and let it slowly drop back into place. Then turning towards Donald, he said briskly but without looking at him, 'I must phone for an ambulance.' He rapidly arranged the instruments in his case before closing it.

'An ambulance?' Donald was still mopping the bleeding scratch on his face.

'Yes, an ambulance.' David now looked straight at him and asked pointedly, 'You don't think she can stay here, do you?'

'No, no.' Donald's voice was flat. 'Where will you send her?'

'To Rockforts if I can get her in.'

'Rockforts?' Donald's eyebrows moved upwards.

'Yes, Rockforts, where else? I suppose you are aware that something has snapped.'

Donald said nothing, only stared at David, and as David returned his look he saw the protective skin close over the vicar's eyes. He had seen this look before and he wanted to shout at the man, 'For God's sake come clean! Come into the open. Isn't this lesson enough for you?' But he knew the futility of such an appeal. If the girl on the bed hadn't been able to get through the barrier there was little chance that he would succeed. The man's pride and ego were a protection stronger than armour plating.

'What are they likely to do with her?'

David was moving towards the door as he said, 'Put her to sleep, I should suppose, for as long as she can take.'

'And then?'

David was at the door, and he turned and confronted the minister and said flatly, and now without the semblance of any sympathetic feeling for the man, 'Try to undo twenty years of strain, I should think . . .' The straightening of Donald's body did not check his closing remark, for as he turned from him he said, 'And I wouldn't count on her coming back here. In fact, I would go so far as to say the knowledge that she won't have to return will be about the one thing that will bring her back to normality . . .'

But here David was wrong, for a year later Grace returned to Willow Lea.

15

Yet, as David had foretold, it was the knowledge that she was not going to return to the house that helped Grace's recovery. She always looked back on the first three months at Rockforts as her initiation into hell. For the first week there she had slept; she would wake and be given food, then go to sleep again, and this pattern seemed to go on for years in her mind. But when finally they allowed her to wake up and she realised where she was, the shock wiped out any good the long sleep had achieved. She became a bundle of visibly trembling nerves. She was in an asylum, she was going mad . . . if she wasn't already mad, she was going mad. Nothing could convince her otherwise; even the electric-shock treatment only succeeded in dulling the fear for short periods. Until she came under the youngest of the three resident doctors. She took to him because he was not unlike David, or rather as David had once been. Brown-headed, slight of stature and bouncing with energy. It was he who first took the now intensified fear of swearing away from her. What was swearing, anyway? She could swear if she wanted to, it was her only weapon, that's why she had used it. He encouraged her to talk about her childhood. He came to know Jack

Cummings and the coal depot. But it wasn't until he learned about Andrew that he saw the whole pattern, and the pattern became clear-cut in outline when she hesitantly told him of her first meeting with Andrew on the night she had tried to lure her husband by standing naked before him.

Another thing the young doctor managed to reassure Grace about was that her power to love would return to her, for now all feeling had left her, all feeling of affection and love. She thought of Andrew, but not with love, only with fear because she felt she loved him no longer. She had no feeling for anyone, not even Jane. And she couldn't cry.

It was not until she had been at Rockforts for six months that the desire to regain complete normality began to stir within her. But even so she had no desire to go back into the world. She had a very nice private room; she walked for long periods alone in the grounds; and the thought that she would one day have to leave this place became as frightening in its way as when she first realised that she had come into it.

Andrew was the first person she saw from that other world, for her past life appeared now as if it had been lived in another world, and she was amazed at her reaction to him. She sat on the seat by the stream that ran through the grounds, her hand in his, but no thrill of love stirred in her. She felt dead inside. It was as if she had had an operation and the organs that registered emotion ripped out of her. Vaguely she felt comforted in Andrew's presence, yet strangely undisturbed by his nearness, or his sadness.

When some time later she asked to see the children, only Beatrice came. Stephen was at college and Jane was at boarding school. But Beatrice came and their meeting roused in Grace the first stirrings of maternal feeling again, accompanied by one of surprise, for Beatrice, never demonstrative, flung her arms around her neck, and not only kissed her again and again but hung on to her while the tears streamed down her face. Grace could not help but be touched, yet she did not cry with her.

It was during Beatrice's third visit, when once again with her arms round Grace's neck and the tears streaming down her face, that she begged her to come home. Because . . . because . . . and then it had come out in a garbled rush. She wanted to get married, she must get married . . . she must . . . she must. Grace had pressed her away and looked at her, and then she knew the reason for Beatrice's need of her.

She did not send for Andrew; it was David she sent for, David would know.

Yes, David said, Beatrice was pregnant and the shock had caused Donald to have a heart attack. He was in hospital. It was the first time anyone from outside had spoken of her husband to her for a year, and David assured her that should she come home again she would not be likely to meet Donald, for he was in a bad way and there was a possibility that he might never come out of hospital.

It was some time before the fear of returning to the house itself – even knowing that Donald was no longer there – was overcome. But as the days went on Beatrice's happiness became more and more important to her. And on the day she said to herself, 'She is Andrew's daughter, not his' – on this day she informed the doctor of her decision, then phoned David, and wrote to Andrew . . .

Andrew received the letter when he returned home from work. Mrs MacIntyre took it from the mantelpiece and handed it to him immediately he came in the door. It was the first letter Grace had written him since her illness, and before pulling his coat off he sat down and read it. After a moment he said quietly, 'It's from Grace.'

Mrs MacIntyre was standing by the table, her almost sightless eyes bent towards him. 'I had a feeling it might be,' she said.

'She's coming home.'

'Back to the house?'

'Yes.'

'Oh, Andrew . . . why?'

When Andrew told her she sat slowly down, but did not speak, and after a time he put his hand across to her and said, 'Don't. Don't cry.'

'But . . . but she's had enough. Why has this to happen an' all? It's as if there's a sort of . . . influence there . . . in that house, holding her there, bringing her back to it. I thought now that . . . that you and she would have made a fresh start.'

'I'm thinking that the sins of the fathers are not waiting for the third and fourth generation, we are both going to pay in this by being kept apart until we die.'

'Don't talk like that.'

'Well, I can't stand the thought of her going

back there. I imagined she would have gone to the cottage, for a few months anyway, with Aunt Aggie having it all fixed and waiting . . . Funny.' He moved his head slowly from side to side. 'I don't feel any concern about Beatrice. I suppose that's unnatural.'

'No. No, not at all.' His mother wiped her eyes. 'It's just because you're so concerned about Grace . . . I suppose it's that Spencer boy you were telling me about.'

'Yes, it'll be him all right and I can't say anything against him, for who am I to pick holes – in that direction, anyway.'

'It was different with . . .' Mrs MacIntyre did not finish and, as her voice trailed off, Andrew's head came up and he said, 'What is it?' He got to his feet and went and stood by her and again he said, 'What is it?'

Her two hands were pressed tightly on her stomach, her head was bowed and the sweat was oozing out of the pores of her forehead. He put his arms about her, and when at last she was able to speak she pointed towards the ceiling and said, 'Tablets in the top drawer . . . in a bottle.'

Five minutes later Andrew, crouched on his hunkers before her, said in an unsteady voice, 'How long have you known this?'

She let her eyes linger on him before she answered, 'About two years.'

'Good God.'

The two words condensed the searing compassion he was feeling and he bowed his head before her.

*　　*　　*

Grace did not like Gerald Spencer, but at least she thought he had one asset – he was not impotent. The concern in her mind now was to keep any disgrace from Beatrice, and this lifted her thoughts from herself and helped her more than anything else could have done at this time towards readjustment.

Although at times she was subjected to bouts of terrifying fear of the dark, and swearing, and thought she was back to where she had been at the beginning, at others she knew, and knew with certainty, that only now was she seeing the whole situation in its right perspective, for she faced the fact that she would never be free to go to Andrew until her children were settled. Her love for Andrew was seeping back into place, but it was subject, as it had always been really, to the children's welfare.

She had decided also, and quite calmly, that if she heard that there was the remotest possibility of Donald returning to the house she would take a long holiday, and Jane would go with her. This could be accomplished without scandal, for to the village she was still ill. Those who had been in an asylum were never . . . well, the word used was . . . right. They would say, 'They're never right, you know.' To the majority, the stigma of an asylum could only be thrown off by death. Grace was painfully aware of what the villagers thought, but this same opinion, she knew, would relieve her of their condemnation should she remove herself from the needs of a sick husband.

Oddly enough, since her breakdown she had acquired a greater fear of scandal than ever before. Had the truth come out years ago she herself would have been the main sufferer. But not now. Her family were no longer children; they were a young man and two young women at vitally impressionable stages of their lives. Nothing must affect them.

If there was one thing she was grateful for now it was that she had been prevented from screaming out the truth on that dreadful night a year ago.

Yet again things did not work out as she planned. Two months after Beatrice had married, David told her that Donald was leaving the hospital and was going to a nursing home near Hove, for he was still very ill, but the very next day he walked in through the front door and into the drawing-room.

It was one evening early in the spring of 1959. Andrew MacIntyre was doing the garden, Jane was curled up on the couch where it was placed before the window, and Grace was sitting by her side, her hands lying idle in her lap. She was watching Andrew. She always felt soothed if she could look at Andrew; she seemed to draw quietness from him and into herself. His rhythmic movements, which appeared slow, but which speedily disposed of the work, were a kind of joy to her . . . Andrew was good. She would say to herself numerous times a day: 'Andrew is good.' It seemed to sum up his whole character . . . his faithfulness, his reasonableness, and his patience, mostly his patience.

His mother had died three months ago, and it

would not have been surprising, now he was released from that shackle, and knowing that she herself could not again bear to live in the same house with Donald, had he pressed her to go away with him. At times she had a strong feeling, and not only recently, that inside, under his patience, he was straining against the unnaturalness of his life. It would become most apparent when, held tight against him, she felt the not infrequent force of his passion. But when she would say, 'Oh, Andrew, we just can't go on like this', as she had done over the years, he would reassure her, saying, 'Patience. Things will pan out.'

Meetings were no easier to arrange than they had ever been; in fact, if anything they were more difficult, for now there were often four pairs of eyes to be wary of. Only last night, when she had pointed this out to him, he had said, 'Remember years ago, when I told you I could love you without touching you? Well, that still holds good.' Then for a few moments he had loved her fiercely. Andrew, she had learned, was a strange mixture of passion and reticence. She could not fully understand him – and considering that during all the long years of their intimacy the hours they had actually spent together amounted only to a matter of weeks, this was not to be wondered at – she could only be glad in the depths of her heart that he was as he was . . . Andrew was good. The actual words were once again crossing the surface of her mind when she heard someone enter the room.

After she had slowly turned her head, her hands

jerked upwards and clutched at her throat. She could not rise, she just sat in a twisted position, staring.

Donald sat down on the first chair nearest to hand. He looked desperately ill, weird, gaunt and ungainly; there seemed nothing of the suave parson left. He sat looking at her quite impersonally, and in this panic-filled moment she knew he wanted nothing from her, nothing at all, not even pity. Neither had he any for her. She knew that for him she had died quite finally that night of revelation in the bedroom, when she became no longer any use as a face-saver.

Still sitting in the twisted position, and too stunned to move, she watched Jane, who gave an almost agonised cry, fly to him and fling her arms about his neck. The demonstration seemed too much for him, and after patting her head he pressed her from him and asked if she would get him a drink of water.

Taking a long, gasping breath, he once again looked at Grace. Then in a few terse, unemotional words, he told her why he had come back. He knew he was to die soon, and he wanted to do it in his own home.

As in years gone by, there welled up in her a flood of pity for him, but as she continued to stare at him, the man himself, the man in the soul of him, the suave, evasive dispenser of mental torture, pressed against the feeling and it subsided. But strangely, she did not doubt his word. She did not say to herself, 'He has only come back because he knows I am alone with Jane, and he is afraid he will lose his power over her.' No, she believed him.

That his attraction for Jane had lost nothing in his absence she witnessed in the next second. Returning at a run with the glass of water, Jane hovered over him like a mother over a sick child. And Grace knew as she looked at them together that if she went upstairs this minute and packed she would leave the house alone. She could no more take Jane away from him now than she could have taken Stephen years ago. The very suggestion that she should leave her sick father would, Grace knew, lose her her daughter now. No, if she went she would have to go alone. But she couldn't lose Jane, she couldn't. She had lost the others, she couldn't lose Jane. She must talk to Andrew . . . Andrew . . . Andrew . . . She cast her eyes to where he stood rigidly stiff, his eyes riveted on the window, then she pulled herself up from the couch and made her way towards the door. And as she left the room, neither Donald nor Jane seemed to notice her going . . .

Three weeks later, Donald, as good as his word, died, and so prevented her from having to take refuge with Aggie. He did it dramatically one evening on the steps of the altar. And who should be with him there at the end but Kate Shawcross. Grace was not sorry that this should be so, for she had loved him. But what sickened Grace was the significance the postmistress gave to it. Throwing all discretion aside, she declared openly to Grace while her face streamed with tears that God had willed that Donald should die in her arms, and that he had done so with her name on his lips. She was so distraught she made no secret in the village of what she spoke of as the Will of God.

The village buzzed as villages will. Kate Shawcross was a fool, it said, and brazen with it. Fancy saying a thing like that! Then as usual two and two were put together and conclusions jumped to. No wonder the poor vicar's wife had gone off her head. And everyone remembered how often the postmistress had gone up to Willow Lea when its mistress was absent. Well now, would you believe it? And they did believe it. Until Christmas week, 1960, when Peggy Mather opened her mouth.

PART THREE

Grace was the only one seated. She sat at the end of the couch, her head bowed, her eyes fixed on her tightly joined hands resting in her lap. At the head of the couch Andrew stood with his left hand pressed into the padded upholstery. To his right, and both standing with their backs against the end of the grand piano, were Beatrice and Jane, and on the hearthrug in front of the fire stood Stephen. Grace could see his legs and his knee caps twitching from time to time. She could not bear to look at him and see the hate of herself pouring like steam from his bloodless face. His colour was that of rice paper, his skin had the same smooth texture. He had been talking for some time, spewing words out, words coated with venom, words that ill-became a prospective man of the Church. But at this moment Stephen was nothing but a young man fiercely defending his heritage and denying with every pore of his body the claim of this rugged Scot as his father.

'. . . If you . . . if you were to go on your knees and swear on the Cross I wouldn't believe you, do you hear? I know what I am, I know where I came from . . . inside here.' He thumped his chest, and the action, although intent, had nothing dramatic about it. 'I know I'm like my father. My father, do you hear? His thoughts are my thoughts, his ways, his principles, everything . . . everything . . .'

Grace raised her head, and Andrew, thinking she was about to protest, placed his hand on her shoulder. But Grace had not been going to protest. She was just looking at her son to try to convince herself that he was wrong, for listening to him she was imagining that it was Donald who stood once again on the hearthrug, his back to the fire. And it wasn't Stephen's stance alone that conjured up Donald, for even without the slightest facial resemblance to Donald he was, at this moment, almost his chosen father's double. The doubt that had assailed her over the early years from time to time recurred, and if it would have been any help now she would have said, 'All right, there is a doubt, take the benefit of it.' But she knew, even if she could have made the last great effort and brought herself to say such a thing, that it wouldn't have helped in the least. She had talked for what seemed hours trying to tell them the facts while endeavouring not to blacken Donald, trying to put him over as David had always described him . . . a sick man, even knowing as she talked that this was merely white-washing. But in spite of her knowledge she had done it, and with what result? Merely to bring forth Stephen's hate. She knew that her son had never really loved her, but now his distaste of her amounted to loathing. Whatever reaction the girls would make had yet to be seen, but one thing was already certain – she had lost Stephen. Yet hadn't she lost him even as a baby? Yes, but the pain hadn't been like this.

As she unloosened her hands and pressed them to her throat Andrew spoke for the first time.

'Whatever you say, it makes no difference. I know how you feel' – his voice was low and steady and held no bitterness – 'but the fact remains, whether you like it or not, I'm your father.' Yet as Andrew stressed this statement, a point in the conversation he'd had with Aggie after his demobilisation sprang to the forefront of his mind, 'Impotency didn't mean a man wasn't fertile.' Whenever he and Stephen had come face to face in the past few years he had denied this statement entirely, but now, as he looked at the young man he was claiming as his son, he acknowledged for the first time a grave doubt, for he could see no trace of himself or his forebears in the ascetic face that was glaring at him. No-one had spoken in the pause and he now went on: 'If your mother had done as she wished she would have taken you away when you were a baby, but she stayed here for my sake. I was tied here, as she's already told you. But these latter years she has remained here not for my sake, but for yours, all of you.' His eyes moved to the girls. 'She wanted to see you all settled before . . . before she began to live her own life.'

Grace's head drooped again. Yes, that had been her main concern, to see them settled, with no scandal emanating from her to spoil their lives. She realised now that, strangely enough, this had always been the main purpose of her life, to keep herself clear of scandal. Her attempts to leave

Donald she saw now as half-hearted gestures. She had submitted herself to years of mental torture not so much to be near Andrew, but to keep herself unsullied in the eyes of her children.

Even the breakdown and the language she had frothed out at the time had left, as far as she could see, no adverse impression on them. Rather her illness had aroused their compassion. But now here, at the very last minute, she had to be exposed to them and in such a way that it would appear that either fate or God was determined to make her pay for her sins . . . Or was it perhaps the spirit of Donald still at work, justifying himself and his principles? As ye sow, so also shall ye reap. Whatever it was it was weird . . . uncanny, that the instrument chosen to expose her should be Jane's beloved George. That this man she had seen only twice, and for a matter of minutes each time, should be both accuser and deliverer was in itself, she felt, beyond the bounds of ordinary happenings.

She raised her head to look towards Jane, but was caught once again by the glare of Stephen's face, and he was speaking to her. He was answering Andrew by speaking to her. 'No matter what he says . . . what he says, I don't believe a word of it, do you hear?'

He was shouting now, and Andrew put in sharply, 'Don't speak to your mother like that. Say what you have to say to me.'

'You . . . !' Stephen moved from the rug and it seemed for a moment that he was going to strike out at the man before him. But when Andrew neither spoke nor moved he recovered himself, and after turning one last long look of loathing on Grace he rushed from the room, banging the door behind him.

Grace pressed her throat tighter. He would leave the house, he would go back to the college. Her fingers were hurting her neck as she thought, 'That is the last I will ever see of Stephen.' She turned her head quickly and looked towards the door. Stephen. Oh, Stephen. Slowly now her eyes turned on to the girls. Beatrice was staring at her, but Jane was looking at no-one, her head was sunk deep on to her chest and she was so still she might have been asleep on her feet. She looked back towards Beatrice and from the look on her face she could almost tell what she was thinking.

Beatrice's mind was moving rapidly as, fascinated, she stared at her mother. All these years she had had a lover, and he only a farm manager . . . and a mere farm-worker at one time; and now she wanted to say that this man was her father . . . and that Daddy hadn't been capable of giving a woman a child . . . it was shocking. And the things she had said were shocking, really shocking. Yet vaguely she understood the reason for her mother going off the rails, for she knew that life would be impossible without . . . it. It being the thing her mother had inferred her father had lacked. But she couldn't think of Andrew MacIntyre as her father, she never would be able to. It was awful, really awful, and the worst of it was Gerald knowing. Her mind touching on her husband, she thought bitterly, 'He started all this. He could have warned Andrew about the man, but no.' And she didn't believe he hadn't guessed her mother was the woman, he must have. He was getting his own back and all because he couldn't have the money. She had been married to Gerald less than three years, but she knew her Gerald – he was spiteful. But that had given her a shock too . . . there being no money. She couldn't take it in that her mother was broke and there was nothing to look forward to in the way of a legacy, and nothing for the child either. She looked her mother over now, at the quiet elegance of her dress, at the heavy diamond and ruby ring glinting on her finger. She looked a woman of means. Would she mind being poor? No . . . no, she knew somehow she wouldn't; she would be quite content in a cottage . . . the cottage . . . with him. She could not look at Andrew although she knew he was looking at her. Andrew, the superior spare-time gardener, whom her mother liked to refer to as a friend of the family, was one person, a likeable person, but when he turned into your father that made him into another person, a detestable person. She hated him, almost as much as Stephen did. And her mother . . . her mother had made herself cheap, horribly cheap. It was understandable for anyone falling – she had the grace to blush at the thought – but to keep it up for years and years and with a working man like Andrew MacIntyre, it was beastly. She could stand no more, she must get home, even if it was to row with Gerald. She could almost hear him saying, 'That was why she took it all so calmly, us having to get married. Kind . . . huh!' He must get the car out and get them away from here before dark. What a Christmas Day! It was terrible, shocking. And not one of them had had a bite of dinner. She dropped her eyes from her mother's as she said, 'I – I – we'll be going home. I – I can't talk now.' Then, like Stephen, she hurried from the room, but without banging the door behind her . . .

There was only Jane left. As Grace looked at her younger daughter she began to tremble. If Jane turned against her, if her reactions followed those of Stephen and Beatrice, she couldn't bear it. She forced herself to say, 'Come here, Jane.'

When Jane did not move she pulled herself up from the couch and, after a quick glance at Andrew, she went towards her.

'Jane.' She leaned forward to take one hanging hand into her own, but it was jerked upwards away from her.

'Oh, Jane, please, please look at me . . . Please.'

When Jane at last answered the desperate plea, it was as much as Grace could do to meet her eyes. Stephen had looked at her with hate, Beatrice with shocked incredulity, but the look in the young girl's eyes showed neither hate nor incredulity. Grace could see that Jane believed all she had been told and that she was hurt and bewildered, but above all else she was shamed.

'Jane . . .' Grace forced herself to go on. 'You have always liked Andrew, now haven't you? You know you have. Why, just yesterday you defended him to Stephen.'

Jane's eyes dropped from her mother's and her young face became hard as she murmured, 'I – I wouldn't have if I'd known.'

'Don't say that.'

'It's all right.' Andrew came slowly towards them, his voice unusually humble as he said, 'I understand. And you will too, Jane, later, when you're older . . . and married.'

'Married!' Now Jane was looking at him and she repeated, 'Married! I'll never marry now, you've spoiled it all. George will . . .' With a swift movement she turned her back on them and leant over the piano.

'George is a good man, I'm sure of that; everything will be all right.' As Andrew finished speaking he looked at Grace and nodded in the direction of the hall, and she took it to indicate that he was going to speak to George. As she watched him leave the room her thoughts, leaving Jane for a moment, went out to him. Poor Andrew, what he must be feeling to be looked down on and spurned as he had been in the past few hours and to take it all without exploding. Andrew was big; in all ways Andrew was big.

'How could you? How could you, Mammy?'

She was startled when Jane swung round to her a moment after the door closed, and she did not reply for some seconds, and then rather wearily, for of a sudden an overwhelming sense of deflation was sapping her, she said, 'I've told you all I can . . . it's as Andrew says, you won't understand until you're older.'

'I'll never understand . . . Daddy was so—'

'Stop it, Jane.' Grace's voice had a cold ring to it now. 'Don't make me say things I'll be sorry for.'

'Oh.' Jane shook her head helplessly. The tears began to pour down her face and in a broken voice she exclaimed, 'I can't stay here . . . I can't. I'll . . . I'll go with Beatrice.'

'No, you won't go with Beatrice. You'll stay here.'

'I won't . . . I can't . . . Can't you see, it would be unbearable?'

'You were going to George's people on Tuesday, wait until then.'

'No, no, that'll be over.'

'No it won't, darling.'

'Don't touch me.'

Grace almost jumped back, so sharp was Jane's recoil. Then, after one long bewildered look at her mother, she turned from her and stumbled out of the room, her hands covering her face.

'Jane! Oh, Jane! Don't, Jane.' Grace was muttering to herself now as she stared towards the blank face of the door, then almost like someone advanced in years she moved towards the couch. She felt alone as she had never done in her life before; even the thought of Andrew could do nothing to fill this gaping void . . . Jane, Jane. She had relied on Jane understanding . . . it didn't matter so much about the other two, not really . . . but Jane. She put her hands between her knees and pressed them tightly. If only she could cry and relieve this unbearable feeling. Almost the last words of the doctor at Rockforts came back to her: 'You'll cry, never fear, and when you do you'll know you are better.' It was a paradox. If only she could cry now; this was the time she should cry, this moment of realisation that the main efforts of her life had been wasted.

*　　*　　*

Gerald was in the dining-room. He had his back to the wine-cabinet. His chin was thrust out and nobbled with aggressiveness, and he stood tall to enable him to look down on the smaller man, as he growled, 'Who the hell do you think you're getting at? I've told you I didn't know it was her. What bloody business is it of yours, anyway?'

'I should've thought that was plain even to someone as thick-skinned as you.'

'Now look here—'

'Oh, stop your blustering. You can't get away from it, you intended to show him up. You knew when I spoke of his wife he hadn't one, but you couldn't get us face to face quick enough. You know what I think of you? I think you're a nasty swine. A word from you and I would have been on my guard and the man would have played up to it – they both would have played up to it; but no, you let me in there and break up a family . . . You know, I could cheerfully murder you at this moment . . .'

'You'd better be careful.' Gerald had stepped from the cabinet and, stretching still farther, he cried, 'D'you hear what I say? You'd better be careful.'

'Of what?' The cold question was as rebuffing as a blow, and Gerald felt it, but was saved by the door opening.

Beatrice immediately sensed the tension between the two men and the reason for it, also the fact that her husband was getting the worst of it. She said rapidly, 'Get the car out, we're going home.'

'Yes, and I should damn well think so.' Gerald

resorted to the supporting habit of buttoning up his coat, then, turning to the man, he said, 'But let me tell you. I'm not finished with you over this. I'm going to have this out.'

'Any time you like.' The voice was restrained, and as Gerald barged from the room the man moved to the door and held it while Beatrice, with her eyes averted, passed him. He was still holding the door when he saw Andrew.

Andrew waited until Beatrice and Gerald reached the landing, then he walked slowly into the dining-room. After the man had closed the door behind him they faced each other.

'I can't think of anything to say – only I'd like you to know I'm sorry to the core.'

'That's all right.'

'I never for a moment guessed, you believe that?'

'Yes.'

'What can I say, I'm all at sea. I – I—'

'Don't worry yourself, it's one of those . . . well, coincidences they would say. I've always felt it would come out one day, but Grace . . . she felt it was all over when he went, and we were safe – she was just waiting until . . . until Jane was settled . . . will this make any difference?'

'Don't be daft, man.'

For the first time in the past three hours Andrew's face relaxed from its grey grimness. The reply, couched in such a familiar and ordinary phrase, said all he wanted to know.

'Thanks.'

'I love Jane, I mean to marry her. I did the first moment I saw her. I would have come here before, but . . . well, she was so young. She told me she was a year older than she really is, you know.' He smiled. 'But now it can be as soon as possible. The sooner the better, I would say.' He paused now before adding, 'I never, of course, met the vicar, but I'm glad that you are her father.'

He held out his hand.

From where she sat near the bed Grace heard the taxi draw up in front of the house, and she stopped herself from rising and going to the window. Jane had said she would write. Her head bowed as if the shame was hers, she had stood in front of her a few minutes ago and murmured, 'I'll write, Mammy.' That was all. 'I'll write, Mammy.' Jane, her daughter, had left her . . . She put her forefinger between her teeth and bit hard on it.

Would that man be good to her? Yes, yes, he would. As Andrew said, he seemed a good man. He had apologised to her with such deep humility for being the instigator of the trouble that she had to reassure him that he was not to blame. And then he had said, 'Let me take Jane to my home. I can make up some excuse for bringing her . . . suspected polio . . . or something. And I can assure you she will come round . . . I'll do my best to see that she does. Trust her with me, will you?' He had taken her hand, and then he had said, 'I liked your Andrew the first time I saw him. I like him even better today.' Yes, he was a nice man, a good man.

There came now the sound of the taxi starting

up. She got to her feet and began walking about the room. This was what she had been wanting for a long time, wasn't it, for Jane to be settled and them all to be gone. But not in this way, not to scuttle from her as if from a leper. That's what she was to them . . . a leper.

The house was quiet now. There was no-one in it but herself and Peggy Mather. Her head lifted on the thought. Yesterday, even this morning, she had been afraid of Peggy Mather because of what she knew. Now she was afraid of her no more. She would be down in the kitchen now licking her lips over the day's happenings, knowing that her tongue would be free to wag. This past three weeks must have been a torment to her. Was it only three weeks since Andrew and herself had been confronted by her at the door of the cottage? They had just kissed good night, and when Andrew opened the door he still had his arm around her and instead of drawing it away he had jerked it more tightly still when they were enveloped by the light from a torch. It seemed only a split second before he was flashing his own torch on the intruder and she had gasped aloud when it revealed the purple, suffused face of Peggy Mather. Andrew acted as quickly as if his wits hadn't received a shock. In a minute he was facing and talking to the outraged cook. She could hear him now. 'One word from you about this and I go to Miss Shawcross. You're depending on getting what she's got, aren't you? Well, you won't stand a dog's chance if she knows you've done time, and you needn't bother denying it either, for I happened to be passing away an hour in court at

Durham one day when I saw you being sent down . . . stealing from your employer, pilfering here and there. Six months is what you got, and it was your third offence, if I remember rightly.'

Peggy Mather had not denied this. The strange thing was she hadn't spoken at all . . . perhaps the shock had been too much for her. She had pretended for a long time now to hate Andrew MacIntyre, the reason being that Andrew from the first had shown her plainly he wanted nothing to do with her. But why had she gone up to the cottage that night? Neither Andrew nor she could see any reason for it, except a rather delicate one but they would really never know now. Certain they were that it hadn't been to spy on them, for she had been the most startled of the three.

And now she was down there in the kitchen laughing up her sleeve. Well, let her laugh. Perhaps she wouldn't laugh so much after she had heard what she had to say. For she would say to her, 'I won't be wanting you after tomorrow, Peggy. I will pay you an extra week's wages in lieu of notice.' She would pause, then add, 'That is when you return the number of things you have taken from my house over the years . . . there are two rings and the gold watch that disappeared during my illness . . . you ascribed their disappearance to a hawker who passed through the village, I remember. And then there is the set of miniature Georgian salt cellars . . . but you will know what you have taken.' She would be cool and cutting. She'd had to put up with Peggy Mather over the years because her dismissal would have offended

Miss Shawcross. Well now, this is where she could hit back.

But when some time later she entered the kitchen and saw Peggy muffled up ready to go, she said none of these things, she merely looked at her straight and said, 'I won't be needing you any more after tonight, Peggy. I will send your money and cards down tomorrow. You had better take your aprons with you.' She pointed to a drawer.

After returning her look with a dark, venomous blaze for some long seconds, Peggy tore open the drawer and hauled out her aprons. Then, confronting Grace, she muttered, 'To be pushed off like this after all these years . . . by God, I'll have me own back!'

'I have no doubt of that, Peggy, but I should advise you not to start until the end of the week when I'll have left the village. It would be a pity if at this stage your aunt and you had to part company.'

The look that Peggy levelled on her reminded Grace of Stephen, and when the kitchen door banged she went to it and, after locking it, stood with her back against it, her eyes closed and her breath coming in gasps. Well, that was over. Thank God that was over. It was all over, all the secrecy, the lying, the fear. She was alone . . . alone. She opened her eyes and saw the emptiness inside of her widen until she felt she would drown in it. The next minute she was running through the hall and up the stairs and into her bedroom. Pulling the curtains back from the window, she held them wide for a second, then closed them before opening them wide again. Through the gap where the beech had stood she expected to see a speck of light far up on the fells. He said he'd be waiting for her signal. There was no speck of light. Oh, Andrew, where are you? Come quickly, quickly. She turned from the window. The house was so quiet, empty, bare. She walked on to the landing . . . 'As ye sow, so shall ye reap.' 'Ask and ye shall receive.' She had asked for Andrew and she had got him . . . at a price. But where was he? He said he would wait for the signal and come down at once. Oh, Andrew. She stopped at the head of the stairs; it was as if a hand had come out from the ornate frame and halted her. Slowly she turned her head and looked up at Donald. For a moment she imagined his eyes moved. His whole face seemed to be moving, smiling, a self-satisfied proud smile . . . there was a supercilious lift to his lips. 'As ye sow, so shall ye reap.' She put up her hand and crushed the flowers entwined in the frame . . . then slowly her fingers relaxed. She had not sworn. She looked back into the eyes and whispered aloud, 'You can do no more; I will be happy in spite of you. I can even have another child . . . do you hear that . . . another child.'

But no . . . she turned from the picture and went slowly down the stairs . . . no more children, only Andrew.

Andrew! She stood in the centre of the hall; the house was so lonely. Had anything happened to Andrew? What if he had fallen out there on the fells, he could lie there all night . . . Don't be silly, don't be silly. Andrew knew the fells like the back of his hand. She would phone Aunt Aggie and tell her what had happened. What was she talking about? Aunt Aggie was down at the cottage. She had thought it would be a change to spend Christmas there. Hadn't Andrew gone down with her and her friend to see them settled in, and stay with them until Boxing Day? That had been the arrangement. But he hadn't been able to stay away, he had come back. If only he hadn't come back . . . Be quiet, be quiet.

She went into the drawing-room and looked about her. It looked gay . . . tree, lights and holly. This was Christmas night and the house was dead. She put her hands to her head, and as she did so the front-door bell rang. She ran like a child to it, and when she opened it and saw Andrew standing there she fell against him crying, 'Oh, Andrew! Andrew!'

'There. There.'

'I signalled and you didn't answer . . . I was frightened.'

'I've been outside for some time. I couldn't stay up there any longer. I've just seen her go.'

'Oh, my dear, let me take your coat.'

'No, Grace, I'm not staying here.'

'What!' Her mouth was agape.

'And neither are you. We couldn't start our life here. Not in this house. Go and get your coat, wrap up well. I'll put out the lights.'

'Yes, yes, Andrew.' She turned quickly from him and ran up the stairs, and in a matter of minutes she had joined him again. He looked at her for a moment, then, pulling the collar of her coat up around her neck, he led her towards the door, and when they reached it he switched out the last light . . .

It took them nearly half an hour to get to the cottage, and as she stood taking off her outdoor things Andrew lit the lamp and in its first fluttering gleam she saw that he had prepared for her coming. For there before the fire and between the two worn armchairs was a set tea-table, warm and inviting.

'Oh, Andrew!'

'Sit yourself down and leave this to me . . . this is my show.' He was smiling at her. 'No talking now, just sit there.' He pressed her into the chair and touched her cheek once before turning away to make the tea. When he had done this he sat opposite to her, handing her food and pressing her to eat, looking at her all the while, and her heart and spirits began to lift under his look. His face appeared almost boyish again in the lamplight. After some time, during which he still continued to look at her in this odd sweet way, she said, 'What is it, Andrew?' His eyes left hers for a moment and he leant towards her across the flame of the fire and took her hands. And when he looked at her again he said softly, 'I've dreamed of this for years, ever since the day I saw you in the kitchen, and you seemed to hold those roses out to me. It's a fact, night after night I'd see you sitting just there, and I was always pouring the tea, not you . . . Funny, and it didn't end there.'

'No?'

'No.'

'Tell me.'

'Later when I've cleared away.'

And later when he had cleared away he came to her and, pulling her up gently, placed her on his knee, and they talked, not of the happenings of the day, but of the cottage near Buckfastleigh and how he would find work on one of the farms near at hand. She knew this too was part of his dream.

Some time later still, the fire banked down, the lamp turned out, he picked her up in his arms and, walking sideways, carried her up the narrow stairs; she laughed into his neck. And when on the tiny square of landing he placed her on her feet and, chuckling himself, said, 'It was much easier in the dream,' her laughter rose, filling her body, shaking her as if with ague, until with a burst her mirth exploded in a torrent of tears which seemed to spring from every outlet of her face.

'Oh, Andrew! Andrew!'

'There, my love.'

'Nothing matters, Andrew; nothing matters any more. Nothing, nothing . . .'

Only the loss of Stephen and Beatrice . . . and Jane . . .

Oh, Jane. Jane.

THE END

SLINKY JANE

Catherine Cookson

CORGI BOOKS

Chapter One

The village of Battenbun lies on a hillside in
Northumberland. The village proper is shaped
like a half moon, with its back closely wooded,
and houses two-thirds of the population of a
hundred and seventy-four; which number includes
Tilly Boyle's son, Tony the half-wit, seven children of Mamie Spragg, each of whom just fails to
qualify for the pseudonym of Tony Boyle, sixty
women over fifty, fourteen men over sixty, eight
over seventy, and one coming up to ninety.

The last mentioned, Grandpop Puddleton, lives
and has lived since he was born in the central
house of the village. This house forms the key-
stone of the village street, and from the outside
it appears very picturesque, being built of stones
filched from the Roman Wall and the dead quar-
ries, and timber that had once been part of a boat
that traded along the Tyne. Inside, it consists of
seven rooms, each in its own way a death-trap,
with ceilings so low as to brain you with their
beams and floors so uneven as to whip your feet
from under you. That all the Puddletons born
during the past ninety years have survived is a
tribute to their staying power.

From nine o'clock in the morning till the light
fails, except for meals and the calls of nature,

Grandpop Puddleton sits fully dressed and with his cap on before the front window, in his armchair on the raised dais which lifts him a foot above floor level, and watches the milling world of the village pass to and fro, and also what occasional traffic deems to make a detour from the main road three miles away which leads to Allendale.

Cuddled in the nest of the half moon is the village green – without a pump in its middle, for in nineteen forty-four an American lorry under the influence of drink, the driver at the inquiry having denied that he was, dispensed with it. And so now there is just a stretch of grass with a ring where the pump once stood, and the grass is divided in two by the feet that will persistently cross it in the same place. Beyond the green is the road, and beyond this Mrs Armstrong's house, which is also the Post Office and General Stores, interrupts one of the finest views across to the South Tyne. Although some miles from the actual river, the fells that run towards it, billowing with woods, heaths and lush green valleys seem but a cascading overture, spilling and tumbling, for ever tumbling, down to it.

At least that is how Grandpop Puddleton sees it, for when he takes his eyes from the interests of the street he is away once more, striding over the fells after his sheep, his dog at his heels, sometimes in the direction of Allendale, sometimes farther afield to Blanchland. Ah, Blanchland is a bonny place, as near as fine as Battenbun. Some say finer, but this is only because more folk see it, for out of the way as it is, it is easier to get at than

Battenbun. But whichever way Grandpop goes in his mind, eventually he comes to the river, the bonny Tyne. Some folk madden him when they refer to the Tyne as mucky. They are the folk who never push their noses past Jarrow or Newcastle; they are the stay-at-hyems who don't even know that there is a North and a South Tyne and have never heard of Peel Fell or Cross Fell; they know nowt about their country's history, about its castles and abbeys, its Roman Wall, its patchwork of dry-stone walling, evidence of the art of forgotten men. They are 'pluddy numbskulls'.

When Grandpop brings his eyes back to the village he can see, to the left and without glasses, the far end of the crescent where the painted sign of the Grey Hart swings. And when he turns them right, to the other point of the village arc, he can see the garage, owned and run by his great-grandson Peter. Wherever Grandpop's eyes roam between these two points, to Miss Tallow's house-window drapery shop or Wilkins the baker on the garage side, to Bill Fountain's the butcher on the Hart side, or to the numerous grey stone houses that lean, bend over, or stand back independently from each other, invariably they come to rest on the garage.

It was nearly a year now since Grandpop had been to the garage. His legs one day refusing to obey his orders had deposited him quite suddenly on his buttocks opposite the Mackenzies' house, next door. And Grandpop had said, 'Blast 'em!' . . . if they had to give out why had they to do so on that particular spot and why had he to be helped to his feet by that upstart sharp-shooter of a Davy, who was out to get the better of their Peter at every turn. The Mackenzies were town upstarts, the whole lot of 'em. He'd said that twenty-five years ago when they first came here, and he still said it, and if their sickly-looking, psalm-singing, cow-faced daughter caught their Peter he'd give the whole family hell he would.

This reference of warmth to come was not promised to the Mackenzie family but to his own, composed of his son Joe, his grandson Harry, and Harry's family of three sons, the twins, seven years old, and Peter, twenty-eight – and of course, Rosie their mother, whom he hated, the main reason being her refusal to allow a dog in the house, not even to please Peter, and him the apple of her eye . . .

Along the street, Peter came to the wide doorway of his garage and listened – over the years he had developed an ear for 'knockings'. He held his big, dark head to one side until a little anticipatory smile appeared on his face, bringing with it the glad thought that something was wrong there.

He could see nothing of the car yet, for just beyond the garage the road turned in a sharp curve, to become lost for miles on the fells before linking up with a main road again.

The knocking, accompanied by a loud rattling, came steadily nearer, but not wishing to appear too eager for what he hoped would be a job, he did not go to the end of the drive to meet the car.

When it did come into view he almost laughed aloud. No wonder she was rattling. In the past eight years he had seen some has-beens in cars, but this beat them all. She looked older than anything that went into the Old Crocks' race, but without any of the spruceness that was the hall-mark of such cars.

As the front wheels touched the gravel of the drive the car, with one final splutter, gave up and Peter, moving now hastily forward, looked through the windscreen at the owner before saying, 'In trouble, miss?'

He had hesitated between mam and miss. That the girl sitting at the wheel was a town type he could see, but whether she was old enough to be a mam or young enough to be a miss, he couldn't at such short notice make up his mind.

'Yes, she's given up . . . Still, I got her here.'

The voice was warm and high, and, as he phrased it, a laughter-making voice, but he was quick to note that it was in strict contradiction to the owner's face. There was no laughter on her face, not even a vestige of a smile, and it was perhaps the whitest face he had ever seen . . . due, he had no doubt, to smart make-up. Yet why they wanted to look like that he didn't know.

He opened the door and she stepped out onto the drive, and again his mind was taken from the car and he thought, By! she's thin. But it was, he also noted, a smart thinness, accentuated by a grey woollen dress pulled in at the waist with a scarlet belt. She was wearing no stockings, only sandals, and his eyes lifted quickly from the matching scarlet of her toe-nails up to her shoulders, on which lay the ends of her long, straw-coloured hair. It looked damp, even wet, as if she had been sweating, and it lessened a little the effect of her over-all smartness.

'Has she been like this long?' He inclined his head to the car.

'About a mile back. I felt her hit something in the road.'

He nodded understandingly. The car was an Alvis, one of the early type, and likely had a low oil sump. 'I'll push her in and look her over.' As he spoke he went behind the car and with his back bent he slowly edged her up the drive and into the garage.

At the opening he turned and looked back to where the girl was now standing in the middle of the drive. She was slowly and methodically wiping her hands on a handkerchief, and she raised her eyes and, looking towards him, said, 'It's a nice little village.'

He nodded. 'None better.'

'Battenbun . . . the name's intrigued me for days. I wanted to come and see what a place with a name like Battenbun could look like . . . it's pretty.' She turned her eyes and looked over the village green. 'And quaint,' she added.

'Aye, it's quaint all right.' He smiled as if she had paid him a personal compliment. 'Not a quainter or prettier village in Northumberland.'

'It's difficult to get at.'

'Well – aye, it is, but I suppose that's part of its attraction.'

She nodded understandingly. 'It hasn't been commercialised yet.'

'No. No, it hasn't.' But how I wish it was, he thought; then chided himself, No, you don't! You know you don't. No, he didn't want Battenbun commercialised, but what he did want was a bit more traffic through and a few more jobs like this one here might prove to be. It was twelve o'clock in the day and but for Honeysett's tractor he hadn't seen anything on wheels go past the garage. And it was a bonny day, a fine day, a day when cars should be whizzing about. They were whizzing about all right, but miles away on the main road.

'How long will it take you to find out what's wrong?'

'Well, I'll get down to it right away. Perhaps you'd like to have a meal . . . Look, down yonder, at the far edge of the village there's the Hart. Mrs Booth does a good dinner.'

'Does she?'

'Aye, she does.' He smiled as he looked at her; then he took his eyes from her, for she was staring at him in a fixed kind of way. Her eyes, he had noted, were brown, large, like saucers in her white face, but tired, lifeless. Only her voice seemed to hold any animation.

As he looked away from her he happened to see his father running up the green from the direction of the Hart and making for the house. This was so unusual that he lifted his head and his eyes narrowed in the sun. His father never left the Little Manor before ten to one, landing home dead on one for his dinner. And when he waved to him excitedly before entering the gate he was made to think, 'What's up? What's wrong?'

'Do you live here? I mean in the village?' The girl was speaking again.

'Yes.' He drew his eyes slowly back to her and

repeated, 'Yes . . . dead centre. Our house is the black and white one.'

'Are all the houses old?'

'Not all – some. Ours is the oldest, goes back four hundred years. It's got the date on it. There's been Puddletons there for over two hundred years.'

'And your name's Puddleton?'

'Yes, I'm a Puddleton. My great-grandfather's alive, and he's near ninety . . . my grandfather is seventy-two.'

'You're all long-livers then here?'

'Yes, I suppose you could say we are. Plenty of fresh air, peace and quiet. Nothin' much ever happens here . . . you can time everything and everybody nearly every hour of the day.'

She was standing gazing at him, her hands hanging slack by her sides as she asked him, 'Do you like it that way?'

Now he became a trifle embarrassed. If he were to speak the truth half of him would say 'Aye . . . yes, I do. I don't want anything to change,' but the other half would say, 'I want a bit more business, and that means a bit more life.' But whichever way he would have answered her was forgotten, for at that moment his whole attention was brought to the village green again, for there in a huddle, and making their way towards him, were his father, his grand-father and his mother. Now what on earth was up!

So unusual was the sight of his family coming en masse to the garage that he had the desire to go and meet them but courtesy told him he had a customer, so all he did was to move a step or two onto the drive and await their coming.

His father, away ahead of his grandfather and mother, reached him first, and one thing about him was strikingly noticeable. His face was abeam. This was unusual, at midday anyway, without a drink . . . or a woman to chaff.

'What's up?' he asked. 'Won the sweep?'

'Sweep? No. What d'you think?'

'I don't know.'

'Road's goin' through!'

The effect of these words on Peter was electrifying. His six-foot-two long angular body stretched, his head reared up, and the beam that split his face outdid that on his father's.

'No! Who told you? How did you hear?'

'The major. He's just got back from Hexham. Saw his solicitor, Ludworth. Ludworth told him the road business is set. Of course, the major's furious . . . you know what he thinks about it.'

'This is news, eh, lad?' It was his grandfather speaking, and Peter answered, 'Yes, Old Pop, I should say.'

'We're set for life now.' The old man gazed around him from one to the other, until his eyes alighted on his daughter-in-law, and his look, so evidently full of the pints that future prosperity would bestow on him, wiped the bright gleam from Rosie Puddleton's face, and she said, tightly, 'Not so much of the we!'

'Now! now! Ma,' said Peter under his breath.

The 'Now! now!' was an entreaty, but Rosie would have none of it. Looking up at this great big son of hers, she spoke to him as if he were still in his teens. 'Never you mind, I know what I'm talking about.' She nodded at him, then at her father-in-law, then at her husband, and Harry Puddleton exclaimed, 'That's goin' to start now, is it?'

'It's never stopped as far as you're concerned,' said Rosie; 'you never wanted me to buy the garage for him.' She bounced her head towards Peter. 'It was a dry well you said, no good, money down the drain. Forgetting it wasn't your money that was going down the drain.'

Just as Harry, his face darkening, was about to turn on his wife, Peter put in soothingly, 'Now, now . . . look here, there's enough time for all that later. And anyway – ' he threw his glance back to the girl standing in the opening of the garage, and his voice sank, 'Anyway, I'm busy.'

Harry, following the direction of Peter's eyes, stared for a moment at the girl, and the smile slowly returned to his face. Then remembering with a self-conscious blinking the presence of his wife, he turned his attention to the matter in hand again and exclaimed excitedly, 'You'll be busier still, lad. Just think!' He took a step back and his eyes swept over the garage, which had at one time been the blacksmith's shop, then on to the piece of spare ground to the side, and he murmured in something like awe, 'Only garage for miles, and only bit of spare land in village, for it's a known certainty that the major won't let them build on his ground.'

'There's Poynter's tree nursery,' said Rosie; 'he's got a good bit of land there.'

'And a good bit of income coming in from it. He's no fool, he won't sell that.'

'Well, there's the wood . . . don't forget that,' said Rosie, seeming bent on dampening her husband's enthusiasm.

'The wood!' It was Old Pop who turned on her. 'Who's goin' to build on that? The springs have it like a piece of wet yeast. The wood!' he said scornfully.

'They can drain,' snapped Rosie.

'You can't drain springs, woman. They would pop up all over the place, under the floors and everywhere. No, as Harry says, that bit of land—' he pointed towards the side of the garage – 'that bit of land is the only buildable bit for miles, at least where it's needed most, on the main road. The farms can't do nowt, theirs is agricultural land. No, you've no opposition, lad.'

As Old Pop was waving his hand about indicating the absence of opposition, his thoughts suddenly skipped away from garages and land and he, too, became aware of the girl. His grin widened and his eyes brightened, especially the one with the cast in it, and, touching the thin grey tufts of hair on the front of his bony forehead, he nodded brightly and called, 'Goodday, miss.'

The salutation brought all eyes round to the girl, reminding Peter that he had a job in hand, and he moved towards his client, saying apologetically, 'I'm sorry, miss, but we've had a bit of news we've been expecting for a long time.'

'Yes.' She looked from one to the other and smiled faintly; then added, 'I'll go down to the inn as you suggested. Will you let me know the trouble?'

'Aye, I'll come down as soon as I've looked her over.'

She moved away, and as she came abreast of the group on the drive, the cast in Harry's left eye, similar to that in his father's, twinkled and he said, 'Beautiful day, miss.'

'Yes. Yes, it is.'

Their eyes followed her, as if drawn by a magnet, and Peter, standing apart, also watched her go. Her walk reminded him somehow of her voice, lazy yet vital. He couldn't place her at all. She was an odd type, bit of all sorts, he thought. He noticed that she did not take the foot-worn path across the centre of the green but was walking in the grass, and this added to the slight sway at her hips.

It took just this movement alone to arouse the familiar 'Well!' in Rosie. She glanced quickly towards her husband. Like a vulture he looked, as did his father. They were all like vultures, the Puddletons, that is, all except Peter. She glanced towards her eldest son. He was of the same height and build as the other two, big-boned and dark, but not cross-eyed, thank God!

'Well, Dad, what did Grandpop have to say about it?'

This question of Peter's that touched on a still more poignant thorn in Rosie's flesh brought her swiftly from her critical comparison, to put in sharply, 'What he usually has to say, swearing and carrying on.'

Harry, ignoring his wife's remarks, answered

Peter with a laugh, saying, 'Cursing his "pluddy" legs as usual, because they won't carry him no father than the back door. But he's game, he made an effort to come along wi' us, didn't he, Dad?'

Old Pop nodded and laughed as he remarked, 'Aye, he did an' all. Some spunk the old un's got.'

Spunk! thought Rosie, with a whirling of agitation in her stomach that she always had whenever this bane of her life was mentioned. I wish his spunk would bring on a fit and he'd die in it, I do, honest to God! Ninety a week come Saturday, and by the looks of him could go on for another ten years. She turned her back on the group and raised her eyes to Heaven in silent prayer, but quickly brought them to earth again as Harry remarked sharply, 'See there . . . there's Mackenzie.'

They all turned, and in silence looked to where a short, thick-set man was edging himself from a car outside the cottage below their own.

'I bet you what you like he's got wind of this, and not just the day either.' Harry turned and looked at his son. 'What made him come last week and ask you for a share, eh? That was funny, when you come to think of it. And after them always holding us up as nitwits for buying. Aye—'

A loud, sharp sniff cut off Harry's words, and brought his eyes to Rosie again as she said flatly, 'I'd like to remind you, Harry Puddleton, that us didn't buy it. Oh, you can come round now.' She waved her hand airily. 'Oh, I know. I also know that you've been on at me for the last six years for spending me dad's money on it.' And she ended, by saying flatly, 'This is Peter's and mine, and the money it makes will be ours . . . see!'

Harry Puddleton glared at his wife. Sometimes she aggravated him so much that he could murder her. He had to keep telling himself that she was a good mother. She was also a damn fine cook. Oh yes, he would always admit that. And their house was the most comfortable in the village – if only she would let you stay in it in peace! But as she got older she was getting worse. He knew that in his wife's eyes he was woman-mad. She had only to see him look at a woman and in her own mind he was already sleeping with her. All the Puddletons he had ever heard of had had an eye for a woman. It was their natural trait, that is – Harry paused in his thinking – all of them except Peter. He sometimes thought that Rosie had thwarted all natural desire in this strapping son of his, for never, to his knowledge, had he had what he himself would call an affair. He was nice enough with the lassies, but nothing seemed to get beyond that. You couldn't call the business of Mavis Mackenzie an affair, although it had caused a stink in the house last night.

Then there was Miss Florrie . . . But nobody was supposed to know about Miss Florrie, least of all Rosie. Rosie would have a fit if she thought that Peter had any ideas about the major's daughter. He was sure, in his own mind, that Peter hadn't. It was Miss Florrie who was doing the running there. She was a strong character was that young lady and, like her father, usually got what she wanted. But to get back to Rosie. One of these days, if she wasn't careful he'd walk out . . . he would that.

Mr Mackenzie having disappeared into his house, their attention was drawn once again to the girl now nearing the Hart, and to Bill Fountain, the butcher, who was standing outside his shop waving his hand to them while with his hips giving an exaggerated imitation of the girl's walk.

And there's another of them, thought Rosie. Another one that can't keep his eyes at home.

'Look at Bill wobbling his belly . . . mickying her, he is. Oh, he's a lad. Let's go down and tell him.' Harry turned to his father. 'Not that he'll be over-pleased either, for he's got the daft idea the road'll take some of his custom away . . . Come on. See you later, lad, and then we'll talk.' Harry nodded to his son and, followed by his father, hurried from the drive on to the road, while Rosie, nodding after them, said, ' "And then we'll talk!" What have they got to talk about?'

'Now, Mam.' Peter looked down on his mother. 'Don't go on.'

'They make me sick. What have they ever done to help? They've been at you for years about this place. Saying you couldn't give it away, and you should go on the buildings or some such . . . be another Mackenzie and try to own the village.'

'Don't worry, I'll go me own way as usual.' He smiled gently at her. And when she answered his smile the hard lines went from her mouth and a softness came into her eyes, and, patting his arm, she said, 'If you're all right, lad, I'm all right.'

He nodded down at her. 'I know that, Mam.' It

was a shy admission. And then he added, 'But don't go for Dad, he doesn't mean anything.'

Her head moved in small jerks from side to side. 'Doesn't mean anything! Oh, I know what I know. But there, I must get back and see to the dinner.'

'Be seeing you, Mam.'

He smiled once again at her before she hurried away, and he watched her compact body bustling over the green towards the house. Poor Mam. In spite of her iron will and dominant attitude, he always thought of her as 'Poor Mam'. But she should be better, he thought, when the road came through, for with it would come water, and this would mean a bathroom, one to outshine anything Mrs Mackenzie would have, of course. He smiled to himself. And why not? Why not, indeed! He himself wanted something to outshine the Mackenzies, especially Davy, the only fellow in this village or anywhere else who had ever been able to get his goat.

Honeysett's tractor came wobbling back up the village street, and he waited for it to wave an hello to George before turning finally into the garage to have a look at the job in hand.

Perhaps it was the rumble of the tractor that covered up the sound of the approaching horse, for he had just lifted the bonnet of the car when a voice from the doorway said abruptly, 'Hello, there,' and he turned with a definite look of apprehension on his face to confront a short, slim young woman in riding kit.

'Oh! hallo, Florrie.' His voice and everything about him showed his uneasiness and confusion, and as she slowly approached him he bent his head down towards the engine.

'Look at me!'

His head jerked up and he looked at her where she stood at the other side of the bonnet, and he almost spluttered as he said, 'Now, now, Florrie. Now see here!'

'Why did you do it?'

'Do what?' He had grabbed up a handful of tow and was rubbing his hands with it.

'You know what I mean. You took Mavis Mackenzie into Hexham on Saturday, didn't you?'

'Now, Florrie.'

'Didn't you? And out again on Sunday – didn't you?'

Florrie's voice was so tight that she seemed to be finding it a bit of a struggle to get it past her lips.

As if making an effort, Peter straightened his shoulders and, looking squarely down into Miss Florence Carrington-Barrett's face, said, 'Yes, I did. And what of it?'

'What of it! You are a fool. If I'd been here you wouldn't have had the nerve to do it, would you?'

Throwing the tow into the corner and taking up a fresh lump, Peter continued with his rubbing as he said, 'Look, Florrie, we had all this out last week. I told you it was no good . . . never could be. You'll only get yourself talked about.'

'Talked about!' She almost spat his words at him. 'What do I care about being talked about? It's you who are afraid of being talked about. You haven't the guts of a louse. You're petrified of your own shadow . . . and your mother.'

'Now, look here, Miss Florrie!'

It would seem that the mention of his mother had recalled to his mind the title by which the daughter of the manor was spoken of in the house, and it brought a minor explosion from the young lady. 'Oh, for God's sake! Peter, come off it, and stop the Miss Florrying. You know, I could laugh – if I wasn't so mad I could laugh – you're acting like one of last century's melo-dramas. Miss Florrie!'

'Well, it won't do. I've told you afore.'

'All right.' Florrie's voice was getting higher. 'Say it won't do, and say you've told me before. Was that any reason to take up with that nitwit after you had dodged her for years?'

'Mavis is all right.'

'Mavis is all right!'

'She's a good girl.'

'She's too damn good. Sanctimonious little hypocrite. She makes me sick. And you do, too!'

'Well, I'm sorry you feel like that, but as I said last week, me mother would have a fit if she thought I was making up to you.'

'Let her, it's about time she realised you are grown-up. You know, when I look at Old Pop and Grandpop and your father, I can't believe you're a Puddleton. Why, they've got more of what it takes in their left eyes than you've got in your whole body.'

A pink hue crept up under the dark stubble of Peter's face; his head moved slowly from side to side; which other woman or man for that matter, of his acquaintance, would refer openly to the Puddleton morals and the family cast in one sentence? What could a fellow do? All he could think to say was, 'By! you are coarse, Florrie.'

'Coarse!' Florrie's scorn was vigorous: 'It wouldn't surprise me to know that you're an hermaphrodite!'

'Florrie!'

Although Peter wasn't sure in his own mind what an hermaphrodite was, he knew, by the way she had said it, it was bound to be something indecent.

'I'm going to tell you something.' Florrie was now stabbing her finger at him. 'If you hide from me behind Mavis Mackenzie you're in for fireworks. Once that little cat has her claws into you you won't be able to get them out, and now that the road's going through, as I suppose you know, her dear papa and brother, for business reasons alone, will see that she keeps them tightly fastened on you. They're not going to let the only garage for miles slip through their hands. They'll have it, with her help, and you. You'll see.'

'Will they, be damned!' Now there was no nervousness in Peter's voice or manner. 'Will they? That's where you're mistaken. There'll be no Mackenzie get a foot in here, not even over my dead body. The garage, as you know, belongs to me mam and me, and she, like me, would sooner see it go up in smoke than the Mackenzies get it.'

'That's what I couldn't understand. I just couldn't understand—' Florrie was now staring up into Peter's tightly drawn face – 'you hating the Mackenzies like you do and then taking up with Mavis. I just couldn't understand it. Until the reason jumped at me. You hoped to put me off, by doing it. That's the truth, isn't it? You thought I'd have too much dignity to come back at you. Daughter of the major and all that . . . You don't know me.'

'No, now, see here, Florrie.' Peter's fiery countenance was abetting his guilt. 'I – I can't explain.'

'No, you can't explain, you haven't got the guts to. You'll dance at the hops with me, ride with me, but you won't walk with me. I'm too young.' She mimicked his voice. 'Ten years makes a lot of difference. You don't say you haven't got the spunk to face Mammy, or the village.'

In hopeless desperation Peter closed his eyes. But when he opened them his attitude immediately changed and with a quick gesture he turned his attention hastily to the engine again and whispered, 'Here's Miss Fowler coming.'

'Damn Miss Fowler!' Florrie's voice was low, but not low enough that Peter didn't hear her add, 'and you, too!'

Florrie and Miss Fowler passed each other at the entrance to the garage, and no-one would have believed that Miss Carrington-Barrett had just been fighting for a place in the garage-owner's affections, for her voice was airy and not without a little condescension as she said, 'Good morning, Miss Fowler. Lovely day, isn't it?'

'Yes, it is a lovely day,' replied Miss Fowler. 'But the lawns are parched, really parched, I wish we could have some rain.' Whereupon they parted with nods and smiles.

As Peter filled Miss Fowler's can with petrol he,

too, nodded and smiled at her as she chattered, but his mind was not on the one concern of her life, namely, the job of keeping her lawn green, nor yet – although she both worried and scared him with her young, ardent and unmaidenly-like pursuit – on Florrie. But it was agitated, and very much so, by what she had insinuated about the Mackenzies. He knew he had been a blasted fool to take Mavis out, and Florrie had been right about his reason for doing so. He had thought it would put her off, for she was getting beyond a joke. The whole place would soon be talking about him making up to his dad's boss's daughter, and he didn't want that. Why, in fact, the way she had been going on lately, he could see himself waking up one morning in the Little Manor house having to call the major 'Dad' and his old battleaxe, 'Mum', and that scared him properly. Florrie was young and spoilt, and up to now had had her own way in everything. And if she were to yell loud enough the Major and Mrs C.-B. might consent even to her latest whim. That had made him desperate and he'd had to do something. There being no-one of his own age unattached in the village, or nearabouts, he had, against all his better judgement and in a moment, so he told himself, of great necessity, asked Mavis out. The damn fool that he was.

In a sweating bother he tackled the car, and half an hour later he knew all there was to know about it, and none of it was good.

After applying more tow to his hands, straightening his shirt, and trying to flatten down his wiry hair, he gave a hitch to his belt and made his way through the village in the direction of the Hart.

A few doors down below the garage, Wilkins, the baker, was lowering full sacks from the loft, and he turned his white-powdered face to Peter and called cheerily, 'Good news, eh, Peter, lad? This'll set the ball rolling, eh?'

'It will that, Dan.' Peter's voice was equally cheery. Dan was one of them who wanted the road to go through. 'It will that.' He nodded total agreement. But when he came opposite Miss Tallow's shop he could hear, through the open doorway, her thin, piping voice bemoaning the fate of her beautiful village. Miss Tallow was all for beauty – she was a rustic poetess was Miss Tallow. Beauty, and Miss Tallow, rose above everything. Even the Spraggs' cesspool, brazenly fighting its own battle, could not convince her otherwise. Beauty must be preserved with the help of Jeyes' fluid. And she wasn't the only one who thought this way, either. There were a whole number of them in Battenbun, Peter knew only too well, who would rather see the village die a long, lingering death than have one inch of its beauty disturbed.

A shining yellow brake slowed up sufficiently to allow its driver to thrust his head out of the window and with a broad grin yell, 'Happy, Peter?'

'Hallo there, Brian. Aye – aye, I'm happy. Who wouldn't be?'

The car moved on, and Peter, with an inward glow, thought: I like Brian, he's all right. Now why can't Florrie see sense and marry him? He's nuts about her, and no social barrier to worry about there. Farm, money and name. The lot.

'Hello, Peter lad.' It was Bill Fountain, still not in his shop, but standing now across the road on the post office steps talking to Mrs Armstrong, the postmistress. 'Feeling like a millionaire!'

'Well, not exactly yet, Bill. I'll let them get started first.'

He nodded happily in their direction but noticed that Mrs Armstrong did not nod happily back. She was another one of them, for besides the post office she had the only grocery business in the place.

Bill's next shouted remark was lost in a bellow that filled the street, and Peter turned quickly to confront his great-grandfather where he sat in the window of the cottage, the living origin of the cast, hook nose and big mouth; all, in fact, that went to make up the questionable handsomeness of the Puddletons.

'What's pluddy well goin' on? Whole place gone mad and me not hearin' a word. Come here a minute, can't ya!'

'Now look, old 'un.' Peter went through the gate and across the narrow strip of garden to the window. 'I can't stop now, I've got a job in. You would see it coming in.'

'Aye, I saw it, I'm not blind. But I don't want to know about no pluddy car, what about road? Harry's goin' runnin' round as if he'd suddenly found God or summat and Joe, as usual, has made himself scarce. Always was a dab hand at that, he. As for your mother, you try to get her to shut that mouth of hers when she's got nowt to say, but when there's summat to talk about the ornery bitch goes mute.'

Peter smiled tolerantly down on the old man. 'Well, old 'un, you know as much as me. I hear it's going through, and that's all I know.'

The old man's attitude underwent a lightning change; a softness came into his face and his big, bony hand clutched at Peter's arm, and shaking it gently, he said, 'Lad, you're on to summat now. You're set for life . . . you're made . . . thousands and thousands you'll make out o' that garage. I'm tellin' you' – he raised a finger and wagged it in his great-grandson's face – 'that'll be a gold mine, a real gold mine. But mind—' his attitude changed quickly back to its former truculence, and in what he thought was a low tone, but in a voice that would have carried to the neighbours in question, he added, 'But mind you, lad, you look out for them lot.' He thumbed in the direction of the Mackenzies' house. 'They'll be after you like flies in a midden, you're on to a good thing, and anybody that's on to a good thing has the Mackenzies in their way. What do you think?' His voice did drop a shade lower now. 'Joe tells me this mornin' that old Mackenzie's bought shares in the mill – took them by way of payment for repairs. Just like him, ain't it. And Cuthbert's in Allendale is selling their contracting business, and he's after that an' all. I tell you, lad, look out for yersel'.'

'Don't you worry, old 'un, I'll look out for meself where the Mackenzies are concerned.' Although Peter's voice was a whisper it held strong emphasis, and Grandpop nodded and said,

'Ay, ay, you do . . . but lad . . . Here a minute.'
With a backward jerk of his head he beckoned
Peter even closer, and his deep-set misty eyes
fastened on his face and his voice was thick and
rumbling in his throat as he demanded, 'Not true
what I'm hearin', is it, you takin' up with their
dry cow?'

Peter's eyes dropped, his shoulders drooped,
and he sighed, and Grandpop, his voice returning
to normal, cried, 'Well, lad, you must be up the
pole. Dodged her for years you have. Laughin'
stock she's made of hersel', trailin' after you.
What's come over you? My God! do you expect
to bundle with that 'un? I'm tellin' you you're in
for a disappointment, for if ever I saw a dry—'

'Now look here, old 'un.'

'Ah! don't you start arguefying with me about
she, no arguefying in the world'll put any blood
into that 'un.'

Peter straightened up and was about to turn
away, knowing the uselessness of argument, when
old Grandpop, giving the final stamp to his
displeasure, whirled his old lips round and spat
towards the bunch of phlox at the gate. Perhaps
because of his disturbed state of mind his aim was
not so good today and he missed. A suppressed
squeal coming from behind him on the pavement
gave Peter the desire to duck and dive round to
the back of the house.

'You dirty old man!'

The indignant words were almost spat back at
Grandpop, and Peter, his expression a mixture of
sheepishness and dismay, turned and looked, not
without sympathy, at Miss Collins, the vicar's

sister. Grandpop's ammunition had not hit her, but that had been only a matter of luck.

Miss Collins's tight-lipped, narrow, sagging face was pink-hued as, trying to ignore the old man who would not be ignored, she addressed herself to Peter. 'Something should be done . . . one can't walk the street. At least, this particular section of it. It's a disgrace!'

'Yes, miss. I'll speak to him.' Peter's voice was very low.

'Speak to him! He should be—'

What Miss Collins would have liked to do to Grandpop seemed too big to get past her gullet, for her neck, after jerking up and down a number of times, only allowed her to swallow hard, and she walked away, her body twitching.

'Pity it didn't hit she. Who does she think she is? Like to run village, she. Pluddy Bridget!'

'Now, old 'un, you'll do that once too often. What's going to happen when me mam hears?'

'Never mind yer mam. She's another of 'em. All women should be smothered.' Grandpop blinked rapidly, champed his lips, then demanded, 'You on your way to Hart?'

'Aye.'

'Bring me a wet, I'm near parched.'

'I can't now, old 'un, I'm going to see a client about the car.'

Peter walked out of the gate and the old man's voice, now low and wheedling, followed him. 'Ah, Peter lad, bring me a wet. Go on, man.'

Peter smiled to himself as he walked on. By! the old 'un was a tartar. But there'd be the devil to pay as usual when his mam found out, as she would from Miss Collins, about the spitting.

Before he got to the Hart he was hailed a number of times, and he thought, By! the place is like London the day. Never had he known such bustle before, and on a Monday, too. Saturday might see the village street a bit busy like, but the rest of the week it could be dead.

He went into the bar of the inn and Mrs Booth, from behind the counter, asked without any preliminaries, 'You come to see her?'

'Yes, Mrs Booth.'

'She's in the livin' room, havin' a bite. Here—' she leaned across the counter and whispered confidentially – 'what d'you make of her, eh? Some piece that. What d'you say?' She poked at him with her finger. 'I bet you what you like she's just come out of jail. That skin of hers looks like it hasn't seen daylight for months. She looks a type, doesn't she? And what do you think about the road, eh?'

Peter blinked. He'd never had much time for Mrs Booth, never got on with her somehow. Perhaps that was because his mother couldn't stand her. Some talk of her making up to his dad at one time. So without commenting upon her observations of either the girl or the road he said, 'Can I go in?'

'Aye, go on.' Mrs Booth swept the counter clean with her ox-like arm, and he went along the passage towards the 'private' room.

When he reached the open doorway he could see the girl sitting at the end of the table, and she lifted her eyes from her plate and looked at him for a moment before drawling, 'Oh, hallo. You've been quick.'

'Well—' he moved uneasily and gave a little laugh – 'I haven't done anything to her yet.' He went slowly into the room and stood looking across the table towards her. It was as Mrs Booth had said, her skin didn't look as if it had seen much daylight lately and it wasn't the usual pallor associated with blondes either, yet jail! Trust Mrs Booth to jump to the worst conclusion. Likely, as he'd thought earlier, it was just smart make-up.

'Sit down, won't you?'

Peter glanced back towards the door. Mrs Booth was of a funny temper; you never knew how you had her, and him in his dirty clothes. This one here was as easy in her manner and invitations as if she had a share in the place. He smiled to himself and sat gingerly on the edge of the chair before beginning, 'Well, I'd better tell you what I think. You see I could fix her up but it would cost you a tidy bit, so my advice is for you to get another secondhand one. But mind—' he gave a short laugh – 'I haven't got one for sale; I'm not trying to sell you one or anything.'

She was leaning back in her chair, and she looked and sounded very tired as she asked, 'How much would it cost to repair her?'

He bit on his lip as he stared at her, then said hesitantly, 'It's difficult to say at the moment. The big ends are gone. They'll have to be rebored. She'll have to be stripped and reassembled. And the engine's on its last legs. You see, it's hard to say to the shilling what she'll cost. About sixteen pounds, I should think. Perhaps a bit more.'

She stared at him, her dark brown eyes, in sharp contrast to her hair, looking almost black. And then she stood up, and turning her back to him she walked to the window.

He, too, rose to his feet and added haltingly, 'And I'm afraid it'll take some time to get the big ends done an' all.'

'How long?' She spoke without turning round.

'A fortnight. Perhaps three weeks. They have to be sent to a depot. As I said, I think you'd better call her a bad debt and get another. But, of course, it's up to you.'

When she did not answer he thought, you're a blasted fool, doing yourself out of a job. What's up with you? Not a thing in for a week and turning this down. He shook his head at himself and looked at her back and commented privately again. By! she's thin.

As he continued to look at her he saw over her shoulder running from the green towards the bar the twins, with Tony Boyle jangling after them, and Penelope the tame duck, as always, endeavouring to catch them up.

Tony's garbled words came through the open window, crying, 'Le' me Jimmy! . . . Jimmy! . . . Johnnie, le' me! . . . Petter . . . Tell Petter.'

'It's beautiful country here.'

His eyebrows moved up a trifle. They had been talking of cars, but he smiled and said, 'Aye, it is fine . . . Yes, there isn't better. At least, that's what I think. It's wonderful country. Once you've lived here you can't settle nowhere else.'

'I'll stay till she's ready.'

Her abruptness slightly nonplussed him.

She still had her back to him, and he said with a kind of naive surprise, 'Here? . . . But the car, it'll be a fortnight, even three weeks, as I said. It could even be longer, you never know.'

She turned now and looked at him, and her face seemed wiped of all expression, telling him nothing. And when she made no effort to speak he went on, lamely, 'But if time doesn't matter' – he didn't add 'and money' – 'it's up to you.'

Her eyes held his in an odd way until he became uneasy, and there came back to him Mrs Booth's comment regarding time, to be thrust aside quickly, and he heard himself asking, 'Are you on holiday?'

'Yes. Yes, I am sort of.' She walked to the table again and sat down. 'They take boarders here?' She was looking intently down on her half-eaten dinner.

'Yes, they can take two. There's nobody staying at present.'

'Then I'll stay until you put the car right.'

She smiled up at him, and he was quick to notice again that there was no brightness in her eyes, the smile just touched her lips.

'It's up to you.'

'Yes, it's up to me.'

Like the look in her eyes, there was an odd quality about her reply, and he stood awkwardly confronting her. She was the most unusual customer he had come across for a long time. In fact he couldn't remember having met anyone quite like her. And her voice . . . He found he wanted to listen to her speaking. 'You American?' he asked with a grin.

'No.'

When she did not enlarge on this, he said lamely, 'Oh.'

'Psst! Peter! Peter, man!'

He turned sharply to the window, and there, just above the low sill, were the faces of his brothers, and high above theirs the wide, flat, gaping countenance of Tony Boyle.

'Here!' They gesticulated wildly to him.

He frowned at them and said sharply, 'Get away now. I'll be out in a minute.'

The girl had turned in her chair, and from the three faces she looked back enquiringly to him. And he grinned again and said with something of embarrassment, 'Me brothers.' Then added hastily, 'Not the top one, he's Tony. He's – he's just a trifle odd.' Trifle, he thought, was putting it mildly, but people were scared of the word mental.

'We've got sumthin' to tell yer, Peter . . . aw! Peter man.'

The two small heads were thrust well into the room now and Peter, looking distinctly uncomfortable, commanded 'Get away! Get yourselves off. Now! This minute!'

They stared at him in some surprise; then instead of doing as he had ordered they transferred their cheeky glances from him to the girl.

Hastily now he made for the door, from where he turned and asked, 'Will I bring your cases?'

'It would be very kind of you.' Her lips were smiling again. The situation with the bairns seemed to have amused her.

Without further ado he went along the passage

and out of the side door, for he did not want to encounter Mrs Booth. Somehow he didn't quite know what attitude Mrs Booth would take on knowing the girl was to be a guest, but one thing was certain, Mrs Booth would be glad to have someone in, for trade at the Hart most of the week was almost on a par with that of the garage.

As he came out into the sunshine the twins came pelting round the corner with Tony behind them, and he greeted them with a sharp 'Now, look! Quiet a minute! And you listen to me.' He held out his finger and stabbed it at them. 'When I'm talking to anybody you keep your tongues still and keep away, or I'll pay your backsides for you, the pair of you. And you too, Tony.' He looked at the creature who was almost as tall as himself.

'Me, Petter? Me, I found—'

'You shut yer mouth! I'm goner tell him. It's a fish, Peter, like an eel, only bigger. It's in the little lake,' said Johnny in an excited whisper. 'Come and see.'

'A fish?' The sternness slid from Peter's face.

'Aye. A great, long big 'un, a whopper.'

With a smile now forcing its way from the depths of his eyes, Peter looked down on the twins and said, 'A whopper, eh? How big? Like that?' With his large hand he measured about six inches, and the twins cried in chorus, 'No man, no!'

'It's as big as Tony, it is. It's as long as him!' Johnny nodded towards their gangling playmate, and Jimmy added, 'Aye, it is. It's as big as Tony, honest!'

'Big, like me, Petter. Big!'

The smile was hidden behind Peter's narrowed lids now as he said, 'You're having me on. You know there's no eels in the lake, nor fish bigger than me hand.'

'I'm tellin' you, Peter man. Come and see, man, for yersel. It's lying below the bank in the clearing.' Jimmy took on a dignity that doubled his seven years.

Peter, more puzzled now, surveyed them in silence. He knew what type of fish there were in the little lake, but he also knew that there must be something unusual there for the twins were no fools where fish were concerned. They had been bitten with the bug from the time they could toddle. All the Puddleton men were crazy about fish. And so the lure of this enormous one was too much for Peter. For the moment he forgot about his client, her car, and her cases, and in a whisper he said, 'Well, look, we'll have to be slippy, 'cos I'm busy. You, Jimmy, run down and tell your Grandpop to keep an eye on garage. Then come up Wilkins' cut and you'll be there as quick as us. Go on now.'

Hardly had the words left his lips before Jimmy was away, and together with Johnny and Tony, and Penelope quacking her disgust at having to start another trek, he hurriedly went into the road, skirted the wall of the inn yard, and getting under a broken fence ran across the field, and within a minute was in the wood. Another two minutes of running and they were all scrambling in single file through a narrow opening in a high wall of bramble and onto the only firm piece of bank bordering the lake.

Throwing himself down onto the edge of the bank, Johnny pointed into the water, saying, 'It was just here.'

Peter's eyes followed his small brother's fingers, but there was no sign of a fish of any kind. He knew the elusive ripple of the carp, the squiggle of the roach, and the dash of the salmon, but there was nothing here, only a little family of tiddlers sporting in a splash of sunshine.

'It was here.' There was a keen note of disappointment in Johnny's voice. And when Jimmy came pelting through the hedge crying, 'Have you seen it?' he spoke dolefully down into the water, 'No, it's gone.'

'Was it an eel? You know what an eel's like,' said Peter, looking from one to the other.

'No, it wasn't an eel,' said Johnny. 'We know an eel, man. This was big. It was like an eel, but longer, yards longer.'

At this moment the quack-quack of Penelope came from behind the undergrowth, and Peter, nodding in the direction of the duck, said, 'You're not having me for a Penelope, are you?'

It was a family joke.

'No, honest Peter, am I, Johnny?'

Johnny shook his head gravely.

Suddenly there came a spluttering yell from Tony. 'There! . . . there! . . . Petter . . . fish . . . fish.'

'Where? Steady man, where?'

'There! Petter.'

Peter's eyes searched the expanse of water indicated by Tony's great flapping arms. And then he saw it, and he silenced them all with a lift of his hand. He watched it slithering about in a shallow, its long body gleaming like silver against the mud, and he lowered himself slowly down on to the bank and gasped, open-mouthed, scarcely believing what he saw. The length of it! The length of it! Four foot, if an inch. What would it weigh? Ten, twelve pounds, perhaps more. It was the biggest eel he had ever seen – or thought to see. He was actually shivering with excitement. Never had he seen an eel of any size in this lake; in the rivers, aye, in both of the North and South Tynes. He had seen one about two foot long once, slithering past at Featherston's Bridge, but this one here was beyond even a fisherman's nightmare! She must be ten inches round.

The eel slid forward, the light on her turning her to mother-of-pearl; she was like a floating stream within a stream. She moved nearer, and did she look at him? Everything now was wiped from Peter's mind – garage, road, women, and cars to repair. She was a beauty. By, lad! she was – a wonder. Oh! if his dad could only see her. He wouldn't believe it unless he saw her with his own eyes. But they must be careful who they let on to about her, for if the village got wind of her every man jack would be after her. He gave a gasp as she flashed out and away, but his eyes tight on her he managed to follow her to where she went into deeper water against the sunlit bank and became still on the mud.

Their heads were all close together now, their

eyes concurring to the one point, and Peter, letting out an excited hiss of breath through his teeth, said softly, 'Mind, all of you, don't breathe this to a soul, except Dad. Do you hear? And you, Tony?'

'Aye, Peter.'

'Aye, Peter.'

'Not me, Petter.'

'Are you fishing?'

Not having heard the approach of anyone with whom the voice that asked this question could be associated, they almost overbalanced into the water, and Peter, swinging up to his feet, turned to face the guest of the Hart. And his colour rose just the slightest when he thought, Lord! her cases.

'I was passing and I heard you.' Again she asked, 'Are you fishing?'

'No, no, not just at the moment.' He scratched his head, then by way of explanation gave a short laugh and said, 'The lads here told me of something I couldn't believe. It sounded like a Lambton worm story, but it's true all right.'

'What have you found, a ten-pound salmon?' Her voice was slightly mocking.

'No, there's no salmon in this water, but there's something here that I never expected to see.' His eyes narrowed at her. 'And I bet you've never seen anything like it.'

'What is it?' She moved forward, and he, pushing the twins to one side, knelt down on the bank and beckoned her to him. And when she was kneeling by his side he pointed along the bank and down into the water. 'See that, down there?' He felt as well as heard the gasp she gave, and her thrill of excitement went through them all as she exclaimed, 'Why! it's an eel.'

'You've seen one afore?' There was a trace of disappointment in Peter's voice. She didn't look the type who would know anything about fish, let alone eels.

'Dozens.'

'Dozens?' There was open disbelief in his tone, and she turned her face to his as she repeated firmly, 'Yes, dozens.'

'Where did you see them?'

'I was born in Norfolk. I lived by the river for years.'

Well, didn't that cap all! And he had thought she was an American.

She was looking at the eel again, and he looked at the back of her head, not more than a foot away from him, and unconsciously he sniffed. She had a nice smell about her, different from the scent that Florrie wore. But then Florrie only wore scent at a hop, and then it couldn't cover up the smell of the horses. And Mavis's scent . . . He cut off his thoughts abruptly.

'Oh, she's a beauty! Has she been here long?'

'I shouldn't think so. I come here pretty often and I haven't seen her afore. I've never seen an eel of any kind on this lake. Too far from the rivers. I'm wondering how long she'll stay.'

'Not for long, I shouldn't think. She's full grown, ready to go back.' She moved her head in admiration, and her drawl was more defined as she added, 'She's a real Slinky Jane.'

They all looked at her, and Jimmy gave a giggle

of a laugh, and hung his head as she turned her eyes towards him and asked, 'Well, what do you call them?'

'Nowt, miss, 'cept eels.' He looked up at her under his brows and smiled, and she returned his smile and said, 'We always called them Slinky Janes.'

Jimmy giggled again. Then Johnny joined him, and Tony, not to be outdone, let out a high, hysterical yell, which brought the girl's eyes sharply to him. She stared at him prancing like a dervish, until Peter cried, sharply, 'That's enough, Tony!'

'He's perfectly harmless.' He spoke reassuringly under his breath, his face turned towards the water.

'I'm sure he is, I'm not afraid.' She moved casually around and looked in the direction of the eel again.

Her hair fell forward on to her face and caused him to comment privately that she looked better like that . . . younger. Yet he knew now she was no young lass, not with that air and that walk she wasn't. And a young lass couldn't possess that something which lay in the depth of her eyes, like age or —

He stood up abruptly, saying, 'I'd better be getting back. I'm sorry, miss, about your cases. I'll bring them down right away. The trouble with me is I can never resist a fish.'

'No?' She turned her head, and for the third time in their short acquaintance she looked steadily at him, and her scrutiny made him feel as gangly as Tony, as if he were all arms and legs, so it was in a very self-conscious tone that he said, 'There's just a favour I'd ask of you, miss. We're not going to let on about it.' He nodded towards the water, 'Except to me dad. If the men of the village knew there was one of her size here, there'd be open competition to net her.'

'Oh, no!' She was on her feet now, all her casualness gone. 'Oh, no! I wouldn't like to see them do that . . . she's making for home – the Sargasso Sea to breed – she must have a chance.'

His eyebrows moved the slightest. She even knew that. 'Aye,' he nodded, 'that's where she'll be bound for. So you won't say anything, miss, down at the Hart?'

'No, no, of course not.'

'Thanks. I'll get those cases down right away for you. Come on, you lot.'

He marshalled his brothers and Tony and the quacking Penelope through the opening, and just as he was about to follow she said, 'I have nothing better to do, I could sit here and ward off intruders.'

He didn't know whether she was laughing at him or not, but he answered, 'Aye, you could do that, there's worse things than sitting by the lake.' And just for a moment he returned the concentrated look in her eyes before swinging about and following the boys.

Chapter Two

By six o'clock that evening not even its owner would have recognised the Alvis. From the bits of her that lay strewn about the garage one could be forgiven for thinking that she had been shot to pieces. Peter had decided to give her a 'fair do'. If the girl was determined to put her back on the road, well, she would be as good as he could make her, although he realised that, in this particular case, that wasn't saying much, for he was no miracle worker.

The afternoon had been exceptionally hot, and now feeling both tired and hungry he decided to pack up for the day and go home. Towards this end he straightened his back, wiped the sweat from his forehead with his forearm and inhaled a deep breath, and was about to go into the office to get the key to lock up when a low, red MG, coming to a skidding stop almost an inch from his pumps, caused him to turn on it a countenance that was so full of fury as to make him almost unrecognisable. Gone was the loose-limbed, easy-going and, at this moment, tired individual; in his place was a dark, taut, glowering mass of anger. And without any preamble he barked in a voice that almost outdid Grandpop's, 'Now! Davy Mackenzie, I've warned you about that trick afore!'

'Aw! man, be quiet.' The slight, dapper young man eased himself out of the car and came into the garage. 'You're frightened of the death you'll never die, and your pumps an' all. Look, they're still standin'.' He pointed. 'Calm down, can't you?' He stood surveying Peter's convulsed face with a grin that drew up one corner of his thin, clean-shaven lip. Then his eyes slowly, almost insolently, dropping away, he walked round the stripped Alvis, his raised eyebrows clearly showing his opinion of it, and coming to a stop outside the office, he kicked at the upturned beer box which was old Pop's seat. Then from this he turned sharply about, stretched his chin out of his collar and began, in a tone which sounded in direct variance to the one of incitement he had just used, 'Now look, Peter, I'll come straight to the point, I'm after something.'

'You're telling me!'

'All right! all right! don't bawl. I'm telling you. Didn't I say I was? Well, here it is. Dad's bought up Cuthbert's haulage business, and I won't deny we're stuck for a place to park the lorries. I offered you four hundred pounds for a share. Now I'll go further, we'll give you nine hundred pounds for the lot. There, we can't be fairer. And you know me, I don't shilly-shally. It's a darn good offer, let me tell you, for as a garage it's a dry well and you know it.'

When disturbed in any way, Peter's hands became restless, and he was now rubbing them with tow as if they were made of cast iron. And he kept his attention on the process for some moments until he could force himself to say, with a semblance of calmness, 'And you're offering me nine hundred pounds for a dry well, nine hundred pounds just for a place to stick your lorries in! It's not because the road business is settled, is it?' Without raising his head he raised his eyes and looked at Davy, and Davy, blinking rapidly now, had the grace to look sheepish, and he blustered, 'Why man, that's been in the air for years, it's only another rumour.'

'It isn't in the air any longer, and you know it. It's no rumour. I can see you offering me nine hundred pounds for a place you said a few days ago wasn't worth five hundred altogether; I can see you jumping four hundred overnight for a piece of land to stick your lorries on.'

'Well,' Davy wagged his head, 'all right, say it's as you say. What if the road is going through? It's a fair enough offer. And when it goes through, where are you going to get the money from to expand? I ask you that. You might raise what this is worth,' with a disparaging gesture he waved his hand about the garage, 'but I'm telling you money's tight these days and you'd want at least three thousand to build any kind of a show here. Of course, there's always the other side to this.'

'Aye, I know,' Peter put in quickly 'partnership. I think I've heard something of that afore an' all. Now look, once and for all I'm not selling, and I wouldn't have you, Davy, for a partner and you know it, at least you should if you weren't so bloomin' thick-skinned.'

This statement, which left nothing to doubt, did not apparently hurt Davy's feelings for he replied, even soothingly, 'All right, all right, don't lose your rag. Huh! I've never met a bloke like you, Peter – like a lamb with everybody else in the place except me. It's funny, I've never been able to understand it.'

Peter looked at Davy scornfully. Davy Mackenzie would suck up to a cobra if he thought he'd get a share of its venom. Then his scorn gave place to a leaping anger, as Davy in a soft, sly undertone said 'And there's our side to this you know, Peter, for if you're thinking of coming into our family I don't suppose you'll be above taking anything that comes our Mavis's way, will you?'

For a moment Peter found himself unable to speak, but when he did it was like a spluttering explosion, as he roared 'Well, I'm not coming into your damn family, so don't you worry.'

They stared at each other in silence until Davy said, 'Oh! so you're not, eh?' There was no sign of amusement on his face now, nor laughter in his voice. Whereas the refusal of his offer for the garage had not, seemingly, touched him, this second refusal brought a tautness to his whole body which showed that he was not only surprised but, in his turn, angry.

'No, I'm not. And what I do is my business! Get that.'

'But there you are mistaken, lad. It isn't just your business, she's me sister and you're not going to play fast and loose with her.'

'Now look – get out!' Peter's attitude again left nothing to doubt, but Davy stood his ground and the two men glanced angrily at each other, as they had done at intervals since their school days.

As always, Davy was the first to recover, and he

did so on this occasion quicker than usual, saying, 'Aw! Peter man, we're fools. What's between you and Mavis is your business, as you say.' He stared a moment longer at Peter, waiting for a retort; and when all he got was the continued fiery glare from Peter's eyes, he gave a laughing 'Huh!' before turning away, saying, 'I'll look in the morrow.'

'You can save your feet.'

The car roared round the garage drive and away along the village, and Peter, pelting the tow into a corner, cried, 'Damn!' and then again, 'Damn!' Why did he let that fellow get under his skin? There wasn't another person in the whole world who reacted on him as Davy Mackenzie did. And him suggesting that because he had been out twice with Mavis he was thinking of moving into their family. My God! Florrie had been right.

He strode into the office, grabbed up the key, and made for the door, there to be confronted by the subject of his thought in the flesh, Mavis herself.

That Peter was astounded by the sight of Mavis was plain to be seen. It would almost seem as if Davy had willed her out of the air and dropped her here to further both his and her own cause.

'Hello.' Mavis's slightly bulging blue eyes blinked up at him while her lips made a vain but refined effort to meet over her slightly protruding teeth. Everything about Mavis was refined. From her too small shoes to her neatly permed hair there was a tight, prim compact refinement about her. And it had thoroughly soaked itself into her voice, for Mavis did not speak 'North Country' except for a few revealing words. But she spoke a twang of her own, which she considered very refined-like.

'I thought I'd look in and see you . . . I got off early.'

Peter did not speak, he only stared.

'Oh, it's been hot in the office today, sweltering.'

Still Peter said nothing.

Mavis looked up at him through slightly narrowed lids now; then she smoothed down her gently heaving bosom with one hand and, lowering her lids, said, 'Oh, I got annoyed today. That Mr Pringle was on again . . . pawing. Really, I think I'll have to leave there.'

Peter's greasy hands ran through his hair. Why in the name of heaven had he let himself in for this. He had known on Saturday night that he couldn't stand her, yet he had to go and ask her again for Sunday. He must have been barmy, clean barmy. Even Florrie didn't warrant his putting up with Mavis Mackenzie for two nights, and one more night of her would drive him round the bend. She had always got on his nerve, which was why he had constantly striven to keep her at a distance. And then he had let himself in for . . .

'Are you going anywhere tonight?'

The sweat ran down from his tousled hair, and he pulled a lump of tow from his back pocket, muttering as he did so, 'I've got a big job in.' He nodded back to the dismembered car.

Mavis putting her head to one side, looked at the skeleton frame of the Alvis and an understanding, even a maternal gleam came into her eye. For Peter she would even babysit to a car. 'I'll come along after tea and keep you company,' she said.

Her eyelids were drooping again and her lips straining to meet, when Peter's voice, with a distinct note of panic, brought them all wide.

'No! no! you'll not, thank you very much. I've got me hands full. I can't stand anybody – I mean—' What he did mean he couldn't bring himself to say, and he turned from her muttering something about shutting up, and with a great deal of 'to do' brought the garage doors together and locked them.

'What's up with you?' Mavis's voice was slightly off its refined key now, and he answered her over his shoulder, 'Nowt's up with me.'

'I thought we—'

He clipped the lock into place with a loud bang, saying 'You shouldn't think; people take too much for granted by thinking.'

'Well!'

He was compelled now to turn and face her, and he nodded at her and said, 'Aye . . . well?'

'I want an explanation.' Her head was up and her lips had almost accomplished the impossible.

He forced himself to throw out his chest. 'And I want me tea and a wash . . . I'm tired.'

As he marched away another swelling 'Well!' hit his back, and he thought again, Aye, well, you can go and tell your menfolk that. They would have to think again if they were going to try and hook him through her.

But although he was thinking in these strong and firm terms he was feeling anything but strong and firm. As Florrie said, Mavis would take some shaking off; it would take more than a little incident like this to get her off his track.

He was still agitated and was sweating visibly when he entered the house, and he hadn't got his hands under the tap when his mother, from the kitchen door, demanded, 'Who's Slinky Jane – do you know?'

He turned quickly. 'Why?'

'Listen to them.' She lifted her head to the ceiling, and he put his head to one side in an effort to make out what the lads were singing.

Rosie's face split into a grin as she said, 'It's a song of some kind they've made up about somebody in the village, listen.'

'Slinky Jane's a girl with style.
For Slinky Jane I'd walk a mile,
Through a dark wood and over a stile,
All for Slinky Jane.'

'It's a nice tune, catchy. Never heard it before, have you?'

'No.' He grinned back at her, then turned to the sink again. The lads had never made that up. Likely it was the girl. And his mother thinking it was somebody in the village. Funny that.

There followed a short silence before Rosie, her tone now completely altered, put in abruptly, 'Your dad's not in yet. If he's gone to the Hart again the night afore coming home there'll be summat to do here, I can tell you.'

Ignoring now the nice tune which was still going on, Rosie banged the cups onto the tin tray and Peter screwed up his eyes against the soap and her voice, as she gave him a sample of what she would say to Harry when he did come in.

O, Lord! He gave a quiet moan. That was one thing he couldn't bear to listen to – his mother going for his dad, even if she was in the right. The security that the house offered from Mavis tonight would, he saw, have to be waived. Yet as he finished drying himself he realised that he had left it too late for even the bus into Allendale, and also that the danger consequent on a walk was not to be considered, so there would be nothing for it but the Hart. The Hart was one place into where Mavis wouldn't follow him; they were all teetotallers, the Mackenzies, too damn mean to be anything else . . .

He had washed and changed and eaten his meal so quickly that Rosie, suspicion gathering on her brow, demanded, 'Going some place the night?'

'The Hart.'

She had warned him about the Hart in the past, saying 'You don't want to get like him,' 'him' being his father, but now there was a look of undisguised relief on her face. Far rather the Hart than that Mavis Mackenzie, and she smiled at him and there was no sting in her words as she said, 'I'll soon have to take all the meals down there.'

'Aye, you might an' all. That'll be the day.'

They both laughed together now at the improbability of such a happening.

As he let himself out of the front door Grandpop's voice, endeavouring to be hushed, came to him heavy with warning saying, 'Watch yerself, lad. One after t'other's been at the window. On the look-out for somebody I should say. You didn't say to meet her the night, not by her face as she passed here, you didn't, and they're puzzling their pluddy heads as to where you might be off to.'

Peter did not reply, only cast a warning glance in his great-grandfather's direction. Nothing escaped the old 'un. You'd think he'd be past taking an interest in the goings-on, but not he. Although he had a tongue that would clip clouts, he was generally right in all he said. And he was right again this time, for as he went out of the gate he detected a watcher behind the Mackenzies' fancy-curtained windows. This fact lent wings to his heels, and he was within a few yards of the Hart when he heard the unmistakable click of the Mackenzies' gate. He did not turn to ascertain who might have come through it, but it took all his control not to sprint the last few yards to the inn.

Once safely in the bar parlour he glanced through the window to see if his assumption had been right, and yes, there she was crossing the road away from the contamination of the wicked place. He heaved a sigh that released a grin to his face, then he answered the remarks being thrown at him from the regulars, as one after the other they called:

'Goin' to stand us one for the road, Peter?'

'Peter Puddleton, made millionaire through being only one in village with bit spare land and garage.'

'Guess of all the lot of us you're the one who's going to gain by this, Peter.'

'Well, it serves you right,' he threw back at them. 'Old Parkinson was trying to sell that place for years, and you laughed at him. You see, them that laughs last laughs longest.'

'What's yours, Peter?' Mr Booth's flat voice asked of him.

'Oh.' Peter turned back to the counter. 'A burton please, Stan . . . small . . . Dad been in?'

'In, and still is.'

'Where?' Peter looked around.

'Darts with the lady.'

Slowly Peter's eyes moved along the room, but they couldn't go round the corner to where the dartboard was. What they did take in, however, was the fact that nearly all the customers were seated in positions which enabled them to take in – the corner.

Nonchalantly taking up his glass, he walked to a point from where he, too, could have a view of the proceedings, and he was just in time to see the girl poised to throw a dart. He watched her thin body give a slight twist, then jerk forward. For one brief second the chatter and laughter ceased, then one voice after another cried, as if to proclaim the achievement for the first time in history, 'Double twenty! Double twenty!'

'Double twenty! Lordy, lordy. Why, miss . . . not first time you've seen dartboard.'

'Why, I be jiggered! What's she got?'

'Double twenty.'

'Double twenty? No! That's the second time she's done it.'

Peter smiled to himself and turned away. It was evident that his client had caught on.

The dart players were moving from the board now and coming towards the bar proper. The girl was walking with his father on one side and Bill Fountain on the other, and Peter kept his head turned away, but his ears were wide to his father's voice as he said, 'What's it to be this time, miss? Now come on, make it something stronger than grapefruit.'

'Hallo there, lad.' Harry addressed Peter's back, and Peter, turning as if in surprise, said, 'Oh, hallo there,' before adding under his breath, 'been home yet?'

Harry's beam didn't actually fade, but he looked sharply at his son while saying quite pleasantly, 'No, not yet, lad.' Then turning to Mr Booth he added, 'Two bitters and a grapefruit, Stan.'

'Hallo, Peter.'

'Hallo, Bill.'

Bill Fountain looked like an outsize Billy Bunter who had just brought off a scoop of some kind, the kind in this case being not far to seek. Really, thought Peter, both his dad and Bill looked like a couple of old roosters in the spring.

And now it was the girl who said, 'Hello.'

'Oh, hallo there, miss.' It was as if he had only just become aware of her presence, and although he smiled his voice was slightly offhand.

The girl's gaze was full on him as it had been earlier in the day. It seemed an odd trick of hers to look you dead in the eye, and for all his outward seeming casualness it disturbed him, made him sort of uneasy. He didn't know whether he liked her or not, but he felt sure that if he didn't he was the only one in the bar who had come to such a decision. In spite of this feeling he couldn't help but notice things about her, for instance her eyes. Behind their directness they looked tired, very tired: yet in their depths did he detect a hint of laughter? This suspicion made him turn away from her, but determining not to be outdone by his sire, in small talk at least, he leaned his elbows on the bar counter and asked lightly, but under his breath, 'And how's Slinky Jane?'

The girl reached out for her glass of grapefruit and took a sip from it, then looked away from him across the counter to a row of bottles on a high shelf, before answering with equal lightness, 'Very well. Thank you very much.'

He had the desire to laugh at the way she said this, and strangely now he began to feel excited, as if they were discussing in code something of great import.

'When did you see her last?' he asked, still under his breath.

'About an hour ago. Are you going to have a look at her before it gets dark?'

Peter finished his beer in one long drink before committing himself – Mavis was still lurking in the back of his mind. Even so he heard himself say, 'Yes, I think I'll have a dander down and see her.'

No sooner had he said it than he knew he had done a damn silly thing, and he almost twitched the glass off the counter when her voice came softly to him, saying, 'I think I'll have another peep at her, too.'

He turned his head sharply and looked down at her. His mouth was slightly open in an attempt at a protest, then he looked quickly away again, straight ahead and into the mirror, and to his consternation he saw that there was hardly a man in the room who wasn't looking in their direction. If he walked out of here with her the village would be set alight, and if they were seen in the wood together . . . ! Frequenters of the wood were the odd fishers going to the lake, the few children of the village, and courting couples. And at present there were only three couples courting strongly enough to warrant their retirement to the wood.

The pink hue was glowing under the dark stubble of his face when she said very softly, and with an unmistakable gurgle in her voice, 'I'll get my coat and dander across.' She stressed his word dander. Then she turned from him to Harry, saying, 'Thanks for the game.'

Immediately Harry broke off his conversation with Bill and gave her all his attention. 'You're very welcome, miss . . . it's been a pleasure. I'll be happy to play you any time, win or lose.'

'That goes for me an' all.' Bill was swelling visibly with this anticipatory pleasure.

As she smiled from one to the other of the older men and Harry bent towards her beaming his broadest, Peter wondered what it was about his dad that made him get on with women. Apparently they didn't seem to notice he had a cast in his eye, yet it wasn't a thing that could escape anybody's notice. Perhaps it was his un-selfconsciousness – and nerve. He wished he had inherited a bit more of both himself.

As the girl walked out amid a chorus of 'Good night, mam' and 'Good night, miss', Mrs Booth came in from the saloon, and having given her list of orders to her husband, she turned and faced the three men, saying, 'Enjoying yourselves, gentle-men?'

'Now, now, there,' said Harry. 'What'd you mean by that?'

'What do I mean? There's no fools like old 'uns.'

'What do you think of that, Bill?' Harry turned his straight eye, full of assumed indignation, on his pal, and as Bill's stomach rumbled with his laughter preparatory to a juicy retort Peter moved away from the counter. He was in no frame of mind to listen to further gallantries, either from Bill or from his father, though they were directed this time towards Mrs Booth. Moreover, he told himself, he couldn't risk staying here in case the girl took it into her head to look in the bar again on her way out. 'Twixt her and Mavis he saw himself now between the devil and the deep sea.

As he reached the open doorway leading to the porch, Harry called, 'You off, lad?' and without turning round he threw over his shoulder a terse, 'Aye.'

Mrs Booth's eyes were on him as he left the bar, and when they noted that he did not turn towards home she went swiftly into the passage and towards the back of the house, and Bill, turning quickly to Harry, said, 'Say, Harry, your Peter know her afore she come here?'

'You mean?' Harry jerked his head upwards indicating the guest room.

'Aye.'

'No, he never seen her afore the day.'

'Fact?'

'Fact. Why?'

'Well' – Bill scratched his chin and gave a deep-bellied chuckle, which managed to convey a complimentary note – 'he's a Puddleton all right, and miles ahead of you, Harry, though I'd never have believed that possible.'

'What you mean, Bill?' Harry's face was straight.

'Well, didn't you hear 'em, man? Christian names it was, and all very intimate like. Sylvia Jane he called her. "And how's my Sylvia Jane?" he said. Just like that. S'fact. You not hear him?'

Harry had just lit his pipe, and the first full draw went scutting down his gullet like the shot from a gun, bringing him doubled up and choking.

'Steady on, man,' said Bill. 'Gone the wrong way?'

'That's your lies choking you,' said Mrs Booth, now behind the counter again. Then apropos of nothing to do with choking as Harry, red in the face, continued to cough, she said, 'I've just ascertained – ' she liked a long word, an educated word, did Mrs Booth – 'I've just ascertained that our guest has gone for a walk in the wood, and it near on dusk. And she's not the only one what's decided to take the same road.'

With a significant nod of her head Mrs Booth departed with a full tray, and Harry, still coughing and dabbing his mouth, said, 'It's as you say, Bill, he takes after me.' With one long drink he finished his beer, then stated, 'Well, I'd better be off an' all. Missus'll be after me else. So long, you old potbelly.' Harry aimed a sham blow at the protrusion, then went out laughing, and Bill laughing in return, leaned his back against the counter and sipped at his beer. By! Harry was a lad, wasn't he?

His thoughts on Harry, it gradually dawned on him that he hadn't yet seen him pass the window on his way homewards. He must be still in the yard. Or was he? Slowly Bill scratched his head.

After having finished his glass of beer and having joined in sundry bits of conversation without taking his eyes off the window, and still not having seen Harry pass, Bill went out into the yard, but could see no sign of his mate. What prompted him to look over the neat hedge of the Booths' garden down to the fence at the bottom and the field beyond would not have been clear to anyone else but himself. There was a gate in that fence, and it was only a hare's leap, so to speak, from there to the wood. 'Harry,' said Bill half aloud, 'you didn't oughter do it.'

Bill looked about him. There wasn't a soul in sight and twilight was deepening. Nobody could accuse him of anything for walking down the bar garden, could they now? – he was a keen gardener himself – and once through that gate . . .

It is astonishing how fast fat people can move when necessary. Bill certainly moved swiftly down the garden path, and Mrs Booth moved back more swiftly from the yard door into the bar and to her husband, who, behind the cover of a china rum barrel, was measuring whisky into a wet glass.

Putting her head close to his, although the din did not occasion her whispering, she gasped, 'What do you think? Fountain . . . he's gone sneaking up the garden into the woods after her.'

Mr Booth turned his long horse-face towards his wife, but no change appeared in his expression. 'Fountain? That makes two of 'em. Guess young Peter went.'

'Three, if I know anything. Harry Puddleton an' all.' Mrs Booth looked angry and sounded incensed, but the only alteration in Mr Booth's face was that it seemed to stretch to even longer proportions as he commented briefly, 'Safety in numbers.'

'Safety in numbers! I'm not putting up with it.'

'Shut tha mouth.' It was an order. 'The likes of her bring custom. You'll see, the morrow night we'll be packed out. Keep your tongue quiet. Say what you like to them but nothing to her. As for Harry Puddleton . . .' Mr Booth left the statement unfinished and turned away, and after a lift of her chin and a prolonged stare in her husband's direction, Mrs Booth flounced about and into the saloon again.

It was evident that Mr Booth, if not quite master in his own house and of its mistress, was in absolute control of the bar and its proceedings.

*   *   *

As nonchalantly as his long legs would allow him Peter had attempted to saunter through the wood. Should he by chance be seen, he was out for a stroll; or he could be going fishing. Without a line, and it on dusk? No, that one wouldn't do. Anyway, whose business was it what he did? His shoulders went back and his head went up, but its position was uneasy. What if Mavis should . . . To the devil with Mavis! And Florrie as well, for that matter.

This way of thinking was indeed daring, and his native cautiousness questioned it and asked tentatively: but wouldn't it be awkward for him if he were seen at this time of the evening in the wood with the boarder from the Hart? As quickly again he defended himself. She wasn't the reason for his coming here – ten-to-one he wouldn't come across her anyway – he was going to the pond for a minute to see the eel, and then he was going straight home to his supper and an early night. Aye, that was all very well, put like that, but he'd have a job to talk himself out of it if he were seen with her, wouldn't he? This cautious pricking was too much for him, and abruptly he left the main path and made his way over the soggy ground and through undergrowth that was almost shoulder high, and somewhat dishevelled in his appearance and disturbed in his mind he came at length to the path along which earlier in the day he had led the twins, and so to the lake.

There it lay before him, dark-shadowed, beautiful, yet eerie. But there was no sylph-like figure bending over its water. Slowly he walked to the bank. It was funny she wasn't here. He looked across the water to where a small shoal of rudd was feeding, snapping up at the black gnats, which through weariness or fly bravado were skimming the surface. Perhaps she'd lost her way – you could you know. Well, she had found her way here twice already the day . . . Aye, but now it was dusk.

From the far bank a moor-hen skidded into the water, followed by her mate, leaving double rows of light catching thin froth in their wake. They swam towards the great dead oak that lay half submerged, its head almost reaching the middle of the lake. He brought his eyes from them to the darkening water below his feet, searching for the silver line that would betray the eel. But there was no movement except that of the little bleak dizzying about. She had, he surmised, taken refuge out in the middle of the lake, or at the other side where it was deeper, it wasn't likely that she had gone yet. He'd come again in the morning, earlyish, but now he'd better go and see where she was, she, this time, being his client. If she had wandered off the path and into the sog she might get a bit of a fright, and it on dark an' all.

He was in the act of turning about to leave the clearing when her voice came to him. It startled him and at the same time brought his brows together, for she was saying in her soft gurgle, 'That's a real fishy story, Mr Puddleton.'

'No, it's a fact, miss, true as I stand here.'

That was his dad, and not gone home yet. Well really, it was a bit thick. No wonder his mam went on. He felt a sudden unusual anger against his father, and turning quickly to the bank again he knelt down and concentrated his gaze upon the water.

'Well, I'm damned! You beat us to it, lad.'

Peter cast his glance sideways for an instant but did not speak, and the girl, moving quickly across the grass to his side, said eagerly, 'Is she here?'

It was odd but he found it impossible to give her an answer, so shook his head; and when she knelt down beside him with her coat-sleeve touching his arm, he thought, she's as bad as him. It amuses the likes of her to encourage an old fellow. Yet in calmer moments he would be the first to admit that his father carried his age even a little too well, for he could pass for fortyish any day. To his added annoyance he again became conscious that she smelled nice.

'She can't have gone,' said Harry; 'ground's like powder. And there'll be no dew the night either. Look' – he went down on to his hunkers at her side and drew her attention as he pointed to some bubbles on the surface of the water – 'there goes an old stager. I've always wanted to catch she . . . an old carp. Ever seen a carp, miss?'

'Yes. Oh, yes.'

Always wanted to catch she! Peter jerked himself to his feet. His father was always wanting to catch something, even if it was only a smile from a mere stranger like the girl here. Was it any wonder that the Puddleton men had a name in the village. And not only in the village. Oh, give over, he chided himself. What was up with him? He knew his father's ways, and there was no use in getting ratty. But he was ratty.

'I'm off,' he said.

'Here, wait a minute, hold your hand!' Harry turned sharply, almost overbalancing himself, then stood up. And as he looked at his son his face sobered for an instant and something came from his eyes that could have been an appeal, an appeal for understanding of a nature that refused to recognise age. And something of it did come over in his words as he buttoned up his coat and said, 'I'm getting back home, lad, your mother'll be waiting. I'm well over me time the night, but I never could resist a fish, you know that.' He paused, and smiled, then nodding to the girl where she was still kneeling on the bank as if deaf to the conversation that was going on over her head, he said, 'I'll say good evenin', miss.'

'Oh! Good evening.' She turned towards him now. 'And thank you for your company.' She stressed this with a little inclining movement of her head.

'Thank you, miss. It's been a pleasure. So long.' He nodded to Peter, then went through the gap.

The girl remained kneeling, her back to Peter. He did not move from where he was, and with silence hanging between them they gazed over the pond. So quiet did they remain that the night sounds became loud; a rabbit scurrying through the undergrowth, a vole gliding into the water that he was used to, but was she? Yet none of them he noted had had the usual effect. She had not exclaimed at the sight of the rat, or jumped as the bat swooped above her head, which was odd for a town person.

He watched her now slowly rise to her feet.

Then as she dusted down the front of her coat, she said, 'I don't think we'll see her tonight, do you? Not in this light.'

'No.' He smiled quietly at her, for the moment all embarrassment gone.

'We'd better be getting back then.' Her eyes were high up under her lids, looking at him.

'Yes.'

Why couldn't he say something besides yes and no? He managed more than that with Florrie, or even Mavis.

He had turned and was about to lead the way out when the sound of steps breaking harshly through the undergrowth checked him. And then came the sound of a voice, which he recognised instantly as Bill Fountain's, and although it was hushed and held a cautionary note, and was full of Bill's deep rumbling laughter, his sharp ears caught the words clearly as Bill said, 'Aw! you can't hoodwink me man Harry, but you didn't oughter do it.'

'Don't be so bloody soft, Bill.' His father's voice was muffled, yet loud. 'I tell you it was an eel.'

Peter threw a quick glance towards the girl, then away again.

'Ooh! Oh, Harry!'

'Look, you great lumbering, fat fool, come back here a minute.'

As Peter heard their feet scrambling nearer, he chewed on his lip for a moment; then somewhat sheepishly he sauntered back to the edge of the bank. But the girl didn't move, she was standing with her head bowed, and he had the uneasy feeling that she was laughing at him. And then her next words startled him, bringing the colour up to his hair. 'We'd better prove the point, hadn't we?'

He shot a swift glance at her, and she made a little face at him.

'What point?'

Without answering she came with unhurried steps to his side, and, deliberately kneeling down again, she leaned over the bank and gazed into the darkening water.

He stood looking down at her. By! she was a cool customer . . . experienced. He wondered how often she'd had to prove the point. And in the moment before his father and Bill Fountain made their appearance a number of questions raced through his mind. Where was she from? Where was she going? What had she done? Who was she, anyway, with her pale skin and that tired look on her face, which robbed it of what he thought to be her natural youth? Yet she wasn't young, her ways weren't young. Where had she learnt to be so smart on the uptake, on this particular kind of uptake, anyway? With men. Aye, with men. Perhaps in pubs – she threw a dart like a man. Yet she didn't really look or sound like a brash pub-type. And she knew about eels . . .

Harry was not wearing his usual grin when he made his reappearance, closely followed by Bill, but before he could give any explanation the girl turned from the bank and, with slightly feigned surprise, said, 'Oh, hello. You've come back again.' Then to Bill, 'Hello, there.'

It appeared all of a sudden as if Bill's weight

was becoming burdensome to him, for he threw it from side to side. As for Harry, his jaws champed a number of times before he managed to bring out, 'I wanted to show him where we saw the eel, miss.'

'Oh, the eel. Well, it was just about there.' As she pointed Bill moved to the edge of the bank and peered down into the water; then glancing at her, he asked, 'Fact, miss? An eel here?'

'Yes . . . fact. And a real beauty, too.'

'No – can't believe it.' Bill shook his head. 'We're miles from the river. Up above it an' all. Who found her?'

'The twins,' said Harry butting in. 'And it's like this here, Bill: if Mackenzie or Crabb hear of it, it's so-long to the eel.'

'Aye, I see.' Then as Bill looked at Harry his expression became puzzled. 'You not going to catch it yersel', Harry?'

After moving his head impatiently, Harry's eyes steadily avoided those of his son and the girl, and concentrating his gaze on his mate as if Bill were a backward youth who had to be instructed in the rudimentary habits of eels, he said, 'She's on her way back to the sea. She's likely had a tough enough time getting here. I believe in giving any fish a sporting chance.'

'You do, Harry?' This charitable characteristic of his friend where fish were concerned was evidently a new one on Bill.

'Yes, I do.' Harry's head bounced once. 'And for your information her name's Slinky Jane.' He laid some emphasis on the Slinky, making it distinct from Sylvia.

'Slinky . . . Jane!' Bill's lower lip was hanging in an astonished gape.

'Yes, the lady here christened her.' Harry indicated the lady without looking at her.

'Well, I'll be damned! Slinky Jane.' Bill's round, bright eyes rolled in their nests of fat. They went from Peter to the girl, then on to Harry, then back again to the girl. And he chuckled, 'Good name, miss, for an eel. Never heard one like that afore for 'em.'

'No?' The amusement came over in her voice. 'We always called them that when we were children. What name do you give them here?'

Whatever answer Bill would have given to this was checked by the bark of a dog, and from quite near, and the bark caused Harry to jerk his head up. 'God above! that's Felix, and where he is the major's not far behind. I don't want to have to go over all this again, come on.' He nodded to Bill, and Bill, somewhat reluctantly, said, 'Aye, yes;' then touching his forehead in salute, he added, 'Be seeing you, miss – and,' he chortled, 'Slinky Jane.'

Peter's one desire at the moment was to follow on the heels of his father and Bill, the last thing in the world he wanted was to explain about the eel to the major. The major wouldn't believe a word of it. Unless he saw it he would be harder to convince than his father had been this afternoon. And the major would talk. He would talk about the eel not being here, of the impossibility of an eel ever reaching this water; and he would, as likely as not, cap every remark with a quotation, for the major had a known weakness for quotations. What was more, if he found him alone here with the girl, he wouldn't be above putting two and two together and making it a topic of conversation at breakfast tomorrow morning. Peter had a swift mental picture of Florrie descending on him again.

'Come on, let's get out of here.'

In his eagerness to be gone he forgot for the moment to whom he was talking.

'Why the hurry?'

He threw a glance back at her, and then said, 'I'll explain later. Come on.'

When they were out of the clearing he found that he had to make a quick decision. If he went back the usual way he would like as not run into the major, so there was nothing for it but to go down the beech drive which would bring them out by the church.

'We'll go this way,' he said, turning sharply to the right. 'We'll have to go in single file for a bit. You'd better keep close behind.'

They had gone quite some distance before he spoke again, and then it was just to throw over his shoulder the evident fact that it was, 'Almost dark now.'

Her voice sounded very small, as she answered, 'Yes,' and he realised that she was some little way behind, and so he called, 'You'll have to keep up and watch where you're going here.'

He slowed his pace a little but she still seemed to keep her distance, saying nothing. Once he heard her stop, and he turned. He could just make out that she was loosening a bramble from her coat. He knew his father would have sprung back to her assistance, but all he could make himself say was, 'You all right?'

'Yes.'

Somewhat reluctantly, he moved on again, until he came to where the path broadened into the beech drive. Here it was darker still, and he stopped and waited for her to come up, and when she did they walked on, now side by side, but in silence.

All about them was a quietness. There was no wind, there were no night noises here, no rustlings, only the sound of their feet on the leaves. He looked up into the thick, dark mat of the beeches. It was like the roof of night, for he could see no light through them. He cast his eyes sideways at her and wondered if she were afraid, and thought how odd it was to be walking in a dark wood and with her, when only a few hours ago he had never set eyes on her. He found himself wishing she would speak, just say something – anything. But instead she made a noise which sounded like a strangled cough, and he felt rather than saw her grope for her handkerchief. A little farther on she made the noise again. They were nearing the end of the beech wood now and it was getting somewhat lighter, and when they came to where the oaks took over he saw the moon coming up – she was heavy and gold-laden, and almost full. It was, he thought, as if her rising had stilled the wind and silenced the wood. He liked the moon. He could never really describe the feeling the moon had on him; he only knew that he liked her hanging over his village, draping the mountains and washing the valley bottoms with a light that did things to a man and transferred his life momentarily to a dream place, where the secrets of his inner world were no longer secrets but took over with a naturalness that made his days seem false.

Peter had moments when the deep poetry of the hills took hold of him, and this was one of them. His natural shyness and slight gaucheness were sliding away, leaving him with words with which to break the silence. And he did break it, to quote of all things, Wordsworth. Softly the words slipped out as he gazed up at his inspiration:

'She was a phantom of delight
When first she gleamed upon my sight:
A lovely apparition, sent
To be a moment's ornament.'

So beguiled was he in this moment that he saw no double meaning in the oration, but he was abruptly brought from his moon-dream to a dead-stop, and was suffused from head to toe in a hot, prickling glow. In a lather of embarrassment he jerked his head stiffly to the side and peered at the girl. She had stopped, and with her handkerchief pressed over her mouth she was struggling to suppress her mirth. She was standing in a patch of moonlight, and he could see her face plainly. And now she gasped, 'D-don't look like that. Oh . . . ! I'm – I'm sorry.' She seemed in pain with her laughter.

'Go on – laugh,' he said, 'it does you good to laugh.' His voice was cold and had an edge to it. She had one hand round her waist and was holding herself closely, and her head dropped forward as she said, 'I've – I've got to – to – to laugh. I must – I must. Let me laugh.'

His face was dead straight. 'There's nobody stopping you.'

Once more she looked up at him; then turning swiftly to the solid trunk of the oak she leant against it, and to his actual amazement laughter burst from her afresh and mounted, peal on top of peal, and so ringing was it that he had the idea that it stirred the trees, for at that moment the top branches swayed and the leaves rustled, building up a wave of gentle sound to pass over the wood. But her laughter outdid the rustle, and in real panic now he thought, They'll hear her in the village. What was she laughing at, anyway? Just because he had said that bit of poetry? Surely it couldn't have tickled her that much. It wasn't ordinary laughter; it sounded a bit hysterical to him. He went close to her, saying, 'Ssh! Ssh!'

'Oh dear! oh dear!' Her laughter took on a cackling quality, and in spite of himself he was forced to smile, although he looked about him apprehensively as he did so as if expecting the entire village to appear.

He was cautioning her again when he remembered with something akin to horror that it was Monday and the minister would be holding his weekly educational meeting in the church hall, which lay not more than fifty yards to the right of them. This knowledge forced him to entreat her now, 'Look . . . look, steady up . . . be quiet now, you see we are near the church and they'll . . .'

'Oh dear! oh dear! . . . What? What did you

say?' She was drying her eyes but he did not repeat what he had said, only waited for her to quieten down further.

Slowly now she moved from the tree and stood with her head bowed for a moment as if trying to regain her composure before starting to walk along the path again. But although her mirth had lessened, apparently she could not gain control over it altogether, and when they came to the stile that led into the road she stopped and said apologetically between gasps, 'I – I must wait. It will pass . . . in a minute. Oh, I'm sorry.'

He stood looking at her, with the bar of the stile between them. The moon was full on her now, showing her face as it had perhaps once been, pink and rose-tinted. The laughter had made her eyes bright and dark; her lips were wide and very red. He watched the moisture gleaming on them as they moved without framing words.

'Why did you laugh like that?' he asked soberly.

She seemed to think a moment before replying, and then she said, still between little gasps, 'It was a bit of everything. It's been such an odd day. Finding the eel; then meeting your father in the wood; and Mr Fountain thinking . . .' She did not elucidate further on this point and explain what she thought Bill had been thinking, but went on, 'And us all scampering from the major. Then – then Wordsworth – in the wood.'

The heat rose again and he rubbed his hand tightly across his mouth.

'Please—' although she was still smiling, there was a sincere note of pleading in her voice – 'please don't be vexed.'

'I'm not vexed.'

'Yes – yes, you are.' She dabbed at her eyes and added, 'Oh, if I'm not careful I'll start again, and I mustn't. Oh, I'm sorry.'

'Be quiet a minute.' His tone compelled her silence, and she was quiet, but only with the aid of her handkerchief held tightly to her mouth.

'There's somebody coming.'

Her eyes widened and they seemed to say silently, 'Well, why worry?'

There were more than one pair of footsteps, and if Peter had wanted to retreat it would have been impossible now, for stepping off the grass verge onto the road came four people: the Reverend Mr Collins, Miss Bridget Collins, Mrs Armstrong, the postmistress, and Mavis Mackenzie. They were all silent. They all hesitated, and they all looked towards the stile. Then they all, without exception, gaped at the couple behind it. And it was evident from their varying expressions that the source of the unseemly laughter was being revealed to them. Peter Puddleton had been in the wood with a woman, was in the wood with a woman. Had it been Harry Puddleton or even Old Pop, three of the onlookers would have said 'Well, what do you expect?' But when it was Peter who was supposed to have none of the Puddleton ways, it would just show you, wouldn't it? Blood would out! For here he was, before their eyes larking boisterously in the wood in the moonlight with a woman. And such a woman! Long, blond hair and painted!

It was unfortunate that Mavis should have been standing nearest the stile, for she was being given a first-class view of the depraved pair, and her eyes seemed to leap from her aggrieved countenance and take in all that she could see of the girl. Then they were switched to Peter, and, her voice expressing their fury, she exclaimed, 'Well!'

Never had a word said so much.

Peter's reaction should have been a desire to sink through the ground, but, strangely enough, he wished to do no such thing. In this incident, which was the culmination of a strange evening, he saw a ready-made loophole for his escape from Mavis and the implications resulting from his having been a damned fool. So, in a tone quite unlike his own, for it held a ring of cockiness, he called out to her, as if she were at the end of the road, 'Evening, Mavis.'

Mavis, after one sizzling glare, gave voice to another pointed exclamation. 'You!' she cried, before marching off after the rest of the company, with nothing now of her genteel, mincing nature evident in her back view.

'Oh, dear!' This was not the prelude to more laughter but a definite expression of sorrow. The girl's face showed deep concern as she looked in the direction Mavis had taken, and after emitting another drawled out 'O . . . oh!' she turned quickly to Peter, saying, 'What have I done? I'm sorry. It was such a stupid thing to do, to laugh like that. I must explain to her and put things right.'

'No! No! You'll not.' Hastily, Peter put up his hand to emphasise his words. 'No, don't explain anything – please.'

'Are you sure?' She gazed up at him, her brows puckered.

'Yes. Oh, yes, I'm sure all right.' Slowly his body relaxed, a grin spread over his face, and from under his breath he said, 'I might as well tell you, you've done me a favour. And,' he added, 'you've wiped the slate clean for having taken the mickey out of me.'

'Yes?' It was a question.

'Yes, honest. You couldn't have done it better. I should thank you. The truth is—' He took his eyes from her face and, looking down at his feet, kicked gently at the stile support, 'I'm an easy-going type, I always take the line of least resistance. She, Mavis, was the line, in this instance.' He raised his eyes now to hers, and the twinkle in them was deep as he concluded, 'She's aiming to tie me up with it.'

Their gaze held, their eyes laughed into each others; their teeth nibbled at their lips, then like two errant children they clapped their hands over their faces to suppress their laughter, and above the horizon of their hands they stared at each other. And it would seem that the testing period of friendship, without the aid of time, was accomplished, and in the first knowledge of it their laughter died in them, and there came on them a silence, and in the silence the girl turned away and leant on the stile and looked on to the road, while Peter turned and looked up at the moon. He had a 'don't care a damn' feeling, and for no accountable reason that he could see he felt bubbly happy, as if he had caught a fish, perhaps an eel four feet long.

'It's odd, but today has been like a short lifetime.'

'What did you say?' He turned quickly towards her, but she continued to look down on to the road as she repeated, 'I said today has been like a lifetime, a short lifetime,' She lifted her head and looked away over the low hedge on the other side of the road, across the moon-capped fells down to the valley. Her voice held no laughter now but a deep sadness, as she added, 'Nothing ever happens in life as you expect it. Do you know that when I came into this village today I thought I would never laugh again, and I didn't care.' Her voice trailed away, and he moved with a soft step to her side, and his gaze like hers looking away into the moon-flooded night he waited, with a feeling strong in him that he was being taken into her confidence.

And the waiting held no embarrassment. Then she went on, as if she were thinking aloud, 'There was nothing left to laugh about, only things to cry over and questions to ask, and silence for answers – and fighting and proving and longing.'

She turned her gaze from the road now and found his eyes on her, narrowed and puzzled. For a moment she remained very still, returning his scrutiny, then with a little smile touching her lips she asked softly, 'Can I call you Peter? If I'm to be here for two weeks, or more, I cannot Mr Puddleton you all the time, can I?'

Still he gave her no direct answer. Her eyes were filled with moonlight – its soft shadowings had lent to her face a flush – she was beautiful . . .

she was the most beautiful thing he had ever seen in his life. 'What's your name?' he asked.

'Call me Leo . . . Leo Carter.'

'Leo?'

'Yes, Leo, short for Le-o-line.'

'Strange name.' His voice was deep in his throat.

'Yes, it is.'

Suddenly she shivered and pulled her coat closer around her. 'I'll go back now.' She put out her hand, palm frontwards, in a small protesting movement. 'Don't come.' There was a pause before she added, 'Good night, Pee-ter.' She split his name. 'I'll see you tomorrow.'

'Good night.' His voice was gruff.

She had her foot on the stile as she turned and prompted him, saying, 'Leo.'

He leaned forward and took her hand and helped her over; then repeated, 'Good night, Leo.'

She smiled at him once again, but now it was a small, somewhat sad smile. It was the smile that she had worn earlier in the day which just touched her lips, there was no trace of her laughter left. He watched her walk away, and when he could no longer see or hear her footsteps he turned and retraced his own to the beech wood again.

It was queer, but he no longer felt bubbly happy, no longer did he have that don't-care-a-damn feeling, but the feeling that was in him now he would not recognise, he would not say that he was afraid. Would his father have been afraid? Or yet, in their time, his grandfather, or great-grandfather? No, they would have known how to deal with her and all her strange facets. They certainly wouldn't have let her walk off without an effort to stop her – and the night so young.

But there were two weeks ahead, and there was one thing he was now certain sure of . . . there was something coming about between him and her – an affair. Aye! an affair. He paused and looked up at the moon and became lost in it.

Chapter Three

As he dressed Peter whistled softly under his breath, but before opening his bedroom door he abruptly cut off this expression of his feelings and went quietly out onto the landing. His intention was to make himself a cup of tea and slip out without waking any of them, but, on creeping downstairs and entering the kitchen, who should he see sitting at the table, a pot of tea between them, but the old 'uns.

'Hello, what's up with you two?' he asked.

'Oh, hallo there, lad,' they answered him, almost together. Then Old Pop, sucking at his tea, added, 'Couldn't sleep. Never do when moon's full.'

Although he had heard it before, this remark, for some reason, annoyed Peter, and he exclaimed, 'Don't talk daft, Old Pop.'

'Daft? Nothin' daft about it.' Old Pop sounded huffy. 'Affects old 'un' an' all, even at his time, don't it?'

'Aye, it does that.' Grandpop wagged his head, then raised his bleared eyes to Peter. 'And your dad, it does – oh, aye, your dad. Ah well—' he gave a throaty laugh – 'them days are gone for half'n us, any road. What d'you say, lad?'

Peter, looking towards Grandpop's thin, bony, multi-coloured legs, where they stuck out of his nightshirt, remarked, 'You know what'll happen if me mam finds you out here like that, don't you?'

This threat brought forth no nervous murmurings from Grandpop; instead it released a mixed torrent of resentment and warning. 'Blast yer ma!' he said. 'And all women. And you'll get caught – aye, you'll see me lad, with one or t'other. And not in till ten past twelve. Aye, I heard you. Moon's got him an' all, I said. Aye, I did. Never been late like that afore. Were with that buckteeth after all, weren't you? You wasn't with t'other one, for close on dark she went galloping along street as if devil was after her. Waved to me, she did. Aye, she's all right, but too young and silly. Not for you, lad, not for you. But that other one . . . God above!' Grandpop's eyes roved around the ceiling as if searching for the Deity, and Peter, knowing that any comment whatever would only succeed in getting him more deeply involved in this conversation, made his escape to the scullery, where he washed hastily, made himself a cup of tea and slipped out of the back door.

And that was the beginning of a very odd morning.

At nine o'clock he had a visit from an agent. The man had breezed in, said his name was Funnel and offered him two hundred and fifty pounds for the spare bit of land. And he was hardly gone before old Mr Mackenzie himself put in an appearance. Like oil he was – he had come to warn him about the agent. He stayed half an hour doing this, and Peter went through three handfuls of tow.

Then from ten o'clock onwards he had visits from his neighbours. Their sociability he laid down to curiosity about his intentions regarding the future of the garage; yet funnily enough most of them never mentioned the garage, they just stood about watching him tearing at the car, and laughed and joked, as far as he could see, about nowt.

It had also been a good morning for petrol. If he'd had nothing to occupy him he wouldn't have sold a gallon, but he had been from his knees to the pumps on and off all the morning.

But most important of all was the fact that the twins had visited him twice to report that the eel was still there, but that they hadn't seen 'the Miss'. And he himself hadn't seen 'the Miss', and it was now eleven-thirty. You would have thought, after what had taken place last night, that she would have dandered down towards the garage, wouldn't you? He asked this of himself during one of the quiet spells, and when by twelve o'clock he still hadn't seen her he began to ask himself further questions, such as had he been daft to imagine what he had done last night? Had his father and Bill Fountain jumped to similar conclusions because she had smiled at them? Had they thought, I'm on an affair? When he came to think about it he must have been a little cuckoo. And not only a little . . . plum barmy, he would say. And then to keep on wandering about in the woods till twelve o'clock on his own!

Perhaps the old 'uns weren't so far wrong after all about the moon.

When another three cars in close succession drew up for petrol, he began to ask himself if the road had already gone through and he hadn't noticed it.

The last one was unusually big and bright. It was a deep blue outside and deep red inside, and it had lent a little of its flamboyancy to its owner who was wearing a fawn coloured suit, a blue check shirt, and light tan sandals, and although, apparently, only in his forties he claimed paternity over Peter straight away in addressing him, 'Fill her up, son, and tell me where the hell I am supposed to be!'

'Battenbun,' said Peter briefly.

'There, I told you, I said it was Battenbun.' It was the other occupant of the car speaking, and Peter, looking through the window at the lady, summed these two up as 'jaunters'. The fellow, likely, had a wife and family somewhere, and the present female was what was left over from a week-end. The garage business created the faculty of tabulating types, and these two were not new.

'I want to get Durham way.'

'Straight through the village, turn right at the crossroads. You can't miss.'

It was after Peter had switched off the last gallon that he noticed that the man had got out of the car and was now walking towards the garage door. He had his back towards him and he didn't turn around when he spoke. 'Here, a minute,' he said. And when Peter got to his side he didn't say what he wanted but walked with exaggerated casualness right into the garage and, of all places, to the back of the office, and there his casualness vanished.

'Where did you get that plate?' he demanded, pointing back to the number plate of the Alvis lying against the garage door.

Peter did not reply immediately but stared at the man, and the man, shaking his head with a nervous movement which did not tie up with his bizarre manner, said, 'Look, I know that number, and the car, an Alvis. Where is it?'

Slowly, and without taking his eyes off the man, Peter nodded towards the jumble of pieces lying at the back of the garage, and the man, after following his direction, jerked round again and exclaimed, 'You bought her! Who off?'

'I didn't buy her.'

'No?'

'No, she's in for repair.'

This statement had an odd effect on the man. He glanced back at the pieces which had comprised the Alvis, then in the direction of his own car, then again quickly to Peter.

'The owner, where is she?' His voice was a low rumble.

Peter's eyes had never left the man, and now there was a stiffness about his jaw that made his words slow of utterance. 'At the Hart,' he said.

'Here?' The man's nervousness increased.

'Along the street.'

The man wetted his lips as he asked, 'She's waiting till the job's done?'

'Yes.'

'What's wrong? At least—' he gave a shaky

laugh – 'it would be easier to tell me what wasn't wrong with that.'

'Big ends.'

'Oh.' He pulled at his tie; then licking his forefinger and thumb in his mouth, he rubbed them together, before carefully following the knife-crease down the front of his trousers.

If for no other reason, this action alone would have aroused Peter's dislike.

'Well, thanks.' He turned to go, then stopped, and with his eyes on the jumble of the Alvis pieces he said under his breath, 'I happen to know the owner, Miss Carter, isn't it?'

'Yes, it's a Miss Carter.' Peter went to the cash box in the office and took out some change, and when he handed it over the man said, 'That's all right.' Then straightening his shoulders and adopting again his jaunty air, he made for the opening of the garage, saying loudly and clearly now, 'Well, thanks for the information.'

Peter jerked his head in acknowledgement, but did not thank him for the tip, for never had he felt so reluctant to accept a tip from anyone. He stood some way inside the garage and watched the man get into the car, and heard his snappy rejoinder to the woman's enquiry as to what had kept him. Then, to his surprise, he saw the car swing round the drive and leap away, not through the village and past the Hart towards the road that led to Durham, but back the way from which it had come.

So he knew her, did he? Well, and what of it? He'd had folks draw up here because they'd recognised the number plate of a standing car as being from some town in the South or in Scotland or as far off as Wales. The fact that someone knew her should make her less of a mystery for, apart from her name, the number plate which indicated Essex and the fact that she had lived in Norfolk was the sum total of his knowledge of her. Yet if it hadn't sounded so daft he would have argued that he had always known her, that she hadn't descended on this village at twelve o'clock yesterday but had been here from the time his memory first started to register. This quaint knowledge was not pleasant to him, for it brought with it a disturbed feeling as if there was something here he just couldn't fathom.

He went onto the drive and looked down the street, and his eyes, skipping over the usual people doing the usual things, came to rest on the Hart. Should he go and tell her about the fellow? The fact that she was acquainted with such a type did nothing to enhance her, and yet hadn't he already agreed that she was well acquainted with all types? She hadn't learned to play darts like she did in Sunday school, not yet cope with men, in the same place. And she could cope with men. She'd had a lot to do with men, he could tell that. His arm went up in an impatient wave to Grandpop at the open window, and almost instantly the old fellow's voice could be heard bellowing, 'You, Jo . . . oe?'

When Old Pop, very short of breath, came hurrying to the garage, he asked, 'What's up now?'

'Nothing very much, I just want you to stay a

minute. I've got to go to the Hart and see the owner.' He nodded back into the garage.

'That all?' Old Pop wiped his forehead. 'I wish you'd get up some signal, lad, when I've got to rush and when I ain't.'

Peter gave his grandfather a wry smile. 'Wouldn't be much use as far as I can see. It's the old 'un's voice you want to alter.'

'Aye, lad, you're right there. Wouldn't surprise me if he weren't to blast them all out of the graveyard when he gets in it. But it's a sure thing there'll be a helluva bellowing that day.'

This comment on Grandpop's future activities brought a short laugh from Peter, and as he went down the street and past the garden he waved to the old man. And Grandpop returned his greeting; then yelled after him, 'You dry, lad? S'm I, begod! mouth like an ash pit. Could do with one an' all . . . a long 'un.'

Peter's answer to this was merely a backward jerk to his head.

At the Hart he went into the main bar. It was empty but for Mrs Booth, and she did not as usual greet him with a 'Hallo, there,' but went on with her occupation of arranging some flowers in a vase in the deep bay window.

'Morning. Nice day again.'

'Oh! Good morning.' Mrs Booth had half-turned as if in surprise; then she turned her whole attention to the flowers again.

'I'll have half a pint, please.'

As if reluctant to leave her artistic occupation Mrs Booth stood back and surveyed her handiwork, and Peter watched her. There was something amiss here – she was on her high horse. He knew the signs all right.

'Half a pint you said?'

'Yes, please.'

Mrs Booth sailed slowly round the counter and drew the half pint, and Peter, putting his money down, said, 'I'll take a bottle for Grandpop.' He looked around the empty bar, listened for a moment to the sounds from the cellar where Mr Booth was busy, and then asked as casually as he could, 'Miss Carter in? I'd like a word with her.'

Now the nature of the high horse was immediately brought into the open, for with her hand covering the top of the bottle Mrs Booth became still, and very slowly through pursed lips, she said, 'Yes, Miss Carter is in. Very much in, if you ask me. It's now twelve o'clock and Her Ladyship has just decided to get up. Asked if she could have tea and toast in bed, if you please!'

At this point Mrs Booth breathed deeply before going on. 'I said people didn't usually stay in bed here until twelve o'clock, and if they didn't come down for their breakfast they went without. And she's gone without, she has!' Her hand grabbed up the money from the counter with such force that the muscles rippled up her brawny arm. 'I've never known the likes of it! Coming in here after we were all locked up last night and then expecting to have her breakfast taken up to her.' She glared at Peter, and he, flushing in spite of all his efforts not to, said, 'Well, it's got nothing to do with me – it's none of my business, is it?'

'Oh!' Mrs Booth drew her chin in, 'Isn't it?'

'No, Mrs Booth, it isn't.'

Her next words brought his mouth open. 'There were two people drunk and roaring in the wood last night – I'm mentioning no names – and if My Ladyship wasn't lit up when she came in at midnight then her eyes belied her and my eyes deceived me.'

'Hello.'

Peter swung round towards the doorway.

To say that he felt uncomfortable was very much of an understatement. His mind was grappling with a number of things at once! Where had she spent her time from when she left him last night? And did Mrs Booth mean she was drunk when she came in? And she'd had no breakfast. And old Ma Booth was a real swine; but the thought which burst the surface of his mind was: That fellow could be her husband.

'It's a beautiful morning.' She was looking directly at him.

'Yes. Yes, it is.'

The girl having ignored Mrs Booth completely, turned away and walked along the passage, while he picked up the bottle, dropped it into his pocket and followed her out.

She had stopped just under the roof porch. Her head was back and she was looking up at the sky, and as he came to her side, her eyes swept over the green and along the street, and she repeated, 'It is a beautiful morning.'

'Yes. Yes, it is.'

They had both said the same thing before.

As he stood uneasily by her side he was conscious that somewhere behind them Mrs Booth was both watching and listening, and that if he wanted to talk to the girl he would have to move away from here. What he would have liked to say to her was, 'Come on down to our house and have a bite,' but he could see his mother's face if he dared to walk into the house with her.

He glanced at her. She was all in red, a soft red dress, sandals, and toe-nails, and the colour made her face look whiter, if that were possible, and her hair more straw-coloured.

In the lowest whisper he could manage, he said, 'Would you step along here a minute? I've got something to say to you.'

She glanced quickly at him, then without further words she walked with him to the far wall of the inn yard, her sandals making a loud clip-clop, clip-clop on the stones. And when he stopped she looked up at him with a smile similar to that of yesterday just touching her lips and said, 'Don't tell me that the vicar has issued an ultimatum that I leave in twenty-four hours.'

He laughed; then stopping abruptly, he said, 'A man called in for petrol this morning. He recognised your number plate. He said he knew you.'

For some moments her expression did not change, and she continued to look at him as if what he'd said had not registered. Then blinking her eyes rapidly she murmured, 'Knew me? Did he say who he was?'

'No. He had a big car, an Austin Princess, blue body.'

From her profile he could see that the description meant nothing to her, but as he went on, saying, 'He was about forty-five, I should say, tall, black hair . . . curly,' he saw her teeth drop sharply into her lower lip, and she remained perfectly still for a moment. Then she looked along the length of the village before bringing her eyes up to him. 'It's a small world,' she said.

'That's what they say.' But instead of this inanity he had wanted to ask abruptly, 'Who is he, your husband?'

'Did you tell him I was here?'

'Yes. I couldn't do anything else.'

'No, of course not. Did he say he'd be back?'

'No.'

He watched her open her bag and take out a handkerchief and dab at her mouth with it. He watched her replace the handkerchief then click the bag closed, and he was waiting for her look as it came to his. But he was both surprised and piqued when all she said was, 'Is there any place where I could get a cup of coffee in the village?'

He seemed to think a moment, although it wasn't necessary, but her changing the subject like that had flummoxed him a little. Then he said, 'Yes, Miss Tallow does coffee on occasions.'

'The little drapery shop?'

'Yes.'

'Well, I'll take a walk down there. Are you coming this way?'

He swallowed before saying, 'Aye – yes, I'm on me way back.'

Together they walked through the village, side by side but not too close. No, he saw to that . . . there'd be enough chipping and chaffing because he was walking with her. He had walked with other strangers through the village, but she was different somehow. She was like nobody that had ever been in this village before, she was one of those people who had only to sneeze to cause an epidemic.

They had an over-hearty wave from Bill Fountain; they had an interesting peer from Mrs Armstrong through the post office window; they had a long following glare from Mrs Mackenzie; they had a loud hail from Grandpop; so it was not without relief that Peter left with just a nod at Miss Tallow's door.

She was a cool customer, he'd say that for her – nothing appeared to ruffle her. Yet when he had first mentioned the bloke she had been startled. But it was only for a second or so, she was a dab hand at covering up.

When he reached the garage, all Old Pop said was, 'Aye, aye!' and Peter, in an unusually sharp tone, asked, 'And now what do you mean by that?'

'Nowt, nowt, lad,' said Old Pop as he walked away, 'just aye, aye!'

It was three o'clock and Peter was standing in the middle of the road trying to carry on a conversation with Josh Turnbull above the rattle of his tractor, when out of the corner of his eye he saw his mother rampaging over the green. Immediately his mind registered trouble, for her walk was such as he had witnessed only when she was on the war-path, going from room to room in the house after a to-do with his dad. This was Tuesday afternoon and Women's Institute. He patted the vibrating machine and yelled, 'All right, Josh, I'll pop over in the morning and have a look at her. 'Bye.'

As Josh raised his hand in farewell and set the tractor moving Rosie came onto the drive. She didn't look at Peter but made straight for the garage, which augured bad, for he knew that his mother liked to fight her wars in private. When he followed her in Rosie was already in the office, the doorknob still in her hand.

'What's up, Mam?' he asked.

'Come in here.'

He went in, and Rosie with some manoeuvring closed the door behind him, which left about two feet of space between them.

'What's the matter? Is it Dad?'

Rosie's bosom took an upward tilt, her nostrils narrowed and she said, 'We'll come to that. Where were you last night?'

So that was it. He commanded his expression to give nothing away. He knew his mother. If he were to speak the truth and say, 'At the lake with the girl from the Hart,' she would not only jump to conclusions but be miles ahead of anyone else in the village, at least where he was concerned.

'Now look, Mam,' he said soothingly, 'I don't have to keep a diary of where I go, now do I?'

'Don't try to sidetrack me, Peter. Do you know what they're saying?'

'They're always saying something, you should know that by now. There's a saying that goes, "They say, let them say . . ." '

'I don't want to hear any sayings,' said Rosie tartly; 'I hear enough. I know full well about sayings, I've had a bellyful of them in this village.

And when they're the truth you've got to put up with them, but this is lies. You weren't drunk last night, were you?'

'Me, drunk!' His eyes widened. 'No, of course not. Not on two half-pints I wasn't.'

'There!' Rosie's breath escaped in a faint hiss of relief. 'That bitch!'

'Who? Mrs Booth?'

'No, Miss Collins.'

'Miss Collins?'

In spite of his determination to give nothing away Peter moved uneasily, and he turned his attention to the petrol-stained ledger lying open on the desk, and this guilty and evasive action sent Rosie's relief fleeing away and she demanded, 'Look here. Were you in the wood last night with her – the woman – the owner of the car?'

'Now, Mam. Look, I can explain.'

Rosie, suddenly covering her eyes with her hand, said, 'I don't want no lies. I've had enough of lies all me life . . . don't you start. You were there and that's all there is about it.'

'There's no need for me to lie, Mam. I just went to the lake to look at—' he salved his conscience in giving the presence of the eel away by saying, 'a fish.'

'A fish?' The unlikelihood of this excuse aroused Rosie's anger again and had a drying effect on her tears. 'A fish?' she cried. 'Huh! I'll say she's a fish, and men's her bait. Did you know your dad was looking for fish an' all – and Bill Fountain?'

Aye,' said Peter now, with a wry smile. 'We were all together.'

'You were all to—!' Rosie's mouth sagged.

'Yes, we were all together.'

Peter was beginning to enjoy her discomfort.

After looking blankly at him for a moment, she asked in a very subdued tone, 'What kind of fish is it?'

Peter moved his feet and he rubbed his hand up over his face, and after some slight hesitation he brought out, 'Look, Mam, it's an eel, the biggest we've seen, and if it gets about Mackenzie or Crabb, or one or other in the village will have her.'

'An eel! But why not?' asked Rosie puzzled. 'Your dad an' you've always been on about the eels pinching your bait and spoiling the fishing.'

'Yes, I know, but this one's such a size and we feel she should have a chance to get home.'

'Home?' Rosie's face slowly screwed up, and Peter giving a patient sigh, went on to explain as briefly as possible where the eel was going – that's if it got there – also who had first seen it and how the girl had come into the picture. 'Well,' he said, drawing his breath in, 'now you know.'

'Yes,' said Rosie. But after a moment's thought she was back to where she had come in. 'Then what made them think it was you who was drunk and carrying on?'

'We weren't carrying on. She – Miss Carter—' Peter stopped. If he were to explain, even if he could, what had tickled Miss Carter it would blow the lid off again, so with a little bit of quick thinking he said, 'She was tickled about the twins. It was her who made up that song about the eel.'

'Oh!' Over Rosie's face spread a slow beam. That's where they got it then. 'Well!' For a moment she looked a little foolish, then again remembering the full text of what Miss Collins had made sure she should overhear, she reverted to her starting point. 'But what made you yell out to Mavis Mackenzie?'

'Yell out? I didn't yell.'

'Well if you didn't, why did you call to her at all?'

Peter's head now swung on his shoulders. There seemed no escape, so he said somewhat grimly, 'Well, this should please you, you've been on about her enough, I did it to shoo her off. We were coming back; we'd got as far as the stile – Miss Carter was laughing – then that lot came past and I saw in the situation an opportunity I'd been, I suppose, looking for. As I said, Miss Carter was laughing, we were by the stile, the moon was shining and the whole set up was something I couldn't have manufactured or put over with my tongue, not in a life time. I might as well tell you I knew I'd been a blasted fool over Mavis, even when I took her out the first time, but when I went and did it again, well, it looked as if I'd jumped in with both feet and I couldn't see how I was going to pull out. And then – well . . .'

There was no need for Peter to go on, the beam was flowing like oil now over Rosie's whole body and she was slumping with relief. 'I knew you'd have sense, lad,' she said softly.

Again Peter's feet moved, and so much breath left his body that he felt his ribs cave in. 'Well, now that's cleared up,' he said briefly, 'I'll get back to work.' He squeezed towards the door, but before opening it he turned to her saying, 'But mind, you won't say anything about the eel, will you, Mam? Don't even let on to Dad that you know – or the lads.'

She nodded her head in small jerks and laughed as she said, 'And that explains that, an' all.'

'What?' he said.

'The twins hammering a couple of the Spraggs and chasing them out of the wood. About ten minutes afore I went to the meeting I had Daisy Spragg at the door asking if we were joint owners of the village along with the Mackenzies, and what she was going to do if I didn't do something with the lads. Well' – she smiled at her son – 'I'll send you some tea along.'

The air was clear again. He smiled back at her and nodded and watched her go out, then returned to his work. But he hadn't been at it more than ten minutes when Florrie's voice, coming from just behind him, startled him, causing the spanner to squeeze out of his hold like paste from a tube.

'Ah! guilty conscience . . . Be sure your sins will find you out!'

'What—' he swivelled round on his knees, then got clumsily to his feet – 'what are you talking about now?'

'What am I talking about now!' She smiled at him with a funny little smile that deceived him into thinking that perhaps she wasn't on the warpath this time.

'So you took my advice, did you?'

He returned her crooked smile with a grin, and said, 'You mean Mavis? Aye . . .'

'No, I don't mean Mavis.'

'You don't?' His brows puckered.

'How long is this going to take?' She kicked at the mudguard of the Alvis none too gently.

'I don't know.' He turned and grabbed up a handful of tow and began to rub his hands vigorously.

'That's a pity.' Florrie was holding him with a straight stare and there was a quirk on her lips, as she went on, 'You might find yourself with a maintenance order if you don't hurry up and get rid of it – and her.'

Like a thermometer plunged into boiling water, Peter's mercurial colour shot up, and with it his anger, startling both himself and Florrie; as did his words when he barked, 'That's enough of that! If you want to make such comments, then do so, but keep them for your social set at the Hunt Ball or any other place where it fits, but don't direct them at me.' He threw the tow against the wall.

Florrie's quirk was no longer in evidence, but the look she now bestowed on him sustained his anger and caused him to surprise himself further when he faced her squarely and said, 'I've had just about enough of this business all round, and I'll thank you to leave me and my affairs alone, Florrie, and do your hunting in the proper quarters.'

After this unchivalrous delivery his anger died quickly away, too quickly, for it left him sapped and thinking, 'That was a nice thing to say; you needn't have gone that far.'

The insult, however, did not seem to worry Florrie unduly, for she remarked, with a maddening casualness that she could adopt at will, 'It's a free country. And that, too, is what I said when I heard you were drunk and disorderly in the wood last night.'

'I was neither drunk nor disorderly.' His colour deepened.

Florrie, straddling her legs a little, pursed her lips. 'But you were in the wood with a certain lady of questionable aspect, weren't you?'

Slowly Peter's eyes screwed up, and he peered at her as if bringing her into focus as he repeated in a tone from which all the heat of his anger had died, leaving it cold, 'Questionable aspect?'

'Well, I understand she's a type – blond, trailing hair—' Florrie's hand demonstrated just how trailing – 'dead white face, skin-fit frock – the lot that one usually associates with that type.'

On Peter's face now was an expression Florrie had not seen there before, and in his tone a quality that annoyed her as he said, 'Have you seen Miss Carter?'

Florrie's chin jerked. 'No, I haven't seen Miss Carter, and I have no wish to.'

'That's as may be. Miss Carter is no more of a piece than – than you are. Not so much if the truth were told.'

Florrie stared at him in open amazement. That the lazy, indolent Peter Puddleton should take a stand like this for a woman – she did not class the owner of the car as a girl – whom he had known but a few hours added significance to the conclusion that was forcing itself on her. Something, almost with lightning speed, had changed him, and it certainly wasn't Mavis. And, with equal certainty, she knew it wasn't herself. This last admission was humiliating to say the least, but being fundamentally her mother's daughter, she drew herself up and for the first time in their acquaintance she put on an air, and the air was prominent in her tone as she said, 'Indeed? you must have been busy to find out so much in so short a time.'

'Now look here.' The hauteur of her manner must have escaped him, for he actually took a step towards her. And if she needed anything further to convince her that something drastic had happened to him it was this – this mild form of attack coming from him constituted a revolution. But after the step, her stare held him and checked what further defence he would have made, for at this moment she was looking an exact replica of her mother, and with much of her mother's manner and her flair for carrying off the honours of battle, whether as victor or vanquished, she now turned from him and without a word of any kind left the garage.

'Damn and blast!' He stamped into the office. What was the matter with everybody the day? He had never known people behave like it, not all at once he hadn't. Could he have done otherwise than defend himself against such an assumption? He went hot under the collar. What if the others thought the same. But no, nobody would think things like that, except Florrie. She was as racy as

– He would not give a definition of her raciness, but said to himself: If it's got as far as the Manor the whole place must be yapping about me – and her, and the lass not in the place five minutes.

'Where are you?' Old Pop came stumbling into the garage. 'Ah, there you are. Tea's here. What's up with your ma? Saw her come dashing up here like a retired greyhound. Owt wrong?'

'No, nothing.'

'Ah! you can't tell me there's nothin', she don't leave the wives inferno for nowt. Ah! you can't tell me. Tale going around you were blind drunk last night. You weren't lad, were you?'

'No, I wasn't.'

The bawl caused Old Pop to put his hand up and scratch the sparse hairs behind his ears. Then he commented, 'No, I thought you wasn't would have heard you else. We none of us were ever quiet when we was bottled. Not the first time of being bottled, we wasn't. No, by gum.' He grinned at Peter and handed him the mug of tea he had poured from the steaming jug. Then pouring out one for himself, he went to the box and sat down. After taking a long drink he wiped his mouth and remarked, apropos of nothing that had so far been mentioned, 'She's nice lass that, that miss at the Hart. She is an' all. What she don't know about eels ain't worth learnin'.'

Peter's mouth fell into a straight line, and he said, with a frankness he rarely used towards his grandfather, 'You like to nose, don't you?'

'Me? I wasn't nosin', Peter. Just taking a dander in the wood, and there she was with the young 'uns. The lads made me swear not to say a word, and it's all right with me. That's not saying I'd not like to catch she . . . the eel. There's some flesh on her and there's nothing tastier than a bit of eel. Though I have a fancy for them a bit younger, more tender then. And you know summat? The young lady knows every step of her road back – Saggassen Sea she makin' for, so she says.' He cocked his squint eye at Peter's stiff profile. 'She comes from Fenlands way, she says. Not the eel, her I mean. Says she used to fish the river with her grandda, and the young eels used to pinch the bait. Knows all the different flies, an' all. Never met no woman what didn't look like a sack an' talk fish like she. Started from scratch, so to speak, she did. Used to dig worms for her grandda. Fish he did, rain, hail or shine, she said. Had a big umbrella and a lot of paraphernalia. From morn till night they'd stay on the banks. Told me all about it, she did. Any more tea to spare there?' He handed his mug to Peter, who took it, filled it and handed it back to him without a word. And Old Pop, staring down into it, gave a chuckle and remarked, 'Remember like yesterday first time I got real sozzled. 'Twas right here at the Hart. Late summer 'twas, hay smellin' and moon shinin'. At least I remember the moon shinin' and standin' on Green singing at top of me voice. Fine voice I had an' all in those days. But be damned, I can't remember to this day how I reached Layman's Farm, and it three miles on, though when I woke in the morning and saw where I was I sprinted down the drainpipe and away across the fields as if the bull was after me.

Young Miss Phyllis got married two months later and off she went to foreign parts.'

'You finished?'

Old Pop, purposely misunderstanding his grandson, said, 'Aye,' and handed him the empty mug. Then rising from the box he added, 'Some bloke at the Hart's enquiring for the young lady. Booth himself came through the wood to tell her. Seemed in no hurry to go back, neither, he didn't. Talked like I never heard him afore . . . Well, you had enough?'

'Yes,' said Peter with some stress, 'I've had enough.'

Old Pop gathered up the things and, placing them in the basket, gave his grandson a cheerful leer. Then going to the doorway he turned and delivered his advice without any diplomatic coating. 'Remember, lad, time's flyin'. There's no time like the present. You leave your fling much longer and you'll lose the taste. An' I'm tellin' you.' He nodded solemnly before adding, 'Me, I could look back at summat at your age, I'll say. Though I don't blame you for steering clear of the Mackenzies' cow and Miss Florrie. One's as dry as the Methodist Chapel; as for t'other – she'd be another Bill Fountain's doe. Pregnant forty-seven times a year.' After which exaggeration of nature's bounty Old Pop departed, leaving Peter bursting, but speechless.

In the past, it had always been a source of satisfaction to Peter when his old Austin was out on hire, but tonight he was deeply regretting its absence. If it had been on hand he would have got her out and gone off somewhere.

He walked up the street, in the opposite direction from the Hart, past Miss Tallow's and past his own garage, which to him now looked somewhat unreal and not a little dilapidated. The closed doors seemed to make his name stand out starkly from the board nailed above them: PETER PUDDLETON, Garage Proprietor. He gave a disparaging 'Huh!' as he glanced at it. It was a daft-sounding name if ever there was one. Why with a name like Puddleton had his mother to call him Peter? Arthur, Bill, John, even Harry – but Peter! His life, he felt, had taken the cue from his name . . . there was no sense in it. He hadn't even the sense he was born with. For years now he had been content to slide along thinking that one day things would work out, which meant that one day he would find a lass to suit him and he would marry her. Then last night, because a woman, a strange woman, had laughed at him in the moonlight, he had been mad enough to imagine he was on to something.

He jumped the fence and, skirting the trees, took to the fields. Going by little-known paths and leaping gates and walls as if he had a grudge against them, he came to the lake. There was no-one looking into the water tonight; they would, he thought wryly, all be in the Hart, laying bets with each other no doubt as to what relation the flashy fellow was to her. Yet when you thought of it there was hardly any scope for betting, the relationship was pretty obvious.

The lake was still; the after-glow from the sun lay on it like patches of translucent paint. He stood at the edge of the bank but did not trouble to search the water for a sight of the eel, for in this light nothing could be seen but the reflection of the sky which seemed to have drowned itself in the lake. Soon the quietude and the colour had their effect upon him and he felt somewhat soothed and sat down with his knees up and his hands hanging slackly between them.

'You all on your own, lad?'

The voice of his grandfather seeming to come out of the air, for there was no sight of the old man, jerked Peter out of his reverie and brought him from the bank like a shot.

'I'm in here, lad. Thought you was somebody else when I heard you comin' . . . dashed for cover.' The brambles parted and Old Pop, pulling himself clear, stood before Peter with head downcast, meticulously picking the burrs from his clothes.

With an indrawn breath of exasperation Peter demanded, 'What are you doing here?'

'Just out for a walk, lad.'

'Out for a walk!' Peter's mouth squared itself, and Old Pop, cocking his good eye at his grandson, repeated, 'Just that lad, out for a walk.' Then nodding towards the water he added, excitedly, 'I've seen her.'

Peter, making absolutely sure to which 'her' the old man was referring, said stiffly, 'The eel?'

'Aye, half an hour gone by. She made me fingers itch. What say, lad, we have a shot at her?' Old Pop thrust his head forward. 'I could scoot back for line . . . or rig a few worms on some worsted.'

'You'll do no such thing. You leave her alone. Now mind, I'm telling you.'

Old Pop walked slowly to the water's edge and looked down. 'Pity . . . she'd be something to brag about the rest of your life, lad.'

'Maybe.'

'Heard young lady telling a bloke about 'un, little while gone.' Old Pop did not turn but kept his interest concentrated on the water.

'Where?' Peter was looking at his grandfather's back.

'In the wood here, with the bloke what came to the Hart for her. Said some funny things, both on 'em did, and not all about eels neither.'

'You didn't have to listen, did you?' Peter now sauntered the few steps back to the bank, and he too looked down into the water.

'Couldn't get out of it, lad.' Old Pop threw an amused look upwards at his grandson. 'Was answering urgent call behind bushes when they stopped close by. Was in a pickle, sure enough! But knew 'twould be they would get biggest shock did they see me. So just kept doggo.' He turned his face, now full of merriment, on Peter, but when it met no answering gleam he turned it away again and concentrated his gaze once more on the water. Then, after some moments, he commented, 'Nice girl, she – but fancy she's been in trouble.'

'What makes you think that?'

'Oh, just something what was said, you know.' Old Pop, with unbearable contrariness, now settled himself down on the edge of the bank and completely turned the course of his reminiscence. 'When I looks at this pond some-times,' he said, 'I get creeps. Like now . . . look at the red in it – like blood. The old 'un, he never liked it neither. Ever notice that he never come here when he could get around?'

Peter did not answer this, but waited. He knew it was worse than useless trying to force his grandfather to divulge anything except in his own time. He also knew the old fellow was playing him as he would a fish.

'No, he never did.' Old Pop jerked his head. 'Saw something here when he was around four-teen that put him off lake. It was the day of the riot, you know. That Sunday when the women of the village all went mad, parson's wife an' all. I know you've heard some of it afore, but not all . . . no, not all.' Old Pop moved his tongue over his lips. 'And you don't hear many speak of it now . . . men a bit ashamed of their dads being locked up in church like and kept there at the point of shot-guns . . . want to forget it.'

Peter still remained mute, and presently Old Pop went on: 'Connie Fitzpatrick was an Irish maid in two senses when she came over, but she didn't remain either of 'em long.' He sniggered in his throat, 'No, she didn't by jove, if all tales be true. When she suddenly came into money she had that cottage built, nicely tucked away in the grove. Hard to get at it was then, and still is. Now had she remained like her cottage, hard to get at, she could have carried on for years. But she wasn't one for making flesh of one and fish of t'other. Connie's motto, by all accounts, was "Come all ye faithful!" and they came, including the minister. That last did it! They dragged her, the women did, shriekin' and screamin' through the wood here to the lake and threw her in, and when she tried to get out they pushed her back. Bet you wouldn't believe it, lad, but Ma Armstrong's mother was one . . . Grannie Andrews. A bit lass she was at the time. Did you ever hear that afore?'

Before Peter could answer Old Pop forestalled him by saying, 'But there's something I'm gonna tell you now that I bet you never have heard afore. See over there,' he pointed across the water. 'It was from there that the old 'un watched 'em. Like wild animals he said they were, howling and yelling. He watched Connie swim the lake to yon side. She was more dead than alive, and when she crawled into the undergrowth she fell almost on top of him, and he petrified. Can't imagine the old 'un petrified.' Old Pop laughed. 'And what did he do?' Again he turned an enquiring eye on Peter, but gave him no chance to comment before going on, 'He covered her up under shrub, and then ran out onto the back path making a hullaballoo. And when they came pelting round the lake he led them a wild goose chase, supposedly after her. That was smart, wasn't it? Later he came back and found her almost finished. He got her to shelter in the sheep hut on the far fell. And then, would you believe it, he went at her bidding to the cottage and brought back a deed box which she had hidden under the floor of a summer house. She had her head screwed on, had Connie, and she paid the old 'un in more ways than one, she did an' all.' Old Pop

441

turned and faced Peter now. 'You never heard that bit afore, did you?'

'No,' said Peter flatly, 'I haven't. But it's the tallest one yet.'

'Nowt tall about it.' Old Pop seemed a trifle annoyed now. 'You ever wonder how we came to own our house, lad, and we only farmhands at eighteen bob a week, eh? Just ask yersel that one, all our folks had lived in cottage but it was Squire's. It was Connie who gave the old 'un the cash for services rendered and some et ceteras, which was nobody's business but the old 'un's and hers an' he bought it. But he's always steered clear of this bit water, and always hated the guts of the village women, so much so that he picked me mother from as far away as North Shields.'

This knowledge of how they had come to be living in their own property was indeed a surprise to Peter, for he had always been under the impression that the house was bought with money left to his great-grandmother; he had got that information from his mother. 'Does me dad know this?' he asked.

'Aye, he does.'

'And me mam?'

'Rosie? No, begod!'

'Then I wouldn't ever tell her.' Peter's voice was stiff.

'What, me?' Old Pop threw his head up. 'Not me! Think I'm barmy lad? Like as not she'd walk out. Very respectable is your mother. Look at the fizzle she's caused the day in meetin'. All over the village it is. Raised stink in hall 'cos somebody hinted you was drunk in the wood and havin' a bit of a lark.'

'I wasn't drunk. Nor having a lark. I've told you.'

'All right, lad, don't sound so testy. But if you was, there was nothin' for her to get shirty about, was there? I wish they could still say it of me, I wouldn't have been past a bit lark with she. Which reminds me, I was telling you, wasn't I? Funny how I went off about the old 'un. She sort of put it in me head, the Miss, I mean. Don't know why. Well, there I was behind the bushes when they stopped—' Old Pop picked up the main trend of his discourse as if he had never let it drop – 'and I heard them. "Anna", he said, that's what he called her.'

'Anna?' Peter put in sharply, his brows drawn together.

'Aye, Anna. That's what he called her, that's her name. "Anna," he said, "I tell you you've got to believe me on this one point. You could have knocked me down when they said you had gone three days afore". That's what he said, and she kept saying, "It doesn't matter." And he kept saying it did, and then he said, "You think me a rat, don't you?" and she said, "I don't even think about you, you don't matter any more. You'll never believe that, but you don't." And I stood there with me pants half up, almost seeing his face, cos he didn't speak. And then she said, "I'll be here for another week or so and all I ask of you is to leave me alone." And then he went on jabbering, said a lot and so fast I couldn't get it. But then I heard him say, "What about money?"

443

Sharply, like that, he said it, and she said, "It's too late for that an' all, I have all I need." "Well, what do you intend to do?" he said then, and she said, "That's entirely me own affair." "You can't go on in the old Alvis, let me leave you the Austin." It was at that she walked off saying she didn't want the Austin or anything else. The last I heard her say was, "The Alvis is mine. I started with her and I'll finish with her." What do you make of it, lad?' The old man now looked soberly and enquiringly at Peter.

What did he make of it? Mrs Booth's comment was surging through his mind, and Old Pop sharpened this particular suspicion further by saying, 'This coming out business that the bloke talked about sounds as if she'd been in some-where, along the lines perhaps.'

'Nonsense.'

'Well, it may be. I wouldn't think none the worse of her for that for she's a nice Miss. Take as you find, I say. Still, if you'd heard them 'twould have sounded to you as if there was something fishy. Then later I came along on, strolling like, an' I heard them in here. He was at her again, saying, "You can't stay in this dump" – dump he called the village, mind – "What you going to do with yourself?" An' d'you know what she said?'

Peter waited.

' "I can sit and watch an eel", she said. Yes, she did. "And imagine I'm young again." What d'you make of it, eh? And her just a young lass when all's said and done. What d'you make of it?'

To this repeated question Peter said slowly and quietly, 'It's none of our business.' Then he turned away and went out of the clearing, in case his feelings should reveal themselves to the all-seeing eyes of his grandfather. But Old Pop was quickly on his heels, and on coming to the main path he walked abreast of him, but had the sense to keep his tongue quiet until they reached the main road. And then he asked, 'You comin' along for a glass?'

Half an hour earlier he would have given a definite 'No' to this invitation but now he answered flatly, 'I may as well.'

The Hart was packed, both bar and saloon, for a coach had come in, and after having stood his grandfather a drink they parted company, Old Pop joining his cronies while Peter stood near the counter, as if waiting.

He saw his father and Bill in their corners, and all the regulars, but there was no sign of her, or the fellow. Some of the villagers craned their necks and threw greetings at him, and one bolder than the rest called, 'You on your own the night, Peter?'

He made no answer to this, and the smile that had been on his face slid away and he turned to the counter to be confronted by Mrs Booth. But she, looking over his head, answered the man by saying, 'He's been given the go-by. Anyway, he's one of the nightshift lot.'

A muffled cry from Mrs Booth which indicated her having received a kick on the shins from her husband, who was standing with his back to the counter, did nothing to soothe Peter's feelings. His face had now assumed almost a purple tinge. He had a strong desire to go for Mrs Booth, and he might have done so at that but Mr Booth, turning to him at that moment, asked in a level tone, 'Well, what is it to be tonight, Peter?'

'Give me a whisky. Double.'

Mr Booth showed not a flicker of surprise. Peter Puddleton's drink was beer, and not much of that either; this was the first spirit he had asked for in this house. The only Puddleton whose drink was whisky was the old 'un, and Mr Booth remembered unhappily the results on certain occasions on the old man of an overdose of the delectable fire. But hadn't he said last night that she would bring custom. Her type always did, one way or another.

'And a pint.'

'And a pint.'

The pint and the whisky gone, Peter did cause a slight ripple to pass over Mr Booth's poker face as he demanded, 'The same again.'

'The same again,' said Mr Booth. And when Mrs Booth stopped in her transit to the saloon and watched Peter give a mighty shiver after depositing the second whisky, she remarked under her breath, 'What did I tell you!' and Mr Booth, addressing a miniature keg of cider, replied, 'Get on with it!'

Catching sight of Mrs Booth's fixed stare upon him Peter now had a great desire to spit in her eye or to produce the equivalent effect in words, and these words presented themselves to him with such force that, for safety's sake, he was urged to put some distance between himself and the mistress of the inn. And this he did, much to the disappointment of Mr Booth.

Outside once more, he stood for a moment looking about him. The night was young: it was barely nine o'clock, too light to go to bed, too light even to go home, for his mother would still be about and she'd likely start on one thing or another, and he couldn't stand that the night.

To save passing the house or going back through the village he returned up the road along which he had come earlier with Old Pop. The whisky was now glowing soothingly inside him; he felt in some measure comforted and took on himself not a little of the blame for being so edgy. Folks were all right. He had always got on all right with everybody; that was all except Davy Mac. The name in his mind coming at the same time as he caught sight of Mavis checked his step and made him gulp. He had reached an opening to the wood where once had been a gate, and standing almost hidden behind one of the old oak supports was Mavis.

He'd had no intention of going into the wood, and with Mavis about he would have shied like a hare from it but now, for some unexplained reason, he made straight for the gap, and when he came abreast of her he stopped, for if he hadn't she would undoubtedly have brought him to a halt in some way.

Mavis, from the shelter of the gate-post, looked at him hard, very hard, and her eyes on this occasion did not appear doll-like and her tone was not just one of enquiry, as she asked sarcastically, 'Off some place?'

'Aye,' Peter replied slowly, softly, and very definitely. 'Aye. Yes, I'm off some place, Mavis.'

The reply and the manner in which it was said was certainly not what Mavis had expected. But her good sense coming quickly to her aid told her she must change her tactics as he had so obviously changed his, and so she assumed an expression of having just been struck . . . her face crumpled, her lips strained to meet, and into her eyes came the look of a woman betrayed, and she whimpered, 'How could you, Peter!'

Peter, the Peter warmed with two double whiskies and two pints was on top. 'How could I what?' he grinned at her.

The whimper turned into a sob and she said, 'You've changed. Why – why did you ask me out last week?'

'God knows!' This answer, by its boldness, tickled him, it also checked Mavis's tears. Her eyes narrowed now, their pale blue turned to steely grey; she moved a step nearer to him, and after staring up into his face for a moment she exclaimed in horror, 'You're drunk!' then added, 'Again.'

This accusation brought no denial from Peter. Strangely, he had no desire to get mad and deny his supposed previous lapse, and what he was led to do next made him laugh loudly inside, for he opened his mouth wide, breathed hard on her, and uttered one word, 'Whisky!'

This flippant action together with the strong aroma of spirit caused Mavis to react naturally, and she cried, 'You!' and it was the same kind of 'You!' she had thrown over the stile at him last night. Then again she delivered it, but followed it now with a spluttered, 'Don't – don't you think

you'll get off with it, I'm not as soft as you think
I am. As for your tart—' Peter's eyebrows shot up,
he hadn't known she had even a nodding acquaintance with the word – 'do you want to know
where she is? She's in there!' With a thrust of her
arm Mavis indicated the depths of the wood.
'Lying full length on the grass. And who with?
The major. Yes, the major. I saw them with
my own eyes . . . they couldn't get closer. The
things I saw and heard! Quoting poetry to each
other . . . love poetry! The major at his age! You
were always a fool and she's made a bigger one of
you. You're the laughing stock of the village.
Everybody's sniggering at you. You know what
they're calling her? Slinky Jane. And you let
yourself be taken in, you big galoot!'

'You finished?'

'Oh, you can appear cool and pretend you
haven't been taken for a ride, but you're not
taking me for a ride. You haven't heard the last of
this, Peter Puddleton. You're not going to make a
fool out of me. You wait, I'll have me own back,
you'll see.'

After one bounce of her head that should have
ricked her neck, Mavis turned and flounced away,
and not until the heels of her shoes tapping out
her indignation on the road could no longer be
heard did he move on into the wood.

This was getting beyond a joke. Eel or no eel
. . . things would have to be made clear. Damn
the eel! No eel was worth her losing her name for
– the eel must be brought into the open. Aye. Aye,
it must. Its presence must be proclaimed to the
entire population of the village and its name an'

all. Damn silly name anyway. Why had she to go and give it a name like that? And the major lying on the grass with her! Bloody silly thing to do, lie on the grass. You should never lie on the grass with a woman, even he knew better than that. By! if this got about it would take some explaining. He knew why they were lying on the grass; the eel must have been on the move, tucked itself away under the bank perhaps. The major had likely gone into the clearing and she had told him about it, and only seeing was believing with the major. But lying on the grass together, and Mavis to spot them. What if it had been him? On this thought he stopped abruptly, not brought to a standstill by his thinking but by the sight of Leo at the other end of the beech walk. She was coming towards him, and alone.

He moved on again, slowly, almost casually now, and as the distance between them lessened his thoughts toppled over themselves. She looked whiter than ever. Had she done time? Who was the fellow? If Mavis spread the rumour that she was lying on the grass with the major there'd be the devil's own dance in the village about her, and there wasn't much doubt but that Mavis would. She was beautiful, but she wasn't good looking, not really. But she was beautiful. And the way she walked, not throwing her feet about as if they didn't belong to her. Who could the fellow be?

'Hullo.' It was he who spoke first.

'Hello.' She sounded tired and did not smile.

He looked steadily at her for a moment, and then remarked, 'You look tired. Walked too far?'

'Yes, I do feel a little tired.' With the faintest of smiles now she added, 'But not with walking, it's all the hard work I do. That eel takes some watching. I've just seen her. Your major was there. He got very excited, he couldn't believe his eyes. He's a nice old fellow, don't you think?'

'Yes, the major's all right.' He stood smiling blandly down at her and blinking.

With a sharp, amused glance she asked, 'Have you been celebrating?'

His grin stretched. 'Well, not exactly celebrating, but I went off me usual. Can you tell?'

The smile came to her lips again, wider now, and she said, 'A little.' Then with a movement of her head to each side she tossed her hair back from her face, and looking about her, asked, 'Do you mind if we sit down?'

Sit down! This was going to be the major over again. What if Mavis should decide to come back? Damn Mavis!

Pointing to a tree with a fallen branch lying at its base, he said, 'There's a seat over there.'

As she left the path he moved ahead towards the log and snapped off some of the side branches, with their dead foliage still clinging to them, to make a seat for her. She watched him for a moment, then sat down on the part he had cleared. Slowly she leaned her back against the trunk, and after drawing in a number of deep breaths she sighed and then she asked him a very odd question. 'When did I come here?' she said.

He looked at her as he laughed. 'You need me to tell you? Dinner-time yesterday.'

'Dinner-time yesterday. If you had said dinner-time ten years ago I should have said it was even longer than that. Yesterday I liked this place, I had made purposely for it. I was fascinated by the name, I had heard it somewhere years ago. And then recently I heard it again and felt I must come here. Yesterday I wanted to stay – the car seemed a good excuse – now I don't know.' She remained quite still but her eyes moved swiftly about, seeming to encompass the whole of the wood and the village beyond, and she finished, 'I feel I must go.'

The warmth of the whisky left his bowels and he said 'I thought you were going to stay put until the car was finished.'

'I thought I was, but I can always come back for it.'

When he made no reply to this she looked up at him and said, 'You're a very nice person, Peter. Why you're at large I don't know, somebody should have snapped you up. Come and sit down—' she tapped the trunk – 'you look too big standing there, like one of the trees. And you must be tired after working all day.'

He did not do as she ordered, and again, not a little to his own surprise, he heard himself saying, 'Don't talk like me mother.'

Suddenly she laughed, not the loud, free laugh of last night, but a soft, gentle laugh of amusement. 'All right, I'll drop the maternal role. Nevertheless, come and sit down.' She chuckled now. 'You know, that sounded funny coming from you . . . "Don't talk like me mother." You must go off your usual more often. Have you got a cigarette?'

As he pulled out his cigarettes he said, 'I've never seen you smoke.'

'No. I gave it up some time ago, but I feel the need of one now.'

She put the cigarette to her mouth, and he struck a match and cupped the flame for her.

'Do sit down.' It was now a request, and slowly he took a seat beside her, but not close.

'Where's your father?' she asked.

'In the Hart.'

'And Bill?'

'Yes.'

'They're a nice pair . . . refreshing.'

'Do you think so?'

'Yes. Don't you?' She blew the smoke gently upwards.

'They're all right.' He would not commit himself.

'Have you ever thought of leaving here, Peter?' The question brought his eyes to her face. They seemed to press on it, so hard was his stare.

'No – not really.'

'Then don't. Stay here until you're old, like your grandfather.'

'Now, you are talking like me mother again.' He said this not as he had done before, but quietly, almost under his breath. Then bending forward, with his hands between his knees and his eyes straight ahead, he asked, 'How old are you?'

'What a pertinent question!' She was laughing gently at him now. 'You'll be sorry for all these questions in the morning and you'll chide yourself for having dropped your guard, that's if you remember.'

453

With his hands still between his knees, he turned his head towards her. 'I'll remember . . . and look, I'm not drunk, not really. I've had two whiskies and two pints. You don't get drunk on that.'

'No,' she cast her eyes sideways at him, 'only curious.'

'Yes,' he repeated boldly, 'only curious.'

She did not pick this up but asked, 'Do most visitors to the Hart arouse the entire interest of the village?'

'Not usually. But then they're mostly very ordinary.'

She smiled a little at the covered compliment, and her head fell back against the tree. Then she blew the cigarette smoke upwards into the leaves, and remarked in a polite tone which dissociated itself from the content of her words, 'Mrs Booth is what is commonly known as a bloody bitch, isn't she?'

Now it was his laugh that rang through the woods, and he was past caring who heard it.

'You've said it there; we're agreed on that point anyway.' He straightened his back and brought his shoulders into a line with hers, and she turned her face full to his as she said, 'If I were to know you long, I should insist that you had two whiskies and two pints every night, and then everything I did or said wouldn't shock you.'

His brow gathered, 'What makes you think you shock me?'

'I know I do. Last night you thought I was much too free with the men, didn't you?'

The silence hung between them for a moment before he said, 'You know too much. But I wasn't shocked as you call it, just puzzled and—' he became bold – 'set wondering where you'd learnt all you know.'

She did not answer immediately; then she said offhandedly, 'You pay very questionable compliments, Peter. But I learnt what I know as you call it in America and repertory – and in a garage.'

Ignoring the first two he exclaimed in open amazement, 'In a garage!'

'I used to help sell cars.'

'You did?'

'Yes. What's so very surprising about that?'

'In America?'

'No, here in England. I was evacuated as a child to America, to the south. Hence the touch of accent. I came back when I was seventeen.'

'But cars, how did you get into that business?'

Her lids dropped and her lips fell together, and she stretched her arm forward and tapped the ash from the end of her cigarette. 'That's a long, long story.'

'The fellow today – was he part of that story?'

She looked slowly back at him again. 'Yes, he was.'

Peter ran one dry lip over the other. 'Is he your husband?'

Again the silence came, longer this time. 'No, he's not my husband.'

Did he detect regret in the admission . . . longing. His mouth was still dry as he asked, 'Who is he then?'

'Someone I know.'

'In the car business?'

'Yes, in the car business.'

She turned her face away and it looked to him almost transparent now, standing out like chiselled alabaster from the tree and the deepening shadows of the wood. And as he stared at it there leapt into his body an urgent longing to hold her. He wanted to pull her towards him and bury himself in the whiteness of her. It was no gentle urge but a fierce demand that sought to wrestle with something that was embodied in the pale thinness of her. Almost imperceptibly he moved a fraction along the log; then after a short lapse, during which neither of them spoke, he moved again. It was at the third move that her voice, quiet and with her drawl more pronounced, said, 'Don't come any nearer, Peter.'

Nothing she could have done or said could have had a more douching effect. His boldness, created by the whisky, deserted him, and with it fled the last vestige of stimulation the drink had afforded. Her quiet command knocked him sober.

The manner in which she had exposed his urge, which some delicacy told him should never have been made plain with words, shook him, and for the moment he had the uncomfortable feeling of being stark naked . . . and added to this the very strong feeling of having stepped out of his place. Even Florrie had never made him feel like this.

He got to his feet, humiliated and angry. Not for him the stalling tactics of 'What do you mean? Who's doing anything?' Nor yet the charm his father might have used. In this moment he was as he imagined himself to be, gauche. His face was scarlet; his hands were searching for tow; his long legs refused to be still, yet would not carry him away. So much, his lacerated vanity told him, for the affair he'd dreamed of last night. He was no more capable of handling such an affair than would be any village idiot.

When she, too, rose to her feet with a swift movement that was not in keeping with her lazy attitude, and stood so close to him that the tiny beads of moisture on her brow below her hair line were visible to him in the fading light, he became rigidly still, and it wasn't of the smallest consolation to him to note that it was now she who was disturbed.

'Peter—' she touched his sleeve – 'I'm sorry I said that, but—' She paused and her head moved downwards in a troubled, bewildered fashion. 'This is mad, utterly, utterly mad. Twenty-four hours. It's crazy and it can't happen, even in fun.' She pulled her eyes upwards towards him now, and fixed them on him, and with her drawl hardly evident she said rapidly, 'Peter, you're nice, and a little fun with you would be nice, too. There was a time when I would have enjoyed it, then driven on, but not now. And don't think I can explain why – I can't. I'm not snubbing you when I won't let you start anything, believe me. I like you, Peter. I liked you the moment I set eyes on you. I like to be near you – you make me want to laugh, and that signifies much more than you think. Even when you're not uttering a word you make me want to laugh. I felt I knew you from the word go, but I'm not going to get to know you any further or in any other way.'

When he did not answer but continued to stare at her, she closed her eyes and her body slumped until she appeared to lose inches, and her voice sounded as tired as she looked when she said, 'You don't understand a word that I've been saying or why I've had to say it. And how should you? I knew last night I shouldn't stay here . . . I'll go in the morning.'

'You needn't go because of me.' He could hardly press the words past his tongue, which seemed to be filling his mouth. 'I can keep out of your way.'

'Oh Peter! Peter.' There was a break in her voice, and her words as she went on were mostly unintelligible to him. All he could make out of them was: 'I'll bring you misery . . . tired . . . tired to death. Can't explain anything . . . not a thing . . .'

She swayed as she stood; her hands were over her face now pressing back her sobs. Last night she had laughed as if she would never stop; now she was crying as if she would never stop.

When his arms went round her and drew her to rest against him she made no protest but came almost as a weary child and moved her face into his coat as if searching for a place to rest. His hand was on her hair, the loose, wanton yellow hair; his chin could feel the smoothness of her cheek; her body lay close to his, yet it fired no urge. The feelings of the previous moment did not retrace their steps and leap back into him, but as he stood thus in the wood, with night fast closing about them forming a cloak which could be turned into a world to hold them alone, he felt for her only a great tenderness that had its birth in pity, and this tenderness had in it no ingredient for an affair; it brought him no promise of ecstasy, not even a small scrap of comfort, for in some quite inexplicable way he sensed he had linked himself to sorrow. How or why, it was beyond him to explain.

Chapter Four

The post office was full. Six people were in the shop, four at the stamp counter and two at the grocery. One of the latter was Miss Collins, and when it came her turn to be served, with prim condescension which she would have termed humility, she waived her priority to Mrs Fellows, and after watching the ungodly woman – for Mrs Fellows had never set foot in the church and it was her proud boast that she never intended to – being served, and with narrowed eyes having watched her leave the shop, she turned to the waiting Mrs Armstrong and said, 'Ah, well now, what do I want?'

With a robin-like movement Mrs Armstrong put her head to one side, and she smiled and waited.

'I'd better have some biscuits, quarter pound of wholemeal – I'm visiting Grannie West. And yes, of course, I want extra sugar – we picked about twenty pounds of blackberries yesterday.'

'You did?' Mrs Armstrong bustled to the tins lined up with gaping tops behind a glass frame. 'I wish I had time to go picking, the weather's so lovely. The wood must be full.' The lid of the case clicked open. Mrs Armstrong grabbed up a handful of biscuits from a tin, dropped them into the bag, put down the lid again and returned to her position behind the counter before Miss Collins gave an answer to her remark.

'Not so much with blackberries as with people.' Miss Collins's pupils were large.

'Really?' Mrs Armstrong did not look at the scales.

'You haven't heard the latest?'

'No.' The scales bounced gently. Still without looking at them Mrs Armstrong took off the bag, gave it an expert twist and placed it on the counter in front of Miss Collins. Her eyes had never left the minister's sister, and she endeavoured to keep from her expression any sign of the malicious amusement she was feeling, for whatever the latest Miss Collins was about to impart it would certainly not be the same latest that she herself had already heard. The vicar's sister, she imagined, wouldn't be looking so smarmy if she knew that her lamb of a brother walked two solid miles along the main road yesterday afternoon with the piece from the Hart and was so taken up with her that he forgot to make his usual weekly call on old Mr Taplow, and there was Mrs Taplow waiting at the window when she saw him stalk by, stepping out like a spring gobbler – that had been Ray Sutton's expression. Ray had seen them from the byres in the farmyard, across the way from the Taplows. No, whatever she was going to hear from Miss Collins, it wouldn't be this.

'You wouldn't believe it, you really wouldn't.'

'No?' Mrs Armstrong's eyebrows moved up expectantly.

'The major.'

'The major! No, Miss Collins.' Mrs Armstrong's chin came in and Miss Collins's chin went up.

'It's a fact, and what do you think?' Miss Collins leaned across the counter, bringing her head down to Mrs Armstrong's, and her whisper was heavy with the insignia of sin, 'They were lying on the grass together—' there was a considerable pause – 'sporting!'

The result of this information on the postmistress, who was steeped in tattle, was most gratifying. Her upper plate jerked loose in her gaping mouth and she saved it from bouncing on to the counter only by some expert lip contortion. With a final flick of her tongue, Mrs Armstrong got her teeth into place.

'You don't mean to say, Miss Collins!'

'I do. Mavis saw them with her own eyes. And something else, too . . . Peter Puddleton, he was in the wood looking for her . . . the . . . the woman, not her, not Mavis. And what do you think? He was drunk again! Oh, that poor girl, she was so upset. I happened to be in the vicarage garden as she was passing and I had to bring her in and console her. And that's not all.'

Mrs Armstrong was beyond speech; nor could her eyes stretch any wider. She waited for Miss Collins to continue; and Miss Collins continued, her whisper getting deeper and more ominous.

'What do you think we saw on the road? This was later when I was escorting Mavis home.'

Mrs Armstrong did not move a muscle.

'Mr Puddleton, Mr Harry Puddleton—' she

emphasised the Harry – 'and Mr Fountain creeping furtively into the wood. We saw them jump the ditch by the cottage, and with them the old man, Joe. He couldn't jump the ditch but went scurrying round by the gate, hoping to avoid being seen. And they couldn't say they were going fishing for there wasn't a line between them. Can you believe it?'

Mrs Armstrong's head moved very slowly from side to side; then contradicting her reaction she said hastily in an undertone, 'Yes, yes I can. That type drives men mad. Me mother here—' Mrs Armstrong jerked out her chin and thrust her head back towards a half-glassed, thinly curtained door behind which could be faintly discerned the figure of an old woman sitting in an armchair – 'me mother saw her go up the street yesterday, and you know she's not much interested in things now at her age but she was when she saw the Hart piece. Stared after her she did for a long time, and then she said a funny thing.' Mrs Armstrong turned towards the glass door as if to make sure it was closed, then leant across the counter towards Miss Collins and her voice was a whisper now as she went on, ' "Who's she?" she said. "Don't see many like her knockin' about. I know that sort – had some dealing with 'em – always cause upsets, that sort." Then you know what she said? She said, "Puts me in mind of somebody she does." "Who?" I asked. "Can't say right off," she said, "but it'll come. But I remember this much, she was no good." '

The two women looked at each other. 'And

then,' concluded Mrs Armstrong, 'have you heard what they're calling her?'

'No.'

'Slinky Jane.'

Mrs Armstrong's round face was an expanse of glee, but the joke found no response in Miss Collins. Her mouth was drawn to a button, bringing her lined face into furrows as she emitted, 'Slinky Jane! Well, whoever named her that knew what they were talking about, I've never heard of a name that suited anyone better. A Slinky Jane . . . she certainly is that!'

Mrs Armstrong's head was nodding and her smile broadening when, as if pulled by a string, it slid suddenly away, and with her eyes directed over Miss Collins's shoulder she said in a clipped undertone, 'Mrs Carrington-Barrett. She's just stopped across the way. She's talking to Mr Johnston.'

Miss Collins did not turn round to ascertain where Mrs Carrington-Barrett actually was, but her eyes did a swift circular exercise. Then in a voice loud enough to proclaim the legitimacy of the excuse for her hurry she patted the biscuits and said, 'I'll settle for these later when I call for the sugar, I don't want to carry it round with me. Grannie West looks forward to her little tit-bit.' She shook the bag and smiled. Then, bestowing a parting and somewhat detached nod on Mrs Armstrong, she turned with an air of casualness and left the shop.

Mrs Armstrong remained still while she watched the vicar's sister make a bee-line for the major's wife. If she wasn't mistaken there was going to be a lid blown off this morning. Miss Collins had been looking for some dynamite to throw at Mrs Carrington-Barrett for years, and now she had it. Mrs Armstrong suddenly hugged herself and waited and watched. And she did neither in vain, for within less than three minutes she saw that Miss Collins had struck.

It was about an hour later when Miss Collins passed the garage. She had no need to pass the garage but she was drunk with the battle of righteousness. During the past hour she had not only paid a sick visit but achieved two victories over the pride of her neighbours, for after having seen Mrs Carrington-Barrett's blood being drained from her face to leave it a sickly grey and the lady's vocabulary momentarily paralysed, she had encountered Amelia Fountain. Now Mrs Fountain was a fluctuating Christian, sometimes she was Church, less Church than Chapel, and because of this she was a source of irritation to Miss Collins. Moreover, there was something else Miss Collins held against Mrs Fountain. During the war and after, gratis choice cuts had now and again found their way to the rectory table; in fact, these little kindnesses of Bill's had continued up to two years ago, when they had ceased, and such was the situation that nothing could be said about the matter. Miss Collins, in her mind, had put the blame wholly upon Mrs Fountain and had only been waiting an opportunity to pay the butcher's wife out for her meanness.

Amelia Fountain was a thin, sharp-faced little

woman, the complete antithesis of her husband in everything, including temper, but such was the shock she had received that morning on hearing the vicar's sister hint more than broadly that her Bill was one of the infatuated males who were chasing through the woods after the piece from the Hart that her retaliation almost choked her; it had left her, like Mrs Carrington-Barrett, speechless. Amelia had experienced an almost overpowering desire to jump on the long, thin piece of skin and misery that was Miss Collins, but her thoughts, leaping back to the middle of the night, had further paralysed her, for she could feel the great whale-like proportions of her husband tossing to and fro as he muttered over and over again, 'Ee! she's lovely . . . beautiful . . .' and a word which she couldn't catch. She had dug him with her elbow and he had woken up puffing and blowing as he always did. Then from Miss Collins's lips Amelia was supplied with the missing word – it was Jane! She recognised it immediately, and without even a word in her husband's defence she had left Miss Collins in the middle of further information and made straight for the shop.

After victory number two one might have thought that Miss Collins would have rested. But no, she wasn't done yet – there were the prime movers in this affair to be brought to book, the Puddletons. Yet she was wise enough, following on the events of yesterday afternoon, not to visit Rosie and inform her that her husband, too, had been running loose in the wood – that could wait, she would get that over to Rosie later – but to finish this morning's work there remained Peter and the vindication of Mavis. What she would say to that young man he wouldn't forget in a hurry.

Miss Collins was happy, very happy, and it could be said to be unfortunate for her that she should encounter the twins playing a game to which they resorted only when bored – they were, like their Grandpop, spitting to pass the time. Lying in the ditch bordering the road of the spare piece of land, they were whiling away the time until Peter should return and they could pass on the message that 'the Miss' had given them. The time seemed to hang less heavy when they played this game of attempting to register hits on passing vehicles. Tony's efforts they did not count as he was always in command of an unlimited supply of saliva. As traffic could not be called heavy they lay and sucked the long hollow stems of the grasses between bouts, but would return to the job in hand with enthusiasm on the sound of wheels coming from around the bend. Being unable to see what type of vehicle was actually approaching until it was almost on top of them made the game all the more exciting. They could, however, distinguish between farm machinery and cars, and the awaited victim now was un-doubtedly of the farm variety, as was denoted by its loud rattling and the slowness of its approach.

Flat on their bellies, they got ready, jaws work-ing in anticipation. There it came, its mighty wheels shaking the earth, the noise deafening them . . . splatch! splatch! splatch! Jimmy got in one direct hit, Johnny none. Tony a number he couldn't count. The tractor rumbled past, its driver ignorant of the assault, and the twins, collapsing from their efforts, rubbed their faces down into the warm grass again. But not Tony. Tony continued, at short intervals, to spit at a point in the road, and it was more than unfortunate that Miss Collins's light and sprightly step should bring her around the corner to that point and afford a direct hit for Tony, low it must be admitted, but nevertheless direct.

The squawk emitted by Miss Collins had the power to shoot the twins out of the ditch. They had no need to wait and enquire what had happened, their flying legs, followed by those of Tony, showed without doubt how well informed they were.

Miss Collins, after rubbing at her thick lisle stockings with a handkerchief which she then threw away in disgust, stormed up the drive to the garage and into it, to be confronted by Old Pop sitting on the box with his paper and his pipe.

Old Pop did not look at Miss Collins; he appeared deeply engrossed in the paper which, he realised, was upside down but which he couldn't right without giving himself away. From the garage door he'd had a view of the bend of the road hidden to the twins, and had not only witnessed the whole affair but had anticipated it, and now he was shaking with suppressed laughter.

'Where . . . where's Peter?'

'Eh?' Now Old Pop lowered the paper, folding it as he did so. 'Oh! Mornin', miss. You want Peter?'

'Yes. You heard me.' Miss Collins looked around the garage with a really ferocious glare.

'Ain't here, miss.'

'Well, where is he?'

'Farm . . . mending tractor. You want petrol, or summat?'

As the vicarage ran to neither a car nor a motor-mower this was obviously a stupid remark, and was met with compressed lips by Miss Collins, until she sprang them apart to declare, 'I'll put a stop to this.'

'What, miss?' Old Pop had risen solicitously.

'This.' Miss Collins pointed to the wet stain on her stocking, 'Though it's no good talking to you, you're as bad as they are, and . . . and, that dirty old—' now she was spluttering in her anger – 'your father, who eggs them on. But I'll put a stop to it once and for all, I'll see Constable Pollard, I'll get the police to deal with this, I will. I will.'

'I wouldn't do that, miss, t'ain't Christian.'

Miss Collins swallowed, drew herself up to her full height, and looked for the moment as if she were about to demonstrate on Old Pop the complaint in question. Then swallowing twice more she turned about and seemed to leave the ground and fly, so quick was her departure.

The happenings in the village during the day were usually reiterated in the Hart at night, and there had certainly been enough events in the past few hours to keep the conversation at a high pitch of stimulation. For had not Miss Collins bearded the major's wife in the street. Major, so it was rumoured, had been larking on the quiet with the

469

guest at the Hart. What was more, 'Melia Fountain had gone for Bill for not keeping his eyes at home, and then the 'Pudd' twins had spat on Miss Collins and she had gone to Pollard and reported them. But the best piece of all concerned Peter Puddleton, for he had been seen coming out of the wood at eleven o'clock last night with the lady who was setting the village on fire. Mrs Booth said she'd had to come downstairs and let her in and had given her the length of her tongue. That was a funny one that, as the Booths were known never to get upstairs afore twelve at the earliest. Ma Booth apparently didn't cotton on to her guest. And now the guest had gone to Newcastle. Everybody knew she had gone to Newcastle for she left a message with the Puddleton twins to tell Peter, and they had told him in front of Dan Wilkins, but they hadn't said when she was coming back.

The question that was covertly going round the room now was: Who was really getting her favours – Harry Puddleton? Bill Fountain? Major? or Peter? It was a big laugh when you came to think of it. But the laughter subsided when Peter made his appearance, yet the greetings thrown to him were even heartier than usual.

His father, Peter saw, was not in the bar, nor was Bill. But as he took a seat on the broad window-ledge Bill came in, and, after nodding briefly here and there and calling for a drink, he came and joined Peter. And it was plain to see that he was not in his usual form; there was no grin fastened on his face tonight.

After taking the top off his beer he nodded and remarked, somewhat dolefully, 'Hallo, lad.'

'Hallo,' said Peter, and as a conversational rejoinder he added, 'been a grand day.'

Bill, lifting his drink again, took another draught and said, 'For some, likely.' And on this simple, yet significant, statement he rested for a moment; then moving nearer to Peter and in a really subdued tone for him he went on 'Been a hell of a day for me, all through that damned eel.'

Peter, his face crumpling with enquiry, said, 'The eel?'

'Aye, seems like I shouted out her name in me sleep, then that old bitch, parson's sister, collared the wife this mornin' and told her I was off last night sneakin' through the wood. And who to see?' He leaned nearer. 'You won't believe it, but the wife's got a bee in her bonnet. She thinks that it was Miss here I was after.' He raised desperate eyes to the ceiling. 'Talk I've done this day till I've been near blue in the face tellin' her 'twas the eel that took me through the wood and that it was her name that was Slinky Jane. "Eel, be damned for a tale!" she says, and if I told that to a cat it would scratch my eyes out; and I was a clever dyed-in-the-wool so-and-so to think up such a thing: "Go and see for yersel," I says, " 'tis in the lake." And you know what, Peter?'

Peter shook his head just the slightest, and Bill wiped his entire face with his hand before resuming, 'She went and came back as mad as Downey's bull. You know what?' Bill's face looked pitiable now. 'The twins were there and they swore there was no eel in the lake. They played at the lake all the time they said, and they'd never seen no eel. Can you believe it?' After staring at Peter with popping eyes Bill wiped the sweat again from his face. 'And that's not all, no, not by a long chalk. You know what those limbs of Satan told her when she asked them if young lady came to the lake? "Aye," they said. "And who else?" she asks. "Sometimes our Peter or me Da," they says, "and sometimes the major, and sometimes – and sometimes Mr Fountain." "And what do they do?" she asks.' Bill paused and stared at Peter over the handkerchief that half covered his face, and his voice dropped to a groaning whisper as he said, ' "They just laugh and lark a bit," they said. My God!' – Bill's face was lost for a moment behind his handkerchief – 'I could kill the pair of them.'

It was in Peter now to laugh, to throw back his head and bellow, but he could see that Bill was in a stew and was seeing no funny side to the affair.

'Wednesday night, an' all,' Bill began again. 'Always take her in to a show, Hexham, Wednesday night, but she wouldn't budge.' He drew in a deep breath. 'One thing I do know, I'll never put me foot inside that wood again as long as I live.'

Bill took a long drink, and Peter, looking at the mountain of flesh, wondered just how far a woman could become self-deluded. Love, in this case, had not a thousand eyes, he thought, but must be stone-blind. A woman who could imagine that Bill could be found attractive to anyone like Leo must be both blind and daft. Yet he had always thought Mrs Fountain a very sensible woman. Looking at Bill, he wanted to laugh again and he was pleased that he could feel like this. It was good to find something to laugh about in this business. The whole thing should be funny, an eel and a girl, and a village getting them all mixed up. But somehow it hadn't turned out like that.

Last night he had held her in his arms; he had felt her body almost melting into his; he had buried his lips in her hair; and what had he felt? Only a sadness. She had seemed to inject him with the sadness that was filling herself. Where had she gone today? Newcastle, the message had said. Why hadn't she come and told him herself? She could have done so. And no word of when she was coming back. What if she didn't come back?

This thought brought him to his feet, and Bill, looking up at him, quickly asked, 'What! off already?'

'Aye. Think I'll take a trip into Allendale.'

'Do.' Bill nodded warningly. 'Any place is better than the wood. But,' he added, 'that's not your worry. You're free to go into the wood if you like, but it won't see me again, eel or no eel. Oh, no!'

Peter grinned down on to the worried butcher and said, 'So long, Bill.'

'S'long, Peter.'

Under the covert gaze of the regulars, and of Mrs Booth in particular, he made his way out of the inn, and down past the yard to the bus stop.

There was one other person waiting for the bus, it was Miss Tallow, and she greeted him in her perky fashion as usual.

'Good evening, Peter, good evening.'

'Good evening, Miss Tallow.'

No-one ever called Miss Tallow anything but Miss Tallow.

'Been a beautiful day, hasn't it?'

'Yes, it has, Miss Tallow.'

Miss Tallow coughed, pulled her white cotton gloves farther up her wrists, then said, without any preamble, 'I do like your client, Peter. The young lady. She came in for coffee yesterday. Oh, it is nice to talk to someone other than the villagers. Not that I am saying anything against the villagers, you know what I mean, Peter.'

Peter stared down at the tiny little woman and nodded his understanding.

'A most intelligent girl. Remarkable looking, too. Of course, other people may not think so. You can stay too long in one place and your ideas of the world become very narrow, but I found her most exhilarating. We talked of poetry. She knows such a lot of poetry.'

Miss Tallow stared up at Peter, waiting for some retort, and all he could find to say was, 'Does she?'

'Yes, very well-versed. It's a pity she's only staying a fortnight. If there were one or two more like her here – I mean of her mind—' Miss Tallow made the distinction soberly – 'we could start a literary group. You know, Peter—' Miss Tallow's voice sank down to her small depths – 'there's very little culture in the village. Mrs Carrington-Barrett does her best, and, of course, there are one or two others, but the rest, dear! dear!' Miss Tallow shook her head, then asked brightly, 'Are you going into Allendale, Peter?'

'Yes, I was thinking of going there, Miss Tallow.'

'Ah, here's the bus.'

The bus rumbled to a stop, Peter put out one hand to help Miss Tallow up, and automatically his other hand went out in surprise and excitement to help Leo down.

Miss Tallow cooed words of recognition, while from the platform the conductor demanded tersely whether Peter was coming or going. And Peter, as if coming out of a dream, exclaimed hastily, 'No, no. I'm not getting on.'

The bell tinkled sharply; Miss Tallow's perky face looked through the window and she raised her hand in a little fluttering salute which Leo answered.

They were left standing looking at each other.

'So you've got back?'

'Yes.' Her voice sounded gay, and he noticed that her eyes were bright, laughing bright. She looked altogether happier, and he wondered where she had been and what had happened to cause the change.

'Were you going into Allendale?'

He smiled shyly. 'Yes, I was.'

'And I changed your mind?'

'That's about it.'

He could not help but notice that she seemed excited, and somehow this depressed him. And then she said, 'Would you wait until I put my case inside?' She nodded back towards the inn and, her voice dropping very low, she added, 'I've got something I want to ask you.'

'Ask me?'

475

She nodded slowly. 'We'll go to the pool, eh?'

'As you like.'

She held his gaze before turning away, and his neck became hot under her eyes. He watched her moving without hurry towards the inn, and he knew that she would not make her entry unnoticed, nor yet her exit, nor would it go unnoticed that they were making for the wood. Well, what of it; he didn't care a damn what they thought. And in this frame of mind he did not walk up the road so that their meeting would go unobserved, but he waited for her where she had left him. There was a recklessness in him that he was beginning to enjoy. But when she did rejoin him his recklessness did not move him to words; he could find nothing to say to her. He could only smile at her and suit his long strides to hers.

He should have felt uneasy walking in silence the length of the road with her but he didn't, and not until they entered the wood did either of them speak. And then it was he who asked, 'Had a nice day?'

'Yes, very.'

'Somehow I didn't expect you back the night.'

'Didn't you?' She glanced up at him. 'It's odd, but I didn't expect to come back either.'

'No?' Their eyes held, then again they walked on in silence, which lasted until they came to the lake.

As if by common consent they made straight for the edge of the bank and looked down into the water. There was no sign of the eel, and they did not mention her, but after some moments Peter, being unable to restrain his curiosity any longer, said, 'Well?'

'Yes? Well?'

Her eyes were cocked sideways at him, and he turned full to her now and said, 'You wanted to ask me something.'

For a second her gaze flickered over the water, then turning swiftly to him she thrust out her hands impulsively towards him, saying softly, 'Oh, Peter.'

His nerves were jangling. He held her hands tightly for a moment, then he lifted them and pressed the palms to his cheeks, so drawing her nearer to him, and when her face was beneath his, he said again softly, 'Well?'

Staring at him, she swallowed then asked, 'Could you enter into a game for the next fortnight, Peter?' Her voice was small.

'A game?' His brows contracted slightly but he was still smiling. 'It would all depend upon what the game was.'

'Loving me.' It was an even smaller whisper.

The colour that flooded over his face seemed to sweep the happiness from it. He could feel it rushing down to the soles of his feet, then up again to form a film over his eyes that blotted her from his sight.

This is what he had wanted on Monday night, an affair; and now it was being offered to him and nothing in him welcomed it. To love her, yes. But the time limit which gave it the stamp of the thing he had first desired aroused in him a feeling of revulsion. He was, to say the least, embarrassed at such an approach. In cases of this nature it was the man who suggested the rules, dictated the pace – took, then moved on – and that, to put it in a nutshell, was what she was proposing to do.

'Peter.'

He saw her face again. Not joyous now, and the apprehension she was feeling came over in her voice as she said, 'Oh, Peter! you think me awful, don't you? Fast as they come – a real tart in fact.'

'No! No, I don't.' He was strong in his protest – all his qualms and his ideas as to the fitness of things were brushed aside. 'I – I think you're the most wonderful creature on earth. That's what I think, and it's true. I've never come across anybody like you. I love you Leo.' His arms went about her and his thoughts took wings in words and rolled off his tongue: 'I do love you, and it's no use saying I haven't had time yet to get to know you. But I don't want just a fortnight of you, I want a lifetime.'

She moved within his hold, and his tone changed and he entreated, wistfully now, 'Leo, listen to me. I know we never clapped eyes on each other until Monday but you know and I know something has happened. And it's no light thing, nothing you can docket in days. Look at me, Leo—' he pulled her face round to him – 'you must feel this . . . you must. Look, tell me.' He was holding her chin none too gently now. 'Is there another man? I can't get the idea of that fellow out of me head. Is there? Don't lie to me, whatever there is, tell me.'

Her eyes, as she looked back at him now, held a dead expression. 'I give you my word there's nobody. Nobody,' she repeated.

'But there has been?' He made himself ask this.

Her gaze did not flicker from his and her voice was cool and steady as she said, 'Yes, there has been.'

He stared at her, refusing to let his mind dwell on this but knowing that later the thought would eat through him. 'Do you love me?' he asked.

He felt the uneasy movement of her body again, and now it spoke to him of impatience. And this was verified when she lifted her chin from his hand and said, 'I asked you to love me, doesn't that answer you?'

'No.'

With another movement she indicated that she wanted to be free, but his arms still held her and she looked up into his face again and said, 'What you mean by love may not be the same as what I mean – I like you—' she brought her eyes from his and looked over the lake – 'I like you a lot, enough to want to make you happy. I cannot promise you a lifetime of happiness which you seem to expect – that would be silly in any case – but I'm offering you something that is sure . . . a few days. There!' She looked back into his face again, and her tone had a flippant air. 'If you don't want it that way there is no harm done . . . none.'

Looking at her he knew he should be thinking, 'She is hard-boiled. This isn't the first time by a long chalk that she has done this'; but the face before him set up a defence for itself. In spite of the look of age or knowledge that the eyes possessed, the face below his was young – there were no lines of calculation, the mouth was generous, and it spoke silently to him now telling him to delude himself no further for whatever his opinion of her might be his answer to her was inevitable.

His lips fell to hers, hard, tight, demanding, and hers yielded hungrily. Their bodies pressed fast, they swayed together oblivious of time, and when at last they drew apart their eyes held the bond they had sealed.

His arm about her, they moved to the bank, and when they sat down it was in a single movement so close were they.

For a long while they said nothing but sat, their cheeks together, staring across the water; then of one accord they turned their heads and gazed at each other. At first their faces showed only the light of their happiness, until Leo, dropping her cheek against his again, began to chuckle. It was soft at first and Peter's smile widened with it, then with a sudden burst she laughed outright, as she had done the first evening, and between gasps she cried, 'Oh, Peter! Peter—' She pressed against him, and his arms held her tightly and he did not try to check her mirth as he had done on Monday night, but he joined his laughter to hers, and it spread through the wood until its echo reached a pop-eyed Miss Collins in the vicarage garden; and Mavis, too, as she patrolled the main road. But Florrie, where she stood within listening distance a short way along the bank, it hit with its full impact and caused her to bite her lip until the blood came. And when the laughter died away each had her own mental picture of what was happening now and was urged to put a stop to it.

Chapter Five

While subjects varying from politics to the Church can raise hot blood in a town, the village verdict as a whole, excluding the Women's Institute, would be 'Let they get on with it,' but the contrary happens when the fundamental urge of life is touched upon. Whereas sex can be indulged in without undue comment in a town, in the village it stirs up a strange and strong reaction . . . let it be admitted, mostly in the women. But even in them, passions come under a certain control if the offender be one of themselves, but should she not be of the village or thereabouts their feelings are liable to rise and flood over. Virtue is outraged where virtue never was, enemies are for a time linked together, and life before the particular event appears to have been good, almost holy. And this feeling touches the mildest of women.

To the extent it had touched Rosie can be guessed at, for she was no mild woman, and it had brought her on this Saturday morning to a stand behind the curtains in her bedroom, waiting to see 'her' come out of the Hart, and where she would make for when she did come out. But after half an hour, owing to the pressure of her house duties, Rosie was forced to give up her watch, but going downstairs and into her front room she approached Grandpop aggressively and without any prelude whatever ordered, 'Keep your eye on the Hart and if you see that – that Miss Carter come out, let me know.'

'What for?' Grandpop turned sharply and in doing so set the screws in his legs working, which caused him to explode with a 'Damn and blast them!' And then he added in much the same tone, 'What you want to know for?'

'Never you mind, just you call.'

Rosie, stalking into the kitchen, decided flatly that if 'she' was going to the garage she wouldn't get there alone. She wasn't going to stand by and see her lad made a fool of; she knew that type, unsettle him for life that one would. There had certainly been something in the wood business. Eel! Really! What did he take her for? He must think she was simple. Which just showed how simple he was and how easily he could be caught.

Grandpop watched Rosie out of the room, and then he thrust his head out of the window and called, 'Joe! . . . here! D'you hear? Joe!'

But not until Grandpop's third bellow had filled the square did Joe appear, and Grandpop, almost foaming at the mouth, bawled, 'You stone deaf?'

'No,' said Old Pop testily. 'Who could be with you around? Can't you see I'm busy?'

'Aye, if I'd eyes that went round corners I might. Here!' He beckoned his son nearer to him, and when Old Pop stepped over the flower bed and brought his head close to his father's, Grandpop, his voice now as near as he could get it to a whisper, said, 'Feel owt?'

Old Pop's eyes narrowed and his face screwed up into folds.

'Feel owt?' he repeated. 'What do you mean? About it being sports day?'

'Sports day! Don't be so pluddy gormless,' admonished his father. 'You know as well as me, summat's up.'

'You mean with the lad?'

'Aye, and with 'ole village. Look at yesterday, Miss Florrie going past and never a "Hallo there" – made on horse was mettlesome, didn't turn her eye, she didn't. First time in her life. Then old Ma Andrews comin' sittin' outside the shop.' Grandpop nodded in the direction of the post office. 'Never done that for years, she hasn't six or more. Then Pluddy Bridget goes in twice in afternoon again. And who else waddles in but Katie Booth? What Harry ever saw in that old sow. Flabby, fat—'

'Shut up man!' said Old Pop sharply.

'She's in kitchen—' Grandpop jerked his head backwards – 'she'd have to hoick her ears out to hear me.'

'She could be as far gone as Hexham but she'd hear summat like that, so let it drop.'

Reluctantly Grandpop let it drop and reverted to the condition of his feelings. 'I tell ee summat's up . . . feel it . . . all this week I feel it.'

'It's yer screws.'

'Screws, be damned!' Grandpop reared and made an effort to straighten out his rheumaticky joints. 'And don't start talkin' pappy. Ain't no screws inside here,' he tapped the top of his cap, 'nor here,' he nudged the centre of his waistcoat.

'Couldn't sleep last night, thinkin'. Mind went right back years. Funny it was, as if it was yesterda'.'

''Twill do at your time,' said Old Pop, aiming to soothe, 'it's what to expect.'

For a moment it looked as if Grandpop was going to lift his arm and land a backhander on his son, but he changed his mind and bawled at him instead, 'I ain't dead yet.'

'Who's a-sayin' you are?'

'Then don't talk as if I'd been screwed down. Pay some in this village if they'd a head clear as mine.'

'Yes, 'twould that.' Old Pop agreed readily now for he could see that his father was on his high-horse. And there was no doubt that he was right about summat funny being up in the village, and he knew who was the cause of it. Yet she was a civil-spoken Miss, as pleasant as you could hope to find in a day's march – she made you feel young, she did. There was no denying that she had that queer something that made an old 'un feel young and a young 'un feel old – old enough to matter at any rate. And that's how the lad now felt.

Old Pop suddenly rubbed his hand over his eyes as if trying to shut out all he knew. Who would have thought it? The apple of Rosie's eye – him that was so far removed from the rest of her menfolk. It would serve her right in a way and level things out a bit if she was to know that her lamb was the fastest worker of them all and he'd like to bet that included the old 'un himself.

'Get your head out of the way.' Grandpop

suddenly pushed at Joe to get a view of the Hart, then exclaimed in excited tones, "Tis the Miss comin' out and makin' for this way. That's another thing, she—' he jerked his head towards the kitchen again – 'she's been on the look-out for her. Spent God knows how long upstairs she did at window, heard her creakin' on boards. Then down she come. "Tell me when Miss comes out Hart," she says. She didn't say, "Tell me if she makes for garage," but that's what she meant all right.'

Old Pop looked narrowly at his father. 'You gonna tell her?'

'Not damn likely – what d'you take me for? What'll she do if I tell her, eh? Skip down garage and say to Miss to leave him alone, as if he was Wee Willie Winkie. No; lad's to have his fling . . . 'bout time he started. She's had him lashed to her back for years. If he don't make a move he'll end up with that sick cow—' his head moved violently now in the direction of the Mackenzies' house – 'and what she'd give him wouldn't tint the white innards of a black beetle.'

With a chortle of laughter in his throat Old Pop was about to make for the gate to watch the approach of Leo when Grandpop said angrily, 'You make off round back, you ain't got the sense you were born with. What if she stops for a word? Rosie'd be on her like a wasp on jam.'

Ignoring the insult to his intelligence, Old Pop turned away muttering, 'Aye, aye. Perhaps you're right,' and with some reluctance went round the back, leaving Grandpop apparently immersed in the scraping and filling of his pipe. His good eye appeared to be in attendance on this occupation while the one with the cast seemed to be roving at will. Whether this was an illusion or not, Grandpop was able to discern the Miss as she looked towards him and at almost the same time he followed the approach towards the post office of both Miss Collins and Mrs Booth, walking side by side. And the excited rumble in his stomach, translated, would have said, 'Never happened afore in my time, Church and pub together; summat's up somehow or I'm a Dutchman.'

It is true that Mrs Booth and Miss Collins had come through the village together, but that was five minutes ago. Now within the cramped space of the post office they were standing as wide apart as they could possibly get, and Miss Collins was endeavouring to widen the distance even farther. But only at the risk of stepping into a box of oranges could she do this, and so she turned her outraged expression down onto the fruit, then back to Mrs Booth, and that lady, her fat moving gently with satisfaction, said, 'Well, I was only pointing out that she doesn't even leave a minister of God alone, I wasn't suggesting anything. But Mrs Armstrong here can tell you it's all over the place. Isn't it, Mrs Armstrong?' She appealed to the red face of the postmistress. 'Aren't they saying that the Reverend forgot to call on old Taplow all through him talking to her? Walked right past the door he did, so they're saying. And as I was saying, I wasn't looking for it nor yet thinking about her – I've better things to do with me time – but I just slipped down the bottom of the garden for a bit parsley and there I saw them. There's no mistaking the minister, is there, Miss Collins?' Mrs Booth smiled a little smile before torturing the minister's sister still further. 'There he was, like any gallant, and as perky as you like, helping her over the stile bottom of Reed's cottage, and held her arm right to the wood he did. As jaunty as a cricket he looked. But that's over an hour gone, and now she's just gone up to Peter Puddleton. Allots her time seemingly. You should hear what they say in the bar.'

Mrs Booth stopped for want of breath, but Miss Collins did not nip in as might have been expected and deny the implications being levelled against her brother, and a very uneasy silence fell on the shop. When it could be borne no longer, Mrs Armstrong busily rearranged some of her merchandise on the counter, and remarked in a sad voice, 'It's getting awful, it really is . . . even Tony Boyle. All the years I've been in the village I've never known anything like it.'

The eyes of the two women turned now on Mrs Armstrong, those of Miss Collins somewhat reluctantly, as she appeared to have to drag her attention away from the turmoil of her mind.

'Tony Boyle?' said Mrs Booth, her face screwed up.

'Yes, Tony Boyle. It's right. Stan Dolton saw her yesterday, nearly at the crossroads they were, walking hand-in-hand.'

The faces of the women now all showed a tinge of horror and disgust.

'With Tony Boyle?' repeated Mrs Booth again.

'With Tony Boyle,' said Mrs Armstrong in sad,

awe-laden tones. After nodding significantly she continued, 'And Stan stopped the car and spoke to them, for, as he said, he thought he'd better. He said perhaps she didn't know about Tony. He even offered them a lift, but she said no, they were looking for the twins. The twins that far, huh! And he said Tony was laughing his head off. I told Mrs Boyle when she was in not long since. I told her "If you don't want no trouble you look out." Say he turns on her, she'll have you up, her kind would.'

'You did quite right. What did she say?' asked Mrs Booth.

'She said she'd give him his hammers, and she will an' all, she'll lather him.'

At this point the glass door leading to the living-room opened and old Mrs Andrews, with the aid of two sticks, made her appearance. But her daughter did not look overjoyed at this interruption and she called loudly to her mother, 'Now, Ma, what you about?'

Ma, hobbling round the counter, grunted, 'Gonna sit out front.'

When the old woman came to Mrs Booth's side she tried to straighten her back and look up into her face, but this being too great an effort her words were directed floorwards as she said, 'Nice folks you're housin'.'

Apparently Mrs Booth had not to ponder to find out what the old lady meant, for she answered immediately, 'We've no choice, we're an inn.'

The old woman gave a long significant sniff, then asked, 'Where's she this mornin'?'

Mrs Booth now bent down to her and jovially shouted, 'Gone up to garage. What do you make of her, Gran?'

'Whore.'

Mrs Booth's body jerked up and her head went back and her laugh rang out, but Miss Collins did not laugh, for the word, besides shocking her, conveyed to her the complete seduction of her brother, and she looked for the moment as if she would collapse.

The old woman, conscious of all eyes on her, now said with authority, 'Wondered who she minded me of, an' it just come up in me mind not five minutes gone.' She turned her eyes towards her daughter. 'Connie, her that caused riot. Afore your time it was . . . same type as this 'un. They ducked her they did. Had no more bother with her after that. Saw it meself, I did.' She chuckled.

'Who ducked who?'

They all turned towards the open doorway and there stood Florrie, sombre and haughty-looking this morning, with the steely light of battle in her eyes.

'Oh! Good morning, miss,' said Mrs Armstrong, with just a touch of obsequiousness.

'Good morning, Mrs Armstrong.'

'Good morning.' The greeting moved around the shop as Florrie came in, and Mrs Booth, with a wiggle of her body preluding the slightest narrowing of her eyes, said, 'We was just talking of a certain lady, and Gran here says she reminds her of somebody that was like her . . . Connie Fitzpatrick. Perhaps you've never heard of her though?' The suggestion was malicious, to say the least, for it had been Florrie's great-grandfather who had built the cottage for the same Connie.

'Why should you imagine I haven't heard of her?' Florrie did not like Mrs Booth. She looked down on her for various reasons and her feeling came over in her tone.

As usual, it was not lost on Mrs Booth, and her quick reply held her retaliation, 'Oh, well, if you've heard of her that's all right then, you've nothing to learn. Only Gran here says my visitor's another like her and 'twould seem she's right, with Peter Puddleton at the head of her calling list.'

Florrie stared at the big woman for a moment and her slim body seemed visibly to lengthen, then with a small drawing together of her brows she went towards the grille that denoted the post office section, and with her head slightly turned she threw a question over her shoulder: 'Do you know where your husband is this morning, Mrs Booth?'

In spite of the polite way in which the question was asked Mrs Booth was not unaware that this was an attack, and she thrust out her bust and advanced a step towards Florrie's back, snapping, 'In bar, getting ready for opening. That's where my husband is, miss!'

'There you are mistaken, Mrs Booth.' Florrie's eyes flicked round and met those of Mrs Booth before turning to the grid again.

'What you meaning, miss?'

'Do you know where Miss Carter is?'

'She's up in garage with Peter Puddleton by now. I told you.'

'She's not, you know, Mrs Booth.' There was a vicious snap in Florrie's words. 'She didn't go to the garage, she turned up Wilkins' cut, and there I saw her meet and speak to your husband. It seemed as if he were waiting for her. And you know where Wilkins' cut leads to; it leads to the wood, Mrs Booth.'

It looked as if Mrs Booth might explode, but for once she could find nothing to say, mischievous or otherwise, and old Mrs Andrews who could not have heard all that was being said but who judged the substance, from the expressions of those about her, gave Mrs Booth one long look before moving towards the shop door, and there she cast her eyes towards the clear, hot sky and stated, 'Rain – smell it. Always rains sports day, an' it'll rain the day. And more besides water it strikes me. Aye, it will that.'

Back in the shop, Mrs Armstrong, with feverish haste, was trying to attend to her customers all at once. She had an urge to be rid of them, for, as she told herself, she liked a bit of gossip as well as the next but Katie Booth was looking as if she might get rough with Miss Florrie at any minute, and she didn't want that, not in her shop she didn't. Let her do what she liked outside, and good luck to her. 'Twas as her mother said, it would rain more besides water afore the day was out.

Chapter Six

Peter tried desperately to hold on to his temper as he looked from the older to the younger Mackenzie. Taking yet another deep breath he said for the countless time during the last half hour, 'I'm not selling.' Then in staccato tones he added, 'I've told you I'm not selling; nor am I letting out any shares, do you hear?' He thrust out his chin. 'I'm not selling, and I don't want to hear any more of it. And you needn't worry about the agent if that's any solace to you. I'm not selling to him, an' I'm not selling to you. I'm not selling at all, I've told you. Why should I? Would you? I'm not a damn fool altogether, you know.'

'No, no, lad,' said Mr Mackenzie soothingly, 'we know you're not, but as we see it you need money to expand. This—' he waved his hand round the old blacksmith's shop – 'this won't do for the future, it'll have to be rebuilt, and where are you goin' to get the money from?'

'That's my business.'

'Yes, yes, we know that, an' all.' Mr Mackenzie's voice was as smooth as butter. 'As you say, lad, it's your business. So all right, we'll leave it for the time being. You never know what changes a man's mind – never. Ah, well, we'll away, but we'll be seeing you, lad.'

As they departed Peter's voice hissed out at their backs, 'I won't sell a stone, so you needn't bank on me changing me mind.'

'We heard you.' Davy's reply, thrown over his shoulder, was not as smooth as his father's, and turning at the garage door he added, 'There's one thing I will ask, and that is if you do change your mind you'll let us have the first refusal – you won't go and do another dirty trick on us.'

Before Peter could make any retort to this, Mr Mackenzie reprimanded his son with a loud, 'Come on, come on, enough of that.'

Peter almost sprang to the garage door, the urge strong in him to get at Davy, but he was forced to restrain himself on the sight of his mother coming out of their gate, sails all out. Even at this distance he could detect the signs, and when he saw her heading up the street he returned hastily into the garage and began busying himself.

Rosie swept upon him. Nothing else could describe her entry, and without any lead-up she began where she had left off at breakfast time. 'If you think I'm putting up with this, you're mistaken.'

Peter said nothing. He went on greasing the steel rod in his hands.

'The place is on fire, everybody's talkin' . . . Are you mad?'

There was still no retort from Peter.

'If you don't think of yourself, you should think of me. Three of 'em I've had to put up with in this way. All me life I've had it, and now you start. God in Heaven! It's unbearable. And with a hussy like that.'

'Shut up!'

The bark almost lifted Rosie from the ground. It lifted her hand to her mouth and she gasped, 'Don't you dare speak to me like that!'

'Well, be careful what you say.' He was looking at her in a way that he had never done in his life before, as if he hated her.

But Rosie, refusing to recognise any change in her son, went dauntlessly on. 'Well, don't think I'm going to stand by and let you make a fool of yourself, as big as you are. I've still got some say in this family, and you'll find that out. And mind you—' she raised her finger to him – 'if you take her to the sports the day you won't see me there, and there'll be summat to do.'

'Well, there'll be summat to do, because she's going.'

For a moment Rosie was silent and startled; then through tightly drawn lips she brought out, 'You can't be serious, lad, not with her. I think I'd rather see you take up with Mavis after all. Better the devil you know. At least she doesn't look like a—'

'Shut up, will you!'

Rosie stared at her son. He hadn't barked this time, in fact she could only just make out what he said, but it was the way he had said it. It wasn't her lad speaking. For the first time she began to doubt her power over him, and it made her afraid, but she showed none of her fear as she cried, 'You can't do it, you can't! You'd be worse than any of them. The ones that they took at least looked decent.'

He swung round on her, his face ablaze and

his anger choking him, and they glared at each other until she wrenched herself about and went out, her body shaking with unintelligible sounds.

Slowly he passed his forearm over his wet brow. He would never have believed that this could have happened between his mother and him – never. He put out his hand and gripped the doorpost to steady the trembling of his body. Oh, this business was damnable, damnable. If he knew where he stood he could have said firmly, 'There's nothing you can do about it, I'm going to marry her,' but he didn't know where he stood. He couldn't think that he was to have Leo for only another week, yet he knew without doubt that when the car was put together again she would go. For a moment he wished that he had never set eyes on her. Then he refuted this thought sharply. She was the most wonderful thing that had happened to him in his life. He also felt now that there hadn't been a moment in his life when he hadn't known her. Yet what did he know about her? Nothing. He could only keep guessing. He was tortured by the thought of the men in her life. He had the constant desire to find out just what this last one had meant to her, but he had not the courage to bring up the subject boldly.

In the space of a few days his life had be- come a sort of sweet hell dominated by her. And on the outskirts stood his mother and the villagers watching his every move . . . and there were the sports this afternoon. God! He groaned aloud.

* * *

Since he was sixteen, apart from the two years he was away on National Service, Peter had on sports day run in the race over the fells; he had also manned one end of the tug-o'-war, had a shot at climbing the greasy pole, and had been successful on three occasions in getting the goose from the top, and yearly he had attempted to beat the record at mending a puncture. Also he invariably had his fortune told by Miss Tallow, who wore a mask and a gipsy costume, and the reading of his fate had always been accompanied by guffaws and side-chat from the listeners outside the tent. And finally he had danced on the uneven grass to Ned Poole's fiddle and Harold Casey's melodeon, and altogether always thoroughly enjoyed himself. How much of this enjoyment had been derived from popular acclaim and from knowing that, the Mackenzie men excepted, he was without an enemy in the place, he never questioned. He only knew he liked the sports. But today was different, he was afraid of the sports. He did not want Leo to go to the fête at all, and there be the focal point of sly interest on the men's part and something not so pleasant on the women's, for he, like his great-grandfather, was feeling that all was not as it should be, even outside his own home. To some extent he could understand his mother's attitude, but not that of the other women. What is it? he asked himself. Why don't they like her? And to this question he gave himself the answer: Well would they now, with she as she is and they as they are?

The race over the fells did not start until two o'clock. But shortly after one Peter left the house.

Rosie was in a silent-martyr mood, which was worse than her yelling, and unbearable to him.

Grandpop looking somewhat soberly from the window, said, 'Early off, aren't you?'

'Aye,' replied Peter briefly.

'Gonna be rain.'

'Yes, it seems like it.' He looked up at the grey-tinted sky. 'Could be a storm.'

'Aye, it will be, an' be a bad 'un, I can tell yer.'

'So long.'

'So long, lad. Take care of yersel'.'

Peter turned at the gate and paused for a moment and looked across the garden at the old man. He did not feel annoyed at the caution inferred, rather did he feel a tenderness rise in him towards this querulous and still sensual individual, and he smiled across at him and nodded, saying, 'Never fear, old 'un, I will.'

He was going to the lake, and the nearest way from the house was up Wilkins' cut. There were several people on the street but he made no effort to hide his destination. Let them talk; they would talk in any case. But in spite of this bold way of thinking he was thrown into some confusion when turning sharply into the cut he almost fell on Mavis and Florrie. His colour went soaring, but without a word or nod of recognition he passed them both; and was acutely aware that their eyes remained hard on him until he cleared the stile.

It was common knowledge that only one thing existed between Mavis and Florrie and this was condescension which one bestowed and the other refused to recognise, but now seemingly they were one, and Peter had not the slightest doubt who was the cause of this affinity. It said much for the change that had come about within him that this meeting, apart from making him blush, did not worry him. Three days earlier he would have been in a stew, with his tow technique in action. But that was three days ago, the only thing that now remained of the old Peter Puddleton was, he knew, his name.

When he stepped into the clearing Leo was lying on her back on the grass, a book by her side, and she didn't rise but turned her head lazily towards him and held out her hand. In a moment he was down beside her, his arms about her and his lips tight on hers, and when he released her she gasped for breath, then laughed gently and touched his cheek saying, 'No-one will convince me but that you had your training in the big city.'

He took her hand from his cheek and rubbed her fingers across his lips, and as he looked down into her eyes he said, 'The big city came to me.'

After allowing him to hold her gaze for a moment she eased herself up into a sitting position, and with a small laugh she said quietly, 'I couldn't make you or anyone else believe that I'm not big city, could I, Peter?' She was looking across the water as she said this, and in spite of the smile that was still on her face he thought he detected a sadness in her question and a drooping in her whole attitude. It reminded him of the night when she had cried, that night that now seemed so very far away in the past, and he checked the retort of, 'No, you couldn't,' and replaced it with, 'Big city or small town, you came and that's all that matters to me.'

She put out her hand gropingly for him, and he pivoted himself round to her side. 'You're nice, Peter.' She squeezed his fingers. 'Do you know—' she turned her face to his – 'now don't contradict me when I say this, for it's true – that you can love someone without liking them, but if you like them and love them, too, then you have the world . . . I like you, Peter.'

'And love me?'

She dropped her head towards his shoulder and rubbed her cheek against his coat. 'First things first.'

Such a reply could have plunged into mute silence the man he had once been, and that individual would have thought, 'There can be no half measures, you either do or you don't.' But into this association had come so many shades of feeling that now he just clutched at whatever she gave and tried to bank down the fire that was demanding more fuel.

As she lay against him she nodded towards the water and said, 'I haven't seen her today, nor have the boys – I felt sure I'd see her again, and if the storm breaks she will certainly go. Somehow I feel she knew me. I'll miss her.'

'I'll bring my line and you can sit and fish.'

'That's an idea.'

'You like fishing, don't you? I never imagined I'd ever meet a girl who liked fishing.'

'I like sitting.' She laughed, and the thought

intruded into his mind that she was right there, she liked sitting. She was as indolent as a sun-drenched native, only there was no evidence of the sun on her – she was the palest thing he'd ever seen. This thought swung open the door that was never really closed, and Mrs Booth walked through it again, and although he banged it shut in her face she managed, as always, to shout at him. 'Well, where has she been this last year? She doesn't say, does she? And you're afraid to ask her. You haven't the spunk.'

In an effort to get away from his thoughts, he said, 'I must go.' But he made no effort to rise, instead he reached for the book that was lying at her other side and asked, 'What are you reading?'

'Oh, just a book. I liked the title.'

With his free hand he turned it over and read 'Words of a Woman in Love', then looking down at her he asked, with a twist to his lips, 'Had it long?'

There was some laughter in her eyes as she replied, 'Since Wednesday,' and his eyes, betraying a leaping hope, held hers a moment before he began to scan the pages. When he stopped flicking them and began to read she eased herself away from him, and putting her arms around her knees she looked about her at the lowering sky now seeming to rest on the tops of the trees on the far side of the lake; and after a time, during which he had made no comment, she asked, 'What are you reading?'

He gave her no answer, and there followed another pause. Then somewhat self-consciously

and without having looked at her, he began
to read aloud, his voice low and thick and halt-
ing:

> 'Would I like woods without you?
> And bird-song and pollen-laden bees,
> And trees;
> And the night sky, and dawn,
> And young things just born;
> And eating out of doors,
> And a hundred and one chores;
> And autumn with its flame of dying
> And wood to chop and leaves to burn,
> And coals to lug and the fire to hug
> And lights ablaze about the house
> And steaming water in the bath;
> Thick snow on the winding path;
> And bed, and sleep, and dreams . . . ?
> What are they without you?'

As he finished the last line he brought his gaze
to hers. And she turned and looked at him, and he
repeated, 'What are they without you?' There was
so much compressed passion in his voice that
when he cried, 'Leo!' and made to pull her
towards him she shook her head quickly and,
sliding with an unusually swift motion to her feet,
said, 'Now, Peter, don't let's get involved. Not
like this – not in this way.'

She took the book from him, and holding her
other hand down to him said, in a matter-of-fact
way, 'Come on . . . up! What about the sports?
Listen to that noise over there.'

'Leo.' He stood before her, his face set now, his

laughing façade ripped away. 'Leo, I've got to know where I stand.'

'You've got to know nothing.' Her voice was suddenly harsh. Even the semblance of the drawl had gone, and her words came tumbling out rapidly as she went on, 'It was a bargain, wasn't it? So let us leave it at that. Why can't you be satisfied? You're like them all—'

'All?' His face looked grey, and suddenly old, and his voice had a rusty sound.

'Oh, I didn't mean that.' Her head rocked. 'I meant all men in general, honest I did. Oh, Peter! Why can't you leave things as they are?'

There was no vestige of fond light in his eyes now. His look constituted a glare as he ground out, 'Leave things as they are! What do you think I am? Have you like this for a week . . . two at the most, then off you go and I forget about you? I must have been daft.'

'But it's what we agreed on, remember. Or would you rather things hadn't been like this at all?'

He did not answer, and with a weary gesture she put her hand to her hair and pushed it back from her brow, saying, 'Oh, why must you start on an afternoon like this, so heavy and close! And we're fighting!' This statement seemed to surprise even herself and she closed her eyes. When she opened them it was to stare up into his tense face, and her voice was weary and flat-sounding as she said, 'I'll tell you something, Peter. Perhaps this might make you see. I never expected to have an affair in my life again. Yes, I know you can raise your brows, you don't believe me. But I can tell you honestly I wanted this no more than you did, it was just one of those things. And I tell you again it's not for good. I'm being brutal, I know, but it's best that way. I know it's best that way.' She stood back from him and said gently now as she surveyed the anger mixed with pain on his face, 'Do you want it to go on, or would you rather not? Whatever you like, I'll fit in. You've just got to say.'

He stood staring at her, fascinated, bewitched by her. He seemed to suck into his body everything that came from her, pleasure and pain. What had she done to him? Her last words appeared to him to be as hard-boiled as anything he had heard, yet, as always, her face, her eyes, belied them. With an intake of breath he turned from her towards the gap, but as he did so he thrust his hand out behind him and drew her after him.

Peter came sixth in the race he had won for two successive years, and was greeted with such laughing remarks as 'Losing yer grip, lad?' and 'Eeh! love always plays havoc with the legs.'

As he stood wiping the sweat from his neck, his eyes searched for Leo, but he could not see her anywhere in the crowd. After leaving the clearing she had gone back to the inn with the promise to be on the field around four o'clock, at which time he was likely to return from the race, and now it was nearer five. It wasn't until after he had joined his half-hearted effort to the tug-o'-war and made an attempt at the greasy pole that he saw her. He had, in fact, just finished cleaning himself up at the tap that fed the cattle trough when he glimpsed her coming in the gate. A quick dive behind the hedge and he got his trousers and made his re-appearance in a matter of seconds. Tucking in his shirt, his coat under his arm and without any hesitation, he wended his way towards her.

When he came up to her she was still standing by the gate, there was a look of uncertainty about her that was unusual, and her greeting suggested relief at seeing him. 'So you're back. Did you break any records?'

'What do you think?' He paused. 'In my condition?' He smiled as he said this, his eyes looking into hers, and she answered his smile and shook her head. Then together they walked on to the field.

As they moved through the groups, heads were turned here and there, and here and there voices called, 'Hello, Peter,' as if they had not seen him before. And eyes moved from him to Leo. He was not unaware of the nudging, winking and bobbing heads, but he took no notice, and it would seem that Leo was oblivious to anything that was going on around her.

Coming to the children's races he saw Florrie. Her face was red, almost purple. The heat was now oppressive, but her colour was not caused by the heat alone, for as she raised her eyes to his he was conscious of her sending out to him a blaze of hate. And when the twins, galloping at him, complained to him of her unfairness in handicapping them in the races, he found he could not laugh at their discomfiture. He had not expected

Florrie's reaction to take this form towards himself and spite to the twins, to whom she had on all other occasions shown prejudiced favours. If he had considered what her attitude would likely be, he would have expected her to adopt her mother's manner and treat him and the whole business with cool condescension.

To get away from the vicinity of Florrie and incidentally to soothe the twins he took them to the White Elephant stall, where after picking ticket No. 13 he was presented with 'The Monarch of the Glen'. This picture was the village joke, for it went the rounds every year. It was after this incident that Peter seemed to sense a change in the atmosphere about them, for they were now greeted with loud hilarity wherever they went, a hilarity that he found it difficult to join his easy laugh to. For instance, when Dan Wilkins stood on a box and yelled out about a mystery raffle, drawing a crowd around him, and then to the consternation of the twins produced a half-smothered squawking Penelope. The laughter became hilarious, but it was mostly, Peter noticed, coming from the men. If it hadn't been too silly to consider he would have sworn that the fellows were showing off, and all for Leo's benefit. It would seem too that for the moment they had lost the fear of their women-folk, for even Bill came up and greeted Leo. But it must be said that his Amelia was nowhere to be seen. Rosie too had kept her word, and this saddened him more than he would admit.

But Leo seemed happy. She had entered into the spirit of the sports; though not partaking in anything she seemed to be enjoying everything. And then she said, 'I'd love a cup of tea.'

There was a tea stall close at hand, and he looked towards it, but she had already turned her gaze towards the marquee. And she asked, 'What about it?'

To take her into the marquee would constitute an act of bravery. Teas in the marquee were reserved for the cream of the parish, none of the lads ever went into the marquee. But now, walking by her side, he went towards the tent.

Teas in the marquee and all they entailed came under the supervision of Mrs Carrington-Barrett, and her second-in-command, as in the Women's Institute, was Miss Collins. From a vantage point inside the marquee Mrs Carrington-Barrett was now keeping a trained eye on the trays of cakes, making sure that the two-pennies did not get intermingled with the three-pennies and that a solicitous mother, as most of the waitresses were, did not slip a plate of cakes under the upturned brails to a young member of her family – it had been done.

With the exception of a table for four which was, at present, seating only the major – here today under protest – and the vicar – here as a duty and part of his cross – the rest of the twelve tables were occupied. And this was instantly evident to Peter when, Leo going before him, he entered the marquee.

Whereas the reactions to them on the field had been somewhat covert, now they became definitely visible. Interest could be seen running like a swelling wave around the tent, and the crest hit the major and the vicar with seeming force.

The vicar's reaction was writ large on his face, for the poor man was still shaking with the implications levelled at him by his sister a few hours earlier. The major was of sterner stuff, though a battle had raged in his drawing-room only yesterday when, admitting he had lain on the grass with the lady now sailing straight towards him, he had at the same time stoutly denied any monkey-business but had bravely threatened it should he hear another word of such nonsense, by God! And then at lunchtime today Florrie, who had always been his ally, had had to lean across the table and ask him out of the blue, 'Do you remember the tale of Connie Fitzpatrick?' Connie Fitzpatrick! Had they all gone mad?

Now the major rose and smiled a greeting, and Leo, returning the smile, said with a familiarity that was seldom used towards the village autocrat, 'Hello there, Major,' and the major, inclining his head into a bow which as a rule he reserved for high occasions only, replied, 'How d'you do?' Then reaching forward he pulled out a chair, adding 'Hello there, Peter.'

'Hello, sir.'

Try as he might, Peter could not prevent some nervousness from coming over in his voice. And who wouldn't be nervous with Mrs C.-B. and Miss Collins looking at her like that . . . He had been stark raving mad to let her come in here.

'You have met our vicar?' The major levelled

his gaze on the obviously writhing and wilting man, and Leo, sitting down while at the same time with a swansdown tap touching the vicar's sleeve, said, 'Oh yes, we have met – and talked.' She stressed the last word, then added with a bubble to her voice, 'And not of pews and steeples and the cash that goes therewith either.'

On this quip the major let out a staccato and bullet-cracking roar that filled the marquee and brought a sweat to Peter's brow while seeming to cast a spell on all the other occupants, and in the stillness the major's voice sounded as if he were speaking into a tunnel as he boisterously finished the quotation: ' "But the souls of Christian peoples. Chuck it, Smith!" Good old Chesterton! Well put, miss.'

The major was now fully aware of his wife's eyes beating a tattoo of signals towards him, and he took a gleeful delight in ignoring them. All the years he had been married to her she had never been able to cap a damn line of his, nor understand one of his quotations, yet she played the learned lady to those who knew no better, and it served them damned well right for being taken in – they didn't read, nobody read these days – but this girl here, she might look like a Floosie but, by damn, she had a mind. Look at the other day when he had come upon her in the wood and said, 'You all alone?' and she had quoted Dickens as pat as pat: ' "Lo the city is dead. I've seen but an eel." ' It was odd but she seemed to know he had a weakness for quotations. Ah, he had enjoyed that hour. But would he have done so had he known he was being watched? Watched!

The thought infuriated him still. Blast their eyes, for sneaking, brainless busy-bodies.

'What d'you say?' There was a bark in the major's voice as his attention was brought to the Reverend again.

'Nothing . . . nothing. I wasn't speaking.' And Mr Collins wasn't speaking, he was choking. His sister was not more than three yards away and the look she was fastening on him was causing him to experience a most odd feeling, as if he had been caught committing an indecency, like in a dream.

He coughed into his handkerchief, and the major said, 'Take a drink of tea, man. It's that cake, it's dry. Well now—' he looked at Leo again – 'you'd like a cup of tea, wouldn't you? Where's everybody?' As he raised his hand to beckon one of the tea-bearers, Peter said hastily, 'I'll get it, sir.'

'Oh, all right. And bring me another one, too, will you, Peter? What about you?'

This simple question seemed to startle the vicar still further and he stammered, 'No . . . no thanks. I was j-j-just about to go . . . prizes.'

'Let them wait, man, they won't run away. Well, what do you think of our sports?' Once again the major gave Leo all his attention, and she smiled widely at him as she said, 'I think they're excellent. It's very well organised.'

'Hm! Nothing like it used to be. Real races at one time . . . horses, from here to Blanchland, round Bannock Fell Farm and back. Grand day! Fine do it used to be! They came from all over the county, and beyond, to compete. Now folks are too busy – or no money. Or if they have they do show jumping – nothing for the sport of the thing. Have us put down the hunt they would . . . Don't be cruel to the foxes – bah! What d'you say, Vicar?' There had come into the major's eyes a deep, humorous glimmer.

'Well – well—' the vicar stretched his neck in an attempt to assert himself and to make a show of his principles even under these very trying circumstances, 'you know what I think of racing . . . of – of any kind, Major.'

'Now, now, what about it?' The major pointed to the open end of the marquee where could be seen the races in progress, and when the vicar shook his head, dismissing such a trumpery comparison, the major leaned towards Leo and said, 'What about one to fit racing, eh?'

Returning his twinkle and entering into his mood, Leo put her head back and looked up thoughtfully towards the apex of the tent; then after a moment of consideration, she shook her head saying 'No, I can't think of one. No.' Her head still back she turned it to the side as if still thinking, and from this position she watched Peter threading his way back towards them with a tray of tea, and over the distance she sent him a look that caused the blood to flood up into his face, and as he neared the table she called playfully to him, 'Do you know a quotation for racing, Peter?'

'Quotation for racing? No, I don't.' He wished she wouldn't act like this. She was doing it on purpose, a sort of teasing. Something had got into her. She looked as if she was in love with him, and the major, and the vicar and all mankind. Why was she doing it? There seemed to be a kind of devil in her, an egging-on, teasing devil. He'd had glimpses of it before, in the bar when Mrs Booth was behind the counter.

The women were furious. He was thankful his mother wasn't here after all. It was bad enough to see Mrs C.-B. She looked as if she was going to take off through the roof at any minute – it was evident that Mavis had talked. As for Miss Collins he wouldn't be surprised to see her have a fit, or pass out. And there, near the door, was Mrs Fountain, with Mrs Booth of all people. Like thunder they both looked.

'It's a lovely cup of tea.' Leo sipped at the tea, pushed the damp hair back from her forehead, then said musingly, 'Races. You know, I can't think of one to fit races.' She bit on her lip, her eyes laughing into the major's over the cup brim. Then putting the cup down, she exclaimed excitedly, 'Only that one about the human race.' She leant across the table towards him:

' "I wish I loved the human race,
I wish I loved its silly face."

'You know that one?'

The major, placing both his hands on the table, bounced his head to each word as he joined it to hers now:

' "I wish . . . I liked . . . the way . . . it walks,
I wish I liked the way it talks,

511

And when I'm introduced to one
I wish I thought what – jolly fun." '

They emphasised the last two words, and, but for their joint merriment and the buzz of noise from outside, for the second time within a few minutes there was absolute silence in the marquee, a shocked silence. It even enveloped Peter. Why had she to do it? And the major acting like that . . . he'd never imagined the major could go on like that . . . like his father or Bill Fountain when they were tight. He could well imagine him getting drunk, roaring drunk, or going mad on a horse, or raising hell in the house, but to act this way . . . silly, daft like a bairn. But she was egging him on. Why was she doing it? This would really set the place on fire.

It certainly brought the vicar to his feet, but not for the reason that Peter and the rest of the gathering imagined – they could not know that the Reverend Collins was not shocked at this unseemly display between the first gentleman of the village and this unusual-looking girl from the Hart. He was shocked at himself: first because it had taken him all his time not to join in and show them, particularly the major, that he wasn't the only one who knew Sir Walter Raleigh's rhyme and, secondly, the discovery had been thrust upon him that he was jealous because the major was finding so much favour in her eyes. Really! really! He wiped his brow, and with a brief nod which included them all and singled none of them out and vindicated himself somewhat in the eyes of his sister, he left the tent.

In the hushed murmuring that crept gently into the silence following the vicar's exit, the major, seemingly oblivious of anything unusual in the atmosphere, took a long drink of his tea. And as he did so there came the first rumble of thunder. 'Ah! been waiting for that.' The major nodded at Peter. 'It'll be some storm when it breaks . . . swamp everywhere. I'd best be getting back – horses don't like it you know. Will you excuse me?'

He inclined his head towards Leo, who smiled at him fondly as he stood up and came round the table. Then bending over her he whispered, 'What d'you say Slinky makes her getaway tonight?' And Leo, as if playing a game with a child, strained her face up to his and whispered back, 'Almost certain.'

In an attempt to do the right thing Peter had risen to his feet with the major, and he now stood looking gloweringly uncomfortable. Yet it was nothing to what he was feeling, for he was now as mad at her as he had been at the major for acting the goat. She had, he felt sure, gone out of her way to encourage the old fellow.

'Pity.' The major's smile lingered on her as he straightened his waistcoat. 'Fine sight. Well, goodbye. Bye Peter.'

'Goodbye, sir.'

He sat down again opposite her, his face straight and Leo, ignoring his look said, 'I like him. I think he's grand. I can understand your father swearing by him, can't you?'

When he made no reply her face lost its laughter and she said softly, 'I'm a wicked woman, a hussy, because I laughed with him?'

His answer came from deep in his throat: 'It's not that.'

'It is that.' Her voice was as low as his. 'And I did it on purpose. I admit it. Do you think I am blind and insensitive to the feeling about me?'

She swallowed painfully as she stared at him. Then dropping her eyes to her cup she went on, 'I'm sorry if I've upset you, but I want to laugh – I must laugh. I told you, and you can't laugh with women, they won't let you . . . I shouldn't have come here, you shouldn't have asked me to, I see that now. It was like flaunting me under their noses, and they won't forgive you.'

He pushed his shoulders back as he said, 'What I do is my business. As for me bringing you here, where I go, you go.' He leaned towards her now as he added, 'You know that.'

He had almost become oblivious of the eyes upon them. But she hadn't, and softer still she warned, 'Be careful.'

What answer he would have made to this was checked by a rumbling of thunder following on a flash of lightning, and within seconds it became so dark as to seem almost like night.

There was a lively stir all about them now, and getting to his feet, he said, 'You'd better be getting back. You haven't got a coat, you'll get drenched.'

She glanced about her before saying, 'Let them get out and then we'll go.'

Another flash of lightning, followed immediately by a deep roar of thunder, acted like a spring and gave speed to everybody's legs, and in a few moments the marquee was empty but for the helpers, feverishly packing up.

'Come on.' Peter took her firmly by the arm and led her to the door of the marquee, where a blinding streak seeming to cut the heavens checked their steps and caused her to turn her face towards him for a moment before moving on.

Outside, as far as the sports field was concerned, they stepped into a changed world. Stalls were already stripped bare and their goods were being borne by willing helpers to the big tent adjoining the marquee. In the far distance the last of the spectators could only just be discerned crowding through the gate before making a dash to the village and home.

Another flash of lightning and an ear-splitting burst of thunder caused Peter to exclaim in some anxiety, 'This is going to break any minute; we'd better run for it while we can. Come on.'

'I'd rather walk.'

'Walk?' He hesitated for a second and looked at her. 'But you'll get drenched.'

'It doesn't matter. I don't want to run.'

Her tone was one he had not heard before. It was utterly flat-sounding and had about it a stiff finality which tended both to puzzle and irritate him. He was tempted at this precise moment to treat her as he would do one of the twins if they were being unnecessarily trying under such similar circumstances – clout her ear, grab her by the hand and gallop her over the field. She was, he told himself, just being contrary, and as far as he could see there was nothing he could do about it. Not trusting himself to speak, he moved in silence to the gate, and there the first drops of rain came, large, slow drops, spaced wide apart. Then one minute there was only the darkened sky and the heavy stillness in the atmosphere about them and the drops of softly falling rain; the next the wind was sweeping the field with the intensity of a gale, and Peter, having to shout now, looked down on Leo in some bewilderment, and demanded, 'You still want to dander?'

'Yes.'

He could not hear her voice but the movement of her head accompanying the words made her meaning clear to him.

'All right—' he made himself smile grimly as he yelled 'we dander!'

Buffeted by the wind they walked on, Peter suiting his pace to hers, while past them now most of the helpers were running madly for shelter. This was crazy – daft. When the storm really broke God alone knew what it would be like, and they had to go through the fields yet.

Then as if the lock gates of heaven had been opened a deluge of water seemed to fall in a complete sheet and envelope them, and in as short a time as it takes to say, they were both drenched to the skin. As she huddled against him he decided grimly that he was having no more of this damn nonsense, and so putting his arm about her, he began to run. Bringing her feet almost off the ground he propelled her forward, and he had managed to get her some way before he took any notice of her hands clawing him, but even then his determination to get out of the storm made him ignore them, and it was not until they had covered quite some distance and her hands had ceased their clawing that he looked at her. And then he was brought to a dead stop.

'Leo!' His voice was carried away from him. 'Leo!' He tried to raise her rain-drenched face, but her chin was dug into her chest and her shoulders were heaving as if she were swimming, and he shouted now in panic. 'Leo! Leo, what is it?'

Firmly he pulled her face upwards. Her hair was plastered across it, her eyes were closed, and but for the rise and fall of her breast she could have been dead. Her face had the alabaster look of death, and he cried out in real fear, 'Leo! Leo! What's the matter? For God's sake tell me! Look . . . Leo! Leo!'

He stood braced with his back to the wind, sheltering her. The water was pouring down his neck as if from a spout but he was not conscious of it.

'Leo!' He shook her gently. 'Say something, for God's sake. Do you hear?'

When she made no effort to answer he looked wildly about him. They were on the main road just clear of the fields, but so dense was the downpour of rain that he could barely make out the banks on either side. He held her to him, and at that moment a car, turning from the field path, moved slowly past them. It was, he saw, packed to capacity. Naturally it did not stop. After one more moment of hesitation he stooped and, picking her up bodily in his arms, stumbled along the road.

The wind, really at gale force now, drove him into the ditch, and it took him all his time to save them both from falling headlong. Fortunately the ditch was shallow, and propping one leg on the bank he rested for a moment, holding her inert form tightly to him. He was frightened, filled with panic. He couldn't ever remember feeling like this. He peered down into her face. But there was no movement from her, even her breast wasn't rising as it had done, so hitching her up to him again he went on.

He was now nearing the vicarage gates when another car coming from behind rounded slowly in front of him and turned into the drive. It, too, was packed, and through the opaque windscreen he could just make out Florrie at the wheel. He knew, too, that she had recognised him, but he had ceased to care what she or anyone else might think. He yelled out to her, but if she heard she took no notice, and the car within a moment was lost in the gloom.

He had covered another few yards or so when Leo moved and spoke. Although her lips were against his ear he could not make out what she said, but the movement of her body indicated that she wished to be put down.

Almost faint with the feeling of relief he gently eased her onto her feet, and his arms still about her he mouthed the words, 'Are you all right?'

There was no change for the better in her face, and she made no effort to speak but inclined her head once slowly, then dropped it against him.

'Can you walk, or shall I—?' He made a motion to carry her again, but she put out her hand to check him, and leaning heavily on him she moved forward.

He wasn't conscious that his own shirt was clinging to his back and his trousers sticking to his legs, but he was very much aware of her wet body beneath her soaked clothes, he could even feel the squelch of the water as he moved his hand at her waist. A terrible crash of thunder rending the heavens brought her round to him, and he stood pressing her face into his neck. They were within sight of the Hart now and after a moment he urged her gently on again, and at last brought her to the side porch. Once under its shelter, and prey now only to the slant of the driving rain, she stood leaning against the wall gasping for breath, but she made no immediate effort to go in through the side door and up the stairs. It seemed as if she were fighting, besides for breath, for composure before entering the inn.

He took her hand and, holding it between his own pressed it gently to his chest. 'Are you ill, Leo?'

She made a small movement with her free hand, and he said, 'Look, go straight up to bed.' It took some effort for him to offer this advice which would send her to her room, for once she was there how could he know just what was happening to her.

She dragged her eyes up to his face, then murmured, 'I'll . . . have . . . a bath.' There was a considerable pause before she added, 'I'll try . . . to come down . . . later.'

He released her hand, and she touched his arm, saying, 'Don't worry . . . I'll – I'll be all right.' He could say nothing, so full now was his heart of an odd fear, but he pushed open the door for her and helped her into the passage, then watched her go slowly up the stairs. And not until he heard her door close overhead did he turn away and make for home.

Free now to run or gallop as he wished, he did not tear along the street towards the house but walked through the deluge at much the same rate as that which had brought him to the inn.

At the house, Grandpop, opening the window just the slightest, yelled, 'You aiming to become a duck?' And when Peter passed him without as much as a look in his direction the old man blinked, banged the window and said over his shoulder, 'I wouldn't stand there with me mouth wide open, I'd get a tub of hot water ready. Strikes me he's in for summat.'

For once Rosie did not retort in her usual vein to the old man's orders, but turned away and went into the living-room. He was in for something all right! For the past few minutes she had been standing at the window behind Grandpop watching his coming. The twins' account of the sports, and their Peter and the Miss, had worked her up to fever-pitch. She'd had enough and was going to put a stop to this business or else she'd know the reason why.

The light was on in the living-room, and on one side of the flower-filled hearth sat Old Pop reading, and on the other side was Harry. He too was reading, but evidently just to while away the time until the storm should ease and he could go out, for he was fully dressed even to his cap which lay on his knee. As Rosie bustled through the room towards the kitchen, the two men lowered their papers and glanced in her direction, then looked at each other before resuming their reading again.

Rosie reached the kitchen as Peter entered from the back door and she looked at him as he stood on the mat, while the water ran down him and made a pool at his feet. He returned her look and saw that she was in a fury of a temper such as, at times, he had seen his father arouse in her. And strangely enough it hardly disturbed him, for his mind was full to overflowing with a feeling of anxiety that was utterly new to him – something was the matter with Leo; what, he didn't know. She was young and she didn't run, and when he had forced her to, it looked for the time as if he had killed her. He was worried, puzzled – and frightened, and so his mother's reactions at this moment touched him hardly at all. And she sensed this in his tone when he said, 'Will you bring me some dry things down?'

Rosie's bust swelled and she answered meaningly, 'Yes, I'll bring you some dry things down.'

As she stalked again through the living-room, Harry lowered his paper and followed her to the foot of the stairs, and there, standing with his palm covering the knob of the banister, he said under his breath, 'If you take my advice you'll keep your tongue quiet.'

'I don't want your advice, thank you.'

Harry punched at the paper as he watched her mount the stairs, then returned to his seat in the living-room, and after giving his father one signficant look he punched at the paper again. They both raised their eyes ceilingwards to where could be heard her voice going at the twins, ordering them to stay up in the attic and play. When, within a few minutes, she again passed through the living-room they were both deeply engrossed in their reading.

In the scullery Rosie placed the clothes slowly on a chair and said with deep emphasis, 'Now!' Then joining her hands tightly at her waist she waited.

Peter, already stripped of his coat and shirt, was rubbing himself with a towel. He did not stop, and Rosie, keyed up to bursting point, cried, 'It's no use you stalling. I want to know what's going on.'

'I thought you knew . . . everybody else does.'

Did Rosie hear a chuckle from the living-room? Her eyes flashed in that direction for a second, and she said as if she were still speaking to her lad and chastising him for backchat, 'Now I'll not have any of that.'

'Look here, Mam, leave me alone.'

The words crisp and cutting, so unlike Peter's and so like her husband's, left Rosie with her mouth wide, and when she saw him grab up his dry clothes and go swiftly past her she could say nothing; she just gaped at him, seeing, she felt, the death of the only joy in her life.

Slowly she walked to the window and stood staring out at the driving rain. And ten minutes later she was still standing there when Peter, in mac and cap, came through the kitchen and went out without a word to her. The lump that came into her throat threatened to choke her, and when Harry, following almost on Peter's heels, stood behind her and said quietly, 'I told you, you'll never learn', she rounded on him, her expression teeming with words. But all she could bring out was, 'Damn you! Harry Puddleton.' Then diving past him she ran through the living-room and up the stairs, leaving Harry standing, turning his cap in his hands, his face showing a concern that would have surprised her had she seen it. He wanted to go and tell her to have patience, that this business was only a bit of fun, an affair if you like but one that would fizzle out. These things always did. No man took a girl like the Hart miss seriously. She and her like were to Harry's mind the type that gave a man that . . . that lift that was so necessary to his self-esteem, but as for getting serious about them, no fellow would – well, certainly not country-reared blokes who had inbred in them a sense of the fitness of things, and by that he meant the choosing of a mate for life. If he had dared he would have said to Rosie, 'She's the type I meself liked to have a lark with. But lark was the limit. And it's the same with the lad.' But he knew it would be no use. Rosie saw indecency in a laugh if there was another woman present. And if she went on in this way at the lad she would, as she had done with himself, make him give her something to worry over.

Harry looked down at the cap; he turned it over and examined it without seeing it. He was himself worried, but he would not admit that there was really anything to worry over. He told himself he was as bad as her, yet he was not at all happy in his mind about the business and the way it was going. Slowly putting his cap on to his head, he pulled the peak well down and went out.

7

Peter did not go straight into the Hart but stood looking at one of the two cars parked in front of the inn, and as he stared at it more confusion was added to his already over-burdened feelings. He had seen the car before . . . twice. It was – the car. That meant . . . What it meant he did not explain to himself but entered the bar, his eyes flicking about him, and almost immediately they found what they sought. The man was standing at the bar counter with his back to it and holding a glass of spirits in his hand, and although everyone in the packed room seemed to be immersed in conversation he was neither talking nor listening to anyone in particular but rather was he taking in all that was going on around him. And he took in Peter immediately and whereas he had appeared somewhat bored, his manner now showed a spurt of interest, for as Peter made his way to the counter he purposely pushed to one side to make room for him, and over a number of heads he nodded and called, 'Hello, there.'

When Peter, not taking advantage of the offer of space, merely nodded in answer to this greeting, the man jerked his head and said, 'Here a minute, will you?'

Skirting a little group, Peter joined him at the

corner and looking levelly at him asked pointedly, 'What is it?'

'What'll you have?'

'Nothing thanks, I'm joining . . .' His vague indication could have been meant for anyone in the room behind them.

'Well have one with me first.' The man threw off his whisky and calling to Mrs Booth, who was serving along the counter, said, 'A whisky and . . .' He glanced at Peter, and reluctantly Peter added, 'A beer – small.'

'A small beer. There now.' The man leant his elbows on the counter and nodding backwards towards the window said, 'Hell of a storm, this.'

'Yes, pretty bad.'

As Mrs Booth placed the drinks before them she looked at Peter with a look that was more in the nature of a glare, and it did not go unnoticed by the man, who dropped his gaze to his drink, which he picked up. Then turning his back on the counter, he muttered, 'That's what's commonly known as a cow, and udder no circumstances to be trusted.' He gave a silly sounding giggle at his own joke.

Peter made no comment. But when the man went on, 'The Sunday Rags aren't in it – thinks she knows the lot,' he knew that Mrs Booth had been talking, and about him and Leo. And this was immediately verified when the man in a soft, insinuating tone, added, 'You both got wet?'

Peter, in the act of taking a drink, stopped. 'Anything wrong in that?' It was a challenge.

But the man did not take it up; his voice was even conciliatory, as he said, 'No . . . no, but not very wise of her. But then—' he sipped at his whisky – 'Anna was never very wise. She might give you that impression – oh, yes, she would – but she never was, and never will be.' He shook his head sadly.

'What are you getting at?'

'Me? Nothing.' He half turned away and looked about him as far as he could see; then almost eagerly he exclaimed, 'Look there's two seats in the window. Those people are just off. Must want to get home badly to go out in this, but that's their look-out. Come and sit down.' And not waiting for any answer, for or against, he pushed through the throng and Peter, determined now that he had got this far to know all there was to know, followed him.

When they were seated on the broad sill the man said, 'There now, what were you saying, son?'

'I wasn't saying anything, you were doing the talking. And I'm not your son.' The last sounded petty and childish but he could not restrain himself from, as he put it, getting at this fellow.

The man, after looking steadily at him, gave a short laugh and said, 'Only a saying, no harm meant, and as you said I was doing the talking . . . you were quite right. Well now—' he leant forward until his face was near to Peter's – 'you won't believe it but I'm going to try to do you a good turn. Oh, I knew you wouldn't believe it, nobody would – I wouldn't meself in your place – but nevertheless I am, and it's this advice I'm going to give you.' His voice dropped. 'Keep away from Anna.'

Although Leo had already said that this man was not her husband Peter found he was doubting the truth of it now, so much so that had the man claimed to be her husband he would unreservedly have believed him. As if sieved through his teeth, he brought out the questions, 'Why should I? What's it got to do with you? Who are you anyway – her husband?'

The man's eyebrows seemed to move up into a point before he said, 'No, I'm not her husband . . . well—' he wiped his trim, short moustache with the tips of his fingers and his eyes slid sideways to Peter – 'not in name. Now! now! look here.' His manner underwent a lightning change and he put out a restraining hand and said under his breath, 'Don't get on your high-horse, lad, for let me warn you I can shoot as straight a left as anyone for my age. Don't let this deceive you.' He patted his flabby paunch. 'What I'm saying to you is for your own good. You asked a question and I gave you a straight answer. I was her husband of sorts, but that's over. Even so, she's not for you, and if you'll take my advice you'll cut loose and save yourself some heartache.'

'And leave the field to you?'

The man drew in his breath. 'I don't want the field, as you call it, but I happen to know it better than you. Anyway—' he threw off his whisky with a touch of impatience – 'why the hell am I bothering! I'm just wasting my breath and—' His words were cut short by the screeching of brakes as a car was brought to a standstill almost in the porch itself, and swiftly turning his attention to the rain-smeared window, he cleared his vision somewhat by rubbing vigorously at the misted pane, then exclaimed, with definite anger now, 'Blasted fools! ripping her guts out.' He kept his eyes on the blurred outline of the car as it backed from the porch and disappeared into the yard. He seemed to have forgotten Peter and the very personal topic in hand, for he turned his eyes towards the door and waited, the look on his face much darker now. And when four internally soaked young men came into view, debating loudly in the passageway whether to go into the bar or the saloon, he muttered, 'Bloody young fools!'

'In here, fellows.'

'No, in here.'

'No, come on in the bar – beer, skittles, girls and victuals.'

So hilarious was their laughter, so loud their shouting that in one after the other of the groups around the bar the talking died down and smiling and interested faces were turned towards the young men.

The newcomers seemed to be between the ages of twenty-five and thirty-five, and all except one were far advanced in their cups. This one happened to be the smallest among them, and although he was apparently in the merry stage he was still in command of himself, and also, it seemed, of his companions, for he hustled them now bodily into the bar and to the counter, but not regardless of the human obstacles in the way, for the people who moved aside he thanked with courteous and even elaborate thanks.

Peter's angry mind was momentarily drawn

from the man at his side to the tallest member of the party, who stood well over six feet. He was blond and big-boned and could, when sober, have represented a travel advertisement for Sweden, and it soon became evident, not only to Peter but to the entire room, that this young man's name was Tiffy.

'Come on, Tiffy, sing,' the other two urged, while their apparent leader between giving the orders for drinks, added his plea, 'Yes, Tiffy, you show 'em. You show 'em.'

Tiffy, his body swaying and his face one great beam, appealed to the entire company, 'You want a song?' And when there were a few restrained murmurs and nods from one or two quarters, Tiffy received these as wild acclaim and cried, 'All right! all right! What d'you want, eh? Come on tell us. Rock an' Roll to Rigoletto – come on, what's it to be?'

But there seemed a reluctance on the part of the company to put forward their requests, and one of the men, addressed as Max, turned to the bar, saying, 'Aw, let's drink. They wouldn't recognise good music if you injected it inta them – let's drink.'

Whereupon, with much laughter and embracing of shoulders, they turned to the bar and drank. And over on the window seat the man, too, drank, throwing off his drink as if in disgust. It was evident that he had no use at all for the types at the bar, and he said so, taking Peter into his confidence as if they were buddies: 'That kind makes me sick. Ah, don't I know them. Meet 'em every day in life, without a penny to rub against the other. Get to colleges on grants. My money, and your money. Then look down their bloody noses.' He snorted. 'Ah well, the quicker they get out of here the better I'll like it.' He turned his attention fully to Peter again, and, pulling his neck out of his collar and squaring his shoulders as if to regain his poise, he said, 'Well, where were we, son? Oh! sorry, I'd better say lad, eh?'

Ignoring this latter remark, Peter answered his question, 'You had decided against giving me any more advice.'

The man gave a short laugh and through narrowing eyes said, 'You're not such a fool as one might think. You sound as if you'd been around yourself, country boy or no country boy.'

Peter's lips fell into a tight line, and he kept them there for a moment before saying, 'Your kind always underestimate the other fellow. There's no country boys, as you call them, left. There was a war on, remember? But if there were any they'd still be able to show you a thing or two. You don't like that lot over there' – he nodded at the merry group at the bar – 'because they see through you, because they won't stand for you and your sharp-shooting car deals or, given the chance, they can outshoot you any day in the week. And they're young.'

This last remark seemed to sting the man more than anything else Peter had said. His eyes narrowed considerably as he got to his feet, and it was evident to Peter that he was going to make a parting shot, one which wasn't going to be softened by any pseudo-paternal feeling. Knowing it would surely be connected with Leo he braced himself for its impact by getting to his feet, too, but as he did so a loud command came from the leader of the group at the bar, and such was its tone that it had the power to draw their attention.

'Order! Order! You are now about to hear the golden voice of Brother Tiffy.' The small fellow endeavoured to hold the blond young man's hand up as far as his reach would allow, which seemed to convulse Tiffy.

'Order! for Brother Tiffy, the star of the theatre – Steven's Theatre.'

On this last remark the other two men, now known respectively as Max and Shaggy, turned to each other in a paroxysm of laughter. Their arms hanging around each other's necks they roared, until the small man cried, 'Stow it! you two, you're holding up proceedings. This is to be a major operation. Brother Tiffy is about to show his larynx as never before.' He turned to his widely grinning and befuddled friend, and after crying once more, 'Order! Now order!' he said, 'All right, Tiffy, off you go, it's all yours. Take it away.'

The room became still. Max and Shaggy broke away from each other and stood supporting themselves quietly against the counter. The only noise was the background din from the saloon; all faces in the room were turned on the great blond man as he straightened himself, took a deep breath and soared without prelude into *Samson and Delilah*.

'Softly awakes my heart, as the flowers awaken
To Aurora's tender zephyr.

But say, O well-belov'd, no more I'll be
  forsaken.
Speak again, O speak for ever!
O say that from Delilah, you will never
  part!
Your burning vows repeat; vows so dear to
  my heart! vows so dear to my heart!'

At this point Peter forgot about the man at his side; he even forgot himself and his churned-up feelings long enough to think, My God! what a voice.

'Ah! once again, do I implore thee!
Ah! once again, then say you adore me!
Ah! I here implore thee,
See, I implore thee.'

And it could have been Samson, the giant himself, singing to his Delilah, and in a voice so pure and strong that his love was forced into the ears of his hearers. A power was filling the room, and without exception it had caught the attention of everyone present; every face was focused on the singer. So fine was the voice and so unusual the range of tone that even movement was captured and held enthralled, for not a hand went towards a glass. And within a few minutes even the noise from the saloon was stilled. And it seemed to the onlookers that the singer's voice had enraptured even himself, for although he would turn his head here and there his eyes looked unseeing, or were seeing beyond the walls, as on and on he sang:

'So sways my trembling heart, consoling all its
   pain,
To thy voice so dear, so loving.
The arrow in its flight is not swifter than I,
When, leaving all behind, to your arms I
   fly!
Unto your arms I fly.'

Mr Booth, content for the moment to stop adding to his till, stood behind the bar, his hands
characteristically touching the edge of the
counter. A little way to the left of him Mrs Booth
had allowed her buttocks to rest against a barrel
and her face had taken on an almost tender
look, and who knew what thoughts were ranging
through her mind as she gazed at the Adonis-like
profile of the entertainer. He looked to her too
good to be true, and she sighed.

Oddly enough, Peter was thinking much the
same thing. The blond man seemed to be
possessed of everything – looks, voice, and charm,
but most of all, a voice. He was likely some big
actor – a star, and this was just a lark, they were
all out on the spree. His eyes were riveted on the
mobile face. One minute he saw the singer's
mouth wide open, sending passionate words out
on golden notes, but the next moment, the mouth
still open, the song had abruptly ceased and the
expression on the singer's face was not far away
and lost in the realms of love but was showing
wildly delighted surprise. He was looking over the
heads of the others towards the door leading into
the passage, and as Peter's eyes flashed in that
direction the blond fellow's arm shot out and he

cried, 'God Almighty! See what I see, fellows – look!'

Standing in the doorway was Leo. She looked fearfully white and slightly spellbound, but when, as if recovering herself, she turned to make a hasty retreat her escape was cut off by those behind her, and with a loud scuffling and whooping she was immediately surrounded by the four men.

So unusual was the scene that the other occupants of the room and those in the passage remained quiet as if witnessing another part of the entertainment set up by these strangers. Nor did Peter move, he seemed fixed by his unblinking stare.

'Leo! Why, Leo! Well, who would have expected to see you here.' The small man's voice could be picked out now from above the rest. He was holding one of her hands, her other being lost in the two great paws of the singer, who was crying in an emotional voice, which was undoubtedly aided by the load he was carrying, 'Aw Leo! Leo, my love. Aw Leo!'

A pain, like a thin blade piercing his chest, struck Peter as he watched Tiffy, with his arm about her now, draw her to the counter. He was still effusing maudlinly for all to hear, 'My day is complete, my life is complete. Leo of all people! Leo!' He looked around his companions for confirmation of his pleasure, and Max, walking backwards in front of her, cried, 'What are you doing here, Leo?' But before she could answer, Tiffy cried, 'Breaking hearts, I bet. What do you say, aren't you?'

'You're drunk, Tiffy.' Her voice was low, but it seemed to be caught up by everyone in the room.

'Yes, I'm drunk, Leo. I've been drunk all day – we've all been drunk. Come on, you have a drink, anything you like, it's an occasion . . . Let me look at you.'

The silence fell heavy on the room as Tiffy, holding her at arm's length, stared down into her face. Then in an even louder voice, he cried, 'You're looking grand – grand.'

On the face of her appearance this seemed rather a strange remark to make.

'Quiet, Tiffy. Let her have a drink. Is it grape-fruit, Leo?'

It was the small man again, and Leo turned to him and said, 'Still keeping order, Roger?' And he, smiling somewhat soberly back at her, answered, 'Someone's got to do it in this outfit, Leo. How are you really?' This last question was hardly audible to Peter, even in the silence.

'All right.'

'That's it.'

Peter watched the little fellow as his eyes lingered on her. Then Roger, his voice louder now, asked, 'You passing through?'

'No. I'm staying here for a time.'

There came a quiet uneasiness among the four men following this statement. Max and Shaggy drank; Tiffy, his eyes on her all the while, took occasional sips from his glass and made occasional unbelieving movements with his head while repeating her name from time to time, as if he still couldn't believe his eyes.

As the room came slowly back to normal Peter,

his gaze riveted on Leo, willed with all his might that she should look at him, and when turning with her grapefruit from the counter to answer a remark of one of the group her eyes came to rest, not on him, but on the man standing at his side, he saw that she was startled and he watched her turn quickly to the counter again.

His companion's face, he now noted, looked grey, and he, too, was holding her with his eyes. In spite of Peter's concern for her, a sudden revulsion of feeling against her came over him. She could handle drunks that was evident. Four of them, all milling round her! And how many men had she known like this fellow here beside him? The question did not shout in his mind but probed him with deadly insistence, more powerful than flashing anger. It was like a slow injection of blood, proving itself as it ran through his veins, gradually giving him strength to reject this mania that had come upon him. Perhaps he wasn't a blasted fool altogether . . . Perhaps they were right. He forgot that just a short while ago he was worried sick because he thought that she was ill.

People were beginning to drink and talk again in a somewhat desultory fashion. Remarks could be heard about the rain, and when another crash of thunder came some weather sage propounded, 'Travelled ten miles, the storm has, since that last crack.'

It was just when people were seemingly falling back into the tempo of the room as it had been before the appearance of the group at the bar that Tiffy's voice ringing clearly out aroused their interest more so than before as it cried, 'Aw, come on, Leo. Come on, sing. Remember Christmas Eve? That was a do. Come on. The duet? Come on, love.'

At this moment Peter's view of the bar was suddenly blocked out by the bulk of his father and Bill. They were standing dead in front of him, and Harry's voice said quietly, 'Let's go, lad. We could get the bus into Allendale, or go Blanchland way – it'll be passing in a minute.'

'Aye, do that Peter,' urged Bill. 'This place is too crowded the night by half – no enjoyment in it. Come on, lad.'

'Kiss me – come on, give me a kiss.' This demand, shutting off the chatter like a sound-proof door, caused all eyes to turn in the direction of the counter again, and Mr Booth, thinking it time to assert his authority, cried, 'Now, gentlemen! gentlemen!'

'Come on, Leo . . . my love.'

It was a slow, drawn-out plea, and although it sounded laughable no-one laughed, there was not even a snigger.

The little man, Roger, intervened quickly now, his voice no longer merry. 'Don't act the goat, Tiffy. Stop it! D'you hear?' He pulled at his friend's arm, but was pushed laughingly aside, and Tiffy, encircling Leo with his arms pleaded again, his voice filling the stillness as he lisped, this time in baby talk, 'Just a leetle peck – just a weeny, teeny little peck. Ah! kiss Tiffy, Leo.'

Tiffy was apparently unaware of the scuffle going on near the window, and not until he was dragged round from Leo did he show any surprise, and then he was still full of good humour.

'What's up? Who are you?'

'You'll know in a minute. Get out!'

'Oooh!' Tiffy's face seemed to brighten with knowledge as he blinked heavily at Peter. 'You a friend of Leo's?' He nodded his head in great bounces, denoting his understanding. 'Well, I'm a friend of Leo's an' all! We're all friends of Leo's, aren't we, ducks?' He looked towards Leo, where he held her at arm's length now with his big white hand. 'But me, I'm a special friend, aren't I? You see—' he leant forward and with his free hand thumbed Peter in the chest – 'I know Leo as you don't know her, nor nobody else . . . Oh! you would, would you!'

In spite of the drink Tiffy knew when he was going to be hit, and ducked, and as Harry, grabbing at Peter's raised arm, cried, 'Give over, lad,' Tiffy's smile vanished completely. His brows darkening, the whole expression of his face altered and he said thickly, 'It's like that, is it? It's a fight you want. Well, I'm game – game for anything. Stand back!' He pushed his friends aside.

'Stop it! Do you hear! Stop it!' It was Leo's voice high and pleading, but it was not directed towards Tiffy but to Peter. And to it was now added the man's. He was standing by her side and he cried in anger, 'Yes, stop it! I should damn well think so. You're taking too much on yourself, you are, far too damn much. I'm the one to deal with this.'

'Oh! you are, are you!' Peter's furious glance swung from Tiffy to the man, but Harry, tightening his grip on his son, urged sternly, 'Come on out of it. Come on, lad.'

The man, with his hand on Leo's arm as if to protect her, now set the spark to Peter's fury when he addressed himself pointedly to Harry, saying, 'That's it. Get him off home before he gets ideas about himself and his capabilities.'

In that moment no-one could have stopped Peter – his father, nor Bill, nor yet the combined efforts of three of the four merry-makers, not Mr Booth, who with the agility of a gazelle had leapt the counter – for his arm swung up and out, and under the blow the man was flung back among the tables. Immediately, there was pandemonium. Two women sitting nearby screamed, and to their screaming was added more from the passage; there were cries from Mrs Booth, who, as she saw the man righting himself preparatory to making a dive for Peter, yelled, 'Get outside! Outside, the lot of you!'

She was herself unable to get into the room for the crush of men blocking the let, and this infuriated her further. Her eyes searched out Leo where she stood with her back pressed against the counter, and rushing towards her she grabbed at the back of her shoulders, twisted her round and screamed into her terrified face, 'You! This is you! Get out! Go on, before I knock your bloody jailbird face in for you, you dirty—!'

Mrs Booth's elucidating epitaph was lost in the fury of her voice as with a ferocious shove across the counter she pushed Leo almost into the mêlée of shouting, swearing, struggling men. It was only Harry, separated for the moment from Peter where he was now being held by Bill and Roger, that saved her from falling to the floor. Grabbing at her, Harry steadied her against him, and she clung to him, gasping.

The room now seemed to be divided into two groups: those around Peter and the rest hanging on to the man; only Mr Booth seemed separate and only his voice could be heard crying repeatedly, 'Get on outside with you. Outside! Outside! I'll call the police, mind. Outside! Get them outside!'

There was no escape for the girl, Harry saw, through the passageway. But his mind, as confused as anyone's at that moment, was clear about one thing: he knew he must not leave her with Katie Booth or else there'd be trouble of perhaps a more serious nature. The girl looked scared, almost petrified. She no longer looked the miss he had got a kick out of knowing, she looked as if she would collapse at his feet.

'Come on.' He drew her round the outskirts of the shifting shouting mass and to the window, where just a few minutes before Peter had been seated. Thrusting up the sash he assisted her over the low sill and out into the rain-swept porch. Then a quick glance back into the room showed him that Mr Booth, with the use of his own brawn and the help of the locals, was persuading the combatants into the passage. So he followed Leo through the window.

The shouting and yelling filled the street as the men came struggling out of both the main and saloon bars and milled about under the porchway, reluctant to be pushed into the downpour. And Peter's voice came clearly above the din when in a roar that would have done credit to

Grandpop, he yelled, 'Leave go of me! Leave go, do you hear!'

Shaking himself like an enraged bull, he flung himself clear of the hands holding him. It was unfortunate that in doing so one of his thrashing fists should contact Bill. In a twinkling Bill was measuring his full length in the road.

The sight of the momentarily prostrate figure with the rain beating down on him seemed to inflame still further the tempers of those directly concerned, for Tiffy, taking up the cudgels of the man lying on his back, now pushed his way to Peter, and lifting his huge fist, aimed a blow at him. It was as well that the direction of the blow was drink-controlled or Peter, too, would have joined Bill, but the blow, skidding past him, incensed him as much as if he had met its full force, and he struck back with such ferocity that within a second Tiffy and he were in the road bashing it out, blinded with rain and rage.

Harry had left Leo against the wall at the far end of the porch to rush to the aid of Bill, and he had just managed to get him to his feet when two things attracted him simultaneously: his lad was fighting in the middle of the road with the singing fellow, and the man, who, in Harry's mind, had started all this, had broken away from those who were trying to deter him and was making for the combatants, not, Harry knew, to assist Peter.

'No you don't!' Harry left the dazed and rocking Bill and practically threw himself at the man, and in a second he, too, was engulfed and hitting out in desperate self-defence.

The road outside the Hart now showed a

scene that had never before been witnessed in Battenbun, and every door and window that could look upon the inn was filled with its shocked spectators, and it seemed to them that their village had suddenly gone mad. For the peacemakers who had been endeavouring to separate the combatants were themselves drawn into the mêlée, and blows, whether used for attack or defence, are hardly distinguishable to the lookers on.

It was only after a great deal of yelling, tugging, pulling and shoving, that the parties were separated. But the noise covering the green was like that of a cup final and one that had not pleased the majority of the crowd. Even with the two contesting groups spread apart the noise still went on.

It was with some element of surprise that Peter found himself neither giving nor receiving blows, but standing round the corner in the inn yard with his back against the wall, gasping for breath, and with blood running into his eyes and almost blinding him. He knew there was someone on each side of him, and dimly he recognised the little fellow's voice as he said, 'Take it easy. Sit down here.'

Dazed and still panting as if his lungs would burst, he allowed himself to be drawn forward and down to a seat which, experience told him, was the step of a car.

'I'll put that right for you. Max, get me the kit. And you, Tiffy, get inside and keep your mouth shut. See to him Shaggy, I won't be a minute.'

'There!' Peter felt a painful sting that hurt more than the blow that had cut open his eyebrow. Then slowly his vision cleared, and close above him he saw the master of ceremonies. The little man's dark thin face seemed to have changed entirely in the past moments, and his voice had a commanding ring as he said, 'Rest easy now till I stick something on it.' There was a pause while his fingers moved round the cut; then he muttered rapidly, 'That'll stop the bleeding . . . it won't need stitching.' Another pause and then he went on, 'I'm sorry this has happened. Tiffy's a fool but he meant no harm. You know when all's said and done you asked for what you got . . . we're all fond of Leo, Tiffy particularly. He did a great deal for her, it made a difference – he got to know her rather well.'

The mention of Leo's name seemed to have as astringent an effect on Peter as the stuff that had been applied to the cut for it brought him lumbering to his feet. He stood swaying slightly as he rubbed his hand roughly over his face; then he said thickly, and not without sarcasm, 'I can believe that.' Then, try as he might, he could not resist asking, 'And what did he do for her that was so different from all the others?' His tone, like his lips, was curled in a sneer.

The small man blinked, then in a somewhat off-hand manner, he said, 'Oh, well, he was in the theatre and attended her for months afterwards. She was an interesting case besides being a damn fine girl.'

It was painful to screw up his eyes but Peter's bewilderment slowly puckered his face as he exclaimed thickly, 'You're not actors then, you're . . . ?'

'Actors? What gave you the impression we were actors? – we're doctors.' There was a crispness about the reply.

'Doctors?' In amazement he repeated the word, yet it was as if he were giving himself a long-awaited reply.

'Yes, doctors.' Roger gave a small laugh now. 'I don't suppose we appear quite the accepted idea but you've got to let your hair down sometimes in this business or you'd blow your top. Don't you know about Leo?'

Peter was standing quite still, looking down at the smaller man but not seeing him.

'She's ill, you know that?'

Peter's lips moved without emitting any sound, and when finally he did speak he could scarcely hear his own words.

'Ill? How?'

'Come on, let's get out of this blasted dump.'

Roger turned to where Max was leaning out of the car window and said curtly, 'Calm down, I won't be a minute.' Then putting his hand on Peter's elbow he guided him away, and when they reached the comparative quietness of the corner of the yard he looked up at him and made a statement, followed by a question: 'You're in love with her. Seriously? Now don't—' he raised one finger sharply – 'now don't say that's your business. Give me a straight answer.'

Here was no merry drunk. Looking at the man now it was hard to believe that he had touched a drop that day, and Peter did as he ordered and his reply came firmly as he said, 'Yes.'

'And you hadn't guessed she was ill?'

He shook his head in a pathetic fashion. 'No – not really. Only this evening she couldn't run out of the rain and . . .'

'Well.' The doctor bit on his lip, stretching it down behind his teeth. 'Well.' He moved uneasily. 'There should be time to tell you this. Not in this fashion and here—' his eyes flicked around him – 'and after this set-up. Still, you'd better know for I think you're in earnest about her – I'm coming!' He turned an angry face towards Max who was once again calling from the car window. Then resuming slowly, he said, 'When she left the hospital, four months ago, she had, at the outset, a year to live. She was supposed to report back at regular intervals, but once she was out she never came again. From something she let drop to Shaggy he got the idea that she was going to drive that old car of hers until she could go on no longer, then finish it. Of course, we could do nothing as it was just a surmise of his, and then when she didn't turn up and we didn't know where she was, we felt it had been no surmise and perhaps, after all, she knew what she was doing. Now and again her name would crop up because she was one of the gamest creatures we'd had through our hands. And then to come across her like this . . .'

The urge to punch and bash, fear of what he didn't know, fear of what he did know, even his blind jealousy of the man whom he knew definitely had been part of her life, were swept away, driven before a flood of compassion and love – and weakness. The weakness made him want to put his head in his hands and cry, cry with loud pain-easing sobs. Almost conquered by this feeling, he turned away and looked down towards the bar garden, and saw beyond it, in his mind's eye, the wood and the lake and the eel. She had been content to sit and watch the eel and wait for its going, and what had she thought as she sat there all alone? Of dying? Of the quick end she was going to make of it? Always in her mind must have been that thought.

Sweat suddenly enveloped him, outdoing the rain that was streaking his face. Then the doctor's voice, brisk but full of sympathy, put an end to his weakness: 'If you love her you'll stand by her. Not that that'll be easy, for unlike most women of my experience she rears from pity like an unbroken colt, but that's merely because she thinks it's her role. She's always been taken lightly, she's the type that's always good for a laugh and a lark, but she's got another side. We found that out during her long stay in hospital.'

Peter was forced round. 'What is it? What's wrong with her?'

'Growth . . . malignant. Here.' The doctor pointed to his chest.

Peter's mouth was bone dry and he rubbed at his swollen lips before saying, 'But there are cases where they—'

'There are miracles. You could pray for one, but as things stand I've told you what to expect. Still, as you say, there are cases, and pharmacy has no medicine that I know of to come up to the stimulant of love – a good love.'

'Hi there, Peter!'

Peter turned to the entrance of the yard where his father and Bill, now joined by Old Pop, were standing.

'Come on.' Harry did not advance any farther. His voice was harsh and he looked very much the worse for wear. But his face had escaped lightly, whereas Bill, besides a cut lip, was already showing signs of a beautiful black eye.

'We'll be off now.' The doctor turned towards his car, adding as he did so, 'This has been a strange half-hour to say the least. Goodbye. Tell Leo I'm sorry for all this, will you? Tell her I'll write to her here.'

From where he stood Peter watched the doctor get into the driving seat, and as the door banged behind him he moved hastily forward and, bending to the window, he brought out somewhat haltingly, 'I'm sorry . . . I'm sorry this happened. It was my fault.' Then turning his gaze on to the back seat to meet the scowling face of Tiffy, he repeated, 'Sorry about it.' Whereupon, as if an oiled rag had wiped it away, Tiffy's bad temper cleared and he shuffled his huge body saying, 'Oh, it's all in a day's work. We'll call in again some time.' He even laughed, and to the astonished gaze of Harry, Bill and Old Pop, and equally to a number of men still standing under the porch, the occupants of the car waved to Peter as it moved out of the yard, and, more astonished still, they watched Peter answer with one self-conscious lift of his hand.

'Well, I'll be damned!' Harry squeezed the wet out of his hair, then again repeated, 'Well, I'll be damned!' And turning on Peter as he slowly advanced towards them, he demanded, 'What d'you mean by waving after such a bloody do, all pals together like?'

Peter, ignoring the remark and the blame attached, asked, in an oddly quiet tone, 'Where is she?'

Harry held on to his temper and said, 'Round the corner, drenched and scared.'

'And the other bloke?'

'Oh, he's gone. Thought it best . . . got a bit too hot for him.'

Peter moved past them now and past the lingering men, and as he reached the front of the inn, Mrs Booth, pushing her way out of the door, confronted him and, her face convulsed with fury, cried, 'You'll pay for this. You'll see. You and your cheap street—!'

'Shut your mouth!'

For a moment it looked as if he might hit her, and she, too, must have thought this for she recoiled a step, then screamed, 'You would, would you! You try it on and see what you'll get. You're a disgrace. A disgrace to the place, you and her, and don't you show your face in here again, ever – ever!'

After giving her one long, contemptuous look that spewed her words into an unintelligible gabble he moved past her and went through the men and to Leo, where she stood against the wall, her face turned away, like a child in trouble. And when, without a word he took her arm and led her slowly into the street in the direction of home she made no show of resistance but walked by his side with her head lowered.

Peter's intention of taking her home hit Harry like a brick in the neck and brought him, in a spurt, to his side. Yet any protest he was about to make was stilled, not only by the look on his son's face but by the awful look of the girl, and so with a helpless gesture he dropped behind them and joined Bill and Old Pop as they came up. The lad was mad, stark, staring mad; this could only lead to trouble – Harry drew in his breath through his teeth – and some!

Although there were only five of them on the green, the village had never seemed so full of people, for the doors and windows were crowded, and when Bill, paring off from the cortege, went towards his own door his wife's tirade swept into the street and caused Harry to wince.

Not only was the Mackenzies' doorway blocked by Mrs Mackenzie and a now even more virtuously indignant Mavis, but the men were braving the rain to stand at the gate. But whether it was Peter's look or Harry's or Old Pop's, or the combined looks of all three, they were allowed to pass in silence to their own garden gate, and to Grandpop.

For once the old man was not seated at the window but was standing just inside the front door. He had his back to them and was brandishing his stick and yelling.

Before reaching the gate Harry had taken in the situation, so stepping briskly to the front he pushed by the old man and confronted Rosie, who was blocking the passage, to be greeted with a stammering ferocious protest of rage, 'How dare you! How dare you! She's – she's not coming in here.'

Following a movement from her husband that could be defined as a violent push, Rosie found herself in the living-room with an equally ferocious Harry bending over her and hissing into her face, 'Not a word out of you, d'you hear! It'll keep.'

'Don't you think you're—'

'Shut yer gob!'

'Shut me gob, d'you say? You'll see whether I'll shut—'

Rosie stepped back from Harry, and as she did so her eyes swung to the doorway where now stood her son and . . . the woman. For a moment she was afraid, not of her husband's threats, but at the sudden wild leaping feeling inside of her, for she had an almost unconquerable desire to spring on the girl and tear her to pieces. And when she saw her lad gently lead her towards a chair she had to turn away in case the feeling should get the better of her, and as she pressed her hand over her mouth to still the moaning sound that was rising from her stomach there fell on the room a dreadful quietness, which not even Grandpop's garrulousness could break.

The men's eyes were meeting and questioning. What next? Then they all, with the exception of Peter, looked towards Rosie. Peter had turned his eyes again to Leo, but she, too, was looking at his mother. He saw her fighting for words. Then, her voice breathless and cracking in her throat, she brought out, 'I'm sorry for this, Mrs Puddleton but I won't stay long – just until I can get my things from the Hart.'

Her words made no apparent impression on Rosie, other than to stiffen her back still more, but to Peter, through his new knowledge of her, they spoke of her utter solitariness and twisted this feelings into knots. And he bent over her saying, with a gentleness the sound of which was unbearable to his mother, 'Come on and lie down for a while until we get things straightened out.'

Lie down? Lie down, indeed! Furious indignation reared in Rosie. Not if she knew it. The only place she could lie would be in his room and she wasn't having any of that. No, she wasn't!

She swung round, her mouth already open, but it seemed that Grandpop had been waiting for exactly this reaction, for he pelted his own words into it as he endorsed what Peter had said, 'Aye, aye – shut up, you!' He glared at her. 'Best place bed. Best place, strikes me. You go on, miss, and nobody'll say you nay in this house. No, they won't, not as long as I'm alive and kicking. Don't stand there, you lad. Go on up with you. Take her up.'

Even while giving this last daring order Grandpop still kept his eyes on Rosie. Harry and Old Pop said nothing; as strong as they might be they would not have had the nerve to do this.

Once again Leo looked up at Rosie and there was pleading in her eyes, but Rosie's answered it with what almost amounted to a blaze of hate. And when Peter, his face stiff and hardening, assisted Leo to her feet and felt her trembling under his hands, he turned a look on his mother that matched her own and sent a weakness through her limbs. It made her feel physically sick and caused her to moan inwardly, 'All through that piece. Oh, God in Heaven!'

She watched him showing such tenderness to the girl as he led her out of the room that she became embarrassed by the sight of him. Her big, casual, easy-going son had in the course of a few days shown her so many new sides that she was bewildered by them, but this one, this soppy goofiness, as she put it, was unbelievable and – and unbearable.

When she heard the click of the bedroom door she raised her eyes to the ceiling, then brought them flashing down to her menfolk and demanded, 'Well! nice, isn't it! Suits you, doesn't it, the three of you? It's a wonder you didn't think of starting it years ago yourselves.'

'Now look here.' Harry moved towards her, at the same time pressing his hand back on his father to still his retort, and standing facing her he said, quietly but with hard emphasis, 'He's always been the apple of your eye, hasn't he?' There was a covert accusation in this. 'You've given him a long apron string, but you've kept it fast about his ankle. Well now, he's snapped it and whether you like it or not you've got to face it. He's on his own and for good or bad he's done his own pickin'.'

'You're glad, aren't you? You're glad it's happened.'

The words came brokenly from Rosie now, and Harry, shaking his head, said, 'Lass, have some sense. You may not believe it but I don't think he's even glad himself the way things have turned out. And I know better than you what he's going through at this minute.'

'Yes, I'd believe that all right.' Her voice was strident once more. 'You can tell all right, you've had experience. You and your affairs! And now you've got him like you, the lot of you.' She brought the two old men into her distracted glance. 'Now you're all satisfied.'

Harry's face darkened and he drew in his breath, but instead of making the biting retort that this last merited he let his breath slowly hiss out as was his way and was turning sharply about with the intention of going from the room when the sound of a door closing above checked his steps, and he waited. They all waited. Grandpop eased himself into a chair and Old Pop followed suit, but they all kept their eyes turned in one direction. And when Peter came into the room he did not, as they expected, face their glances angrily but went slowly to the table and sat down, and after a second he rested his head on one hand while they all looked at him.

The sight of him thus, wet and blood-stained, brought the mother-love sweeping back into Rosie – his poor face all cut and knocked about and that gash above the eye, it should be stitched – but when he raised his head and said with quiet firmness, 'I've got to talk to you all,' she stiffened again.

'Go on, lad. You have your say.' Grandpop drew himself to the edge of his seat and bounced his head, and Harry swung a chair round, to sit on it without a word but in a way that proved his willingness, even his eagerness, to listen to his son.

As Peter looked from one to the other the words crowded in his throat, cutting off his breath. He passed his hands over his eyes; then getting swiftly to his feet he brought out in a mumble, 'She's ill . . . very ill. She's . . . she's dying.' And with this he moved with blind steps into the scullery, leaving them all motionless.

The men, with shocked, darkened glances, looked at each other, but Rosie looked towards the scullery.

Dying! Huh! that was the best bit yet. It was a cheap trick of hers to catch him, and he had fallen for it . . . dying! The bigger they were the softer they were. Dying! Huh! Then Rosie's cynicism faltered, just the slightest, urged in that direction by unashamed hope. When she came to think of it there was something wrong with her – that look. But what? Anyway if she was dying there wasn't much future, was there? Slowly, as if she were being drawn there step by step, she moved towards the scullery.

He was standing by the window, and he did not show that he knew she was there, but his head dropped to his chest and she knew he was crying. As she watched him she seemed drained of all emotion, good, bad or indifferent. When a man cried over a woman . . .

After a moment or two she watched his head lift, and he turned to her, unashamed of his tears, and with a deep sense of shock and renewed loss she saw that her lad had gone from her for ever. Not even figuratively would she be able to apply the name to him again for here, before her, stood a man, stronger in spite of his tears than the three back in the room, stronger even than Grandpop. Dead or alive, the girl had done her work, and when he said thickly, 'I must talk to you, Mam – I'm leaving,' she made no protest, but sat down in case the rapid beating of her heart should cause her to collapse.

Chapter Eight

It was just sixty minutes later, but to Peter it could have been sixty years, so much had happened, so much decided. Yet on the other hand he knew that it hadn't taken any length of time to establish his plan, for from the moment the doctor had spoken to him in the bar-yard everything he was going to do was already in his mind, it only needed formulating, and that had taken place when he'd said to his mother, 'I'm leaving.'

When he had stood at the other side of the table and added, 'I want to sell up, straightaway,' Rosie had made no protest whatever, and in her very silence he was made to realise the depth of the hurt he was dealing her. Yet, in this moment, he had no compassion to spare for her.

After a seemingly long time and in a voice he hardly recognised Rosie had said, 'If she's bad, why go?' and he had answered, 'Even if she would stay it wouldn't work. And, anyway, this place has suddenly become—' he had stopped and glanced in bewilderment about the room, but his look had embraced the entire village, yet he did not finish what he had been going to say – 'too small for me.'

But Rosie knew what he meant, as she also knew that if she didn't agree to selling the garage he would go in any case and with bitterness which might prevent him from ever coming back, whereas if the girl died . . . She had not let her thinking go any farther at the moment but had said, 'Selling's not going to be easy. Although they've got nothing to do with it—' she inclined her head towards the kitchen – 'they'll be up in arms, they'll go mad.'

And Rosie's statement turned out to be correct. Although Harry, Old Pop and Grandpop had been touched to the heart by Peter's words, for the girl upstairs was fundamentally their kind of woman, yet from the moment Peter and Rosie had come back into the kitchen and Peter had thrown his news with the effect of a hand grenade into their midst, the girl was thrust aside by the disaster facing them, for it would be a disaster for all of them. The loss of the garage just at this time would mean the loss of money and prestige. With each of them the prestige came first, but things being what they were they knew they couldn't have the second without the first; to have a strong financial footing in the village was power, and power was prestige. Each in his own way needed power and each had suffered when watching power growing in, to his own way of thinking, the wrong hands. It was no solace to any of the three men that their neighbours were held in little respect for, say what you liked, in one way or another money talked and always would.

The mere thought of selling the garage was bad, in fact it seemed that nothing worse could happen; then came the greatest blow of all. Peter had almost stupefied them with it when he said,

'I'm going to sell to the Mackenzies.' Even Rosie had gaped, then balked at this. But Peter, the surprising possessor now of cool reasoning, had explained that three hundred pounds was three hundred and he could run them up to that amount over and above what the estate agent was now offering.

From this point had started a non-stop battle of bitter words, which, but for the brief break when Peter went upstairs carrying a hot drink he had himself made, had not stopped. And now Harry, holding the floor, was resorting to compromise.

'Look, what's going to happen when the money's gone? It's only half yours, you know. You'll have to start from scratch again and you'll never have the cash to buy another place. You'll come back here and tear your hair out when you see them sitting pretty on what they're making out of the garage alone. Look, if you must do this bloody mad thing, let them have a share, and they can take over for the time being. But even that makes me want to vomit.'

'I want no shares with Davy Mackenzie – it's sell or nothing!' Peter's face was grim, but he continued to speak quietly.

Old Pop's voice joined in the fray but he addressed himself pointedly to Rosie now and said, 'Mad! Clean, stark, staring mad! Summat should be done – he just can't do it. An' you standin' there and lettin' him get on with it! You've made your mouth go for years 'bout other things, now when it should be snapping like a trap you're standing there like . . .'

'Me!' All the blame for the inner fires which

were consuming Peter and directing him along this mad course was transferred with the inflection of her voice back to the accuser, and his father, and his son.

'Me?' she repeated again on a higher note. 'Who's he following in this, and everything else, I'd like to know? Blaming me! For as many years as this village can remember the name Puddleton has been a byword connected with loose—'

'Shut up!' Harry barked angrily, while at the same time pushing his enraged father back into his chair.

'Be quiet! all of you. Listen!' The command brought their eyes to Peter, where his were directed towards the door, and Grandpop muttered, ''Tis only the lads.'

But it wasn't the lads. As Peter reached the door and pulled it open Leo stepped slowly into the passage from the stairs. She had his coat about her and her face looked more ashen even than when she entered the house, and her eyes seemed to have sunk deep into the back of her head.

'Why did you get up? I was coming . . . go on back.' In a flurry of anxiety he took hold of her hands, and she left them unresisting in his, but she shook her head saying, 'No. No, I can't go back. If my dress is dry I'd like it. And – and I'd like to see your mother.'

He moved his head in perplexity, then guiding her towards the front-room, he coaxed, 'Come in here, there's no-one in here. You shouldn't have got up.'

When she was seated she did not look at him but kept her eyes directed towards Grandpop's empty seat on the dais before the window, and then she said quietly, 'I must see your mother. All this trouble over me, will it never cease?'

'It isn't over you,' he lied firmly. 'Come back to bed. Come on. You can see her in the morning.'

'No, it must be now.'

'But Leo . . .'

'It's no good.' She moved her head with a weary motion. 'If you don't let me see her I'll walk out this minute and go back to the Hart. They can't forbid me entry. I must get my things anyway, and Miss Tallow might put me up for the night.'

'Look at me, Leo.' He had dropped on to his hunkers before her, and there was no indecision in his tone, or in his manner, as he brought her face round to him. 'Whatever you've got to say to me mother makes no difference. I'm leaving here . . . we are going together. It might take a day or two for me to get things settled up but I'll make it as quick as possible.'

'No.' She jerked hastily at her hands, trying to force them. 'Oh, no. You're not coming with me, now or at any time. You don't understand – you understand nothing. I tell you, you're not coming.'

'Be quiet.' He patted her hands as if she were a child. 'Nothing you can say will stop me. Nothing. I love you and that's just that.'

It was a casual sounding comment, and he made to rise on it but she grabbed at him, staring into his face in a puzzled fashion. Then she said, 'You're different. Why – why aren't you pelting me with questions? Asking about Tiffy and Roger and them all . . . why?'

After a prolonged stare she said in a whisper, 'You know already, you know who they are. You know about . . .'

Quickly he pulled her hands to his lips, and pressing them to his mouth he spoke through her fingers, passionately and urgently, in a way he had never imagined himself capable of: 'I only know I love you . . . I worship you. I never want to be away from you . . . not for the rest of me life.'

Slowly she pressed herself back in the chair and turned her face away from his gaze, and repeated in an agonised whisper, 'A moment of your life!' Then bringing her eyes to his again she said, 'You know that's all it will be, a moment of your life. Oh!—' she seemed to regain some of her energy, for she tossed her head and moved as if searching for a way of escape – 'why had this to happen? Why had they to come? They, of all people.'

'Well, they did,' he said gently. 'It seemed as if it was all planned. I've a feeling now that I've been marking time for years, just waiting for this. And I know this much, at least: if I was to see you no more after tonight these few days with you would be equal to a lifetime of happiness with somebody else. So—' he smiled gravely at her – 'in the next few months I'm going to live a number of lifetimes. There is only one thing I'd like to know, and then you needn't tell me that if you don't want to . . . do you love me a bit? It – it wasn't only a passing fancy?'

As her fingers tightened on his, the tears spilled

from her eyes and her words were almost lost in her throat. 'Love you? Oh, Peter!'

In a moment he was kneeling by her side and holding her close and marvelling that the emotions of sadness and joy could at one and the same time flood his mind and body and make themselves equally felt by him. He stroked her hair as he said, 'Don't, darling, don't cry like that. Come on.'

'Peter.'

'Yes?' He waited.

'I feel so tired I can't fight any more.'

'Well, that's one good thing anyway.'

'You may as well know – I've . . . I've loved you from the word go. And so much, so very much.'

She lay against him quiet and relaxed, and over her head he looked about the room. There was Grandpop's seat. There was the sideboard with the dish of artificial fruit situated dead centre. Arranged at angles so that you could move round them were the couch and the other chair belonging to the three-piece suite. There were knick-knacks on the mantelpiece and pictures on the walls. He should know these things – he had lived amongst them for twenty-eight years – they should be familiar, unconsciously loved or hated things. But now they were neither, they were strange to him, and the walls that housed them were surroundings that had held a man who no longer existed. In this moment if he had thought of the niggling worry occasioned by Mavis and Florrie he would have believed that they had never existed either. Never again would there be the path of least resistance for him. That road was closed.

He moved his lips to her hair when she said, 'What'll I say to your mother now? I was so sure a few minutes ago, I had all the words ready. "I'm not taking your son away, so don't worry," I was going to say to her, but now, how can I start?'

'Don't worry, she knows.'

'Everything?' It was a whisper.

'Yes, everything.'

'Oh, Peter!' Then in a voice even lower now she said his name again, 'Peter?'

'Yes?'

'I must tell you about Arthur.'

Arthur. There was no need to question, he knew whom she meant. 'I don't want to know about him,' he said.

He lifted a strand of her hair, and she reached up and caught his hand and brought it between their faces so that she could look at him. 'I want you to know.'

'You can tell me later.'

'No, now. It might be too hard to tell later.'

'All right. But it makes no difference.' He rose from his knees and, pulling a chair close to hers, sat down and took hold of her hands again.

'I lived with him for a year as his wife.'

Involuntarily his fingers stiffened and the joy was pressed temporarily out of him, but he kept his eyes steady and their expression unchanged until hers dropped away and she began slowly and haltingly to talk.

'It happened after I had finished a year touring the provinces. I had saved up a little and I wanted a car. I knew a lot about cars. There was one of the Company, a Mr Fuller. He was getting elderly and had a mania for collecting car brochures and catalogues. On long, boring journeys he would talk cars, and I became bitten with the bug, and it was . . . it was when I went to a second-hand car mart that I met him – Arthur. He tried to sell me one car after another, but I took a fancy to the old Alvis. He was called away at one point and I continued to look round, and I was examining a car when a man came up to me and asked my opinion of it. Perhaps it was because I was hatless and in jeans that he took me for one of the staff. And it tickled me so that I kept it up. And when he got his eye on the Alvis I remembered all Mr Fuller had told me about that particular make, her being a grand car but very spirited on the brakes, and so on, and I was ladling this sort of thing out when I became aware that he – Arthur – was standing listening to me. But instead of being wild he winked encouragement. Well—' her voice became weary – 'to cut a long story short I sold that man a car, and Arthur said that if I'd work for a month in the showrooms he'd give me the Alvis, sales or no sales, he would take a chance.'

She looked up at Peter. 'That's how it started. He was married and soon I got the Misunderstood Husband story. But when I met his wife I could well believe a little of it, for when there was nothing more between us than the business of selling cars she suspected the worst. After eighteen months he asked her for a divorce. She wouldn't give it, so he left her and we lived together.'

She paused here and wetted her lips, and

drawing her hands from his she rubbed the palms together. 'I had a baby.'

Her words caused something to jerk within him, as if he had received a blow in the ribs from inside, but he still kept his eyes, unwavering, on her face. And she kept hers fixed on her hands.

'It was born too soon – it died. I never felt the same after. Not ill, but not well.' Her hands parted and she turned one palm upwards and examined it as if it were new to her, before continuing. 'Then one day I found myself in hospital. And that was that. From then he suddenly developed a conscience, he remembered he had a lawful wife and he hadn't played fair by her.' Her voice trailed off. 'There was never anyone else. Doctor Patterson – that was the short one, Roger – and the blond one, Tiffy, they helped to keep me sane. Tiffy did – did the . . .'

Not swiftly, not slowly, but with a steady sureness he gathered her hands together again and their eyes met as he said, 'It's all past. Forget it, forget everything but you and me.' He smiled, and had he analysed that smile he would have discovered it was, in a way, a smile of relief. There was no-one else, she had said. Somehow, deep down, knowing how she reacted on men he had imagined a train of them.

'Listen, beloved.' He paused at the sound of his own voice softly speaking the endearment, for it was the first time in his life he had used it. Then, his smile growing more tender, he went on, 'You're not to worry about a thing, not a thing. From now on I'll do that. Think for you and—' he nodded – 'talk for you. Just you lie back there while I see about your dress.' He would have liked to add to this: 'My mother'll bring it.' But on this point he could not even let himself hope, so after holding her face for a moment close to his he left.

In the kitchen all was quiet. Old Pop and Grandpop were seated, but taut, in their chairs. Harry was standing, his arm resting on the mantelpiece. No-one spoke when he entered the room, but they all looked at him. And when he saw that his mother wasn't there he just returned their glances for a brief second, then went into the scullery without saying a word.

Rosie was at the table making an effort to prepare the supper, and she did not move or raise her head when he asked, 'Is the dress dry?' but replied curtly, 'You'd better find out.'

With his face now set stiffly he went to the airing rack and taking off the dress felt it, then moved to the table. And there he stood looking at her, watching her hands moving swiftly and fumbling over the dishes.

'Mam.'

She did not look up.

'Do one thing for me, will you?'

'I didn't think you needed me to do anything for you.' The moving of the dishes went on.

'Take this in to her. Talk to her. She needs you . . . someone like you, more than me.'

Rosie's answer was to draw in a deep breath and turn from him to the sink. After a moment of watching her clattering with the dishes, he moved towards the door, and then her voice, gruff and biting, halted him. 'Put it down,' she said.

It was enough. Putting the dress on a chair he

went out of the scullery and through the kitchen again and into the passage.

He was lifting his old mack off the rack when Harry appeared at the kitchen door. 'Where you off to?' he asked, unable to keep the acid note from his voice.

'Mackenzies'.'

'My God!' Harry's chest swelled. 'Can't you leave it for a day or two?'

'No, I can't.' Peter spoke below his breath and drew his father back into the room again by pushing past him. Then he turned and closed the door so that their voices would at least be muted as Harry cried indignantly, 'If you want to act Sir Galahad isn't this as good a place as any for it? If she's in the condition you say, you're mad to move about.'

The quip of Sir Galahad touched Peter to a flashing retort, but he bit on it and said with somewhat heavy sarcasm 'And enjoy the nice, quiet village life? It's no good talking, you might as well save your breath.' And on this remark, which was in no way calculated to soothe, he turned abruptly and swung out, while Harry, after a number of quick movements which appeared as though they might be a prelude to his wrecking the room, strode into the passage after him, and he, too, went out, but down the back garden and over the fence into the sodden fields.

Grimly the two old men sat looking each into his own particular patch of space, and when Rosie passed through the room, carrying the girl's frock on her arm, they turned to look at her. But even Grandpop was deterred from comment, and not until he heard her enter what he termed 'his room' did he speak. Looking at his son, he commented sadly, 'End of summat, somehow, here.'

Chapter Nine

The village street was deserted. There were no longer faces at the windows and doors, for who could have guessed that as a climax to that remarkable day Peter Puddleton would be going to the Mackenzies' to do a deal about the garage.

For the lack of spectators Peter was indeed grateful, for in spite of his high resolve it was requiring all his new-found courage to carry him to his neighbours' front door. He was no longer afraid of confronting Mavis – she had virtually ceased to exist for him – and he certainly wasn't afraid of either of the Mackenzie men, but his fear was that when it came to the final issue he would not be able to tolerate the thought of them having his garage and that this attitude might decide him to wait and see the estate agent. The two things against the latter were time and less money.

He knocked once, a sharp rap, indicative of his feelings to get it over. And when the door opened and Mavis stood before him he could have laughed, had a laugh been left in him, so large was the amazement written all over her. After one gasp, and the usual struggle of her lips to meet, she gave a loud 'Huh!' and went to bang the door in his face for Mavis was no fool; whatever she might imagine was the business of his visit there was one thing certain in her mind now, it had nothing to do with her.

With his foot firmly placed against the door, Peter said, 'Hold your hand a minute, I want to see your father.' His voice was loud and brittle and it penetrated the house, and Mr Mackenzie, coming from the kitchen, said, 'What is it? Who is it?' Then the door was pulled out of Mavis's hand. Mr Mackenzie stared at Peter. His astonishment was no less than his daughter's, and for a moment he did nothing to hide it. Then, his voice almost a splutter, he said, 'Well! well! Talk about surprises. This is one, and no doubt about it. Well, Peter lad, and what can I do for you, eh?'

'I want a word with you.'

'Oh, a word?' Mr Mackenzie's head moved slowly up and down. Then his attitude changing to his usual brisk, business-like manner, he cried to his daughter, 'Get out of the way, girl.' And he pressed back his arm on her, pushing her against the wall as he said, 'Come in. Come in. Well. Well now, come in here. Get by, girl, out of the way. Don't stand there gaping.'

'Davy!' Mr Mackenzie was calling up the stairs. 'Visitor here . . . Peter.'

'Who?'

It was as if Davy had been catapulted out of his room, for almost instantaneously he appeared at the top of the stairs, and in a second he was down them and had followed his father into the sitting-room, where after staring at Peter, he exclaimed, as his father had done, 'Well! well!' then added, 'Hallo again. Some water and blood passed under the bridge since we last met up, eh?'

It took a deliberate effort for Peter to ignore this remark, and forcing his attention round to the father, he said, 'You've got a saying, Mr Mackenzie – "No beating about the bush!" Well I'll use it and come straight to the point. I'm willing to sell the garage and land for fifteen hundred cash, right on the nail. And I want everything settled within the next two or three days.'

Davy's lips had fallen slightly open, but his father's were pressed tightly together, and he nodded while he stared at Peter. Then thrusting his hand within the rim of his trousers, he said, 'Ah, well now, this has got to be talked about. Sit down, sit down. Yes – aye, there's some talking to be done here.'

Peter sat down, and Davy, regaining his breath, said, 'What's bitten you all of a sudden? Oh, I know—' he waved his hand airily – 'it's your own business. But fifteen hundred! Eh, Dad?'

Davy turned to his father, who said, 'Aye, fifteen hundred – we can't do that lad.'

Almost before he'd had time to settle in his chair Peter was on his feet again. 'That's all I want to know. That's the price and I'm not coming down, not a solitary penny, so you can save yourself the effort of bargaining.'

'Now, now, lad.' Mr Mackenzie laid a restraining hand on Peter's arm. 'Don't let us get excited. Business is business and cannot be dealt with in a minute or so, nor yet a day or so. Not a thing like this, anyway.'

'See here—' Peter looked from one to the other – 'you've been pestering me since Monday to sell.

Now I'm going to sell, but on my own terms and in my own time. Do you want it or not?'

Neither of them answered, but after a brief pause Mr Mackenzie, his face working and his hands hitching at his trousers, went towards his desk standing in the corner of the room and sat heavily down.

'Give you thirteen hundred.'

It was Davy speaking, and Peter, turning and looking at him steadily, said, 'Funnel will give me my price if I wait a few days. And —' he nodded – 'he's not the only one interested, let me tell you.'

This last remark was merely a piece of wishful thinking, coupled with an effort to play these two at their own game, but Mr Mackenzie, knowing he was on a good thing, would not have been surprised had Peter named half-a-dozen men were after it, so he pursed his lips and said to his son, 'Leave this to me, lad. Well now —' he stood up – 'you're driving a hard bargain, Peter, for you know, but for the road coming this way you'd be lucky to get a thousand.'

Peter did not at this point remind them that their valuation of the garage had previously not exceeded eight hundred pounds.

'Well now, where are we going to get this amount from pronto?' Mr Mackenzie looked at his son. 'We haven't that much in raw cash, have we?' And Davy, taking the cue from his father, said 'No, that we haven't.'

'We could, with a lot of raking around, let you have half and the rest later on.'

Mr Mackenzie was now fixing Peter with his small bright eyes, and Peter returned his look and said quietly, 'I want it altogether, Mr Mackenzie.'

'Well now, you're setting me a poser, Peter.' Mr Mackenzie scrubbed roughly at his chin with the palm of his hand. 'I'll say you are. You appear set as I've never afore seen you. Changed you are. Looks to me as if you've got the makings of a business man about you.' He let out a chuckle on a long-drawn breath, which took some flavour from the compliment, then exclaimed loudly, 'There then it's a deal. Well I never!' he slapped his thigh – 'and to think after the way . . . Oh, well now, as you're here and that's settled we'd better have a statement . . . pen to paper, eh? Just to make things right, temporary like.'

As his father busied himself at the desk Davy moved into a position where he could look more fully at Peter, and he gazed at him, frankly bewildered as much at the evident change in him personally as at the reversing of his adamant attitude not to let them have the garage. Inwardly Davy was seething with excitement; the garage and land, as it stood, was worth twelve hundred, but to get it for fifteen hundred with its future prospects was an absolute snip. In a few years' time with a bit of titivating they could ask five thousand and get it. His look was pitying. He knew why Peter was making this lightning decision . . . the sucker. Still, they continued to be born every day, even in this age. He would have liked to do a bit of leg-pulling and get him on the raw, but thought it wiser to wait – that piece of paper he was now signing had in itself no binding value. He watched Peter lay down the pen, and noted the greyness around his mouth that spoke of inward strain. He watched him reluctantly shake hands on the bargain. He was about to offer his own hand but again thought better of it, and he did not, with his father, accompany him to the door, but from the window he watched him move heavily into the street.

The door had hardly closed before Mr Mackenzie was back in the room, and father and son regarded each other. Then their hands gripped and held.

'At last!' said Mr Mackenzie. Then buttoning his waistcoat he added, 'Get the car out.'

'What for?'

'We're going to see Tyson.'

'At this time of night? He can't do anything.'

'Can't he? He can. Talking takes time. I've put him on to a good thing recently and he'll do this for me. Anyway, we can get everything settled but the writing. He'll have that agreement all ready by Tuesday at the latest, because, between you and me, I'm as anxious to push things as Peter Puddleton, more if the truth were known for I'll not feel we've got it till it's signed and scaled.' He slapped his son's back and a beam spread over his face. Then his eyes narrowed and his head nodded as he counted his assets. 'The contracting, shares in the mill, and that won't end there either, and now the garage and the land for fifteen hundred! Give us a few years and it'll be a gold mine. He'll want to cut off the hand that signed that paper when he sees what we'll do with his garage.' He thumped Davy in the chest and added finally, 'We'll show 'em who's running what when this village gets on the map.'

*   *   *

Sunday morning came soft and calm. Nature had apparently forgotten her tantrums of the previous evening. That the swelling congregation was not due to the entrancing beauty and the allure of the morning, nor yet to an overpowering desire to hear him speak the word of God, the Revd Collins knew. As he looked down on his flock he knew that those faces he saw only at weddings, christenings, Christmas and Harvest Festivals were present not for the good of their souls but because after the service there would be the one opportunity of the day to gather and gossip, and moreover to do so without censure.

He had heard an account of the fantastic happenings of last night at the inn, and although he had been chivvied for hours by his sister to alter his sermon and deliver a resounding rebuke on all who drank and had dealing with . . . loose women, he had steadfastly refused even to consider such a thing. For the vicar was fighting his own battle. He was profoundly disturbed because he could not rid himself of the memory of sunlit water, a grassy bank, two kind eyes, and a voice that could shut from his mind everything but itself.

As he stood in the pulpit, the minister's thoughts made him feel faint and weak, and it was all he could do to read his sermon, let alone deliver it with any semblance of feeling. So it was to be understood that he wasn't the only one who sighed with relief when he stepped down from the pulpit.

Moreover, the service ended, he was finding it

unbearable to stand and smile and mutter polite nothings to the departing congregation. So picking Miss Tallow as the one who would likely comment the least on his abrupt departure, he left her after a flabby handshake and in the middle of her views on the weather of yesterday.

The major, coming out onto the gravel path from the porch, turned his eyes to where the minister was hurrying away to the side door of the church. The major's nose twitched, and he thought, 'Queer fellow. Bit unsteady really. And what a sermon! not even worth sleeping to . . . no humour. And look at yesterday. Ran like a rabbit because the girl teased him. Damn bad thing about that girl – Harry said she was ill, dying.' He couldn't believe she was as bad as that. A bit pale, but that was her type and the make-up she stuck on. Suited her though, and gave her that added something. But it made the women hate her. By God! yes. Look at last night. The house raised because he sat with her in the marquee and had a laugh, and young Peter there all the time. Florrie had a bee in her bonnet, too. And bringing up the old family scandal of Connie Fitzpatrick again. What had the girl to do with Connie? You'd think she had started a loose house dead centre of the village to hear Florrie go on. She was worse than her mother where the girl was concerned. Of course, Peter was at the bottom of it. She had always been a little too friendly in that quarter, and that would never do really. No, never. Well, that was settled, and a good thing too. Peter, by all accounts, had gone berserk last night because some fellow had tried to kiss the girl. Really!

really! But he wished he had been there. Of course, with her type that sort of thing was sure to happen. Dying? Nonsense! He wished he was younger, by God! he did. He'd give his household something really to worry over.

The major straightened his shoulders, pulled down his coat, thrust his neck out of his tight, stiff collar, and exclaimed to himself, 'Where the hell are they?' He marched down the path that led into the cypress-sheltered graveyard, and there he saw both his wife and daughter the centre of a group of six or more women, and his mouth clamped tightly. They had got their teeth in. Well, in that case, he would leave them to do their tearing and also to find their own way back. With a certain amount of satisfaction he strolled down the path and into his car and drove away.

Both Mrs Carrington-Barrett and Florrie, quite oblivious that their escort had departed, continued to listen to Mrs Booth. Mrs Carrington-Barrett's mouth and eyes mimed her disgust, but Florrie's face showed no emotion other than sullenness as Mrs Booth continued to pour out her venom. 'Four of them larking round her, and she egging them on to kiss her. Talk about disgusting! I've never seen anything like it in all me born days. And the other man, like a vulture, standing there watching them. But as I said afore he hadn't anything on Peter Puddleton! You never in all your born days . . . never. He was like a madman, and him who wouldn't say boo to a goose. Soppy he was, I used to think sometimes . . . nothing in him . . . did what his mother told him. And then, out of the blue, he changes and all in a couple of days. I tell you she turns men crazy. Every man in the village she's been after. Sex, she oozes it!'

'Same as her they ducked.'

'What d'you say, Gran?' Amelia Fountain, who by her sufferings at the hands of the harlot, as she put it, felt entitled to be one of this particular group, even though she was rarely to be seen at church, now bent above Grannie Andrews who was leaning on her daughter's arm, and enquired again, 'What, Gran? What were you saying?'

The wrinkled flesh of Gran ran into patterns as she munched her jaws before repeating, 'I said duckin', that's what she wants. Only way to cool blood like hers. Sent the other one scooting, it did. Cooled her capers.' Gran spoke of 'the other one' as if the incident had happened last week.

Mrs Carrington-Barrett laughed an amused laugh and exclaimed, 'Now, now, Mrs Andrews. We must remember as the saying goes, that "them days are gone". We have to use other methods in these times.'

'What you say?' Gran, detecting a note of censure in the major's wife, suddenly became deaf and exclaimed again, 'What you say?' Whereupon her daughter repeated, in a much higher key, what Mrs Carrington-Barrett had said: 'She says you can't do that now – duck people. She says them days are gone, we've to use other methods.'

All eyes were on Gran, and Gran looked from one to the other, bestowing on each a flash of her eyes before she brought out: 'Aye, you might. Not so 'fective though, by half. Village'll be turned into a land of Sodom and Gomorrah, you'll see.

Mark my words. I've seen the havoc her sort can play. No man's safe, nor never will be. Well, I've had me say. Come on.' She jerked at her daughter's arm. 'Can't stand much longer. Had about enough now.'

'Goodbye, Gran.'

'Goodbye, Gran.'

'So nice seeing you out, Gran. You must try to do this more often.'

'Goodbye, Goodbye.'

The varied farewells sent the old woman and her daughter down the drive and left standing, besides the Carrington-Barretts, Mrs Booth and Mrs Fountain, Mavis and Miss Collins who had both remained singularly quiet during the chatter of Mrs Booth and the old woman. But now Miss Collins spoke, and she brought all eyes round to her as she exclaimed, 'I've never before wished that I wasn't a Christian.'

This remark was so potent in its meaning that the group with eyes slightly widened, waited, and Miss Collins's next words caused each one of them to react by some movement – the scraping of a foot, the shifting of a bag, the lifting of a shoulder – as she said, 'If she settles in this village no man will be safe – no man.'

There was a pause during which no-one made any comment, they just waited. And she went on, 'I know it, I feel it. Slinky Jane. Never was anybody more aptly named, for she'll slink under each man's skin. There'll be no peace, not as long as she stays. No woman will know where her man is . . . or perhaps she'll know only too well.'

'Who said she was settling here?' Florrie's voice was thin and vibrating, as if her words were strung on a taut wire.

'Mavis.' Miss Collins nodded to where Mavis stood. 'She says he's going to marry her.'

'Marry her!' The exclamations formed a chorus in which Florrie did not join, but she brought out, sharply, 'Who told you that?' She was confronting Mavis squarely as if the issue lay between their two selves, but Mavis, now the centre of interest, became evasive. 'I don't know who said it exactly, it was something I heard.'

It was evident to the group that Mavis was holding something back. It was also evident to Mrs Carrington-Barrett that her daughter was giving herself away. She wished she would use more control and not bring herself down to the level of the villagers. For more reasons than one she herself would be only too glad if Peter Puddleton did marry the girl. At least, if she was married there'd be no further sporting in the woods – there was never smoke without fire.

'Come, Mavis,' she said. 'You couldn't have forgotten such an important thing as that.'

'Oh, leave me alone. I tell you, I must have made a mistake.'

'Really!' Mrs Carrington-Barrett was definitely offended by Mavis's tone, and she did nothing to hide it. 'Really!' she said again.

Mavis, now red to the ears, struggled valiantly in her embarrassment to cover her teeth. If only her dad hadn't gone on so, she would love to tell everything she knew, but it was more than she dare do to mention a word of the pending business transaction, for, with his eye on her and his finger thrust into her chest, her father had warned her before leaving the house what would happen should she let out anything about the garage affair.

'If anything leaks out,' Mr Mackenzie had said, 'Funnel will likely as not be on the spot first thing in the morning offering him God knows what. So mind, you open your mouth if you dare. You know nothing, you've heard nothing, understand?'

Mavis knew she had been a fool and said too much already, but she hadn't thought Miss Collins would go on like this. She was definitely puzzled at Miss Collins's attitude, for had she herself wanted Peter she couldn't have gone on worse. Her attention was brought from Miss Collins to Mrs Booth as that lady declared, in vibrant tones, 'Well, that settles it, something's got to be done.'

After delivering this statement, Mrs Booth's mouth snapped shut and her eyes rolled upwards; indeed they were turning inwards looking at the situation, for, in her own mind, she was certain that something would have to be done. If that piece stayed in the village the Hart wouldn't see her again nor many of the men; they would go farther afield. After all, the Crown was just a mile as the crow flew, and you could, from Battenbun, follow the crow's flight through the woods and over the fells. And Mrs Booth had a mental picture of Leo, in the guise of the Pied Piper, leading the entire village of men over the fells to the Crown, for, as her husband had put it, that one attracted custom like a strip-tease artist. Something would have to be done.

Away over the gravestones and the sloping grassy bank Mrs Booth caught sight of the heads of Grannie Andrews and her daughter slowly bobbing above the hedge as they made their way back to the village, and she murmured something to herself, which Mrs Carrington-Barrett failed to catch. And so that lady prodded, as was her custom, 'You were saying, Mrs Booth?'

'Aye. Yes.' Mrs Booth seemed to come back from a long way. 'Yes, I was just thinking, it's a pity we don't live a little earlier back. Grannie Andrews was right, rough medicine often proves the best purge.'

Mrs Carrington-Barrett's thin laugh trailed away among the cypress trees. 'Now, now, Mrs Booth. We mustn't resort to that. Dear, dear. Must we, Miss Collins? Not in this day and age.'

Miss Collins did not reply for a moment but remained still, staring away into the distance as Mrs Booth had been doing. Then as if answering her own thoughts she said, 'It's right. Things can't go on as they are. She's affected this village like a plague. I don't have much time for the devil—' her eyes now flicked around the group, giving the evidence of her modern outlook – 'but it seems to me past the bounds of iniquity to concoct a story of an enormous eel in the little lake miles from the river. And it is funny, isn't it, that no woman has seen this eel, except her. She's clever. An eel would attract the men, not the women or children! Why didn't she make up a story of elves and pixies to fetch the children, or a male film

583

star retreating to a cave on the fells to fetch the women? One is as likely as the other. But no, it had to be a simple and subtle attraction for the men, so we have an eel.'

With the exception of Florrie's, there was a ripple on the faces around her as if her audience had a desire to laugh, but Miss Collins's expression forbade laughter. This was a very serious matter to all of them, but to her it was of the most vital importance. She was about to resume, perhaps to answer the sugar-coated urgings of Mrs Carrington-Barrett and the insane ravings of Mrs Booth, when Mr Fraser, the verger, came hurrying round the path, and before reaching the group he called to her, 'Miss – miss. I think you'd better come, vicar's in a bad way.'

'What!' Miss Collins had already sprung away towards Mr Fraser, and Mr Fraser, turning on his heel without stopping, went back the way he had come talking over his shoulder to the vicar's sister, 'Sick he's been, throwing up. My! never seen vicar in this state. Upset he is about something. Talking twenty to the dozen, and how!'

As the voice of the verger faded away the women looked from one to the other. Then Mrs Carrington-Barrett said, 'Poor man, nerves, I suppose. He did seem a little unusual during the sermon, don't you think? Overwork.'

They all looked back at her and in their eyes was the same knowledge. Nerves . . . nothing. Overwork? That was funny in this village. It was her; she had even got the vicar now, it was history repeating itself.

Florrie was the first to break away from the circle, and she summed up all their thoughts as she said, 'Well, that would indeed seem to be that!'

Chapter Ten

Rosie's outside world was, through necessity, centred around her family. That it had been rent and thrown into a state of chaos by the events of the last few days was not altogether surprising, but that her inner world, the tower wherein she housed her unbending self, should be brought to the same pass was both surprising and distressing.

She was given to firm opinions: a thing was right or it wasn't; people were right or they weren't. There were no half measures with Rosie, no interwoven patterns of grey. With people, she had thought she could judge them right away. But now, this belief had undergone a severe shaking.

Last night when she had gone into the front-room she had known exactly what she was going to say; it was to be brief and to the point. The girl might be ill; she might or she might not be dying – on this last point Rosie's mind had swung in a very short space of time towards doubt. And then, when she had been confronted by the girl, she had said nothing. It was the girl who had done the talking. And when someone blamed herself for all the worry that had come upon you, what could you say?

Rosie had found herself thinking, 'She doesn't talk like she looks'; and she also found herself thinking, 'I can see what got him.' Yet what it was she couldn't exactly explain, but it was something, and it was there confronting her. She could feel it, that something that the blond bedraggled hair and Peter's old top coat did nothing to diminish. If Rosie had been capable of clear thinking she would have associated the elusive quality with one still more elusive, which was honesty. Anyway, the result of the meeting had been that she had, somewhat tersely, ordered the girl back to bed and with the promise to bring her something up. And finally she had heard herself suggesting that she stay in bed the following day. This last charitable act had not been without motive though, for no matter how much her feelings had been toned down she still couldn't bear the thought of seeing her lad and this girl together. No matter how much she now appeared to have in her favour, dying and all that, the fact still remained that this time last week he hadn't known her, hadn't even known she existed . . . and now he couldn't exist without her. Everything had been thrust aside on her account, everything, even herself – mostly herself. No, Rosie decided, she couldn't stand to see any carry on. Bed was the best place for her while she was in this house, for what the eye didn't see the heart didn't grieve over. Yet, when Peter had come back from the Mackenzies' and had gone upstairs, she had felt worked up. And when she did not hear the drone of his voice her imagination ran wild and presented her with shuddering scenes, so that she wondered if her suggestion had been right after all.

But on Sunday her feelings were again molli-
fied, for Peter scarcely stayed in the house at all.
From early morning he had been in the garage,
and two short visits upstairs was all the time he
had spent with the girl. It was as if he had sensed
how she felt about this facet of the matter and
was going out of his way not to upset her unduly.

It was late evening now and Peter was still at
the garage. This, in a way, was to be expected
as he wished to leave everything as straight as
possible, from his books to the storeroom, mostly
the storeroom. But what was now puzzling and
testing Rosie's mental powers to the utmost,
and had done since lunch-time, was not the girl,
or Peter, but her husband's changed attitude
towards the selling of the garage, and not his
alone, but that of the other two as well.

Harry's temper had not improved when he
returned home last evening, and most of the night
he had tossed and turned and muttered. She knew
this to be a fact, for she herself had hardly slept. It
being his Sunday on at the Manor, a self-imposed
task that she had always quibbled at, he had gone
out first thing with a face like thunder. She had
prophesied to herself that it was going to be a nice
day, with one thing and another. Then, knowing
her menfolk as she did, she had been immediately
openly suspicious when, on Harry's return, his
whole attitude towards the affair was changed
and he had not only offered to give Peter a hand
but had, for all to hear, openly declared to him
that perhaps after all he was doing the most
sensible thing in selling.

To an outsider it might have looked as if Harry

had, after thinking things over, changed his mind about something that was inevitable anyway; it might appear to the same outsider, that he was a sensible man; but Rosie had for a great number of years been on the inside of Harry, and his mellowed attitude put her straight away on her guard and she felt, and naturally, that there was something behind all this. Oh, yes . . . and more so when the other two had by tea-time come to follow his suit. Instinctively she was reminded of the time she had made her bid for liberty.

Eight years ago, when she was forty-four, she had made a stand against the band of Puddletons. She had decided that in future they would look after themselves – all, that was, except Peter. She would supply them with what she called a skeleton service, for she had decided she was going to get out and about and see the world, as far as Hexham each week, like every other woman. And even Durham or Newcastle on a cheap day trip. But she made one mistake. In a glorious row one night she made her plans known to the Puddletons, all three of them, and she could swear to this day that they got together and planned what later developed to crush her revolt; for from the day following her rising her husband began unashamedly to court her all over again. He ceased to dive into the house, swallow his meal and dive out again to the Hart, or fishing, or . . . to them others, as she thought of the women she imagined he was for ever consorting with. Instead, he plied her with his attentions. And she wasn't saying it wasn't nice and refreshing for a time – she blossomed again . . . people noticed it. And then, bang! She woke up one morning to find she was pregnant. She was forty-four and past it, things were safe. But she was to find nothing was safe. She had counted without the exception, and in due course she was presented with twins, and, insult to injury, boys again, each with the hooked nose, Puddleton mouth, and the cast. Aye they had buttered her up then, and now they were buttering Peter, and she was on to them and as suspicious as a newly-made detective.

Although she would have given anything in her world to undo the present state of affairs she was only too well aware that, for good or ill, her lad's life was tied up with that of the girl's upstairs, and that the girl, for a number of reasons, could not stay in this village, so Peter must go, too, and the garage must be sold. That it was sold, and to the long-standing enemy of the house, was what had embittered them all so, particularly Harry. Yet here he was, with his father and grandfather, abetting Peter now, and saying it was likely all for the best. No, no, such an attitude was against all reason. She knew the Puddletons, oh! she knew the Puddletons, only too well did she know the Puddletons. They were up to something again, something to keep him here.

As bad as things were now Rosie saw they could be even worse. For instance, if the selling of the garage fell through Peter would have to stay; if he hadn't any money he would hesitate to take her away, at least until things could be reshuffled. That would mean the girl and herself in this house all day, with the old 'un openly on her side.

No, no. God in Heaven! no, she couldn't stand that.

When at last at the end of the longest Sunday she had ever known Peter and his father and Old Pop came in, tired, and, she noticed, somewhat more saddened than they had appeared earlier on in the day, she hurried them over their washing so that, as she said, they could get their supper and she could get cleared away before midnight. And when, with surprising docility, they obeyed her and marched into the room, she tapped Peter on the arm, giving him a nod to indicate he should wait behind. Then closing the door and drawing him away from it towards the sink, she whispered, 'Do you smell a rat?'

He looked at her, his eyes screwed up. 'Smell a rat? What about?'

'Them.' She nodded back to the kitchen. 'What's made your Da change his tune? He could have killed you last night for selling. And when it was the Mackenzies I thought he'd go off his head. You should have heard him in bed, he kept on and on. And now look at him and the other two. I tell you there's something afoot.'

Peter looked away from her and out of the window, his mind moving rapidly now. She was right, they had all changed their tune and he had thought it was because they didn't want to part bad friends. And after the scene of last night he had been only too glad to accept this attitude. But now he could see, as she said, they were up to something. But what?

He looked at his mother again: 'There's no trick in the deeds, they're straightforward?'

'As far as I know.' She was whispering now. 'But there's something. Ask yourself. You're taking away the thing they were all building on and they act like angels. 'Tisn't natural, not with them. Last night was, but not the day. Could he have got at the Mackenzies this morning?'

'What good would that have done him?' said Peter soberly. 'They want the garage as they never wanted anything. Anyway, I saw them both going off around ten o'clock, Hexham way, and if I know them they'll hurry this thing up as fast as a deed can be written out. They know they're on a good thing. Trust the Mackenzies. They wouldn't have agreed to the fifteen hundred else.'

They looked at each other; then Rosie, turning away, sighed and said, 'Well, there's something.' Then, on the sound of a low chortle of laughter from the other room, she looked sharply back at Peter and said, 'See what I mean. And the old 'un's never barked at me nor nobody else since dinner-time. I'm telling you, you'd better keep your wits about you.'

As his mother bustled out of the scullery Peter remained where he was, considering her words. She was right, but what could they be up to? He racked his brain, but could find nothing that they could do to stop the deal going through.

Whereas last night, for financial reasons alone, it had been necessary that he should sell the garage, the happenings of today had now made it doubly so, for it seemed that the entire population of the village was against him. Previously he had only to walk down the street any number of times in a day to be hailed with a smile, a wave, or a call of 'Hallo, there, lad', from his elders, or, 'Ho! Peter', from his contemporaries. But today he had seen people turn indoors or cut over the green to avoid him. The entire blame of last night's brawl had been put down to him, and if not to him, then to Leo, and that amounted to one and the same thing. Then the scene in the Hart this morning when he had gone to collect her things would take some forgetting.

His mission had at first been delayed by Mr Booth, who had endeavoured to bully him into paying the damage done the previous evening to two chairs, the leg of a table and ten broken glasses. And he was standing in the passage with Leo's cases at his feet, his way obstructed by Mr Booth, who was threatening him with a summons, when Mrs Booth came in. It wasn't clear then, or now, what she had said, but what had impressed itself on him was the almost terrifying force of her vindictiveness, for she had acted like someone possessed. She had gabbled about the vicar being ill and the major forgetting his position and making a fool of himself, of Amelia Fountain going to leave Bill, and others. She kept referring to 'others' with her popping eyes on her husband, until he, with some force, pushed her into the living-room, and in doing so allowed Peter to make his escape.

The slighting by his friends and the scene in the Hart had somehow upset him even more than last night's business. For him the village was finished, as, indeed, apparently was the village finished with him, and although he would not admit it he was hurt by this rejection.

He passed through the kitchen, answering Rosie's look from the table with a murmured, 'I won't be a minute,' and went upstairs.

When he opened his bedroom door Leo's eyes were waiting for him, as if they had not changed their direction since he had left her at tea-time. Without a word he went to the bed and took her into his arms. And she clung to him with a strength that was in contrast to her thinness. Then with his lips against hers he gently pressed her back onto the pillows, and after gazing at her for some moments he asked tenderly, 'Been a long day?'

'No.' She shook her head. 'The boys have been so good, keeping me company.' Her fingers outlined his cheekbones. 'I've been learning all about you and this room. All your life seems to be bound up in this room. Peter—' her voice became urgent and she clutched at his hand now – 'I feel so guilty. If it wasn't for me you'd still be happy here. This is your place – this house, this village . . .'

'Be quiet.'

'No, I can't.'

'You just will. Look—' he held her face between his hands – 'let me tell you something. I've just realised these past few days that I've never felt alive before; I was easy-going, even lazy, I was neither happy nor sad. I just wasn't alive, not aware of living, not really.'

As his eyes moved lovingly over her face she said, 'You can talk but I know.' Then she asked, with an eagerness she tried to hide but which did not escape him, 'When do we go, Peter?'

'As soon as I sign that paper.' He rubbed his knuckles gently up and down her cheek.

'Your mother cannot forgive me, she never will.'

'Yes, she will. I know her. She'll come round. She's working that way now.'

Leo shook her head, then said, 'I wouldn't in her place. Where are we going, Peter?' After she had asked this question she gave a little laugh and added, 'See? I don't know where I'm going any more.'

With a swift movement he slipped his arm under her shoulders and, drawing her up to him again, he said softly, 'That's how things should be, I'll be driving from now on. And I can tell you you'll be safer in our old Austin than ever you were in the Alvis. We'll find a little place somewhere, a cottage or a flat, and I'll start the business of getting you better.'

'Oh, Peter—' her face took on a look of pain – 'don't hope like that, it'll make things harder. I used to, then I had to—'

He brought one hand to her mouth and placed his fingers gently over it, and smiling down at her, he said with such firmness that he almost believed it himself, 'You'll get better, or your name won't be Mrs Puddleton. Aw there, don't – don't cry. Leo, darling, don't.'

As he dried her eyes, Rosie's voice came from the bottom of the stairs, startling them. 'This supper'll be stone cold.' They looked at each other understandingly, and he whispered, 'Smile . . . come on. Just another day or so and then . . .'

And when she smiled and kissed his fingers

with her wet lips he had to leave her swiftly in case the pain of his love should overwhelm him and he should join his tears to hers.

There was silence at the supper-table when he sat down, and he did nothing to break it. But after some moments Harry spoke, and his question brought all eyes in his direction.

'How're you having your money?' he asked. 'Cash, or in a bank?'

His fork half-way to his mouth, Peter said, 'Cash. Why do you ask?'

'Nothin'. Nothin' . . . . I just wondered.'

'Why?' asked Peter again, his fork still poised.

'Now can't I just ask a question?'

'Funny one to ask, strikes me.' Peter bolted his mouthful of food.

'Well, I could say it's funny you having cash, couldn't I?'

'No. Because I don't know where I'm going to settle, I may want ready cash at any time. But when I know where I'm going to stay I'll open an account.'

In deference to Rosie's feeling he kept to the 'I', omitting the more personal 'we'.

'Lot of money to be carrying around with you,' said Old Pop quietly.

So that was it, they wanted to hang on to his money for him. Rosie's knife clattered to the plate as she cried, 'He's not a child! If he can't look after his own money now he never will.'

'That's right. You're right there, he's not a child.' This stressed agreement coming from her husband took the strong wind out of her sails and left her more puzzled than ever. She was about to resume her supper when Harry, chewing on a piece of sirloin, looked up at her and asked, in a still, quiet, even conversational tone, 'And what are you doing with your share, lass?'

Rosie's chair scraped backwards. So this really was it, she hadn't been mistaken. If they couldn't get his they'd go all out to get hers. So nodding her head at her husband, she cried, 'I'm putting it into the new War savings, the minute I get it. Get that!' Her indignant gaze swept the three men. And when they all, in quite a docile manner looked at her and nodded agreement she felt completely stumped. But when Harry added, 'Good for you, lass,' the situation went beyond her powers of understanding, and she rose from the table and flounced into the scullery, and Peter, glancing at his father tucking heartily into his supper with apparent renewed appetite, thought, 'She's right after all, they are up to something.'

Chapter Eleven

Grandpop was feeling sad, so sad that he hadn't the list to bellow at the twins and Tony for dashing out and leaving the front gate open. And there it was, swinging wide now, a challenge to all the village dogs looking for pastures new. There'd be pluddy hell to pay when Rosie came back and found any of her flowers trampled. At any other time he would have thought gleefully, 'Let she get on with it'; but today he would, if he could, have so arranged life that Rosie would find no cause for any complaint, at least through him or the delinquency of dogs, for just about this minute she was, he surmised, in Hexham signing away the garage.

Slowly Grandpop turned his eyes up the street. From today onwards, he felt, all interest in the street would be gone – he wouldn't want to look at the garage any more. And yet . . . and yet, if things turned out as they should, perhaps he could sit here and get the laugh of his life. But still, Peter wouldn't be there. His things were all packed up, and hers, too. The morrow they'd both be gone. He'd miss the lad mightily . . . and she. Now why in the name of fortune couldn't things have worked out sensible like, and she could have stayed here. Lay on the couch by the window, she could, and what she couldn't see he would have told her about. And some laughs they'd have had and no mistake, for she had a bright spirit . . . aye, she had. She might be ill, but she wouldn't say die until they shut the lid on her, that 'un. Look at her this mornin' as she had sat just there. Gay she was. That was when Rosie wasn't nigh – she'd made very little headway with Rosie and she knew it, aye, she did. She was sharp. Well, not sharp but wise. Aye, she was wise for her years. Reminded him of someone. His mind started groping. Now who did she remind him of?

'Grandad.'

At the sound of her voice he turned quickly towards the door and automatically adjusted his cap to an angle. 'Hello, lass. I was just this minute thinkin' on you. Come an' sit down, me dear.'

Leo came a step into the room, but said, 'Not now, Grandad, if you don't mind, but when I come back I'd like to. I've got a feeling I'd like to see the lake once more and see if the eel has gone.'

'Oh, she'd be gone after Saturda' . . . all that watter.'

'Yes, perhaps, but it'll be a little walk and it's such a lovely day. I won't be long, Grandad.' She spoke his name gently and her eyes smiled at him.

'Wish I could come along of you, lass.' He returned her smile, wistfully, and the flesh on his cheeks fell into folds. 'Take it easy, mind, and don't be gone ower long. They'll be back soon and that scarecrow of a Peter'll be sayin', "Where she be?" ' He cackled softly and knowingly, and now she smiled at him almost lovingly and her eyes lingered on him before she said, 'I'll be back before they are. Bye, bye, Grandad.'

'Bye, bye, lass.'

As he watched her go out her yellow hair seemed to take the light from the room, and when she was halfway down the path something prompted him to call to her.

When she came back to the window, he said, as quietly as his voice would allow, 'Don't go through village, lass, go up street by cut, side of baker's shop. You know—' he nodded at her cautiously – 'best keep clear of 'em, eh?'

She nodded soberly and somewhat sadly back at him as she repeated, 'Yes, best keep clear of them.'

When she had gone through the gate he waved to her, and she answered it with a small salute of her hand that left him with an added sadness, and jerking his cap to the other side of his head, he exclaimed, 'Blast! Damn and blast the pluddy lot of 'em!'

Now that she had gone there seemed to be nothing for him to do but stare, so settling himself in his chair he prepared to doze . . . just a nod, not real asleep. He never slept any place other than in bed, at least so he believed.

It seemed to him only some seconds later, but was actually fifteen minutes, when the sound of the gate being banged back and almost off its hinges brought him out of a deep sleep and upright in his chair, and through his bleared eyes and with fuddled mind he saw the twins galloping up the path and round the side of the house. And before he could collect himself and let forth a bellow they were in the room yelling, 'Grandpop! Grandpop!'

'Name of God! What is it? Shut up yer screamin'. Here! here! You'll have me on the floor.' He thrust away their hands.

'Grandpop.'

'What is it, I say?' He took as firm a hold of Johnny's shoulders as his rheumaticky hands would allow. 'Stop gibbering an' tell us.'

'You tell him.' Johnny turned to his brother, and Jimmy, swallowing and spluttering, gabbled, 'We was playing round back of Institute, spot the tiger with Tony and young Betty and Clara, an' it was our turn for tiger an' we got into the lav at the back. And then the women came round and we couldn't get out cos they would have clouted us, an' they started talking, Miss Collins and Miss Florrie . . .'

Jimmy paused for breath and Johnny put in, 'Mrs Booth was there an' all. An' Mavis, cos she'd been to the doctor's and she said she'd got nervis bility and was put off for a week.'

'Aye, she did.' Jimmy took up the tale again. 'But it was Mrs Booth what first said "Duck her", and she had seen her going across the fields to the lake, and she called her brazen, Grandpop, and said she was wicked. She's not, is she, Grandpop?'

Grandpop's hands came off the boy's shoulder and on to the arm of his chair and he asked quietly, although he knew the answer, 'Duck who?'

'Miss. Our Peter's miss.'

'Where are they . . . the women?' Grandpop

601

had pulled himself to his feet with the help of his stick.

'They went back in the Hall, cos Miss Florrie said the more that was in the better, an' Mrs Armstrong would be with them. An' Mavis said, "What if she swims away?" an' Mrs Booth said she couldn't swim, she had told Mr Booth she couldn't. And Mrs Booth said three times under would give her a good chance to try and she'd think twice about staying here. They think she's staying, Grandpop. An' Miss Collins said they should tie her hands.'

'God Almighty!' The old man looked wildly around the room, then his gaze came back to the two youngsters who were looking to him for guidance, and he barked, 'Why the hell didn't you go straight to garage for Old Pop?'

'We did, Grandpop, but he weren't there, an' 'twas shut up.'

'Weren't there? Did you look round back?'

'Aye, an' we couldn't see him nowhere.'

The old man looked down at the legs that would carry him, and then only with great willpower, as far as the lavatory and back, and lifting one foot slightly he attempted to shake it. When it responded with no more than the merest wag he thumped his stick on the floor, then drawing in his mouth until his nose almost touched his chin, he demanded, 'Could you knock down bottom palins?'

'Garden palins, Grandpop?'

'Aye, that's what I said, garden palins.'

Blinking bewilderedly together, they said, 'Aye, Grandpop.'

'All right, go on then . . . But listen—' he stopped their rush to the door – 'once they're down, you Johnny, double back to garage and find Joe. Tell him to come back of lake where elm tree is, he knows the place. Come on, then.'

'You comin', Grandpop?' They halted.

'Course I'm comin'. What you gonna knock palins down for? Use yer napper.'

They blinked at him again, then dashed ahead, through the kitchen and scullery and down the garden, to do a job they'd always longed to do, for you could go almost in a straight line from the bottom of the garden to the wood.

Fencing that has stood for forty years and whose posts have rotted in the ground doesn't take a lot of knocking down, but as the railings were wired together it required the uprooting of quite a number before they could be pushed flat enough on the nettles and brambles in the field beyond to allow Grandpop to slither over them.

With burning impatience he had stood watching what was to him their fumbling and slow progress, and when, finally he was in the field beyond, to his own amazement he found that his legs were moving, if not as they once did, at least as good as they had done two years ago. And with Jimmy darting in front of him to clear the obstructions he made the outskirts of the wood within a few minutes of leaving the garden. But once under the shelter of the trees he stopped, and supporting himself against a broad trunk he took his breath, for he was both gasping and shaking.

After a moment or so he dropped his head to

one side in an attitude of listening, and Jimmy said, 'Can you hear owt, Grandpop?'

The old man shook his head.

'Perhaps they'll have their meetin' first?'

Again Grandpop shook his head. 'There'll be no meetin' the day, lad.'

Jimmy stared up at his great-grandfather. Somehow he seemed to have changed; he didn't look old here, like he did when he was in the chair.

It was odd, but at this moment Grandpop did not feel as old as when he was in his chair, for in his mind he had skipped back over seventy years to the time when he had scrambled through this very wood on much the same errand as he was on now. Love had been in his heart that day and curses on his lips, and it was much the same today. On that bygone day he had first called women 'pluddy buggers and bitches', and today they still merited the names.

Although it was now some years since he had been in the wood, he knew, as well as he did his own house, every inch of it. He knew where the best courting bowers were; what had once been the best rabbit runs; the badger sets and the short cut to Top Fell Dyke.

It was of this now that he spoke to Jimmy: 'If we can't see Miss afore we get to lake we are going round t'other side, and when we find her you take the road till you come to Top Fell Dyke.'

'But she'll be in the clearing, Grandpop.'

'Well, if she is, all to the good, but it's no use us makin' for there. Once that lot get their eyes on her we couldn't be all that use . . . summat would happen. They'll have to do summat to her to get her out of their systems for she's made of the same stuff as Connie . . . knew she minded me of somebody.'

Jimmy looked puzzled and asked, 'Connie, who, Grandpop?'

And the old man, wiping the question away with a flick of his hand, said, 'It's no matter. What we've got to do is to get her across to t'other side, if she's in clearing.'

Jimmy pulled a briar from the old man's path and let it swing back behind him, then asked, 'But how'll we get her across, Grandpop?'

'Cross tree trunk.'

'Tree trunk?'

'Aye.'

'But you can't get down to tree trunk, Grandpop, it's all tangle in there.'

'We'll get through . . . you'll get through.' Grandpop looked significantly down on Jimmy. 'Badgers still got their run down there?'

'Aye, Grandpop.'

'Then where badgers can go, you can go, eh?' He smiled down at the boy, and Jimmy, without much conviction said, 'Aye, Grandpop.'

'That's the lad. Move that bit wood.'

Jimmy moved the rotting branch and Grandpop, slithering on again, said, not without pride, 'Legs doing fine, eh?' Then stopping, he raised his hand with a warning gesture. And as Jimmy listened there came to him the faint crackle of feet on undergrowth and he glanced up apprehensively at the old man.

'Come on.'

Not only to Jimmy's, but to Grandpop's further astonishment, his legs began to move faster, with his feet actually clearing the ground, and when Jimmy exclaimed in admiration, 'Grandpop, your legs are going,' his only comment was, 'An' it'll take 'em.'

They were now on the narrow bramble-strewn path that ran round the far side of the lake opposite the clearing, and after traversing some way, with his eyes darting upwards at every step or so, Grandpop pointed to a tall tree whose top was bare of branches and which was kept upright only by the support of the other trees around it and exclaimed, 'That beech tree. It's hereabouts.' He now thrust his stick about on the ground, until it came into contact with a covered stump of a tree. 'There!' he exclaimed. 'See that?' He pulled Jimmy to him, and tapping the root with his stick he whispered, 'Right opposite here is where oak's fallen cross pond. Go down one of the runs, but keep to the right – your right hand, see?' He tapped the boy's arm, 'If you don't you'll come high up on the bank, away from tree. When you're through, whistle her softly and wave her over – like this.' He gave a demonstration of silent beckoning. 'But don't shout or they'll hear you.'

Jimmy was far from clear in his mind about what he had to do and he looked his bewilderment and said, 'But what if she won't come, Grandpop?'

'Get along the trunk then and swim over to her. You can swim, can't you? Tell her I'm here. And don't make more noise than you can help.

Oh, God Almighty!' The old man's eyes flashed angrily, 'I wish I was young again, I'd be through there . . .'

'All right, Grandpop, I'll go.' The boy got down on his hands and knees to the questionable comfort of Grandpop's words as he said, 'Go on, push. Don't be feared of a few scratches and bit blood.'

Necessity aiding his wits, Jimmy found that if he lay flat and wriggled on his belly instead of crawling he not only made progress but evaded the brambles. Then, with so much relief that he almost shouted aloud, he found himself within a few seconds clear of the undergrowth and its gloom and forced momentarily to close his eyes against the glare of the sun on the water. He hadn't thought of Grandpop's instructions to keep to the right, but not two yards away was the great upended root of the oak tree, so big that he couldn't see over it. But across its trunk which followed a steep grade down towards the middle of the lake he saw on the other side, standing at the very edge of the clearing the Miss, but with her back to the water . . .

Leo had her eyes riveted on the opening from where, at any minute, one after the other, the women would emerge, and then . . . The sweat broke out all over her body and she knew fear as she had never done before. That she was dying she knew; there was no doubt about it in her mind. After the first terrifying and sickening shock of this knowledge she had been more upset at its effect on the man with whom she was living than by the fact that at most she could hope for only another few months of life. As day had followed day she had, unconsciously by her attitude towards living, practised letting go of the reins so that at this time last week she would not have cared if the end had been a matter of minutes away. Yet even then she would, she knew, have been afraid of an end precipitated by mad women, and she felt, and truly, that the women behind that screen of undergrowth were, for the moment, mad.

Not five minutes ago she had been sitting on the bank here, praying in her own fashion, giving thanks for the gift and the solace of Peter's love, and her thoughts had been threaded with a wisdom that did not owe itself entirely to experience and which told her she was glad that this love would only live long enough to keep its vitality and freshness, with its essence of giving always to the fore. Nothing, she determined, would mar the numbered days of their life together, and with an eagerness to be gone and start that life she had risen from the bank, and after bidding a voiceless, sentimental farewell by kissing her fingers to the lake and to the eel that could, or could not, still be there, she had gone through the opening, to be brought to an abrupt halt at its farther end.

In front of her, through the boles of the trees and half hidden by an outstretched branch, she had seen a figure standing, not that of a man, although it was in breeches . . . it was the girl from the Manor. And as she watched she saw her move slowly forward. It was something in the way she walked that had made her turn swiftly, and there, where the path turned into the broad walk, stood Mrs Booth and at her side the vicar's sister. It was the linking of Mrs Booth's eyes with her own that struck instant terror into her, and she had turned swiftly about to make her retreat by the path to the right, only to find standing there more women, three of them. She didn't know them, but one thing she recognised, they had on their faces a reflection of the look in Mrs Booth's eyes, but only a reflection, for if ever she had seen insane hate she had seen it on Mrs Booth's face.

For a moment she had thought, 'Don't panic. Don't run. What can they do? Nothing . . . they daren't do anything. This is . . .' And she had been about to give herself the comfort of this day and age when Mrs Booth moved, just a step, and to her step the others added theirs. She'd had the desire to cry out to them then, to ask them why, why were they acting like it, even to plead with them. But her common sense had told her that talking would be worse than useless; Mrs Booth would act first and talk afterwards because she loathed and hated her.

In undisguised panic she had backed into the clearing again until she came to the edge of the bank, and there she stood, all her small strength draining away from her. She had glanced back once at the lake. Even if she had been able to swim she knew her strength would never have carried her across to the other side. And now it came to her that a casual remark to Mr Booth, in his wife's hearing, that she had never been able to swim had set the seal fixing her death warrant. It was also enabling Mrs Booth to practise the art of suspense.

With her eyes stark wide and her teeth digging into her lip she stood and waited, feeling them every moment moving slowly nearer. As her mind screamed, 'Peter! Oh Peter!' she heard a 'Psst! Psst!' and the low whistle that followed it brought her stiffened head round. She knew that whistle. And when her eyes alighted on Jimmy astraddle the fallen tree, she turned swiftly and waved frantically to him. Then dropping her arms helplessly to her sides she asked herself, what could he do? She could shout to him, she could scream to him and he could run for help. But wouldn't he think it was a game she was having? And if she shouted, 'They're going to kill me,' he would think she had gone mad – her mind used Jimmy's own words for such an occasion, 'up the pole.' And who wouldn't think but that she was up the pole should she shout any such thing – this wasn't the Middle Ages, this was nineteen fifty-nine and people were civilised. They didn't do things like this – it wouldn't be till after she was dead that people would know that they still could and did do things like this . . . Then through her terrified mind it dawned on her that Jimmy was aware of her plight, for he was alternately thumbing the water and beckoning her with wide sweeps of his arm towards himself and the tree.

The tree lay to her right and, it seemed to her petrified gaze, miles away. She had no idea of how deep the water was a few feet away from the bank. She would likely drown if it became so deep that she could not walk through it. But of the choice that lay before her she thought it better now to drown in an attempt to get away than to be mauled about by them, for that would result in death anyway.

She slipped her feet out of her sandals and grabbed them up, then sitting gingerly on the edge of the bank she slid down into the water. It felt cool, almost cold, as it gently embraced her knees, and she shivered but mostly with her fear. And it was fear which thrust her out from the bank and into the water which reached well up to her thighs. As she moved towards the tree her feet began to sink into the soft ooze and drag her steps. But each step took her away from the clearing, and soon she was past it and there was nothing to her right but a high green wall of undergrowth.

Her heart was beating so fast that she thought it might stop. She was gasping and felt she was going to be sick at any moment. Dragging her eyes from the water she looked towards Jimmy. He seemed much nearer now and he was beckoning her with another wide sweep of his arm which spoke of haste. In her fear of getting out of her depth she moved parallel with the bank, and when she was almost opposite the fallen tree the water had receded from her hips to her knees again. But this was no relief, for in order to reach the tree and Jimmy she would have to move now in a straight line towards the middle of the lake, and this spoke to her, not of safety, but of deep water.

'Come on, come on, miss!' It was a hissing whisper from Jimmy, and she nodded to him.

Then testing each step for foothold, she moved tentatively towards him. But she had not gone more than a yard or so before she realised that the particular fear of deeper water near the middle was well-founded, for already it was round her waist and rising with each move forward. Her dress was floating like a ballet skirt about her; moreover her feet were stumping against submerged branches that threatened to trip her. Then for a space she suddenly rose out of the water as her feet touched a silted bank, damned likely by trees and mud. Praying that this would hold until she reached the tree she edged her way forward once more. And then, not six feet from the first broken, bleached, outstretched branch of the oak, she felt the bottom going rapidly downwards again, and in a few steps the water had risen to her breasts. Her arms outspread on the surface like stiff wings, she became so rigid with her fear that she could move no farther.

'Come on!'

'I – I can't. Ji – Jimmy.'

'You've got to . . . come on.' Jimmy hitched himself towards a fork in the head of the tree. He was high above her now, almost looking down on her. 'Aw, come on, miss. It's just a little way.'

When he saw her gulp and shake her head he bit on his lip, and his face crumpled as if he might cry.

'Aw, come on. Grandpop's waitin' for you. He's up the bank.'

There was the sound of tears in his voice, and this caused her to put out a foot but when she did so and it found nothing she hastily withdrew it.

Again she tried to the other side. And when the same thing happened her breathing almost stopped.

Jimmy, seeing the fear on her face and knowing she wasn't going to make it, said helplessly, 'Aw, miss . . . miss.'

She looked up at him and cried softly between gasps, 'Jimmy – I'm – I'm going back. I'll stay under the bank. Go – go and get Peter.'

'Aw, miss.' He could think of nothing else to say, and as Leo, her eyes tight on the water once more and her arms swivelling to help her to turn, took the first step on her return journey there came a churning of the calm water, and the eel, like submerged lightning, flashed round her, catching her with its tail end as if she had been lassoed. The combination of her struggles and its swift, coiling movements flung her face forward, and whether it was the effect of her terror or the jerk that the eel had given her she found herself with her head above water once more, her feet on a submerged branch and her hands upstretched grasping at another branch just beneath Jimmy's knee.

'Eeh! miss. Oh, miss! Eeh! I thought . . . Oh, come on.' He was pulling at her.

Spitting out the water, she gasped, 'All right – I'm all right . . . Wait.' She rested a moment, then working her feet along the branch she gradually drew herself out and onto the trunk.

Jimmy now backing swiftly away encouraged, 'That's it, miss. Come on. Come on.' And, like someone hypnotised, she dragged herself along the trunk towards the root.

As Jimmy went to climb down through the roots, he stopped and exclaimed, 'Don't turn round, miss. They've seen you, miss. They're all standin' watchin' . . . Eeh! no they're not, they're goin'. Come on, hurry.'

Spent and gasping for her breath, Leo lay flat on the trunk. 'I can't hurry, Jimmy, I can't. You go on – and – and get Peter.'

After a moment during which he stood and watched her apprehensively she slid down through the roots and sitting with her back against them murmured, 'I – I must rest, Jimmy.'

'But Grandpop's waitin' for us . . . just here, miss.' He pointed up the bank to the bushes.

'Grandpop? Here? You mean – Old Pop?' She raised her drooping head.

'No, miss, Grandpop.'

'Grandpop?' she said again. 'Grandpop?'

'Yes, miss.'

Her heavy lids stretched; she made an incredulous gesture with her hand; then with an effort she turned on her knees and rose to her feet, and looking at the seemingly impregnable wall of undergrowth she asked, 'How – how do we get out?'

'We've got to crawl, miss. But it's only a little way. If you do it on your bell – stomach, it's easy. Up the badger set.'

'Show me.'

She bit on her lip as she followed him in her bare feet over the thorn and bramble strewn bank, and then she lay down behind him and slowly dragged herself the few yards to the top and Grandpop.

When her head appeared almost at his feet Grandpop bent down and clutched at her, pulling her to her feet, muttering in a broken voice, 'Aw! lass. Aw! me dear. Aw! me dear. Aw! the sight of you . . . For this to happen.' Then in a growl he cried, 'I'll have 'em jailed, so help me, God, every pluddy one of 'em! So help me God, I will!'

'Oh! Grandad.' Leo was leaning within the shelter of his trembling arms and gasping with each breath. 'I'm frightened . . . so . . . so . . .'

'There now.' He patted her shoulder. 'Don't you be frightened of nowt, just do as I say. Go with the lad here. He knows the way to Top Fell Dyke; there's only one road there from this end and it's along this path. Go on now. Aw, your poor feet . . . bleeding.' He looked down at her feet, and she said, 'They're all right. But you – what about you?'

'You leave this to me. Go on now, as quick as you can, lass, and by the time you get there Joe'll be along. Blast him, he should be here now. Never could be where he's wanted, that lad.'

'Listen!' She held her head to one side. 'They're coming. I can hear them.' She looked anxiously up at the old man, and he said calmly, 'Aye, I know. Go on, now.' He turned to Jimmy. 'Go on . . . quick! And when you get clear of the path there's no need to hurry. If those bitches of hell get by me there's three lanes beyond and they won't know which one you've gone, even if they get that far, which they pluddy well won't. Away now.'

Gently he pushed her from him, and Jimmy,

holding out his hand, took hers and led her away.

They weren't out of Grandpop's sight before he turned and, moving with doddering steps in the opposite direction, went along the path to where it narrowed and bent sharply at the head of the lake. Here he quickly selected a patch of earth which was bordered by a couple of stakes, remnants of a fence which had once guarded the high and dangerous bank above the lake at this point, and lowering himself very, very cautiously down, he took up his position with his back to the stakes, his legs across the path and his stick firmly gripped in his hand.

Their approach was not heralded by their voices, but by their feet which sounded to him like the pounding of horses' hooves. They came upon him all in a bunch, Mrs Booth and Miss Collins pulling up so rapidly that Mavis and Mrs Fountain were almost knocked backwards.

Miss Collins let out a stifled squeal, for she couldn't believe what she was seeing: Grandfather Puddleton, who couldn't walk more than a few yards, here in the woods! And Mrs Booth's mouth was wider than it had ever been without anything coming out of it. Then snapping it closed, she exclaimed, 'Good God!'

'Aye, good God. And you keep the Almighty's name out of your dirty mouth, Katie Booth, until you're in court and asked to say, "I speak the truth and nowt but, so help me God". And you'll need help, let me tell you, you pluddy mischief-making bitch!'

The taunt lessened somewhat the shock Mrs

Booth had received, and she cried, 'What are you up to here? And you be careful what you say. Get up out of that.'

'Can't,' said Grandpop flatly; 'legs is give way.'

'Then move yourself round.'

Mrs Booth was the only one so far who had spoken, for the sight of Grandpop and his implied threat of the police court had, it would seem, returned the others some way to normality. Even Miss Collins backed away a step.

'If you don't move I'll get over you.'

'You try. Just you try it on, you big slobbery bitch. An' you see this stick here?' He brandished the stick up at her, then with not a little glee, he watched her evident wilting and listened to the horrified gasps of her companions as he went into minute details of what explorations he would put his stick to should she attempt her threat.

'You filthy old swine you! You should be locked up.'

'Aye, that's a matter of opinion, Katie Booth. You should have been locked up years gone for what you was up to.' Grandpop brought his back from the staves and raised his chin to her. 'And now tryin' to kill a bit lass cos she has the men about her like flies without raisin' a finger. You've had to do more than raise a finger an' not get as far as she, hevn't you? Go on, you as much as lay a finger on me and I'll crack those big, fat, ugly shanks of yours.' He flourished his stick wildly at her, then cried, 'And you there, 'Melia Fountain, shame on you for being in this. Shame on you! And with her – this village whore here – and she after your man. Aye, aye, you was . . . !'

Now he had to brandish his stick wildly to keep Mrs Booth at bay. 'Waylaid him you did, at every turn. Couldn't get rid of you, Bill couldn't. And then you started on Harry. Come on, come on,' he challenged her, as she heaved like some great animal over him. Then flashing his attention to where Mrs Armstrong was trying to hide herself behind Miss Collins, he said, 'And if your man was alive the day Celia Armstrong, he'd tell you a thing or two, an' all. Ask her about the notes she used to leave in orange box near door. Had him petrified, she had, lest you picked 'em up.'

Grandpop suddenly paused for breath and also because his heart was giving him warning. Much more of this, he told himself, and it would be the finish; he'd better steady up. He leant back against the posts again, but as he did so he kept his steely gaze fixed on the purple, suffused face of Mrs Booth, daring her to make a move nearer.

'You! you!' she brought out at last, 'I'll have you up. It's a libel. You dirty . . . you!'

'Aye.' It was a short, sardonical reply which conveyed volumes, and it added to her rage which was so great as to be temporarily suppressing her powers of invective.

Two feet at the back of the group quietly turning round drew Grandpop's eyes to the assortment of legs and to the polished riding boots, and he exclaimed in a voice full of scorn, 'Aye, go off quietly, Miss Florrie, it'll be you what has to face the major. And as long as I'm alive don't look my way agen. Hear that? Nor put a step inside me door. And the rest of you'd better get along with her. And as for you, Miss

Collins—' he paused – 'I told you years ago when you came here you'd better settle in your mind to stick to God, being a little too long in the tooth to harness any lad hereabouts, and place running wild with young heifers at the time. But you wouldn't listen, an' you've gone sour on yersel. Aye, you can rear your skinny neck, but I'd call in me church and go down on me knees if I was you. So I would!'

There was a great tiredness on him now and his words were coming slower, and it was with relief that he saw them, without parting shots of any sort, turn one after the other and glide cautiously away as if afraid now of the sound of their own footsteps. All, that was, except Mrs Booth, and she remained, glaring at him as if she would jump on him and tear his flesh apart.

Grandpop was finding that he hadn't even the strength to outstare her when he heard Joe demanding, 'What's up here?' And never had his son's voice sounded sweet to him before. 'What you up to, Katie Booth, you knocked him down?'

Mrs Booth turned her bloodshot eyes on Old Pop, and her spluttering was near idiot jabbering as she cried, 'Kno – knocked him down! He should be dead . . . dead and buried alive, and you along of him . . . all of you, all the Puddletons, all of you. The – the dirty old swine! The—!' Her lips white with froth, she spluttered in his face. Then like someone drunk she turned and went running along the path, mouthing her venom aloud.

After turning his astonished gaze from the

departing figure, Joe exclaimed, 'God Almighty, save us! How you got here?' He looked down on his father straddled across the path, and Grandpop, looking scornfully up at him and with only a little punch left in his voice, grunted, 'Don't ask pluddy silly questions, I didn't fly. Where you bin? Never about when you're wanted. Same all your life. Here, give me a hand up.'

With some effort on both sides Grandpop was on his feet again, but it was evident, even to himself, that he wasn't the man he had been before he sat down. That do with Katie Booth had took it out of him and no mistake. His legs were like jelly and he was trembling all over, even his voice now. But in spite of this, it still held a ring of authority, and he commanded, 'Come on, let's get movin'. If I don't soon have a drop of hard I'm for it.'

'Where're you going?' asked Joe, as his father turned and moved slowly along the path. 'That ain't the way.'

'I'm going to Dyke . . . Lass is there.'

'You'll never get to Dyke.'

'Who won't? Got here afore you, didn't I? Lass is near mad. That lot near done for her.'

'They really meant it then?' Old Pop's eyebrows were reaching for his scalp.

'Meant it?' Grandpop turned on his son. 'You stone blind as well as daft? You saw 'em all, and Katie Booth like a witch.'

'Aye. But she always looked like witch when you got at her. Your tongue were never easy on her. But I can't take it in; 'tain't feasible. Johnny says they were gonna duck miss . . . fact?'

'Fact!' Grandpop's voice was withering. 'Why d'you think I'm this far from me chair? Looking for fairies in me dotage? Aw, come on, you helpin' me or is it me helpin' you? Give me yer shoulder.' Slowly, and in silence now, they made their way to where the three paths met.

Chapter Twelve

'I'll kill her if I get me hands on her, I'll kill her!'

Peter, holding the sodden body of Leo to him, looked wildly from one member of his family to another as they all stood in a group on the road bordering the dyke. Then lifting Leo's face up to his he begged, 'Are you all right?'

She did not speak but nodded her head.

'We'll get you home and to bed, then—'

'No – no.' To his astonishment she dragged herself from his hold and backed from him. She backed from them all as she cried, 'I'm not going back there – ever – I can't!'

'But, Leo . . .'

'It's no use – I can't set foot in that village again.'

'But, lass, you're soaked, and you'll catch your death.' It was Rosie speaking, a changed Rosie, for the weird incident had both shocked her and frightened her. In a flash of insight she had seen herself as one of Katie Booth's followers if not in flesh in spirit, and she turned in fear from the picture. And now it was a genuine pity that was filling her, and she said again, 'A day or two in bed, lass—'

'No.' Leo shook her head emphatically and Peter, stepping to her side, said soothingly, 'It'll be as you say, dear. What do a few hours matter anyway. I'll go back and get our things and you can change in the car . . . all right?' He patted her cheek.

'Yes.' Her voice was scarcely audible.

'But you'll catch your death.' Rosie repeated her statement as much now to prolong the departure as because of her concern for the girl, but Harry, who had spoken very little up to now, said firmly, 'It's the best way. Get your things together, lad, and get off.'

Without another word Peter went to the car, and with his foot hard down on the accelerator he headed back to the village. It may have been just coincidence that the entire street was deserted – in fact, the whole place looked dead; perhaps it was as well that he encountered no-one, for the anger in him would have burst over innocent and guilty alike.

It took him only a matter of minutes to gather their belongings up and bundle them into the car before he was once again roaring through the village towards Top Fell Dyke. As he came to a stop opposite the family seated on the grass verge as if on an outing, Grandpop's voice hailed him with, 'Think to bring a drop of hard with you, lad?'

Peter, getting out of the car, drew a flask from his pocket and handed it towards the old 'un, and Grandpop, his eyes sparkling at the sight of the whisky, said, 'Ah, lad, that's the ticket.' But when with trembling hands he filled the lid cup from the flask, he did not gulp it down but handed it to Leo, saying 'Get that into you, lass.'

Leo hesitated until Peter urged quietly, 'Drink it up, it can't do you any harm.'

As Leo drank the spirit she shivered, and Rosie, as if there had been nothing between her and this girl but affection, said gently, 'That'll keep out the chill . . . come on and get those things off.' And then to the surprise of all the Puddleton men, even the twins, they watched her get into the back of the car and hold the door open for Leo to enter, at the same time shouting in an over-loud voice to Peter, 'I bet you didn't think to bring a towel!'

'I did; there's a couple on the front seat.' He opened the front door of the car and leaning over handed the towels to her to be greeted with, 'All right. Leave them there and get away for a minute . . . And look, get that bottle off the old 'un, or we'll have a nice game getting him back home. Go on now.'

Rosie was speaking to him as if he were her bit of a lad again, and he knew the reason. Her shouting and bustling was only a way of covering up her embarrassment.

Grandpop no longer had the bottle. It was being passed now from Old Pop to Harry. And when Harry had had his pull he handed it to Peter, but Peter shook his head and stood for a moment voiceless among them, just looking at them. There they were, five of them, the Puddleton men, and as he looked from the youngest to the eldest an odd feeling flooded him. It was as akin to love as ever he had felt for them and he knew that he would miss them, each one of them, more than he cared to admit.

Harry, imbued with the same kind of feeling, put his hand onto his son's shoulder and said softly, 'Well, lad, this is it.' They looked steadily at each other for a moment before he went on. 'There'll be no chance to talk in a minute and I couldn't say this to you then, anyway. But I'd just like to say that when you are . . . alone again, come back, will you? This is your home, lad. This ground, these rocks and hills. And you won't be able to throw them off lightly no matter what you think. And what's more, in a short while folks will have forgotten anything ever happened, and if anybody talks about it later on, it'll just be like another fable, with a smattering of truth in it – or something to laugh at.'

Peter's face hardened immediately and his voice was stiff as he said, 'I'll never laugh at the day's business.'

'No, lad, no. I wasn't meaning that. You know what I mean. But you'll come back, won't you?'

After a long moment, during which he looked from one to the other and saw in their eyes an intensified reflection of the feeling he bore them, he said, slightly non-committal, 'I may do. But it won't be for years – not for years.' His voice was hard with emphasis as he repeated this.

'Aye. Yes, lad. Aye.' It was a chorus joined with shaking of heads. 'We know that. We understand that. But we'll see you . . . perhaps you'll settle not so far off.'

This last was from Old Pop, and Peter said, 'Perhaps. Anyway, I'll let you know.'

'Give us a hand up, one of you.' Grandpop held up his arms and they all went to his assistance.

And when he was standing between Harry and Joe he put out his trembling hands to Peter, and, gripping his, said, 'She's a fine lass. Be happy, and later on you can remember the words—' his voice was shaking and his eyes were full of the unusual moisture of tears as he quoted brokenly – ' "And often glad no more, we wear a face of joy because we have been glad of yore." '

The whisky as usual had revived Wordsworth, and Peter said softly, 'I'll remember, old 'un.'

They stood now, saying nothing but watching the twins scampering in the hedge, then the car door clicked and Leo stepped down into the road. The difference in her appearance that a change of clothes and her hair rubbed near dry had made brought the first touch of relief to Peter's face.

'That's better.' He touched her hair and said softly, 'You look yourself again, like a million.'

Leo's smile was wan, and full of disbelief, and still a little fearful.

Now came the goodbyes. Under ordinary circumstances Peter hated the business of leave-taking and always avoided it if possible, and now the urgency to make the break and be gone caused him to bustle almost as much as Rosie.

'Well, we'd better get a move on,' he said to no-one in particular, 'no use hanging about.' He turned to the car and, putting his head inside, fiddled with the ignition key. As he did this Rosie's busy-busying ceased and he said, without turning his head to look at her, 'All fixed, Mam?'

'Yes, I think so.' Her voice was quiet now and she slipped out of the car and into the road.

Leo was standing surrounded by the three men

and the twins; the twins were holding on to one of her hands while with the other she held Grandpop's; Old Pop was patting her arm and Harry was saying, 'Well, don't forget us, lass. And don't go too far away, now, will you?' He waited for a reply, and when her lips moved without sound and she swallowed, he said hastily, and thickly, 'There now, there now . . . Go on, there's that big goof of yours straining to be off.'

Grandpop's gums were champing up and down, and when she leant forward and kissed him he looked deep into her eyes and muttered softly, 'We'll meet up again, lass, you'll see. I've a sort of feeling this isn't the end. God bless you. Go on now.'

He pushed her as he had done earlier, and she turned away towards the car, and there she was face to face with Rosie – Rosie standing close to her son. It was a testy moment. Slowly she held out her hand and Rosie took it. Then to the further surprise of all the family they heard Rosie mutter, 'Always wanted a daughter.'

Leo gazed at the little dominant woman, then swiftly she bent her head towards her and pressed her lips to her cheek before turning bindly away and into the car.

Now Peter was shaking hands and receiving pats and advice from his elders. Lastly, as he knew it would be, he came to his mother. After a moment of eye holding eye he pulled her awkwardly into his arms and held her close and whispered, so that only she could hear, 'Thanks, Mam.'

'There.' Her voice was shaking and her eyes

blind with unshed tears and she stepped back from him. 'Off you go the pair of you.'

When he was in his seat and the engine throbbing she put her head through the window past him and addressed Leo: 'Take care of yourself, lass,' she said, before adding diffidently, 'Perhaps I could come and see you when you settle.'

'Yes. Oh, yes.' Spontaneously Leo's hands went across Peter and touched hers.

'Get him to write.' Rosie nodded at her son. 'He's the world's worst letter-writer.'

'I will, I promise. And soon.'

'Goodbye, lad.'

'Goodbye, lass.'

'Goodbye, miss.'

'Goodbye, Peter . . . Bye.'

'Goodbye. Goodbye.'

The farewells were mixed and toppling over each other; then the car was away and Leo's voice, stronger than it had been yet, could be heard for the last time calling, 'Goodbye Grandad.'

'Goodbye, lass.' Grandpop spoke aloud to himself, for she could no longer hear him. He stood unsupported, the receding car lost in the blur of his eyes. 'Reckon we'll meet up on the road out. Aye, reckon we will, somehow.' His words were clear and firm and brought a quick exchange of glances between Harry and Joe.

The sound of suppressed crying turned them about to see Rosie, their hard-bitten Rosie, her back to them, standing at the side of the road crying her heart out, with the twins, silent and disturbed, one on each side of her.

'Aw, lass. Now, now, don't give way.' Going to her Harry put his arms about her shoulders and turned her towards him adding, 'It's a pity to say this and I wish it wasn't so, but you'll have him back afore long, aye afore very long. So come now.' Then giving a silly laugh, and his voice high, he said, 'You've still got me.' He paused now, and an odd look came over his face and he murmured under his breath, 'Perhaps you'll remember I'm here now, Rosie, eh?'

Rosie, slowly lifting her wet face up to her husband, looked at him, and he held her look, and even through her blurred vision she saw that something had gone from him. Was it the jealousy of their son? For a moment she forgot the presence of the others and a flicker of tenderness passed over her face. Then she turned from him, sniffing and saying, 'It's no use standing here, is it? We've got to get him back.'

'Him,' in his wisdom, had called the twins to his side and was engaging their attention, as well as that of Joe, by describing graphically just what he was going to do and say to Katie Booth and the rest of them murdering bitches. He was going to the Hart the night, he was that, and he'd show 'em, every pluddy one of 'em.

'Come on, old 'un.' Harry approached his grandfather, and Rosie rubbing her face quickly with her handkerchief said, with some regret for what appeared like past splendour, 'No garage to send to now for a car, unless we hire one from them. Huh!'

The three men had turned as one and were

surveying her, and Harry asked, tentatively, 'You so sorry, lass, that the garage has gone?'

Rosie's head wagged a little as she said, 'Well, if you want to know, I'm sorry that them lot's got it, as sorry as you are. And we'll be more sorry still yet, you mark me.'

'Tell her, lad.' Grandpop's eyes were twinkling, and he chuckled, 'Tell her.'

'In a minute. Here.' Harry called the twins to him and bending over them, said, 'Look, run back home and bring the barrow. We'll take Grandpop home in it.'

There was a sort of minor explosion from the road. 'Push me in a barrer! No pluddy fear. No you won't, be God! . . . No, be God! I won't be ridden in no barrer.'

'Sh!' Harry laid a restraining hand on his grandfather's jerking and indignant shoulders and whispered, 'Got to get rid of 'em.'

'Ah. Ah, well, that's as may be, but send 'em for summat else, not barrer. No pluddy fear.'

Harry did not change his order but said, 'Go on now and hurry.' And the twins scampered off, glad to be sent on such a pleasant errand with the ultimate prospect of a laugh to see their Grandpop wheeled in a barrow.

'Now,' said Harry slowly nodding his head at Rosie, 'I've news for you.'

''Bout garage?'

''Bout garage.'

Rosie looked puzzled. The garage was sold, Peter'd had his share and she'd had hers, and Peter was gone with every penny in his pocket, for Harry had not tried to borrow a farthing from him. Yet, as she had felt since Sunday, there was something up. 'Well, let's hear it,' she said.

'How much d'you think you'd have got for it afore the road was going through?'

'Aye, how much?' added Old Pop.

'Eight, perhaps nine hundred. That's what Mackenzie said, but they'd skin a louse for its hide, them skinflints.'

'And how much did you get?'

'That's a silly question, you know what we got – fifteen hundred.'

'Aye.' Harry paused, and the old 'uns nodded. 'That was 'cos road was going through. But there was no mention of that in the deeds, was there? Old Mackenzie didn't make a hullaballoo about it and yell, "I'm giving you fifteen hundred 'cos road's going through," did he? No. He knew that when road went through that piece of land and garage would be worth three times what he paid. He felt he was cute not to harp on about it and put it in writing.'

'So what?' said Rosie puzzled. 'Ain't road coming through?'

'Aye, it is. But not through Battenbun, it ain't.' There was a wave of glee connecting the faces of the three men.

'Not coming?' Rosie blinked. 'Not coming? Who said?'

'Major.'

'But 'twere major who said it were.'

'Aye. And he were right then, but apparently committee were divided all along. And then it were found that if they built the road running through Downfell Hurst they could build houses nearly all along its length but not if they built it through Battenbun. You know major, he wouldn't sell an inch and they were stumped. They could run the road by the side of his land but that's all they'd get out of him.'

'But – but won't they come back on us?' said Rosie, looking scared.

'Come back on us? What for?' asked Harry. 'The cat won't be out of the bag for near on two weeks, next committee. Major only told me because he saw I was in a bit of a state about the lad selling, and it was him, hisself mind, who said, "You sing dumb, Harry." He was tickled to death about the whole thing. You know what he thinks of the Mackenzies. And, of course, he's over the moon about the road not touching us . . . Mackenzie's got a place for his lorries, and that's what he said he wanted, isn't it? But as for the garage, when the road goes through not a damn car will come this way at all. And now he can't do a thing about it, it's all been done in good faith. Them was Mackenzie's own words – good faith.'

'He won't make out our Peter's gone off on purpose and sue him?'

'Let him try.' Harry's face became grim. 'And anybody in the village who doesn't know what's happened the day will by the night, and their lass was one of them who tried it on. Peter took his future wife away because of this village's women's murderous attack on her. 'Twould make good reading in the Sunday papers . . . let 'em start anything.'

Harry drew himself up, and after gazing up at

him for a moment a smile spread over Rosie's face and she gave a little hick of a laugh.

'That's it, lass.' Harry slapped her on the back.

'Eh, what a shock!' Rosie's smile was broad now and Grandpop's and Old Pop's chuckles were deepening.

'She – she turned her nose up at me this morning, Winnie Mackenzie.' Rosie put her hand over her mouth to still a chuckle; then she laid her fingers on Harry's arm and tapped it twice saying, 'But it's good job lad's gone, he would have taken it back. The money and the garage.'

'Yes. Aye, that's what were worrying us, weren't it?' Harry looked at his father and grandfather, and they nodded and slapped each other. Their laughter mounted, and to it was joined Rosie's. For the first time in her life she was laughing with the combined force of her menfolk, and this knowledge did not escape them and gave further rein to their mirth. Grandpop's sides were cracking with it, his body was rocking. Then one minute he was standing as firmly as any of them and the next he was on the road all of a heap.

'Blast 'em! Damn and blast the pluddy things!'

'Aw, old 'un, your legs?'

'Blast 'em!'

'They give way?'

'Blast . . . blast you!' Grandpop punched at his useless legs. Then glaring up at Harry he cried, 'I ain't goin' in that barrer. Hump me on your back, back through the woods. I ain't gonna be no laughing stock, not at my time, I ain't.'

'I couldn't carry you back all that way, old 'un,' said Harry. 'What d'you take me for – Samson?'

'Well, I ain't pluddy well goin' in barrer.'

'You are so, and here they come with it now. And thank God for it.'

Swearing and protesting loudly, Grandpop was hoisted into the barrow, and, supported on all sides by his family, set off down the road to the village. As they neared it Rosie, with her tongue in her cheek, remarked, 'You won't get to the Hart the night, old 'un, so I would have your say about Katie Booth and the lot of them as you go through. And the slower Harry goes the more you'll get in.'

Grandpop's protestations ceased and he cast a bleared eye up at Rosie. Then giving a rumbling chuckle, he exclaimed, 'You've said summat there, Rosie, lass, summat that I agree with. After all these years you've said summat that I agree with.'

THE END

THE GOLDEN STRAW
by Catherine Cookson

The Golden Straw, as it would be named, was a large, broad-brimmed hat presented to Emily Pearson by her long-time friend and employer Mabel Arkwright, milliner and modiste. And before long it was to her employer that Emily owed the gift of the business itself, for Mabel was in poor health and had come to rely more and more on Emily before her untimely death in 1880.

While on holiday in France, Emily and the Golden Straw attracted the eye of Paul Steerman, a guest at the hotel, and throughout his stay he paid her unceasing attention. But Paul Steerman was not all he seemed to be and he was to bring nothing but disgrace and tragedy to Emily, precipitating a series of events that would influence the destiny of not only her children but her grandchildren too.

The Golden Straw, conceived on a panoramic scale, brilliantly portrays a rich vein of English life from the heyday of the Victorian era to the stormy middle years of the present century. It represents a fresh triumph for this great storyteller whose work is deservedly loved and enjoyed throughout the world.

0 552 13685 9

JUSTICE IS A WOMAN
by Catherine Cookson

The day Joe Remington brought his new bride to Fell Rise, he had already sensed she might not settle easily into the big house just outside the Tyneside town of Fellburn. For Joe this had always been his home, but for Elaine it was virtually another country whose manners and customs she was by no means eager to accept.

Making plain her disapproval of Joe's familiarity with the servants, demanding to see accounts Joe had always trusted to their care, questioning the donation of food to striking miners' families – all these objections and more soon rubbed Joe and the local people up the wrong way, a problem he could easily have done without, for this was 1926, the year of the General Strike, the effects of which would nowhere be felt more acutely than in this heartland of the North-East.

Then when Elaine became pregnant, she saw it as a disaster and only the willingness of her unmarried sister Betty to come and see her through the confinement made it bearable. But in the long run, would Betty's presence only serve to widen the rift between husband and wife, or would she help to bring about a reconciliation?

0 552 13622 0

THE MALTESE ANGEL
by Catherine Cookson

Ward Gibson knew what was expected of him by the village folk, and especially by the Mason family, whose daughter Daisy he had known all his life. But then, in a single week, his whole world had been turned upside down by a dancer, Stephanie McQueen, who seemed to float across the stage of the Empire Music Hall where she was appearing as The Maltese Angel. To his amazement, the attraction was mutual, and after a whirlwind courtship she agreed to marry him.

But a scorpion had already begun to emerge from beneath the stone of the local community, who considered that Ward had betrayed their expectations, and had led on and cruelly deserted Daisy. There followed a series of reprisals on his family, one of them serious enough to cause him to exact a terrible revenge; and these events would twist and turn the course of many lives through Ward's own and succeeding generations.

0 552 13684 0

THE YEAR OF THE VIRGINS
by Catherine Cookson

It had never been the best of marriages and over recent years it had become effectively a marriage in name and outward appearance only. Yet, in the autumn of 1960, Winifred and Daniel Coulson presented an acceptable façade to the outside world, for Daniel had prospered sufficiently to allow them to live at Wearcill House, a mansion situated in the most favoured outskirt of the Tyneside town of Fellburn.

Of their children, it was Donald on whom Winifred doted to the point of obsession, and now he was to be married, Winifred's prime concern was whether Donald was entering wedlock with an unbesmirched purity of body and spirit, for amidst the strange workings of her mind much earlier conceptions of morality and the teachings of the church held sway.

There was something potentially explosive just below the surface of life at Wearcill House, but when that explosion came it was in a totally unforeseeable and devastating form, plunging the Coulsons into a excoriating series of crises out of which would come both good and evil, as well as the true significance of the year of the virgins.

'The power and mastery are astonishing'
Elizabeth Buchan, *Sunday Times*

0 552 13247 0

THE SOLACE OF SIN
by Catherine Cookson

As soon as she saw the house on the wild moorlands near Hexham, Constance Stapleton was attracted to it. With her marriage to Jim on the brink of collapse, she had already decided to sell the large flat they shared. And a further visit convinced her that she could live quite happily at Shekinah Hall, despite its isolation and lack of basic amenities. Connie also sensed that the move would initiate the separation from Jim she knew was inevitable, especialy now that her son Peter was old enough to go off to university.

Connie was told she must negotiate with Vincent O'Connor if she wanted to buy the house, although his abrupt manner and insistence that the papers must be signed the following day took her by surprise. She was to discover that mystery was a way of life for Vincent and began to rely on him increasingly as she settled into her new routine. However, when shocking revelations about the man with whom she spent so many years came to light, she realised that her life at Shekinah could be under threat . . .

'Dame Catherine has done it again . . . a rattling good story with a satisfying ending, plenty of gritty dialogue, a tricky affair of the heart, and a strong, honourable heroine'
Val Hennessy, *Daily Mail*

0 552 14583 1

A SELECTION OF OTHER
CATHERINE COOKSON TITLES
AVAILABLE FROM CORGI BOOKS

THE PRICES SHOWN BELOW WERE CORRECT AT THE TIME OF GOING
TO PRESS. HOWEVER TRANSWORLD PUBLISHERS RESERVE THE RIGHT TO
SHOW NET RETAIL PRICES ON COVERS WHICH MAY DIFFER FROM THOSE
PREVIOUSLY ADVERTISED IN THE TEXT OR ELSEWHERE.

All Transworld titles are available by post from:
Book Service By Post, PO Box 29, Douglas, Isle of Man IM99 1BQ
Credit cards accepted. Please telephone 01624 675137,
fax 01624 670923, Internet http://www.bookpost.co.uk or
e-mail: bookshop@enterprise.net for details.
Free postage and packing in the UK.
Overseas customers allow £1 per book (paperbacks) and
£3 per book (hardbacks).